"Fast moving. . . . A compelling read about the seedy underworld of crime and the crime fighters who wage wars against it."

—*Indianapolis Star* on *Chicago Blues*

"Readers looking for a good escapist fantasy . . . won't find a better one than Holton's latest."

—*Booklist*

"His gift for retaining suspense is golden."

—*Chicago Sun-Times*

"Where in the world did Hugh Holton come from? He is a true, immensely talented writer."

—Dorothy Uhnak, *New York Times* bestselling author of *False Witness*

"The most exciting storyteller I've encountered in a long time. His novels have everything—suspense, mystery, fascinating characters, and an insider's knowledge of the streets of Chicago. He is extraordinarily talented."

—Andrew M. Greeley, bestselling author of *Irish Gold*

"A macabre thriller about the underbelly of Chicago . . . Holton has written an imaginative first novel."

—*Kirkus Reviews* on *Presumed Dead*

THE
LEFT HAND
of GOD

HUGH
HOLTON

A TOM DOHERTY ASSOCIATES BOOK
NEW YORK

This is a work of fiction. All the characters and events portrayed in this book are either products of the author's imagination or are used fictitiously.

THE LEFT HAND OF GOD

A Forge Book
Published by Tom Doherty Associates, LLC
175 Fifth Avenue
New York, NY 10010

Forge® is a registered trademark of Tom Doherty Associates, LLC.

ISBN: 0-812-57084-7
Library of Congress Catalog Card Number: 98-47004

First edition: February 1999
First mass market edition: January 2000

Printed in the United States of America

0 9 8 7 6 5 4 3 2 1

I dedicate *The Left Hand of God* to Mr. and Mrs. Kevin Cook and to any future offspring they have, who will be my grandchildren.

CAST OF CHARACTERS

THE COPS
Larry Cole—chief of the detective division
Cosimo "Blackie" Silvestri—a lieutenant assigned to Cole's staff
Judy Daniels (aka the Mistress of Disguise/High Priestess of Mayhem)—a sergeant assigned to Cole's staff
Manfred Wolfgang "Manny" Sherlock—a sergeant assigned to Cole's staff

THE PRESS AND AUTHORS
Kate Ford—investigative journalist
Orga Syriac—WGN news commentator
Sven-Erik Voman—WGN news director
Dave Spurgeon—WGN news cameraman
Barbara Zorin—author
Jamal Garth—author

OUR LADY OF PEACE CATHOLIC CHURCH
Father Philip Cisco—pastor
Sister Mary Louise Stallings—school principal

THE HUMAN DEVELOPMENT INSTITUTE
Dr. Gilbert Goldman—director
Virginia Daley—executive assistant
Thomas Kelly (aka Father James Lochran)—operative

THE MOB
Jack Carlisle—the fixer
Sonny Balfour—henchman

SIGNIFICANT OTHERS
Larry "Butch" Cole, Jr.
Paige Albritton

ACKNOWLEDGMENTS

I would like to acknowledge some of my friends in the news media, who have given me their support over the years of both my police and my writing career. To Art Norman and Allison Rosati of NBC Channel 5 and Allison Payne and Randy Salerno of WGN Channel 9 News. Also, members of the Saint Columbanus Church-School community, who gave me technical advice and spiritual support during the writing of *The Left Hand of God*, especially Father Philip Cyscon, Mrs. Sandra Wilson, George and Blessing Bohra and Family, Gracie Banks, Seymonia Smith, and Ray and Edna Taylor.

The support of my police colleagues never ceases to amaze me from book to book. I would like to say a special thanks to Chicago police second district officers Lieutenant Mike Byrne, Lieutenant Mike Johnson, Sergeants Gordon Lohrman and his wife (a big fan) Darlene, Larry Pasco, Christopher Coleman, Dorothy Knudson, Christina Dzido, John Kenny, Donald Januszyk, Carolyn Connelley, Caroline Armstrong, Eugene Warling, Bob McDonald, Janelia Freeman, Milton Marshall, Maurice McCaster, Lamont Johnson, William Ogletree, John Fason, Melvin Powell, Gerald Szymanski, Mike Lazzaro, and Bob Kirchner.

I would also like to thank police officer D. Michael Hines of the second police district and Evie Bevins of USA Basketball for their technical assistance.

Again I would like to thank my editor Robert Gleason, my agent Susan Gleason, and the members of my writers critique group, Barbara D'Amato and Mark Richard Zubro.

PROLOGUE

The black Buick Roadmaster threw up a cloud of dust as it rocketed down the gravel road. Behind the wheel was a barrel-chested man with a prickly head of blond, crew-cut hair. He was wearing a loud Hawaiian shirt and possessed eyes of a washed-out brown. He gazed at the world with a cold indifference. He was a man of action; however, before engaging in any act he carefully deliberated its consequences.

The woman beside him was thin to the point of appearing haggard. She wore her gray hair cut short and had the darting, watchful eyes of a hunted animal. She wore a plain white cotton dress, which hung almost to her ankles, and plain black leather shoes. She didn't seem like the type of spouse the blond man would select, but odder married couples had been known in this part of the country.

In the backseat of the Buick was a red-haired, freckle-faced young man in his mid-teens. He was a muscular lad with deep blue eyes and an easy smile. He bore no resemblance to either of the adults, but in their travels they had occasionally passed him off as their son. He was not.

Darkness was falling rapidly, and the dense forest lining both sides of the road added a deeper shade to the shadows enveloping the black car. The man flipped on the bright lights to negotiate the dark strip. He handled the Buick with relish, although it did not belong to him. He had driven over four thousand miles since they'd left Chicago. He never let the woman or the boy behind the wheel.

They had been on the road since daybreak, when they'd left New Orleans. They had stopped twice for gas and once for lunch. The poor quality of the roads had made their progress slow. They were searching for a small place called Diggstown. It didn't appear on any map and there was no available documented evidence indicating that it existed at all. Diggstown was a legend, possibly no more than a fantasy, but searching for it was the job of the people in the black Buick.

"We're wasting time," the woman said testily. She stared out through the windshield at the ever-increasing blackness of the Mississippi night closing in on them.

"It's on the way," the man said without taking his eyes off the narrow road in front of them.

She turned to stare at him. "There are better highways than this connecting New Orleans and Chicago."

"This one will get us there eventually."

The woman turned back to stare out the window. "That old woman back in New Orleans was stringing you along to see if she could get a couple of extra bucks. Diggstown is just something she made up and you bought it lock, stock, and barrel."

The young man in the backseat recognized her mocking tone. Soon, he figured, they would begin arguing. He hated it when they did this. Back in the orphanage the nuns never bickered openly like these two did. The rules of the house also prohibited the kids from arguing or fighting, but sometimes they did so anyway. Then they were punished. Punished severely, but it was a punishment which they deserved.

But the driver of the Buick was not in an argumentative mood. He knew that when they got back to Chicago, the woman would complain about this side trip and the money he'd spent on the old woman back in New Orleans. And, as always, the director would listen to her patiently before telling her that a full investigation would be forthcoming. But there would be no investigation. In fact, the director would probably compliment the man on his initiative. So they'd spent a couple of extra dollars and driven a few miles out of the way to check out what could amount to no more than a myth. That was the job they'd been sent out to do by their employer.

A light appeared on the road up ahead. It was actually caused by the illumination from an open flame. A number of open flames. As the Buick approached, the light source's origin became evident. The road ahead was blocked by twelve men on horseback carrying torches. Men wearing the white robes and hoods of the Ku Klux Klan.

The man took his foot off the accelerator and tapped the brake. He slowed the car to ten miles an hour when they were still fifty yards from the Klansmen. The woman reached for a secret compartment hidden inside her car door. The young man in the rear seat reached for a similar compartment located in back of the woman's seat. The driver ordered them to stop.

"Let's not go getting antsy and be forced to kill any of the locals," he said with the calm conviction of the combat veteran. "At least until we have to."

They glided to a halt twenty feet from the line of horsemen. "Stay in the car while I talk to these boys."

Since they'd left New Orleans, the man had not spoken with an accent, but rather with the speech patterns of a native of Sausalito, California, who possessed a master's degree from the University of California at Berkeley and a Ph.D. in sociology from the University of Chicago. Now, as he instructed the woman and the boy to stay in the car, he had adopted a deep southern accent, which was so authentic not even a native of the region could tell that he was an imposter.

He put the car in park but left the engine running. Spying the shotguns and rifles the Klansmen carried, the man kept his hands in plain sight as he got out of the car. Slowly, adopting a slight shuffle, he walked around in front of the car. He addressed the center of the line before him.

"Good evenin'."

"Evenin' to you, friend."

"Nice night."

The same voice came from beneath the hood saying, "Sure is. You out for a drive with the family?"

"Sure am."

"Going someplace in particular?"

The two horsemen at the far opposite ends of the line peeled off and moved toward the Buick. The man barely glanced at them; however, he said a silent prayer that the woman and the boy would remain calm. The horsemen disappeared behind him. He knew they were checking out the car.

In response to his hooded questioner's inquiry, he said, "Lookin' for a place called Diggstown. Heard tell it was down this road a piece."

"Heard tell from who, friend?" There was a slight edge in the interrogator's voice now.

The man shrugged and smiled at the man in white. "I don't know. I think it was somebody in New Orleans."

"Where you from, friend?" another voice asked.

"Baton Rouge," the man lied convincingly. The Buick possessed Louisiana plates affixed with a Baton Rouge tag.

The hooded head of the second questioner straightened just a bit as he looked past the man at one of the Klansmen checking out the car. Apparently, his companion signaled back the accuracy of the car's identification.

Now the first speaker resumed. "There ain't nothing for a good Christian white man in Diggstown, Mississippi, friend. You is a Christian, ain't you?"

"Praise the Lord," the man said, keeping his friendly grin in place. "But maybe I could ask you fellas a question?"

No response came from the line of masked night riders.

The man was far from intimidated by them, but he didn't show it. "Is there something wrong in Diggstown?"

There was a long moment of silence. Then the second speaker said, "Diggstown is a nigra settlement. Most white people aren't welcome there, which is just as well with us."

"It's also haunted," a new, younger voice piped up with a definite note of fear. "Them nigras worship some kind of she-devil."

The man managed to keep himself from nodding, as this

information jibed with what he'd been told in New Orleans. However, there had been a significant difference from the tale he'd heard in the Crescent City. In New Orleans the woman in Diggstown was not described as a demon, but rather as an angel. An angel who protected the town's occupants from the Ku Klux Klan.

Now the man was faced with a dilemma. He had to get past the Klan. He could do it with force, but he'd rather use persuasion. He couldn't tell them the truth, but maybe what he did tell them would be enough to get them out of the way without it becoming necessary for those white robes they wore with such pride to become stained with their own blood.

It was as he was composing a halfway plausible lie that a scream echoed from the depths of the dense forest surrounding them. The sound, shrill and high-pitched, wasn't a noise that anyone on the road could easily categorize as having been made by a human being. The horses reacted violently, and one of them, a gray mare, reared up on its hind legs and tossed the rider onto the gravel road. The unhorsed man lost control of his torch and tossed it into the chest of the rider next to him. The Klansman's robe ignited and he howled in terror and pain. This added to the confusion raging among the night riders. Then there was another unearthly scream from the forest. This one was more the howl of a predatory beast. The man felt the hairs on the back of his neck bristle, and with the Klansmen in confusion, he ran back to the Buick.

"What was that?" the woman said, her eyes bright with fear.

"The hell if I know." He yanked the car into gear and floored the accelerator. The rear tires kicked up gravel as the car rocketed forward. He spun the wheel to avoid one of the agitated horses and fishtailed before getting the car under control. In the rearview mirror he checked the hellish scene they'd just left. Four of the Klansmen had dismounted and were attempting to extinguish the flames consuming their comrade. Then a dark shadow loomed up behind one of the

Klansmen and the white-robed figure was snatched into the forest.

The Buick's driver was forced to turn his attention back to the forest road, but he knew that whatever was back there was not something he ever wanted to encounter. However, the boy was looking out the back window and had gotten a good look at what had snatched the Klansman into the woods. That sight scared him into bloodless shock.

Ten minutes later they were still on the road. Now night had fallen and outside the steel cocoon of the black Buick the world was dark and menacing. They had left the Klansmen miles behind, but what had occurred back there remained with them.

At one point the boy began reciting the Our Father, but the man shouted for him to shut up. Now no words had passed between them for some time, adding another dimension to the already unbearable tension in the car. Then the sky began brightening ahead of them.

"What city is that?" the man said, noticing that now the whole sky was illuminated.

The woman removed a map of Mississippi from the glove compartment and examined it under the dome light. "There's nothing on this. The closest city is Jackson."

As they got closer the sky continued to brighten. A quarter of a mile later the gravel road became a blacktop. Then the blacktop became lined on both sides by wrought-iron electric streetlamps set at hundred-foot intervals. A sign appeared above the road. The Buick stopped beneath it. The banner was tied between two lampposts. The lettering, in white Old English script on a black background, proclaimed, "Welcome to Diggstown—Population 2,015—Isaac Diggs, Mayor."

Slowly, the man drove down the lighted road. He was forced to make a right turn before stopping suddenly.

"I don't believe it," the woman said in a voice barely above a whisper.

"This is impossible," the man said.

The boy leaned over the backseat and looked at the sight through the windshield with unbridled awe.

They were on the main street of Diggstown. It was tree-lined, brightly lighted, and incongruously modern. Every-thing looked new and clean, without any dirt or trash in evidence. There were businesses lining the two-block stretch. The trio in the Buick noticed a watchmaker, a tailor, a grocer, a butcher, a café, a candy store, and a ladies' dress shop. At the far end of the street facing them was a red-brick building with a white steeple. As they looked on, a man stepped out-side this building. Even at this distance they could tell he was black, muscular, and extremely tall. Then he began walking toward them.

"Just take it easy," the man said. "Let's find out what he's up to."

"You mean what they're up to," the woman said, as doors up and down the street began opening and more people emerged.

"Stay sharp," he said. "I'm going to have a little talk with these folks." The man had again adopted his southern accent.

After he got out of the car, the woman opened her secret door panel and removed a .45 Army Issue Colt, while the young man opened up a rear seat compartment and removed a Thompson submachine gun. They were both extremely good with these weapons and were also ready to use them.

A hundred and fifty people were now on the street. Most of them were Negroes, but there were a couple of whites and a few Orientals. Not one of them said a word, but mingled around the Buick, staring passively at the new arrivals.

The man took up a position at the same distance in front of the car that he had when he'd faced the Klansmen, and waited for the tall Negro. The black man was the largest human being the man had ever seen. He had to be close to seven feet tall and possessed a wiry, muscular body with a hint of formidable strength present. He had ebony skin, which bore no wrinkles, and it was impossible to guess his age. However, the eyes told the tale. He had been around for a long time and seen a lot.

"Good evening," the Negro said as he stood towering over the man, "and welcome to Diggstown." He extended a huge work-hardened hand. "My name is Isaac Diggs."

*   *   *

Isaac Diggs invited them to share refreshments with him in the café. The crowd that had gathered dissipated a bit, but at least twenty people were milling around outside. The interior of the café was of varnished wood, and all the tables were equipped with marble tops. They were attended by a good-natured, heavyset woman who fussed about serving coffee, cake, pie, and a glass of milk for the young man. The guns were once more concealed in the car, and Isaac Diggs was proving to be a gracious host.

"Diggstown is something of a model community," he said in a bass voice which rumbled from deep in his chest. "We are self-sufficient, growing our own crops and raising livestock on the rich farmland we own surrounding the town."

The man and woman were listening closely. The youth was busy with a second glass of milk and a third slice of apple pie. In fact, a place like Diggstown, Mississippi, was of great interest to them and their employer back in Chicago.

"How do you produce the electricity to light this place?" the man asked.

"We have our own powerhouse."

"It must be pretty big," the woman said.

Diggs smiled, revealing large, startlingly white teeth, and responded, "It is."

The man paused a moment to sip his coffee. Before he could return the cup to the saucer, the waitress was there refilling it. The man smiled at her and said to Diggs, "We couldn't find this town on the map. We stumbled across it purely by accident. In fact, we ran into a few of your neighbors who tried to discourage us from coming here at all."

Diggs frowned. "Neighbors wearing white hoods?"

"The same. They said something about the people in Diggstown worshiping some type of she-devil."

The waitress was on the other side of the café, but she heard what the man said and dropped the coffeepot. The sound of the glass breaking made them look up. She began cleaning up the mess and did not approach their table again.

Isaac Diggs turned to the man. "In Diggstown we only worship God."

The door to the café opened and a woman walked in. She appeared to be in her mid-twenties, was of above average height, and displayed a slender figure. She was dressed in a simple gray denim skirt and a black sleeveless blouse. She was barefoot. However, none of the new arrivals were paying any attention to what she was wearing or her lack of footwear, as she was the most stunningly beautiful female that any of them had ever seen.

She stopped just inside the entrance to the café and stared at them. She was a light-complexioned Negress with flawless tan skin. Her hair was jet black, worn loose to hang to the small of her back. Her eyebrows were arched and well defined, but not thick. Her eyes, haloed by long black lashes, were dark and had a bright luminosity indicating keen intelligence and something mysterious, possibly even frightening.

"Orga," Isaac Diggs said with his booming voice, "come and meet our guests."

She moved across the room like a panther approaching its prey and took the seat next to the boy. He reddened and looked down into his empty pie plate. The man and the woman felt a sudden apprehension, which they couldn't identify. But they did realize that they were now in the presence of something extremely dangerous.

"Our friends were just telling me about an encounter they had on the road with the Klan," Diggs said. "They were also asking if the people in Diggstown worship a she-devil."

Orga stared at the man and woman long enough to make them nervous. Now the woman wished that she'd brought the .45 from the car.

"Where did you hear about Diggstown?" Her voice was strong, but had a soft, melodious quality.

The man responded, "A woman in New Orleans told us about it."

"And what were you doing in New Orleans?"

"Sight-seeing," he said flatly.

"Did you enjoy the French Quarter?"

"It was very nice."

"And your investigation into voodoo, which led you here, did you like that too?"

The woman glanced nervously at the man. He had gone rigid, and the boy bloodless.

"You seem to know a great deal, Miss . . . ?" the man's voice trailed off.

"Syriac. Orga Syriac," she said. "And I assume that you are Mr. and Mrs. Smith, or today is it Jones?"

"Smith will do," he said, regaining some of his casual composure.

Orga Syriac leaned forward and fixed him with a gaze of such intensity he was forced to look away. "What do you want here, Mr. Smith?"

He thought for a moment and then exhaled a long sigh. "Okay, I'm going to come clean with you folks." He dropped his phony southern accent. "We work for the Human Development Institute at the University of Chicago."

"But you are funded by the United States government?" she asked.

"We receive government assistance, but everyone nowadays is getting a slice of the federal pie." The man looked at Isaac Diggs, who never took his eyes off the mysterious black woman. The apprehension on the huge man's face was evident. Mr. Smith continued, "The Institute is interested in advancing the living conditions of humanity on this planet. We study advances made in one part of the world and explore how they can be employed to help people in some less fortunate place."

"How will voodoo and she-devils help humanity?" Orga's tone had turned hostile.

Quickly, the man changed the subject. "As Isaac said before you came in, Diggstown is a model settlement, which just one look will verify. What you've accomplished here is indeed miraculous. You people are in the heart of Mississippi, oppressed by the Ku Klux Klan, and you still manage to prosper. Have you any idea what you could accomplish with a little help?"

"I don't understand what you mean by 'help,' " Diggs said.

Mr. Smith leaned toward him. "We could make the story of this place public. Show how a Negro community can be self-sufficient in a hostile environment. You would become famous overnight. The world would beat a path to your door-step."

"Sir," the black man said solemnly, "one of Diggstown's greatest strengths has been its anonymity. If that anonymity is violated, then the outside world will not come to help us, but to destroy us as the Klan has so often tried to do."

"But the Institute can protect you," the man protested.

"We don't need protection," Orga Syriac said, "from the Klan or from you and your Institute. Back on the road did you see what happened?"

The man and woman exchanged nervous glances. The boy refused to raise his eyes from the table.

At that instant something changed in her face. Something unusual and terrifying began happening in the Diggstown, Mississippi, café.

"Now what do you want to know about the she-devil?" Orga said, but her voice came out sounding like the snarl of a wild beast.

Later the boy would remember running through the forest. There was a fire raging behind him and rapidly consuming the woodland. But the fire was not his problem; the fact that *she* was pursuing him was.

The young man realized that there was blood on his hands. A great deal of blood. He also knew that the man and woman who had answered to the name Smith back in Diggstown were dead. He knew that *she* had killed them and wanted to kill him for what they had done. However, he couldn't re-member exactly what it was that they had done, and he was rapidly losing any memory of everything else that had hap-pened in the past twenty-four hours. Everything that is except *her*.

The unearthly howl he had initially heard during their con-frontation with the Klan an eternity ago echoed through the woods. Startled, he looked back and ran head on into a low-hanging tree branch. He was knocked flat on his back and came dangerously close to losing consciousness. He tasted blood and found that he couldn't breathe through his nose.

Slowly, he managed to sit up. The darkness surrounding him was terrifying and at the same time oddly comforting. If *she* couldn't see him *she* couldn't kill him. Then he heard the sound of something moving rapidly through the forest.

He managed to get up on all fours and listen. The sound was made by something or someone running. Something which was headed straight for him!

Alarmed, the boy jumped to his feet, and although he was shaking and frightened into a near-catatonic state, he began moving away with impressive speed. But he could tell, after he had traveled only a short distance, that his pursuer was gaining on him.

The ground began sloping at a sharp downward angle. He was finding it difficult to maintain his balance as he ran; however, the fact that the noise made by his pursuer was becoming increasingly louder refused to allow him to slow down. Then he fell.

He skidded to a stop in a clearing. He was lying on his stomach, and he'd badly skinned his elbows, knees, and chin on the rough ground. He was winded from running and his face was streaked with blood, sweat, and dirt. For just a minute he considered surrender. Then he remembered the nun's voice back in the orphanage. *"God has something important for you to do."*

These words gave him strength and he struggled wearily back to his feet. He was about to start running again when *she* appeared at the opposite end of the clearing.

All he could do was stare at *her. She* stared back at him and then slowly began advancing toward him. He took a step backward and then another, but *she* was closing the distance between them rapidly and would soon be upon him. He closed his eyes and prepared to see the face of God. He took one more step back and found that the ground was no longer there. Surprised, he opened his eyes as he began to fall. *She* was close enough to reach out and almost grab him, but his plunge was too fast, which saved his life.

He fell through the dark for what seemed an eternity before he struck the top of a tall tree. The branches initially broke his fall, but as he fell through them they tore at his clothing and battered his body unmercifully. He tumbled end over end until he was out of the tree to fall a short distance before striking something hard.

The boy was lying on the corrugated metal roof of a barn. His fall had upset the animals in the barnyard, and a hound began baying at him with a howl that awakened memories of *her* in his fear-tortured brain. A flashlight beam shone up from the ground to envelop him. He merely glanced at it before passing into an oblivion in which *she* was the only reality.

The boy had sustained two broken legs, a severely fractured right arm, a ruptured spleen, and multiple skull fractures, but he was alive. Many times over the remaining years of his life he wished that he had died on that night so he would have no memory of *her*.

However, he would see *her* again.

1

"God Bless All Here."
Father James Lochran

CHAPTER 1

Chief of Detectives Larry Cole stood in the back of the interrogation room watching Sergeant Manny Sherlock question serial killer Dwight Frazier. Frazier was alleged to have murdered fifty-one men, women, and children in Chicago over the past eight years. It had taken Cole and his crew of Lieutenant Blackie Silvestri, Sergeant Judy Daniels, and Manny six months of intensive investigation to apprehend this vicious killer. Now, in the presence of a Cook County state's attorney, a court-appointed defense attorney, and a stenographer, the murderer was candidly confessing to each crime along with providing the minute details of his offenses.

Cole, a tall, broad-shouldered, handsome black man with thick black hair streaked with gray, studied Dwight Frazier with barely concealed awe. The killer was a nondescript type of short stature with gray hair he parted severely to one side. He wore steel-rimmed glasses with thick lenses and looked like a librarian or file clerk. In actuality, like the infamous Richard Speck, Frazier had no occupation but drifted from job to job. He had been a dishwasher, busboy, janitor, and school custodian. Working at the latter job in a West Side school, he had been responsible for the kidnap, brutal sexual assault, and eventual murder of eleven grammar-school children.

"Tell us about the women," Manny said.

Cole noticed that Sherlock had adopted an interrogation manner very similar to that of his former partner Lou Bronson, who had retired five years ago. Bronson had been one of the best detectives Cole had ever met.

In response to the sergeant's question, Frazier smiled. "I don't understand the fuss you people are making about them," he said in a quiet, near-cultured voice. "I did the men of the world a favor by getting rid of those sluts. They were disease-ridden, foulmouthed parasites. Because of them, many a man's life has been destroyed." He chuckled and leaned toward Sherlock, as if he were attempting to tell the sergeant a secret or make him a coconspirator in his crimes. "You know I was very inventive in disposing of them. I drowned a few in cheap motel-room bathtubs. Held them under and watched their eyes glaze over in death. Sent those harlots on the road straight to hell."

Cole noticed the court reporter's back stiffen, but she kept her fingers working rapidly over the keys.

"In a few cases," Frazier continued, "due to time constraints, the weather, or some other thing I couldn't control, I'd open their guts up with a butcher knife or take a straight razor and slit their throats. But that's really messy, Sergeant. Do you know what I mean?"

"I know, Dwight," Sherlock responded.

Larry Cole knew Manny Sherlock well and knew that deep inside, the detective sergeant had nothing but loathing for the serial killer. However, his job demanded that he become as friendly with him as possible in order to get the confession that would send Dwight Frazier on his own road to hell.

A lull had developed in the interrogation, and after a brief pause Sherlock said, "Tell me about your family, Dwight."

The serial killer's attitude changed instantly. He seemed to become smaller, as his shoulders slumped and he lowered his head. He wouldn't look at Sherlock. He said, "Do we have to talk about them?"

"I think we should."

There was a long moment of silence. Finally Frazier sighed and said, "Okay. What do you want to know about my family?"

"Why don't you start at the beginning?" Sherlock said. "Where were you born?"

Dwight Frazier's eyes swung to the ceiling and he squinted as if the memory was difficult for him to recall. "Let's see, I was born in Toledo, Ohio, on October sixth, 1950. I was raised on a farm about a hundred miles from Toledo. My stepfather was named James Townsend. He tried his hand at raising a variety of crops, but nothing ever came to much. Most of the time we were on the dole."

"The 'dole'?" Sherlock questioned.

Frazier's face twisted in a lopsided grin. "That's kind of an old-fashioned term for welfare."

"Did you have any brothers and sisters?"

"There were six of us. Three Fraziers: me, my younger brother, Billy, and my baby sister, Meg. The rest were Townsends: Joey, Beth, and Wanda."

"What about your mother?"

The question hit Frazier hard. He tensed and took in a deep breath. He was obviously going through a fierce struggle for control of his emotions. A struggle that he lost. He let out a wail and began to sob. Tears ran down his face and his entire body became racked by his internal pain.

The cops silently waited him out.

"Would you like a glass of water?" Sherlock inquired when Frazier's crying was reduced to soft whimpers.

"Please," he managed.

There was a metal carafe and a stack of paper cups on the table. Sherlock poured the killer a cup of water, which he took and gulped down. When he was finished, he sniffled noisily and ran the sleeve of his seedy sports jacket across his tear-streaked face.

Cole came off the wall and walked over to the prisoner. From his inside pocket Cole removed a white handkerchief.

"Thank you, Chief Cole," Frazier said, taking the folded square of white cloth. "You are most kind."

"You can keep it," Cole said, returning to his place against the wall.

After giving Frazier another moment to control himself, Sherlock said, "Shall we continue?"

The killer nodded. In a hoarse voice he said, "My mother was a very beautiful woman. I don't remember much about my father. He worked for the railroad and wasn't home much. Then one day, before I had even started school, he stopped coming home at all. Then she, that is my mother, met Townsend."

A bitterness had crept into his voice at the mention of his stepfather. Sherlock waited patiently for him to continue.

"Townsend was a brutal man, but he believed in God or rather God's wrath. We ate, slept, and breathed the Bible on that miserable piece of dirt he called a farm. And for the slightest transgression he'd take us out to the barn, strip us naked, and take a strap to us until he drew blood. He'd even whip my mother when she displeased him, which was often."

For a moment it appeared that Frazier was going to break down again, but he took in a deep breath, expelled it slowly, and continued.

"It was about this time, I was maybe thirteen or fourteen years old, that I began experimenting with animals."

"What kind of experiments, Dwight?"

Frazier shrugged and in that simple gesture was transformed from a man with a troubled past back into one of the most vicious serial killers who had ever operated in the city of Chicago.

"Yeah," he chuckled before responding to Sherlock's question, "I liked to open them up and see how they worked. Chickens, dogs, cats, raccoons. It really didn't matter. I'd catch them in these little cages I made, beat them senseless, and go to work with my knives."

"Didn't you get into trouble with Townsend for doing that?"

"He never found out about it, but my mother knew." Again Frazier began misting up. "In the long run I think that's why she left me there. She'd gotten fed up with Townsend's Bible-beating and abuse, so one day, while I was working the fields with Townsend, she took Billy and Meg and just left. Heard they went to California, but they never tried to contact me. Left me with Old Man Townsend and his litter of Christian fanatics."

Frazier paused for a moment. His eyes glazed over momentarily and he said softly, "So I guess you could say that I had no choice. You see, I realized that with my mother gone Old Man Townsend would eventually get around to blaming me. My life would have really been hell then. So that first night, after my real family left, I slit Townsend's throat. I had to kill his kids too. Didn't want any witnesses. Then I burned the farmhouse down and took off on my own. Been by myself ever since."

The interrogation continued. With Sherlock guiding him, Frazier talked freely. To Cole, the observer, the serial killer was actually eager to tell his story. Like the majority of criminals, he made half-hearted, illogical attempts to justify his crimes. But Cole could tell that Frazier knew that he had committed a number of atrocities and was actually confessing to relieve himself of the guilt he had carried for so many years.

The confession was finally coming to a conclusion. Sherlock asked his final question. "Is there anything that you'd like to add, Dwight?"

Frazier reflected for a moment before saying, "No, Sergeant, I think that's just about it."

Sherlock turned to look at Cole in case there was anything else the chief of detectives wanted him to ask. Cole nodded, signaling to Manny that he was satisfied and that the interrogation could now end.

The sergeant turned back to face Dwight Frazier. "Has everything you have told me been given of your own free will without threat or coercion?"

"Oh yes, Sergeant, and I must say that you are a very good listener."

On that note Cole let himself out of the interrogation room. As he headed back to his office, he felt a heavy fatigue drop over him. This was something he had begun experiencing more frequently of late at the end of big cases. It was as if with each one, more and more of his essence was being drained. That his contacts with the worst society had to offer, such as the likes of Dwight Frazier, were chipping away at his soul bit by bit until someday there would be nothing left.

He reached his office and found Lieutenant Blackie Silvestri sitting in his cubicle next to the door marked "Chief of Detectives." Blackie was going over a report and did not notice his boss approach. Cole stopped outside the cubicle and watched his old friend for a few moments. On Thanksgiving Day they would be friends for twenty-eight years. It didn't seem like it had been that long. In fact, Cole didn't feel any different than he had on that winter day when he'd been assigned as Nineteenth District tactical officer Blackie Silvestri's new partner. In appearance Blackie didn't look much different than he had in 1976. Sure, he was heavier, and his once black hair was thinner and shot with gray. There were fatigue lines etched into his face caused over the years by his perpetual scowl. However, if Cole altered his gaze to take in the whole rather than the specific, his old friend would appear to have aged only ten years as opposed to close to thirty.

Cole recalled reading somewhere that agelessness went hand in hand with how someone felt about and lived his life. And Blackie lived life to the fullest. He loved good food, a few beers now and then, and those funny little twisted black cigars he was always smoking. He had only two passions in life: his family and catching crooks.

Involuntarily, Cole's own life flashed before him. He was as passionate about police work as Blackie; however, the only other thing with any lasting value in Cole's life was his son Butch, who was now a teenager staying with Cole for the summer. Larry "Butch" Cole Jr. lived with his mother in Detroit and Cole did not see as much of him as he liked. So it all came back to the CPD, and Cole realized that his relationship with the department could change in the blink of an eye. A case blown, falling into political disfavor, which had happened to him before, or the appointment of a superintendent who wanted his own man as the chief of detectives and it would be all over for Larry Cole. He had seen it happen to other demoted command officers. Some of them didn't weather well the demotion back to their career service ranks of lieutenant or captain. It had even killed a few.

As Cole had this thought, Blackie looked up. "What's cooking, boss?"

Cole smiled, but didn't respond right away. With that look and those words Blackie had reminded Cole of just how much they meant to each other.

When Cole didn't say anything, Blackie frowned. "Larry, are you okay?"

Cole's smile dimmed a bit. "I'm fine, Blackie. Manny's wrapping up Frazier's confession. It will probably run to about three hundred fifty pages."

"That much, huh? I bet Barbara Zorin, Jamal Garth, or Kate Ford could have a field day with that transcript."

Cole headed for his office. "Someday they probably will, but we've got to try Frazier first."

"You do remember that you're supposed to go to that reception at Navy Pier tonight. It's a command performance. A select few members of the top brass, to include you, must attend."

Cole frowned. "I know."

"You don't look like you're in much of a partying mood."

"Maybe it's because of the people I'm being forced to party with."

CHAPTER 2

JUNE 11, 2004
4:05 P.M.

Thomas Kelly entered the Days Inn Hotel on Clark Street across from the Lincoln Park Zoo. He was a tall man with snow white hair and a ruddy complexion. He walked with a cane, which he leaned on heavily, as he traversed the lobby to the front desk. A man and woman in jogging outfits were on their way out of the hotel and noticed Kelly. The woman remarked that he bore a striking resemblance to Senator Ted Kennedy.

The desk clerk was talking on the phone when Kelly came up to her station. Placing her hand over the mouthpiece she said, "I'll be with you in a moment, sir."

He smiled and replied with a lilting Irish brogue, "Take your time, darlin'. I'm in no hurry."

A few moments later she hung up and said, "May I help you, sir?"

"I'm looking for the Reverend Father James Lochran."

"Yes, sir. Just one moment and I'll ring him for you." She picked up the house phone and punched in a number. Thomas Kelly watched her as enough time passed for the telephone at the other end to have rung at least five times. The call being finally answered caused the clerk to frown.

"Father Lochran?" She paused and then said, "Are you okay, sir?" Another pause. "There's a gentleman at the front desk to see you." She looked at Kelly. "Could I have your name, sir?"

He told her and she announced him.

"Father Lochran's in room eleven oh seven. You may go up now."

He started to ask her what was wrong, but he already knew. With a smile and a wink at the clerk, he headed for the elevator.

Thomas Kelly knocked on the door to room 1107. After a moment, the sound of the chain being released and locks being undone carried out into the hall. Then the door opened.

The man standing at the threshold to room 1107 was short, balding, thin, and quite drunk. The room had recently been made up, but cigarette smoke hung heavily in the air and there was a strong smell of whiskey present. "Good day to you, Thomas."

"And to you also, James."

Slowly, Lochran turned and walked unsteadily back into

the smoky room. Kelly followed him, making sure he shut the door securely behind him.

James Lochran made it to an easy chair over by the window, which provided a panoramic view of Lincoln Park and the western shore of Lake Michigan below. On a table next to the chair was an ashtray overflowing with cigarette butts, a package of Salems, a half bottle of Bushmills whiskey, and a single glass. An ice bucket rested on the floor beside the chair. Collapsing into the chair, Lochran picked up his glass and raised it in salute to Thomas Kelly: "God bless all here."

Kelly took a seat on the bed facing Lochran. He placed his cane across his lap.

"Amen to that, James, but you're not supposed to be on the booze. After all, you're posing as a Catholic priest."

Lochran took a pull of his drink prior to saying, "Some of the biggest drunks I know are priests, Thomas."

"You also have a job to do in a couple of hours. It wouldn't be proper for you to show up in your current state."

Lochran lit another cigarette, coughed as he got it going, and said, "A shower, a bite to eat, and a little mouthwash will have me as good as new."

"I heard that's what you told them in Denver before you passed out and didn't show up at all."

Lochran glared at Kelly. "So I made a mistake, Thomas. After being in this business for twenty years I'm entitled to one."

Kelly, using his cane as a brace, got slowly to his feet. "Do you mind if I join you?"

"Now that's the ticket. Let me get you a glass."

Lochran got up and crossed to the washroom. He flicked the light on and was reaching for one of the hotel glasses when he heard a noise behind him. He spun around in time to catch the full force of Kelly's cane right in the center of his forehead. James Lochran, priest impersonator, fell backward to land hard against the toilet bowl. His skull had been split open and his eyes were already glazing over in death.

Thomas Kelly stepped over him and examined his handiwork. There was no need for another blow. There never was. He could have killed Lochran in the bedroom, but it was much harder to get bloodstains out of fabric than was the case with the cold porcelain and tile of the bathroom.

Looking down at the body of his onetime comrade, Kelly said, "I actually did you a favor, James. The booze would have killed you in a great deal slower and more painful manner." The assassin emitted a sigh. "Now I'm going to have to take your place myself, and I'll be a damned sight better priest than you've ever been."

He returned to the bedroom and picked up the telephone. Dialing 9 to get an outside line, he made a local call. After one ring the phone was answered: "Human Development Institute."

"I'd like to speak to Dr. Walker. Dr. Wendy Walker."

"I'm sorry, sir," a male voice said, "but Dr. Walker is no longer with the Institute. I can provide you with a forwarding address."

"No," Kelly said, "that won't be necessary. Thank you for your time."

He hung up.

Thomas Kelly returned to the washroom and retrieved the clean glass which James Lochran had gone in search of as the last act of his life. On the telephone, in code, Kelly had requested a cleanup team to respond to the hotel to remove the body and every trace of the man's presence, including checking him out and paying the bill. When the operator at the Human Development Institute had offered to provide him with a forwarding address for Dr. Wendy Walker it was an acknowledgment of the cleanup order.

Now Kelly picked up the bottle of Bushmills and poured himself a neat shot. Before downing it he raised the glass and said, "God bless all here."

CHAPTER 3

Cole was dressing for the affair at Navy Pier. The occasion called for formal attire, and as it was late spring, he would be wearing a white dinner jacket. He had already put on everything but the jacket. He went to the closet where the garment bag containing his summer formal wear was hanging. He pulled the bag out, laid it on the bed, and unzipped it. What he found inside stopped him.

"Butch!" he called for his son.

The young man came into Cole's bedroom from the living room. Larry "Butch" Cole Jr. was sixteen years old. He was six feet two inches tall and weighed 185 pounds. Had anyone been viewing Cole and his son for the first time they would have been startled at the remarkable resemblance between the two. It was so uncanny as to appear unnatural. Identical twins were seldom so close not only physically, but also in their every gesture, facial expression, and manner of speaking. And the two men recognized this, as each time they looked at each other it was as if they were gazing into a mirror.

"What's up, Dad?"

"Where is my white dinner jacket?" Cole said, pointing at the bag.

Innocently, Butch said, "It's right there."

Cole reached into the bag and removed the white waist-length dinner jacket with the black buttons. He held it up for his son to see. "This is not my dinner jacket."

Butch smiled. "Actually, it is, Dad. At least it is now. Barbara and Judy bought it for you. They said that the old one was starting to yellow a bit."

"So who picked this one?" Cole said, holding up the new jacket with a frown of disapproval.

"I did." Butch stepped forward and took the jacket from his father. "This is really cool." He held the jacket so Cole could try it on. "It's a Michael Jordan Number Twenty-three."

Cole had to admit that the jacket fit perfectly. "But it makes me look like a waiter, Butch."

"No one is ever going to mistake Larry Cole Sr., the CPD chief of detectives, for a waiter. You're going to be the hit of the ball with this on."

"It's a political fund-raiser," Cole said. "By the way, what did you do with the old jacket?"

"Gave it to Goodwill."

The telephone rang. The younger Cole walked over to the night-stand and picked up the extension. "Hello? Oh, hello, Ms. Ford. Yes, he's right here. By the way, I enjoyed your article on the Cook County Hospital scandal. That was great stuff. You must go undercover almost as much as Judy."

Cole knew that his son was talking to investigative journalist Kate Ford. Cole had met her a few years ago. She'd won a Pulitzer Prize for her work, and she and Cole had been involved in the investigation of the scientific genius Jonathan Gault. Now he wondered why she was calling him.

"Hold on a minute," Butch said, handing the phone to Cole.

"Hello, Kate."

"Hi, Larry. That young man is very polite. He's also got excellent taste."

"I wonder about the 'taste' part," Cole said, fingering the lapel of his new dinner jacket.

"I need a favor."

"If there's anything I can do, you know I will."

"There's a member of Sisters in Crime who is going to the Cook County PAC affair at Navy Pier tonight. She's new in town and doesn't know anyone. She's going to work for WGN next week and—"

Cole completed the statement for her: "—and since I'm going alone you want me to be her escort."

"Would you mind? She's terribly attractive and the people at Channel Nine are saying she's going to be the next Oprah."

"Okay, what's her name and where do I pick her up?"

Cole removed a pen from his shirt pocket and jotted the information down on a pad beside the telephone. After hanging up, he tore the sheet off and folded it. His son stood a short distance away watching him.

"So now you've got a hot date to go along with your new formal look," Butch said.

"I don't know how 'hot' this date's going to be. These electronic-media types are often a little too self-centered for my tastes. What are you going to do tonight?"

Butch had his hand in his jeans pocket so Cole couldn't see him cross his fingers. "Judy's coming over to play chess."

Cole didn't know that the Mistress of Disguise/High Priestess of Mayhem knew how to play chess. He mentioned this to his son.

"I'm teaching her. We might go out for a pizza later. We'll probably be back before you get home."

"Well, I'd better get going," Cole said. "My blind date lives on South Lake Shore Drive. Enjoy yourself this evening and give Judy my regards." With that he headed for the door.

As he rode down to the parking garage beneath his condominium building, Cole realized that he was glad Judy would be with Butch tonight. Although the kid could take care of himself and was big for his age, Cole still would have been uneasy with him being alone and unsupervised. Judy Daniels was like a big sister to Butch and had been watching over him most of his life. However, Cole just couldn't picture Judy Daniels being interested in learning how to play chess.

He reached his car and was about to unlock the door when he glanced at the sheet of paper with his blind date's information on it. Cole read, "Orga Syriac, 5050 South Lake Shore Drive, apartment 1025, telephone number 909-7283."

CHAPTER 4

JUNE 11, 2004
5:02 P.M.

Security for the Cook County PAC affair had been put into place by the Eighteenth Police District watch commander at noon. The heaviest police presence would be in evidence during the affair, when a number of political bigwigs would be in attendance. Now, thirty minutes before the cocktail party was scheduled to begin, two uniformed officers assisted a private security guard at the gate leading out to the pier. A gray panel truck drove toward the gate.

The security guard, a heavyset black man carrying a clipboard, flagged the van down. He walked over to the driver's side. A thin-faced man with a two-day growth of beard rolled the window down. He was wearing mirrored sunglasses and kept his gaze cast stonily to the front. Before the guard could question him, the passenger leaned forward and addressed the guard.

"Good day to you, Officer. I'm Father James Lochran. I'll be giving the invocation for the affair this evening."

The guard took in the white-haired, ruddy-complexioned man in the black suit with the clerical collar. He reminded the guard of someone, but he couldn't place who at that moment.

"You're a bit early, Father. We won't be opening the gates until five-thirty for the guests."

"Actually, I'm not here right now as a guest. I've got a special delivery to make."

The guard consulted his clipboard as the two Eighteenth District cops walked over to see what was going on. "I'm sorry, Father, but all the deliveries have been made."

The priest smiled. "This really isn't a scheduled delivery. It's a gift from the cardinal for the attendees of tonight's grand affair."

"What kind of gift?" asked a young cop, who wore his uniform a shade tight over a muscular body.

"Three cases of fine white wine," the priest said. He turned around and reached into the back of the van to remove a bottle from one of the cases. He held it up for the policeman to see. "One of these will go on every table for the enjoyment of the guests."

The security guard shook his head. "I've got nothing here about any delivery of any wine."

"Could I talk to you a minute?" the muscular cop said to the guard.

They moved away from the van and spoke in whispers. Initially, the guard shook his head in the negative. But the cop was insistent. The guard finally gave in, walked to the gate, and swung it open. The cop walked back to the van. "It's okay now, Father. You can drop the wine off at the delivery entrance on the north side of the rotunda. The waiters will distribute the bottles."

"Thank you, young man," the priest said.

The cop raised a hand to touch the bill of his cap and said, "Saint Rita, class of eighty-seven."

"Bless you," the priest said as the driver rolled the window up, put the van in gear, and drove through the open gate. Throughout the entire exchange the driver never altered his frontal gaze.

The gray van traveled down the north side of the pier but did not stop at the delivery area. It proceeded to the main doors to the rotunda and stopped. The two occupants got out.

Walking with his cane, the priest moved over to the entrance. The driver went to the back of the van and removed a handcart, on which he loaded four boxes. Three of these boxes held wine-label markings; the fourth box bore no markings at all.

At the doors to the rotunda the priest stopped and peered through the glass. There were a number of waiters and service personnel moving around the tables preparing for the dinner. There were no cops or security types in evidence.

The priest turned to his companion. "I doubt if anyone will question you, but if they do, just tell them to see me."

The stone-faced man gave the priest an almost imperceptible nod of understanding. Then the priest opened the door and they entered the rotunda.

CHAPTER 5

JUNE 11, 2004
5:19 P.M.

Larry Cole rode the elevator up to the tenth floor. The doorman had told him that Ms. Syriac occupied apartments 1025 and 1027, which she had made into one large apartment by knocking out a wall. The cop figured that doing such a thing had to be expensive, and he wondered how much money a TV newscaster made.

The elevator door opened and he exited into the corridor. He followed the numbers around to 1025. He knocked on the apartment door and waited. After a moment, when nothing happened, he repeated the knock. Still nothing. He was turning away from the door when a voice with a foreign accent came from behind him: "May I help you, sir?"

Cole turned around to find a black woman, dressed in traditional African garb, standing at the entrance to apartment 1027.

"I'm here to pick up Ms. Orga Syriac," he said, finding that he was smiling. He realized that the reason for his grin was that he thought he was being stood up on a blind date, which had never happened to him before. Then there was the woman. She had the face of a Nubian princess, with soft eyes and an easy smile. She stared noncommittally at him for a moment and said, "You must be Chief Larry Cole. Won't you come in?"

Cole followed her through the door into Orga Syriac's quarters.

The 5050 South Lake Shore Drive building, as was the case with most addresses on LSD, was a fairly prestigious place. A luxury high-rise with spacious accommodations, the condominium prices started at $200,000 for one-bedroom units. Orga Syriac owned two three-bedroom units that had to have cost her over $2 million. And what she had done to the interior of this place stunned the chief of detectives.

The floors were of black marble and the walls were painted white. Lights from the ceiling provided ample illumination for the furnishings, and for a brief moment Cole thought that he had entered an art museum. The entranceway was lined with antique sculptures, all of which were of African origin. As he followed the woman, he gave a couple of the sculptures they passed a quick once-over. One of them, a hand-carved mask, looked to have been made of ivory. Another carving, which resembled a gargoyle, was encrusted with jewels. The sculptures and apparent cost of the double high-rise luxury condo made Cole certain that his blind date was a very wealthy woman.

At the entrance to a sunken living room, the woman stopped and turned to face him. "Please make yourself comfortable. Ms. Syriac will be with you in just a moment."

"You're not Ms. Syriac?" Cole asked with surprise.

"No. My name is Blessing. I'm Ms. Syriac's assistant."

Cole extended his hand and she took it. "Nice to meet you, Blessing."

"May I get you something, sir? A cocktail, some coffee, water or fruit juice?"

"Do you have orange juice?"

"Yes, sir."

"That would be nice."

She was turning to leave the room when Cole said, "Oh, Blessing, please don't call me 'sir.' Just 'Larry' will be fine."

She smiled. "Yes, Larry." Then she curtsied and left the room.

Blessing returned a short time later with a frosted glass of orange juice. When Cole tasted it, he discovered that it was freshly squeezed. Blessing again left him alone. He took a seat on a brocade couch and placed the glass down on a woven hemp coaster on top of the glass cocktail table. He was looking around at the furnishings, which were just as expensive as everything else he'd seen in this place, when he felt a strange unease grip him. He was certain that he was being watched and that whatever was observing him was preparing to attack.

Cole jumped to his feet and spun around. She was standing at the entrance to the living room. She was staring at him with a gaze that initially froze him in place. She was partially concealed in shadow, making it difficult for him to see anything more of her than her silhouette and eyes. Cole found himself reaching for his gun and even taking a step back in case she chanced a leap at him. Then she stepped into the light.

He had never been more stunned by anyone or anything in his life. The woman standing across the room from him was one of the most beautiful human beings he had ever seen. She was a black woman with a medium brown complexion and long black hair worn to hang to her shoulders. Her skin was flawless and she possessed beautifully arranged features. But the thing that intrigued him most about her were the eyes, which had initially frightened him. They were black orbs surrounded by pure whites under long lashes. Her eyebrows were thick and well defined, and if Cole wasn't mistaken, she didn't have on any makeup. She was wearing a black dress accented by a strand of white cultured pearls. On her, this simple ensemble was as elegant as a queen's coronation gown.

"Good evening. I am Orga Syriac." She walked toward him with a fluid motion that exuded sensuality with every move.

It took him a moment to find his voice. "Hello, I'm Larry Cole."

She laughed. "Are you sure?"

"Yes," he said with more assurance. "Kate Ford called and asked me to escort you to the affair at Navy Pier tonight."

"Yes. She is an angel for doing that and she did provide me with a really handsome escort. I love your dinner jacket."

She reached out and touched his arm. It was as if a jolt of electricity passed through him. The entire room became filled with a sexual tension.

"Kate Ford did me quite a favor too."

She gave him a demure smile. "Shouldn't we be going? It's almost six o'clock."

"I'm at your service," Cole said.

She took his arm and together they headed for the door.

CHAPTER 6

JUNE 11, 2004
6:06 P.M.

The Navy Pier reception was being hosted by the Cook County Political Action Committee. Although it professed allegiance to no political party, PAC was decidedly right-wing and had a tendency to back ultraconservative candidates and causes. It had developed a great deal of political muscle in Chicago and had cracked this once solidly

Democratic bastion to succeed in electing five Republican aldermen to the once one-party fifty-member city council. It was rumored that PAC had a war chest in excess of ten million dollars, and with each fund-raising event, such as the affair tonight, it increased its coffers considerably.

Philo Coffey was the chairman of PAC. He was a seventy-year-old lawyer who had spent most of his career plying his profession in the courtrooms of Cook County. He had once been a minor political functionary in the administration of Mayor Richard J. Daley. However, Philo was ambitious and wanted to be slated for national office. Daley refused to do this until the fledgling, but brilliant, young politician paid some dues and spent time toiling in the wards of the city on behalf of the organization. So, in the early seventies, Coffey broke with the Democratic machine and devoted himself to his legal practice full-time.

A rotund, moonfaced, balding man, Philo Coffey was very rich, and was considered to be one of the best civil procedure attorneys in the state. But he wanted more. He wanted a great deal more. He had long ago given up any desire to hold elective office, at a local or national level, but he did want to become a kingmaker. The power behind the throne, so to speak. To that end, he had formed the Political Action Committee, funded it initially, and watched it grow to become a formidable political presence. Now PAC, in the person of Chairman Philo Coffey, had its sights set on slating its own candidate for mayor in the next city elections and a candidate for governor in the state elections. Coffey was confident that his candidates would triumph, but even if they didn't, he and PAC would be a force to be reckoned with. A force to be feared.

In fact, Coffey and his organization were feared. He was upsetting a status quo that had been in place in Chicago and Cook County since the death of Mayor Harold Washington in 1987. A status quo that could affect the power and the fortunes of a great many prominent people. And, as Philo Coffey was not the type of man who could be easily persuaded to abandon his pet project and was impervious to threats or intimidation, more drastic measures were called for to deal with him and his supporters.

It was a few minutes after six when the prominent PAC chairman's chauffeur-driven limo pulled up to the main entrance to the Navy Pier rotunda. More uniformed policemen were in evidence now, and when the black car stopped, a sergeant leaped forward to open the back door. Philo Coffey, dressed in a custom-tailored white dinner jacket to hide his ample girth, stepped out of the car and smiled at the cop.

"Good evening, Sergeant. It certainly is a nice night for a party, isn't it?"

"Yes sir, Mr. Coffey. It's a great night for a party."

"Make sure your men get fed during the course of the evening," Coffey said. "I've had a buffet table set up for them on the second floor over the kitchen. There are plenty of cold cuts, salad, soup, snacks, and soft drinks. No beer, of course."

"Oh no, Mr. Coffey," the sergeant said. "My officers would never drink on duty."

"I know they wouldn't, Sergeant. I know they wouldn't."

Coffey stepped away from the limo just as a twelve-piece band stationed on the pier struck up "Hail! Hail! The Gang's All Here." Flashing a warm smile, which was caught by the throng of print- and electronic-media types hovering around the entrance, he waved and entered the building.

Inside the rotunda a stirring went through the early arrivals when Coffey walked in. He shook hands with a dozen of his supporters and kissed a number of women. There had been three Mrs. Philo Coffeys, but he'd been divorced from the last one for five years and didn't plan to name a replacement. He was starting for the bar when he saw Jack Carlisle walking toward him. Coffey frowned.

"Good evening, Counselor," Carlisle said expansively.

"Carlisle," Coffey responded solemnly.

The younger man came up to Coffey with his hand extended. When the attorney didn't take it, Carlisle dropped the hand back to his side; however, his smile never altered. Coffey turned his back on Carlisle and walked away.

Jack Carlisle was a handsome man with blond hair and

blue eyes. He was tall, slender, and always impeccably
dressed. He presented a face to the world that was perpetually pleasant and always etched with a smile. But the smile
was a mask he wore to conceal what was really going on in
his mind. And if Philo Coffey could have detected what was
going on in Jack Carlisle's mind he would have been
shocked.

Carlisle was considered part of the nouveau riche society
crowd that had become prominent in Chicago during the past
five years. On his annual income tax return, Carlisle's occupation was listed as "restaurant operator," and he owned
one of the more exclusive nightspots in the Windy City,
called the Dragon's Lair, located on the North Side. However, Jack Carlisle was much more than that.

Carlisle was a gambler, a bookie, and a fixer, but not necessarily in that order. He did not participate in games of
chance but instead bet heavily on professional sporting
events. He particularly enjoyed betting on football and basketball games. And he won consistently, as he was adept at
quoting point spreads with an uncanny accuracy, as well as
predicting the most outrageous upsets.

One of his more noteworthy feats had been a huge bet he
placed on a football game between the reigning Super Bowl
champions and a team which had finished last in its division
with a 2–14 record. Carlisle had placed his money on the
losing team and taken any bet he could get. The bookie's
spread was twelve and a half points, and even though the
Super Bowl champs' star running back was injured and
would not be able to play, it was expected to be little more
than a practice game for them. It turned out to be such a
one-sided defeat that it was dubbed the "Upset of the Century," with the underdogs winning by a score of 41–6.

There were cries of fix from coast to coast, and the NFL
commissioner's office issued a statement that a full investigation would be conducted. The amount of money Jack Carlisle won was estimated to be into eight figures, and it was
rumored that some Mob types, backing the Las Vegas book,
were also going to conduct their own investigation.

But in the long run, the investigations conducted by the

National Football League and the Mafia revealed no more than that the world champs had had an off day against an inferior team. There was nothing anyone could do to Jack Carlisle except pay him what was owed.

However, the NFL and the Las Vegas Mob overlooked a couple of things in their separate investigations of the "Upset of the Century." One item was that the head coach of the world champs had split up with his wife the week prior to the game. Another was that the team was experiencing internal turmoil due to an unpublicized racial incident that had divided the team. The final fact was that since winning the Super Bowl, team morale had been extremely low, with cliques developing and confusion being the general state of affairs. Jack Carlisle was aware of each of these things, due to contacts he had developed on not only the Super Bowl championship team, but every team throughout the NFL and the NBA. So he had anticipated a devastating upset and had won.

But the elements which caused the defeat of the championship team were not purely coincidental. In the weeks prior to the game the football coach's wife had been receiving telephone calls from a woman who asked for her husband in a breathlessly sexy voice. By itself this would have meant nothing; however, five years before, when the coach was running a Southeastern Conference college team, he'd had an affair with a woman on the college faculty. The wife had found out about it, which had placed a strain on their marriage. They had managed to survive together, but when the calls started coming in, the wife had been plunged back into an unbearable nightmare. The head coach had denied any infidelity, but the effect on his marriage was devastating. This had a carryover effect on his preparation for that Sunday's game. The coach had been faithful to his wife since that one foray into infidelity. The telephone calls were placed by a woman in the employ of none other than Jack Carlisle.

Now the fixer stood in the Navy Pier rotunda and watched the receding back of Philo Coffey. Carlisle lifted his martini to his lips and took a sip. For a lawyer, Carlisle thought, Philo Coffey was somewhat naive. He thought that his money and power were all that he needed to take over the political machine in Chicago. And although he had no use for Jack Carlisle, Coffey could have employed the fixer's savvy to keep himself from crossing some people whom it was indeed very dangerous to cross.

Carlisle looked around the rotunda. In fact, he was already manipulating PAC. Of the ten prime tables at the front of the room surrounding the dance floor, Carlisle had purchased seven of them at five hundred dollars a plate. He had given the tickets away. When Coffey seated his VIPs, he'd find them surrounded by associates of Jack Carlisle. The fixer wondered how the esteemed PAC chairman would like that.

A young socialite in a tight dress with a plunging neckline walked up to Carlisle and took his arm. "What are you doing standing out here in the middle of the floor by yourself, Jack?"

His smile broadened. "Waiting for you, honey. Waiting for you."

As Carlisle walked away, with the socialite hanging on his arm, his mind was on Olympic basketball, Philo Coffey, and PAC.

CHAPTER 7

JUNE 11, 2004
6:17 P.M.

The doorbell rang in Cole's condominium overlooking Grant Park. Butch Cole raced to answer it. Swinging the door open he looked out at the figure standing in the hall, took a step back and said, "Wow!"

Judy Daniels walked past him into the apartment. Butch closed the door behind her.

She stopped in the center of the living room and turned around. "You know the doorman almost didn't let me come up. I had to flash my badge and threaten him before he finally gave in."

Butch could see quite clearly why Judy'd had this problem. Over the years he had seen this policewoman in many different disguises. She could transform herself into almost anyone, be they young or old, male or female. And she had fooled many people on both sides of the law with her disguises. No one had ever been able to see through the mask of deception she constructed with makeup and a bit of latex, along with changing her mannerisms, voice, and walk. No one, that is, except Butch Cole.

Today Judy had not adopted a disguise so much as she had a persona. To give her appearance an appropriate name would probably get her labeled a "punk rocker." Her hair, arranged into three spikes on top of her head, was electric blue and held in place with a thick gel. She had applied a thick coating of makeup to her face, which produced a ghostly pallor. Her eyes were heavily lined with mascara and her lips were covered with black lipstick. The jewelry she wore dangling from her ears and around her wrists and neck was appropriately gaudy. She was dressed in a black leather outfit that completely exposed her back to the top of her buttocks and was so tight that it looked to have been applied with spray paint. She was alien, bizarre, and a trifle obscene, but to Butch she looked great.

"Can you do something like that to me?" he said enthusiastically.

She patted the large shoulder bag she carried. "I've got everything right here. I figured to give you what they call the Dennis Rodman look."

"Cool!" Butch cried. "Can I have blond hair?"

"You can have chartreuse hair if you want," she said, unslinging the bag and beginning to remove multicolored jars from it.

"Then?" he said expectantly.

She stared at him for a moment. "Then we're going to the Dragon's Lair, but only on the side where they don't serve alcohol."

"Great!" He plopped down on the couch ready for the Mistress of Disguise/High Priestess of Mayhem to change his appearance.

"First, you'd better get me a couple of old towels."

"Yes, ma'am." He leaped up and headed for the bathroom.

"And Butch." Her voice stopped him.

He turned around.

"We have a deal."

"Yes, ma'am. We've got a deal." Then he continued on his way to get the towels.

CHAPTER 8

JUNE 11, 2004
6:24 P.M.

"How long have you been the chief of detectives?" Orga asked.

They were on Lake Shore Drive approaching the Navy Pier exit. Since leaving her South Lake Shore Drive condo, Orga Syriac and Larry Cole had gotten acquainted.

"About seven years," Cole said, finding that, contrary to his expectations, this "electronic-media type" was very much to his liking.

She was gazing out the window at the passing sights of Lake Shore Drive when she said, "Police work must be fascinating."

"It has its points," Cole said. He glanced sideways at her. She was indeed stunning, but there was something about her that was bothering him. He remembered when she walked into the living room back in her apartment. At that instant he was certain that he was in the presence of something extremely dangerous. But he could detect nothing dangerous about this very beautiful woman now.

"How long have you been in broadcasting?"

She turned from her examination of the passing scenery to look at him. "Actually only a very short time. In fact, this job in Chicago is my first in television."

"What did you do before, newspaper reporting or radio commentary?"

"No. I simply sent WGN my photograph and a sample of me speaking on video and they hired me."

Cole was certain that she was joking, but when he glanced at her he found that she was staring back at him in deadly earnest. Before he could question her further they pulled up to the gates leading out to the pier.

There was a short queue of cars being cleared by the security guard with the assistance of the two Eighteenth District police officers. The cop from the Saint Rita class of 1987 recognized Cole and walked down the line to intercept him.

"Good evening, Chief," the officer said. "A number of exempt members have already arrived. It's a madhouse at the entrance to the rotunda. If you'd like, I can get one of our guys on motorcycles to clear a path for you to the VIP parking section."

There were certain privileges that came with being the chief of detectives. One of these was the motorcycle escort service the officer was extending to him. Cole accepted the offer, and in less than a minute a uniformed officer wearing a robin's-egg blue helmet and knee-length black leather boots guided a big Harley-Davidson police motorcycle in front of Cole's black Chevrolet. The motorcyclist turned to look at Cole, gave a thumbs-up, and then turned on his lights and siren. Cole followed as a path was cleared down the pier.

"I'm impressed," Orga said.

"Just routine, ma'am," Cole said with a Jack Webb deadpan. "Just routine.

*   *   *

The motorcyclist left them at the valet VIP parking area at the south end of the pier. Cole walked around to the passenger side to assist his lovely date from the car. She came out regally and took his arm. They began walking toward the entrance to the rotunda.

Two mounted unit cops, astride their horses, stood guard a short distance from the VIP parking section. The cops recognized Cole and sat up a bit straighter. The horses became skittish.

Cole's attention was focused on Orga. "It's my understanding from Kate Ford that the people at WGN are saying that you're going to be the next Oprah."

The exotic woman smiled and said, "Kate is being much too kind. All I'm going to be doing at the start is some traffic and weather reports."

Cole was about to make a comment about this when one of the mounted-unit horses, a chestnut mare, began to rear and buck, making a concentrated effort to unhorse its rider. The other horse, a black gelding, began pawing nervously at the cement surface of the pier, causing sparks to fly from its iron-shod hooves. It was obvious that both riders had lost control of their mounts.

Orga disengaged herself from Cole and walked toward the agitated animals. He reached for her, but she was moving away rapidly and at the same time speaking in a low tone of voice. Cole couldn't hear clearly what she was saying, but he was able to detect that she wasn't speaking English.

As she approached, the horses glared at her with wild-eyed fear; however, their agitation began subsiding and the mare lowered her head. Orga went first to the gelding, who snorted loudly and bared its teeth. She reached out her hand, palm up, and after the horse sniffed the palm, it also lowered its head. She patted the huge animal's mane, said more words in the same foreign language, and moved on to the mare.

The chestnut horse actually behaved like a fawned-over puppy as it nuzzled the woman's hand and sighed deeply. Cole and the two cops, who had managed to stay astride their mounts, were dumbfounded.

She was rubbing the mare's chest when Cole walked up

beside her. "You really have a way with animals."

She turned to look at him. "At times, Larry. At times."

The cop on the mare said, "Priscilla here can get real nervous sometimes, ma'am, but I've never seen her react like this to anyone."

Orga looked into the horse's eyes. "You're a good girl, aren't you, Priscilla. Just trying to take care of yourself and your own the best you can."

The woman lingered a moment longer before turning to Cole. "I'd better go someplace and wash up. You wouldn't want your date smelling like a horse."

As a bewildered chief of detectives led Orga Syriac into the Navy Pier rotunda, the cop on the mare said, "Isn't that the damnedest thing you've ever seen?"

The other officer's face remained impassive. He responded, "Yeah, but what got the horses riled up in the first place?"

CHAPTER 9

JUNE 11, 2004
6:30 P.M.

Father James Lochran, or rather the man impersonating Father Lochran, was mingling with other guests at the reception in the rotunda. He was nursing a bourbon and water. He planned to have nothing else alcoholic to drink tonight. Unlike the dead man he was portraying, the phony priest did not believe in excessive drinking.

Jack Carlisle and the shapely socialite in the low-cut dress were making idle chitchat with the priest. They had discussed little of consequence until the subject of the Catholic Church came up.

"I must say, Father," the socialite said with a slight British accent, which was an affectation she'd picked up while attending finishing school in England, "that I don't see why priests can't marry. After all, this is the twenty-first century."

Father Lochran smiled. "The vow of celibacy was not meant to affect merely one time in history, but was meant as a means of deepening the faith of the most important of God's servants for all time."

Jack Carlisle, perpetual grin in place, joined in. "But surely, Father, things are a great deal different for a priest today than they were a thousand or even a hundred years ago."

The priest played with his plastic cup of booze, but didn't drink from it. "The world is different, Mr. Carlisle, but the priesthood has remained the same as the day Christ named his apostles to be the twelve original priests."

The socialite's cheeks reddened. "Couldn't that possibly be the problem with the church today? Why attendance at mass continues to drop from year to year and converts to the faith are becoming increasingly hard to find?"

Father Lochran cleared his throat. "I don't think that the problem originates with Holy Mother Church, dear lady, but with the world community *she* is trying to serve and save. The precepts that we adhere to, under the enlightened guidance of Our Holy Father the pope, were passed down to us by our Lord Jesus Christ. It is not for us to alter them, but to carry them out in the face of society's adversity and the pressures of modernity."

"Well said, Father," Jack Carlisle said, before the socialite could add anything more to the argument. He noticed she was rapidly turning crimson and that any further exchanges between her and the priest would probably result in a shouting match. At least a one-sided one from her perspective. Taking her arm he began guiding her away from the confrontation. "Come, dear, it's time we found our seats for dinner."

The priest imposter watched them go. For a moment he

stood alone in the massive Navy Pier rotunda, which was rapidly filling to capacity. He noticed a number of prominent politicians present, including the lieutenant governor. Also the core of the people who financed PAC were in evidence. They, along with Philo Coffey, were the reason for the presence of the Reverend Father James Lochran. A presence that would result in this affair becoming a total disaster in the most complete sense of the word.

"Father Lochran," someone called to him.

Turning, the priest came face-to-face with a young man with thinning hair. He extended his hand. "I'm Gordon Harris, Mr. Coffey's assistant. I'd like to escort you to the dais. We'll be signaling the start of dinner shortly."

"Thank you, young man," Lochran said, deepening his accent.

He followed the assistant through the crowd to the dais, which consisted of a head table set for twelve resting on a raised platform. As he walked along with the aid of his cane, the priest touched his jacket pocket. Through the cloth he could feel a small rectangular device about the size of a pocket pager. On this device there was a button, which when depressed detonated an explosive by remote control. This explosive was wired to a table at the center of the dining area. The devastation it would cause would be monstrous, with a number of people killed and a great many more severely injured.

Of course, there would be survivors and perhaps even Philo Coffey would come out of this alive. However, PAC would be severely damaged and a number of its major supporters along with it.

The priest knew that the explosion would be considered an act of political terrorism. Radical groups would be targeted and some fringe fanatical faction would probably take credit for the act. But terrorism was not the reason for the bombing, but rather the realignment of the status quo, which PAC had upset. It was an act to reestablish order, not one intended to impose chaos. And the instrument for this reestablishment of order was the man posing as Father James Lochran.

The assistant led the priest to the center of the dais. There an enraged Philo Coffey was yelling at a small, very pale man wearing a cutaway coat. "I don't care how many god-damned tables he bought! I've got ten of the committee's top contributors I promised that table to and I'm not going to seat them back by the fucking kitchen!"

"Excuse me, Mr. Coffey," Gordon Harris said quietly.

Coffey spun on his assistant. "What in the hell do you want?!"

"Uh, you sent me to get Father Lochran."

"Yes, I did. So what are you doing . . . ?" Coffey looked past his assistant at the man in the clerical garb. Some of the wealthy attorney's anger ebbed away. "How do you do, Father? I have a place for you up here. I'd appreciate your giving us a nice, short invocation before dinner."

"It would be my pleasure, Mr. Coffey. I'll give you a prayer that will perk up the ears of the angels."

"Fine," Coffey said abruptly. "Have a seat." He indicated a chair with the priest's name on a place card on the table in front of it. As Father Lochran hobbled to his seat, Coffey spun back to the man in the cutaway coat. "I've got to take one of Carlisle's tables."

"But, sir . . . ," the little man attempted to protest.

Coffey shut him up with a wave of his hand. The lawyer looked off across the crowded rotunda. "Who do you have at table six?"

The little man consulted a list he carried. "Mr. Carlisle purchased that table for members of the Chicago Police Department."

"Okay, I want the cops moved to table thirty. I'll make the apologies to them personally. Who's at table eight?"

"That table was purchased by Barbara Zorin, the national president of the Sisters in Crime writers group."

"We'd better leave them there. Move the cops to table thirty."

The little man appeared distressed. "Mr. Carlisle will—"

"I don't give a shit about Carlisle," Coffey snapped. "I'm running this show, not him."

"Yes, sir."

"Excuse us, Father," Coffey said. Then he led his assistant and the little man off the dais.

Alone, the priest impersonator looked off across the rotunda at table 30. He knew that there was approximately eight ounces of an extremely powerful plastic explosive secreted beneath that table. When it blew, no one seated there would survive.

The priest had the thought, *The Lord giveth and the Lord taketh away.*

CHAPTER 10

JUNE 11, 2004
6:36 P.M.

Larry Cole was waiting for Orga Syriac in the alcove outside the main rotunda when he heard his name called. Turning, he found Jeffrey MacNeil, the deputy chief of patrol division administration, walking toward him. MacNeil was an overweight man of fifty with thinning hair. He was more politician than cop and had spent his entire police career behind a desk.

"What's up, Jeff?" Cole said.

The heavyset man's face was flushed and he was obviously angry. "There's some kind of flap on inside between Philo Coffey and Jack Carlisle. They've put the CPD right in the middle of it."

"How so?"

MacNeil explained about the table changes. "So they just moved us to table thirty. The first deputy, three deputy superintendents, two assistant deputy superintendents, and four deputy chiefs were just snatched out of their chairs and forced to a table at the back of the room."

Cole did some mental arithmetic. "Hold it a minute. I counted ten heads at the CPD table."

"That's right," MacNeil said, still seething.

"And I assume that everyone is already here?"

MacNeil nodded and then started to catch on. "Uh, you haven't got your ticket yet have you, Chief?"

"Deputy Superintendent Rogers was supposed to have it for me. I still can't figure out why I was singled out for the invitation anyway."

"From what I heard," MacNeil explained, "all the requests were made directly to the superintendent by Jack Carlisle. Also I heard that he especially wanted you to be in attendance. He's supposedly said publicly on a number of occasions that you are his favorite cop."

"I'm flattered," Cole said with a pronounced lack of enthusiasm.

"But as far as the tickets go, there must have been a miscount, because when I left, our table was full."

Cole smiled, "Well, I guess I got dressed up for nothing."

Orga emerged from the ladies' room and walked over to the two cops. Cole noticed that MacNeil was as stunned by her appearance as he had been. After making the introductions, Cole explained the dilemma to his date.

"That really won't be a problem, Larry," she said. "I've got two tickets for the Sisters in Crime table. You can sit with us."

For the second time that evening Cole felt his spirits brighten. The idea of sitting through dinner with the cops that would be at his former table didn't appeal to him at all.

"Enjoy dinner, Jeff," Cole said as he headed for the rotunda with Orga on his arm. "I'll see you around."

The fat cop called after them, "Thanks, Chief, and it was nice meeting you, ma'am."

When they were out of earshot of MacNeil, Orga said, "You were obviously relieved that you didn't have to sit at that table. Do you mind telling me why?"

"I will," Cole said, opening the door to the main rotunda for her, "just as soon as we sit down."

The dais was filling up rapidly. The only remaining vacancies were for Philo Coffey, who was attending to last-minute arrangements down on the rotunda floor, and the president of the Cook County Board, whom another commitment would prevent from attending tonight's affair.

Father Lochran had exchanged pleasantries with a couple of the arriving dignitaries, but as the seats on both sides of him were vacant, he was left alone to gaze around the crowded rotunda.

He couldn't help but feel a certain disdain for these people. They thought they were in actual control of their lives and the events that affected those lives. From the superrich Counselor Philo Coffey, to the manipulations of Jack Carlisle, to the members of PAC, who gave their money so freely to the right-wing causes which the Political Action Committee supported. Causes which they hoped would keep the poor, the homeless, and the disenfranchised out of their sight or at least away from their doorsteps. To keep the rich and affluent blissfully ignorant of those minor blemishes on the facade of the American Dream, such as racism, sexism, and homophobia. Perhaps this was the tragedy of it all, Lochran thought. That if these people simply followed the Word of God and indeed "loved their neighbor as they did themselves," then what he was about to do wouldn't be necessary. A troubling thought invaded his consciousness: *Thou shalt not kill.* He quickly pushed it away. He wasn't committing murder; he was merely doing his duty.

Again he looked around the rotunda. A disgruntled group of cops were being relocated to the new table by Philo Coffey. Lochran recognized most of them and could even call a few by name. There were First Deputy Superintendent Bishop and Deputy Superintendents Rogers, Seidman, and Fitzgerald. He knew the assistant deputy superintendents on sight, but not by name. He had read the files the Institute maintained on each of them. Their presence at the affair was noted because they were also a contributing cause to aber-

rations in the system. This was because, although they'd
never taken a bribe or even so much as accepted a cup of
coffee "on the arm," as it was called, they had long ago sold
their badges to the highest bidder. Instead of working in the
city's crime-ridden slime pits, they had curried political favor
and performed such onerous tasks as chauffeuring and body-
guarding politicians. Any police work they had ever performed was done in the safety of offices, and little, if
anything, of merit was ever accomplished by them. Now, for
the most part, due to the political manipulations of PAC, they
virtually controlled the Chicago Police Department.

However, Father James Lochran's mission against the
CPD was more comprehensive than the simple elimination
of the law enforcement sycophants now seated at table 30.
There was also the opposite extreme to be considered. Someone who, after tonight's action, could pose a threat to those
mounting that action. This individual was Chief of Detectives
Larry Cole.

The priest impersonator felt a twinge of conscience. Cole
had been thoroughly studied at the Human Development Institute, and the threat he presented had been analyzed. Initially, his participation in the PAC affair tonight merely
would have placed him in jeopardy, which his file indicated
he had been in and survived many times before. However,
now that he would be seated at table 30, where the explosive
was secreted, there would be no way that he would survive.
Another thought crossed Lochran's mind: *Indeed God does
provide*.

He was still idly studying the people into whose lives he
was about to introduce so much mayhem and violence when
he turned to look at the entrance doors. A woman entered
the rotunda. She wore a black dress and was stunningly beautiful, although he viewed her beauty from a completely pla-
tonic perspective. His eyes moved casually to the man in the
white dinner jacket walking beside her. Larry Cole had arrived. Then the priest began experiencing a silent psycho-
logical seizure of such violence that he nearly passed out.

In the blink of an eye he was no longer in the Navy Pier
rotunda in the year 2004, but someplace else. Someplace

foreign, dark, and dangerous. A place where evil lurked. An evil that was attempting to kill him. An evil that was female.

"Father Lochran?" The voice of Gordon Harris, Philo Coffey's assistant, came to him as if from a great distance. "Father Lochran, are you well?"

He attempted to respond, but his entire body was frozen rigid. However, his eyes in the present were locked on the beautiful black woman crossing the rotunda floor, while his mind was imprisoned in the past and the memory of the she-devil who had pursued him nearly a half century ago.

Cole was walking beside Orga Syriac across the rotunda floor when she suddenly stopped. He had proceeded a pace or two farther before he became aware that she was no longer with him. He turned around and found her staring up at the dais. And he noticed that in her posture and gaze something about her had changed. For just a brief instant he felt that same sense of peril he had experienced back in her apartment. He took a step toward her and stopped. He followed her line of sight up to the head table, where a thin balding man was leaning over a man in clerical garb, who looked seriously ill. As Cole watched, the priest fell off the chair. Forgetting Orga, Cole bolted onto the dais to lend assistance.

Father Lochran was lying on his back on the floor of the dais. Despite the paralysis, he was aware that he had a mission to carry out. He fought through his agony to reach for the device in his pocket, but he was helpless and his limbs wouldn't cooperate with his brain. A familiar face leaned over him. It was Larry Cole, the man whom only a short time ago he was planning to kill. Cole was speaking to him: "Father, you must lie still. You're having some type of seizure. An ambulance is on the way."

Again, Lochran reached for the remote detonator. Cole grabbed his wrist. "Relax, Father. Help will be here in a few minutes."

Cole's face dissolved into the she-devil's, and as Lochran began losing consciousness, a terrible despair settled over him. He had failed in his mission. In the blackness that closed in on him, the she-devil remained.

CHAPTER 11

Barbara Zorin, Jamal Garth, and Kate Ford were seated at table 8 across the dance floor directly in front of the spot on the dais where the priest collapsed. They also saw Cole and Orga Syriac stop at the center of the dance floor. When Cole leaped up on the dais, the writers got up and rushed over to Orga.

"What happened?" asked Jamal Garth, a distinguished-looking black man in his sixties, whose adventure novels had sold over 100 million copies around the world.

"Is the priest okay?" questioned Kate Ford. The investigative reporter was a pretty blonde who had developed a tremendous reputation in her field.

Orga Syriac did not respond to either question and she never took her eyes off what was happening on the dais.

"I'm going to help Larry," Barbara said, hiking up her dress and climbing up beside Cole. An ambulance crew entered and rushed onto the dais. Everyone in the rotunda had stopped to stare at what was happening to the sick priest.

Jamal Garth turned to look at Orga Syriac and again ask her what had happened when he caught a glimpse of her face. What he saw there startled him to the point that his heart began beating discernibly faster. Then she turned to look at him. For just a moment the author doubted his sanity. The woman standing next to him was outrageously beautiful, not the . . . *thing* he thought he had seen a moment ago.

She smiled. "We haven't been introduced, Mr. Garth. I'm Orga Syriac."

"Yes," Garth said, finding that his mouth had gone dry. "It's nice to meet you."

They were lifting the priest onto a stretcher. Cole and Barbara Zorin remained standing on the dais until they carried the ill man out of the rotunda. Then they joined the other writers and Orga back on the dance floor.

Philo Coffey was making some consoling remarks to the audience about the sick priest along with uttering a half-hearted statement for his quick recovery.

"Shall we take our seats?" Cole said. They began walking to their table.

Orga turned to him. "What was the priest's name, Larry?"

"I think someone referred to him as a Father Lochran, although I didn't catch his first name. Do you know him?"

"No," she said. "He simply reminds me of someone I met a long time ago."

"He appeared to be having a seizure," the silver-haired Barbara Zorin said. "But he looked like he was really afraid of something."

"You're saying you think his seizure was caused by him being frightened?" Kate Ford questioned.

"There's no way I could tell you that," Barbara responded. "Only a doctor could. But I've seen frightened people before, and that man was terrified."

When they were seated, Jamal Garth lapsed into a contemplative mood. He glanced at Cole's date. She looked back at him and smiled. He tried to smile back, but the attempt failed.

Philo Coffey was at the microphone. "In the face of this unexpected emergency, I guess I'll have to bless this affair myself before we have dinner. I'm not much good at this sort of thing, so I'll ask you all to be not only patient with me, but tolerant of my inexperience. Please stand."

As the three hundred diners got to their feet for the PAC chairman's invocation, the explosive under table 30 was still in place.

CHAPTER 12

The Dragon's Lair was located on Superior just off of Wells Street. A line had formed outside and an off-duty cop named Tom Grant was working security at the door when two punk rockers sauntered up to him. He eyed the pair with open disdain. The female had blue spiked hair and the male's hair was a shade the cop could only call lime green. They, like most of those waiting to get into the club, looked to Grant like aliens from another planet. If he didn't need the money so badly, he would quit this job. He was about to tell the bizarrely hued pair to get in line like everyone else when the woman said, "How's it going, Tommy?"

He frowned. "Who in the hell are you?"

"Your ex-partner from the Twelfth District tactical team thirteen years ago."

"Blow it out your ear, sweetheart. Take your boyfriend and—" He stopped suddenly and squinted at her in confusion. "Judy?"

She winked one of her heavily lined eyes at him. "Also known as . . ."

She motioned to her male companion, who was clad in a black leather outfit similar to the one made popular by Richard Roundtree in the *Shaft* movies. He completed the statement for her: ". . . the Mistress of Disguise/High Priestess of Mayhem."

"What in the hell are you doing here?"

"It's a long story."

Grant shrugged and stood back to let them enter. He ignored the protests from those waiting in line.

The noise hit them the instant they stepped into the interior of the Dragon's Lair. The music was blasted from six-foot-tall speakers arranged around a cavernous room, which was divided into three sections by floor-to-ceiling partitions. The section they entered was dominated by a huge dance floor surrounded by tables and chairs. The dance floor was packed. A bar, running along the far wall, was doing a brisk business, although only soft drinks, popcorn, hot dogs, and hamburgers were served. A huge dragon in gold filigree dominated the ceiling, and simulated smoke spewed from the painting's nostrils. There were corridors leading off to the other sections of the club. In those sections alcohol was served, and in order to enter those areas, IDs had to be presented to two huge men stationed at the entryway. Judy recognized the guards as off-duty cops, but she had no intention of approaching them. She and Butch would remain in the nonalcohol section during their visit to the Dragon's Lair.

"Let's dance." Butch had to shout to be heard over the noise.

"Later," she yelled back. "First, you've got to fulfill your end of the deal."

"With all this noise?"

"I've got excellent hearing. Come on, I'll buy you a soda."

They sat down at the bar. A female bartender, clad only in a halter top, a pair of very short shorts, and black boots, stepped in front of them. "I like your hair," she said to Butch.

"Thanks," he said with a broad grin.

She swung her eyes to Judy. "I like yours too, but women aren't my thing." Then she looked back at Butch. "Is this your old lady?"

He was stunned speechless.

"He's spoken for, sweetheart," Judy said with a glare.

"Just checking," she said with a shrug. "I could make beautiful music with a hunk like him. What'll it be?"

Judy ordered them both Cokes.

The bartender gave Butch an obscene gesture with her tongue before walking away.

When she was out of earshot Judy warned, "I don't want you getting any ideas while we're here, Butch."

He hadn't taken his eyes off the bartender. "She was just being friendly, Judy."

"There's a limit to friendliness."

After they were served, Judy turned to him. "Okay, let's have it."

Either the decibel level of the music had decreased or they were getting used to it, because they no longer had to shout.

"You want me to tell you how I always know it's you no matter what kind of disguise you're wearing?"

"That was our deal."

"Okay, there are two things I've always been able to use to tell that it's you."

"And those are?"

Before he could answer, she noticed him stiffen as he looked over her left shoulder at the club entrance. "Judy, look!"

She turned around to see the reason for his surprise. It was obvious instantly. Paige Albritton had just walked in.

Judy and Butch had met Paige during Larry Cole's investigation of Neil and Margo DeWitt, a pair of superrich serial killers. In fact, Butch and Paige had been kidnapped by the maniacal DeWitt woman and barely managed to escape with their lives. After the DeWitt case was closed, they'd kept in touch for a time before drifting apart during the eight years that had passed since the summer of 1996. Now, as Judy and Butch watched their old friend enter the Dragon's Lair, they could see that time hadn't been very kind to Paige.

Prior to their meeting, Paige had been a high-priced Mob call girl. She was rescued from her former occupation by Sergeant Clarence "Mack" McKinnis, who had become one of Neil DeWitt's victims. To Judy, it was obvious that Paige had returned to the fast lane and that it was burning her out quickly.

It wasn't so much that she looked bad as she appeared exhausted with a fatigue that no amount of rest could alleviate. Her hair, when they had known her, had been dark brown. Now it was bleached to an almost platinum blond, worn short, and it looked as if it received little care. Her pearl white skin was pale and lifeless. She had maintained her figure, but she was tall and a few more pounds would not have hurt her at all.

Paige was not alone. Judy recognized the garishly dressed man walking with her as Sonny Balfour, who was Jack Carlisle's righthand man. Balfour was a dark-complexioned black man who still wore his hair in oily jheri curls. He had the face of an ex-pug, and before he'd hooked up with Carlisle, he'd been a contender for the middleweight crown. A title he failed to win during a controversial fifteen-round bout at Madison Square Garden seven years ago. A fight Carlisle had made a bundle on. Balfour was reputedly now a collector for Carlisle's sports-betting operation.

The other person with Paige was also fairly well known. Her name was Vanessa "Fuzzy" Dubcek, a pretty, well-put-together woman who was the wife of Chicago Bulls basketball star Piotr "Pete" Dubcek. Dubcek was the star playmaking guard for the Bulls and had led the Chicago pro team to within a game of going to the NBA finals two weeks ago. He was from Germany, and when the couple had announced that they were getting married on that past Christmas Day it had caused quite a stir in the Chicago gossip columns.

As Judy recalled, Fuzzy Dubcek was twenty-four and had something of a reputation as a party girl in the various fast-track nightclubs around the city. She'd been romantically linked to a couple of professional sports figures in the past and had been involved in a scandal when a fight over her broke out in a Rush Street bar. Two of the participants in this brawl were members of the Chicago Bears, and an innocent bystander was hospitalized in critical condition with a fractured skull. The next time Fuzzy was heard from, her imminent marriage to Pete Dubcek was announced.

Butch got up and started to yell at Paige. Judy quickly snatched him back into his seat.

"But, Judy . . . !" he protested.

She whispered, "Take it easy and let's see what's going on before we start renewing acquaintances."

The threesome walked past them and took a table at the

edge of the dance floor. Judy noticed the vacant expression on Paige's face. She was either high or had gone through so much lately that she was emotionally drained. After sitting down, Paige looked directly at them, but did not display any recognition. Balfour leaned over to say something to her, and she got up and headed for the bar.

"Are we undercover?" Butch whispered. His back was to Paige and he didn't see her until she was standing beside him. Quickly, he lowered his head, which Judy could have kicked him for doing. Paige didn't pay the slightest attention to either of them.

The female bartender came down the bar to wait on Paige, who ordered three soft drinks, which she didn't pay for. Turning with drinks in hand, she returned to the table. Fuzzy Dubcek was already dancing with a husky black guy wearing nothing over his upper body but a skimpy black vest. Sonny Balfour was snapping his fingers in time to the rock tune blasting over the speakers. It was obvious that Paige was considered little more than a servant, and it didn't look like she enjoyed her job very much.

"So what are we going to do now?" Butch asked.

"We're going to watch them and see what they're up to."

"You mean we're on a stakeout?"

She turned to look at him. His excitement was evident.

"We're on a stakeout, Butch."

"Cool!"

CHAPTER 13

The meal served during the PAC dinner was singularly unspectacular. The chicken was bland, the vegetables tasteless, and the bread rolls a bit hard. The guests were saved by a hot minestrone soup, which the chef had obviously taken the time to season properly, and a crisp salad. The dessert was vanilla ice cream with chocolate sauce, which was adequate. However, the company at table 8, where Cole and Orga were seated, made up for the inadequacy of the meal.

Barbara Zorin and Jamal Garth talked about the new novels they had in progress. Cole briefly discussed serial killer Dwight Frazier, which absorbed the attention of everyone at the table. Then, after Orga had maintained an attentive silence for a time, Kate brought her into the conversation. "So when do you start at Channel Nine?"

She dabbed her lips with a napkin and replied, "Next week."

"Are you excited?" Barbara asked.

"I guess I am. It will be an interesting job: however, it will be nowhere near as stimulating as what Larry does."

Jamal Garth was watching Orga. "What part of the country are you from, Ms. Syriac?"

She spooned ice cream into her mouth and took a moment to swallow. She repeated the dabbing with her napkin and said, "The South, but I wasn't raised in America, Mr. Garth."

They waited. She took another bite of her ice cream and added, "I was born in Africa."

"Oh," Kate Ford said, displaying a heightened interest. "What nation?"

Orga uttered a short, mirthless laugh. "I really don't know. My parents were missionaries and we moved from place to place. I've lived in Zaire, Nigeria, Liberia, and Egypt, just to name a few."

"But your English is flawless," Garth said. "I detected something in your speech, but it is so faint as to be almost completely undetectable."

Cole laughed. "You've got better hearing than me, Jamal. She could have grown up next door to me on the South Side of Chicago for all the accent I could detect in her speech."

"You know, Orga, you could probably help me with some research I'm doing for my next book," Kate said.

"You're writing a book about Africa?" Cole asked.

"Actually, I'm writing about some African myths."

"That doesn't sound like your usual line of inquiry, Kate," Barbara said.

"Oh, I am conducting an investigation, but instead of going into corruption in government, I'll be exploring some African lore which has manifested itself in our contemporary society."

The PAC affair raged around them; however, the people at table 8 were becoming totally engrossed in their after-dinner conversation.

"It sounds like you're talking about voodoo, Kate," Garth said.

"Worship of the god Vodu originated in Africa and the practice of voodoo was brought to America with the slave trade. There are still vestiges of it in today's world."

"Such as with your friend Sandra Devereaux," Cole said, referring to the owner of the new Sandy's jazz club on Fifty-third Street in Hyde Park.

"Madame Devereaux will be a part of my book, but I'm more interested in an entity known as an Abo-Esu."

"What is that?" Cole asked.

"A she-devil," Orga said, placing her spoon down beside

her ice-cream dish. "It is also called an Abo-Yorba, depending on which language you are speaking."

Kate was surprised. "You seem to know a lot about the she-devil, Orga. Perhaps you could help me with my research?"

She appeared uncomfortable. "Actually, I don't know much about it. I just heard some stories years ago." Her voice trailed off, but before anyone could say anything she added, "Why don't you tell me what you've learned from your research and I'll see if I can add anything to it."

Kate considered this for a moment before agreeing. "From what I've been able to find out, the Abo-Esu, or as you called it, Orga, the Abo-Yorba, dates back to the time of the ancient Egyptians some four thousand years before Christ. The pharaoh Ramses II reportedly made an Ethiopian princess a high priestess in his court. She was supposed to be capable of changing from a goddess into a demon at will."

"More recent reports date to the sixteen hundreds at the height of the slave trade. A band of pirates was anchored off the coast preparing to sail to America with a load of kidnapped Africans when a woman swam out to the boat. She was described in one of the survivor's accounts, written fifteen years later, as very beautiful. The crew pulled her on board and planned to rape her and sell her into slavery as well, but they never got the chance. She supposedly altered her appearance right before their eyes to become something that the survivor referred to as a 'demon.' She then proceeded to kill or seriously injure a number of pirates, free the Africans, and set the ship on fire."

Jamal laughed. "What is this she-devil supposed to be, a werewolf?"

Kate shook her head. "Not in the terms of lycanthropy or the traditional European werewolf legends, but she is a shape-shifter. Also, werewolves are cursed and stigmatized by the pentagram. The African she-devil does not appear to be cursed, but is rather a being who protects the weak. In some of the tales I've come across she, and those like her, are actually a separate and distinct species from Homo sapiens. They are at times referred to as angels in human form."

"Like aliens?" Barbara asked.

"No," Kate responded. "The Abo-Esu are creatures of the earth; however, they are superior to us in a number of ways, including strength, intellect, longevity, and the ability to change their appearances at will."

"But these she-devils will kill?" Garth said.

"Yes, but only when they, or someone weak or oppressed, is threatened, such as was the case with those kidnapped Africans the pirates planned to sell into slavery."

Cole hadn't said anything for some time. He had been discreetly observing Orga. During the discussion of African she-devils, she had become as tense as a taut violin string. Now Cole asked, "Kate, how did you become interested in researching these she-devils?"

"I was in Sandy's jazz club a couple of months ago and got to talking to Sandra Devereaux, who began telling me the story about a black community in Mississippi called Diggstown. According to her—"

At that moment Philo Coffey stepped to the microphone and announced, "Can I have your attention please? We're going to begin the formal program, which I assure you will be brief. Then we'll have the rest of the evening to party and dance the night away."

At table 8 the discussion about African she-devils halted. Cole noticed that his date was visibly relieved.

CHAPTER 14

A young doctor in the emergency room at University Hospital shined a penlight in Father James Lochran's eyes. The priest was still caught in the grip of a manic paralysis. A nurse assisted the doctor.

"I want to do a brain scan on this man, but I don't think that whatever is causing his paralysis has an organic origin."

"I don't understand, Doctor," the nurse said.

The doctor straightened up and put his light away. "This man looks like he's been scared senseless."

"But what could have done such a thing to him?"

The doctor picked up his chart. "The ambulance crew stated that he was attending a political fund-raiser. Not much there to scare anyone. Well, get him ready for testing."

"Yes, sir."

They left the helpless man alone in the curtained cubicle. A few minutes passed and he remained as he'd been since his collapse at Navy Pier. His face was still frozen in the horror he'd experienced; however, his mind was alive with thought. He was in a fierce struggle to overcome his terror and regain control of his emotions. The image of the she-devil remained etched in his mind, but he had slowly forced it away with another image, one that he managed to place beside that of the she-devil. Then he began to recover.

The paralysis receded. He looked around the hospital cubicle with confusion. He couldn't remember how he'd gotten there. Then he recalled his mission. He felt for the device in his pocket and was relieved to find that he still had it. He realized that the device was useless at a distance of more than two hundred yards from the explosive, so he would have to return to Navy Pier.

His cane was on the floor beside the cot he was lying on. His legs were weak, but he managed to get to his feet, retrieve his cane, and leave the cubicle. He was intent on completing his mission.

Less than a minute later the nurse returned to find her patient gone.

CHAPTER 15

JUNE 11, 2004
9:03 P.M.

Jack Carlisle was about to call it a night. Although Philo Coffey had promised the audience that the formal program would be short, it was turning out to be a long-winded political affair in the true tradition of the Windy City. One politician after another tramped to the microphone to extol the virtues of PAC, themselves, and their individual political affiliations, but not necessarily in that order. Now the fixer who owned the Dragon's Lair was becoming bored. It was also getting close to the time for him to check out his club.

But everything this evening had not been of a boring, humdrum nature. He had enjoyed watching Philo Coffey turn red when he had demanded one of Carlisle's tables for some of the PAC chairman's political cronies. Although Carlisle had displayed a certain degree of polite irritation, he hadn't really cared where Coffey put the cops. There was really only one cop he was interested in anyway, and Cole didn't sit with his fellow cops, but at a table with a bunch of writers. Carlisle had glanced in the direction of table 8 a number of times during the evening; however, this was not because of Cole. It was because of the black woman he was with.

Jack Carlisle was a ruthless man who had made it in this world by doing whatever he had to do, both legal and illegal, to succeed. There had been numerous women in his life, but none of them had ever been more to him than a sex object, such as the socialite with the phony British accent sitting with him at table 2 in the Navy Pier rotunda. A few years ago he had been infatuated with a movie star who was making a film on location in Chicago. They had even discussed marriage. Then she had gone back to California and he had promptly forgotten her.

Now Carlisle found himself inexplicably drawn to the woman with Cole. Finally, when he couldn't endure the speeches any longer, he said a curt good-bye to his phony-British-accented dinner companion, stood up, and headed for the exit. However, first he made a detour by table 8.

Although the rest of them were paying polite, if not rapt, attention to what was being said on the dais, Cole looked up as Carlisle approached. The fixer's perpetual smile broadened. Few people would be able to sneak up on this cop. Then Cole's exquisite dinner companion glanced in Carlisle's direction.

The fixer knew people. His livelihood depended on this. He could size up most people after only brief moments of casual contact. There were a few who were guarded enough to hide their inner self from him completely, but he hadn't met such an individual in a very long time. There were also a few that he could read completely with only a single glance. He initially thought this woman was one of those people.

She was intelligent, honest, and extremely compassionate, Carlisle's sixth sense for such things told him. She was the type who would see an injured stray dog or cat on the street and rush it to the vet, where she would pay for the cost of the treatment out of her own pocket. She would never refuse a street person a handout and she probably gave a substantial amount of her income to charity. In Carlisle's estimation, a twenty-four-carat sucker. Then something else began coming through to him about her. Something that made him actually stop before proceeding the remaining few paces to her table. *This woman was dangerous!*

The distinct impressions he got from her were so incongruous as to make no sense. He decided to file them away for future reference.

A retired judge, who had to be at least ninety and spoke in a low gravelly voice barely above a whisper, was at the microphone rambling on about a subject that the vast majority of the diners weren't paying any attention to when Carlisle walked up to table 8.

"Talent, brains, and beauty all in one place at the same time," he said expansively, and loudly enough to turn heads at a number of tables, as well as draw a scowl from Philo Coffey seated on the dais.

Barbara Zorin and Jamal Garth had never met Jack Carlisle, but Cole and Kate Ford had. The blond investigative reporter had as little regard for him as Cole did. Cole and Kate acknowledged his greeting, but said little more.

This did not slow the fixer down one bit. "It's always a pleasure being in the company of the Chicago Police Department's legendary chief of detectives. I heard you put another notch in the handle of your gun today, Larry."

Carlisle's voice carried over the elderly judge's weak croak, and now a number of people were staring at him. Philo Coffey angrily summoned his balding assistant, Gordon Harris, and whispered for him to go down onto the rotunda floor and shut Carlisle up. Harris hurried to do his boss's bidding.

Quietly, Cole responded to Carlisle, "I don't know what you mean about a 'notch in the handle of my gun.'"

"You caught another serial killer," the fixer shouted. "We should drink a toast to you, Cole." Carlisle snatched an empty wineglass, from a vacant setting at the table and poured from one of the bottles provided by Father James Lochran. Holding the glass up, he said, "To the man who has single-handedly protected this city for the past twenty-five years. Chief Larry Cole."

As Gordon Harris rushed up to him, Carlisle noticed that more than a small number of diners at other tables were raising their glasses in salute. An equal number were glaring their disapproval at Carlisle for disrupting the proceedings.

"Please, Mr. Carlisle," Coffey's assistant whispered, "you're causing a scene."

Carlisle spun toward the little man, grabbed his arm just above the elbow, and dug his fingers into a nerve located between the biceps and triceps muscles. Gordon Harris gasped and went rigid with pain.

Cole stood up. "Let him go, Carlisle."

The fixer turned to stare at the chief of detectives. Carlisle's grin was gone. Now his face displayed a meanness mixed with sadistic cruelty. The judge had stopped talking, and every eye in the rotunda was focused on table 8.

"No problem, Chief," Carlisle said, sarcastically. He released Gordon Harris's arm. "That was just a little payback for Coffey jerking me around and moving some of my guests to another table."

Cole glared back at Carlisle. "The kind of payback you're engaging in is called assault and battery."

Carlisle's phony grin spread slowly across his face. "Who am I to argue with the finest of Chicago's Finest? Now what about our toast?"

"Some other time," Cole said.

For a long moment their eyes remained locked. Finally, the fixer raised his glass of wine, toasted Orga, drained the glass, and said, "There won't be another time, Cole."

Carlisle turned and walked to the middle of the floor in front of the dais, where the confused judge still stood at the microphone. There the fixer bowed to the assemblage, smashed his wineglass on the floor, and strode from the rotunda. At the door he stopped and, raising his hands, said with a flourish, "And to all a good night."

CHAPTER 16

Butch and Judy had moved from the bar to a table not far from where Paige Albritton was seated in the Dragon's Lair. Since they'd come in, Fuzzy Dubcek hadn't left the dance floor. She had worn out two partners and was drenched with sweat. Also, she danced with such single-minded, erotic abandon that few could keep up with her, making it seem as if she were dancing alone most of the time.

For their part, Judy and Butch had danced twice, but were more absorbed with keeping Paige under surveillance. She had not moved from the table since her one foray to the bar to get drinks for Fuzzy and Sonny Balfour. Balfour had also remained at the table. He had donned dark glasses and remained virtually motionless for the past thirty minutes. Judy surmised accurately that he had snorted a little nose candy, placing him in this passive state. For her part, Paige stared blankly at her surroundings, appearing at times either very sad or quite bored.

"So, what do you think?" Butch asked.

Judy noticed that he was behaving more naturally now after the first few moments of self-conscious rigidity in his initial undercover operation.

"We need to make contact with her," Judy said, "but I don't want Balfour to make us."

"Maybe I could go over and ask her to dance."

Judy considered this for a moment. "She's not going to

dance with you, Butch. She's not going to dance with anyone tonight. One look at her tells me that."

"But suppose she knew it was me?"

"That's definitely out. It could end up causing her some severe problems."

"I don't understand."

"Whatever's going on here may not be strictly on the legit, Butch. You go over there and let her know you're Larry Cole Jr., it might end up causing her some problems with her not-so-legitimate colleagues."

"I see what you mean, but—" At that instant Fuzzy Dubcek danced over to their table, grabbed Butch by the hand, and pulled him onto the dance floor. Before Judy could protest, he was gone.

The Mistress of Disguise/High Priestess of Mayhem was starting to get the sinking feeling that this trip to the Dragon's Lair was not only a bad idea, but developing into a potential disaster. If Chief Cole found out that she'd colored his son's hair Kermit the Frog green and taken him out to a hard rock nightclub, she'd be lucky to be assigned to the meter maid detail. Then it was obvious that Paige was into something which wasn't necessarily on the up-and-up, and there was no way that Judy and Butch could walk out of there without finding out if she was okay. *And suppose she's not?* The instant Judy had this troubling thought the answer came to her. If Paige was in trouble then Judy and Butch would have to find a way to help her.

The dance ended and an exhausted Fuzzy Dubcek led Butch Cole back to the table where Paige and Sonny Balfour were seated. As the Mistress of Disguise/High Priestess of Mayhem looked on, Butch sat down next to Paige. With a groan, Judy said to herself, "Now what."

Paige Albritton's body was in the Dragon's Lair nightclub, but her mind was far away from not only this place but also this time. It had been quite awhile since she'd thought of her long-dead fiancé Mack McKinnis. Somehow tonight, since she'd arrived at the club with Fuzzy and Sonny, she couldn't get him out of her mind. Briefly, she wondered what her life would have been like if he had lived. She was certain that their marriage would have worked, because she would have made it work!

Tears welled in her eyes and she blinked them away. It did no good to dwell on the past. This was now and she was what she was. Paige looked around her. Sonny Balfour was seated across the table. His eyes shielded by sunglasses, he was as unmoving as the Sphinx. He reminded her of a snake that could uncoil and strike in the blink of an eye. She looked out at the dance floor, where Fuzzy was dancing with a well-put-together young kid with green hair. Paige mused that for a newlywed, Fuzzy was still as wild as any swinging single she had ever seen, and Paige had seen her share.

Paige considered her position. She worked for Jack Carlisle, but she wasn't a hooker. At least not in the manner that she used to be when she worked in the DeLisa organization. However, it was made quite clear to her that she belonged to the fixer, body, mind, and soul. And occasionally, which came more infrequently of late, Carlisle required her to submit to him sexually, which she did with the same enthusiasm she'd displayed when she was turning tricks for the Mob. Once Paige had also been required to be the sexual plaything of Fuzzy Dubcek, who had appetites which were beyond the scope of even the most depraved imagination.

Now Fuzzy was coming off the dance floor dragging the kid with the green hair behind her. Paige had a pretty good idea what the manic basketball player's wife had in mind for him. The fact that she was noticed wherever she went and was an excellent subject for the city's gossip columns didn't matter to Fuzzy.

The kid sat down next to Paige. All she noticed about him was his green hair and black leather suit. There had to be a couple of hundred people in the Dragon's Lair who were as odd-looking as he was, and she wasn't paying them any attention either.

"Look what I found," Fuzzy gushed in the little-girl voice that Paige hated. "Paige Albritton and Sonny Balfour, this is Butch."

Now Paige looked at him, and what she saw made her eyes go wide. It was *her* Butch, only he was all grown up.

"Hello," he said, receiving no response from the immobile Balfour. Then he looked at Paige. "Hi."

She was too stunned to respond.

There was a stirring in the crowd coming from the entrance to the Dragon's Lair. They turned to look in that direction and saw Pete Dubcek, all six feet six inches of him, standing at the entrance looking around. And it was obvious whom he was looking for.

"C'mon," Paige said, jumping to her feet and snatching Butch up with her. "Let's dance."

"Oh, shit," Fuzzy said when she saw her husband.

This galvanized the previously comatose Sonny Balfour, who spun around to see what was going on.

Paige and Butch had just reached the dance floor when Dubcek spied his wife and started walking rapidly toward her, swatting people out of his way as he did so. It was obvious that he was angry.

Dubcek was dark-haired, had the face of a twelve-year-old and the body of a Greek god, although a slender one. At the age of thirty he was strong, fast, and agile, which his exploits on the basketball court attested to. Now he used his physical gifts to reach his wife. As he came up to her, Balfour stood up.

"What's happening, Pete?" the ex-boxer said.

"Get out of my way," the basketball star demanded with a heavy German accent.

"Hold on, Pete," Balfour said, attempting to restrain the bigger man, but Dubcek tossed him to the side as if he were a toy doll.

Fuzzy was standing, looking slightly confused, when Dubcek grabbed her roughly by the wrist and began pulling her toward the exit. Judy joined Paige and Butch out on the dance floor just as a plethora of flashbulbs went off, capturing the exit of Pete and Fuzzy Dubcek from the Dragon's Lair.

CHAPTER 17

The PAC affair was concluding. An eight-piece band was playing in the rotunda, but there were few people dancing, and the majority of the attendees were heading for the exits. Barbara Zorin, Jamal Garth, Kate Ford, Orga Syriac, and Larry Cole lingered around table 8 for a few moments before saying good-bye and going their separate ways. As Orga and Cole walked to his car in the VIP parking section, Cole noticed how quiet his date had become. He also recalled that her period of silence had begun at the moment they had started discussing African she-devils over dinner.

Once they were in the car she said, "You must excuse my silence, Larry, but I was just thinking about that poor priest who collapsed at the start of the affair."

"Father Lochran?" Cole said, pulling the car into a line of vehicles leading off the pier.

"Yes." Then she turned to lean across the seat toward him. "Could you do me a big favor, Larry. I'd like to find out what hospital they took the priest to. Tomorrow I plan to send him a get-well card. I might even pay him a visit."

"That's very generous of you," Cole said, reaching for the phone mounted on the dashboard. However, he couldn't completely buy her Good Samaritan role. There was something else going on, but he couldn't fathom what at this point. A few moments later he disconnected and said, "The priest was taken to University Hospital, but before they could treat him he walked out."

"Oh," she said. "I guess he was not in as bad a shape as he looked."

"I guess not."

They rode in silence for a time. Then she asked, "Did you get Father Lochran's first name?"

He glanced sideways at her. "James."

She became quiet again. They were just about to exit the gates at the west end of the pier when Cole heard her repeat quietly, "Lochran. Father James Lochran."

Across the parkway from the gates to Navy Pier, a figure stirred in the shadows of a multistoried apartment building. As Cole's car drove past, a man stepped into the light. It was Father James Lochran, who was also known as Thomas Kelly. However, in the few hours since he had assumed his false identity the man who had been Thomas Kelly had ceased to exist and only the priest remained.

Leaning heavily on his cane, Father James Lochran limped toward the entrance to Navy Pier.

CHAPTER 18

JUNE 11, 2004
10:15 P.M.

When Jack Carlisle pulled his Cadillac up in front of the Dragon's Lair, the line waiting to get into the nightclub stretched all the way down the block. Security personnel from the club were outside making sure that those in line stayed orderly and did not block the sidewalk. All of Carlisle's security guards were off-duty cops, and he paid them well.

The fixer entered the club to find it packed to capacity. He motioned for Tom Grant, the cop at the door, who had once been Judy Daniels's partner. "Don't let anyone else in until we clear some of this mob out. I don't want any trouble with the fire inspectors."

"Yes, sir," Grant said, before adding, "We had a little trouble in here earlier, Mr. Carlisle."

The fixer frowned. He didn't like trouble in his club. It was the only legitimate business front he owned. "What kind of trouble?"

"Fuzzy Dubcek came in with Paige and Sonny. She was dancing and Pete showed up. He snatched her outside, but before he could get her in his car she scratched his face and told him to fuck off. She came back inside and Pete stood around on the street for a while before getting in his Mercedes and taking off. A lot of people saw what happened and there were some pictures taken. The story will probably hit the gossip columns and scandal sheets tomorrow."

"Damn," Carlisle said through clenched teeth. "Where is Fuzzy now?"

Grant pointed to the dance floor. There Fuzzy Dubcek was dancing with her usual abandon. Carlisle noticed Paige seated at a table near the dance floor with a couple of punk rockers: a kid with green hair and a broad with blue hair. This puzzled the fixer, as the Albritton woman had never mixed with the rock trade before. But he had other things on his mind at that moment.

"Have Sonny get Fuzzy and meet me in the office," he said to Grant.

"Yes, sir," Grant said, heading for the table where Sonny Balfour remained seated alone.

Jack Carlisle's office was in the back of the Dragon's Lair behind a door marked "Private." It was a fairly spacious room attached to a private bathroom equipped with a shower, sauna, and whirlpool bath. He'd had an interior decorator design the place, and the tables, chairs, sofas, and entertainment console were artfully arranged around a large desk, which dominated the center of the office. When Sonny Balfour escorted Fuzzy Dubcek into the office, Carlisle was seated behind the desk. The professional basketball player's wife was still gyrating to the music; however, when Balfour shut the door the sound was cut off. This and a glance at Carlisle's face made Fuzzy abruptly stop dancing. She forged her face into its shy-little-girl expression and said, "Hi, Jack."

The fixer's hands were steepled in front of his face and he stared at her over his fingertips. "Hi, Fuzzy. Sit down. I want to talk to you."

Slowly, she crossed the office and took a seat on a couch facing Carlisle. Balfour remained over by the door.

"I heard you had a problem with Pete tonight."

"Jeez, Jack!" she said, rolling her eyes at the ceiling. "He's such a big baby. He wants a nice German hausfrau to stay at home, cook his meals, and have babies. I'm not cut out for that."

He continued to stare at her until she looked away. "So is that why you made a scene outside my club and got your picture taken scratching his face?"

She wouldn't look at him, as she again adopted her little-girl voice. "I'm sorry, Jack, but he made me mad."

Carlisle laughed. "He made you mad? Now that's one for the books." He slapped his palms together hard enough to make her jump and got to his feet. He walked to the bathroom, opened the door, and turned on the light. The sound of water running could be heard in the office. Fuzzy looked fearfully at Sonny Balfour, who stood stoically with his back to the door. Then Carlisle emerged from the bathroom. He was carrying a wet towel, which he twisted tightly into a rope. He walked slowly toward her.

Tears welled in her eyes. "Jack, please don't."

"Shut up, Fuzzy," he snarled. "Nobody, I mean nobody messes with my business." He raised the towel over his head and she jerked herself into a protective ball. Aiming for her legs, buttocks, and back he began hitting her with the towel. For a long time the only sound heard in the office was the smack of the wet towel against Fuzzy Dubcek's body.

*   *   *

Initially, Paige had been extremely uptight when she recognized Butch and then Judy. But after Pete Dubcek snatched his wife from the club, causing a brief commotion, Paige had seemed to relax a bit. When Fuzzy reentered the club Paige talked to her briefly. Then the two women parted, with Fuzzy returning to the dance floor and Paige going over to sit with Butch and Judy. Apparently, the Dubcek woman had forgotten the green-haired Butch Cole.

"What happened to her husband?" Judy asked.

Paige laughed. "She told me that she kicked his behind." Her southern accent was evident. Paige was from Oklahoma.

"I don't believe that," Butch said. "Pete Dubcek is one of the toughest players in the NBA. He even took on Shaquille O'Neal once."

Paige shook her head. "Pete physically confronting Shaq on a basketball court in front of thousands of people is a lot safer for him than trying to control that little ball of fluff out there." She nodded at the dance floor, where Fuzzy was again engaged in a manic dance with a skinny white kid sporting orange-and-purple hair. Then Paige looked at Butch. "A little while ago I couldn't believe my eyes. My little Butchie is all grown up. When I first saw you I was shocked at how much you resemble your father. Sometimes when I think about you I still remember the little boy Margo DeWitt tried to kill, not . . . this." She made a gesture that took him in from head to toe.

Judy could tell that Paige was relaxed now. Casually, the Mistress of Disguise/High Priestess of Mayhem said, "So, what have you been up to these last few years?"

Paige didn't answer right away. Finally, with a shrug, she said, "I work here at the Dragon's Lair or, more appropriately, for Jack Carlisle, who owns the place."

"Isn't he a gambler?" Butch asked.

Paige became uneasy. "You're not here as part of an official investigation, are you, Judy?"

"Do you think I'd bring Butch along if I was?"

This didn't satisfy Paige. "Then why are you here?"

Judy looked at Butch. Then she explained. When she was

finished Paige laughed. "I would have thought you'd have figured that out by now."

"Then you know too?"

Paige nodded. "Unlike Butch, I can't always tell, but there are two things I look at."

"And those are?" Judy said expectantly.

At that instant Jack Carlisle walked into the club. Paige went silent and lowered her eyes. Judy and Butch could tell that his presence frightened her. However, Carlisle ignored them, and as they watched, the fixer walked to the rear of the club. A moment later Sonny Balfour literally snatched Fuzzy Dubcek off the dance floor.

"Look," Paige said urgently, "you all have got to get out of here, because in a minute there's going to be trouble."

"We're not afraid of trouble, Paige," Butch said angrily.

She reached over and took his hand. "I know you're not, honey, but I want you and Judy to do this for me."

"It's about time for us to go anyway, Butch," Judy said. "Your father's going to be home in a little while and I've got to get the color out of your hair."

Grudgingly, Butch agreed. As they got to their feet Judy said, "Will you call me tomorrow, Paige? I'm still at the same number."

"I'll call you," she said. Then she embraced them. Butch and Judy were walking away from the table when Sonny Balfour approached Paige.

"Judy?!" Butch said, but she grabbed him by the arm and pulled him along with her.

"Just keep walking. There's nothing we can do now. We'll wait around outside and see if anything develops."

A few minutes later Judy and Butch were sitting in Judy's Toyota across the street from the entrance to the Dragon's Lair when Balfour and Paige came out supporting Fuzzy Dubcek between them. The basketball player's wife could barely walk.

"She must be really high," Butch said.

Judy shook her head. "She's not high, she's in pain. I'd say somebody, namely Jack Carlisle, beat the hell out of her."

CHAPTER 19

Larry Cole walked Orga Syriac to the door of her apartment. "I had a wonderful time, Larry."

"We must do it again soon. Perhaps we could have dinner Saturday night?"

She stared at him for a long moment before smiling and saying, "That would be nice. Why don't you call me tomorrow?"

"I will."

She extended her hand, which he took and kissed gently. He waited until she unlocked the door and stepped inside before he turned to walk down the corridor.

Orga's companion Blessing was waiting for her. "How was your evening, madam?"

The mistress of the spacious apartment on the tenth floor overlooking Lake Shore Drive looked at her companion and a heavy sadness dropped over her. "My time is nearly up, Blessing. I had trouble holding my image during the evening. Once or twice I'm certain a few got a glimpse of the Abo-Yorba, and I frightened a couple of horses. I managed to calm them down, but I should have been in better control."

Blessing walked over and placed her arms around Orga's shoulders. "You haven't been out socially for a long time. You're just out of practice." Blessing began leading her toward the rear of the apartment. "I'm certain that when you start your new job you'll be able to maintain your image effortlessly."

The apartment was in semidarkness, with indirect ceiling lights casting cones of illumination on the floor. The two women passed through these areas and would periodically enter spaces which were dark. Passing from one cone of light to the next revealed that Orga Syriac's image was changing. The beautiful woman who had just come from a date with Larry Cole became transformed into something that some would consider hideous and others beautiful. Blessing thought that the entity she had dedicated her life to was the most beautiful being she'd ever encountered in either human form or the one which Orga had changed into now.

Jack Carlisle was still in his office at the Dragon's Lair when Sonny Balfour returned from dropping off Fuzzy and Paige. Tonight, after he'd beaten her with the towel, the fixer had ordered the basketball player's wife to stay at Paige's apartment. In the morning Fuzzy was to go home and do her best to be the loving, respectful wife that Pete Dubcek wanted. Carlisle owned Fuzzy Dubcek, which her husband was unaware of. In fact, it was on Carlisle's orders that she had agreed to marry Dubcek in the first place.

Before Balfour had left on the assignment for Carlisle, the fixer had told him to return immediately, as he had something else for the ex-pug to do.

Now Balfour took the seat on the same couch were Fuzzy had been physically chastised by Carlisle. The fixer looked across at him and said, "There was a woman at the PAC dinner I went to tonight. I understand that her name is Orga Syriac and that she's going to work at Channel Nine next week. She was with Larry Cole of the CPD. I think they might become an item soon, so I want you to find out everything you can about her."

Balfour nodded. He didn't need any additional instructions. He'd been given assignments like this before. Personally, he didn't possess the expertise to do the work himself. But Carlisle employed a lot of cops who, for the proper cash bonus in their pay envelopes, would be happy to obtain any information the fixer required. Of course, Balfour would carefully select the cop or cops he chose for this task, as this

Orga Syriac was linked to Cole. Also, the sources of information they would utilize would be confidential.

When Balfour was gone, Jack Carlisle went to the fully stocked bar in his office. He poured himself a double vodka on the rocks and returned to his desk. Leaning back in his chair he slowly sipped the clear liquid and stared at the far wall.

Despite what he'd done to Fuzzy tonight and the control he exerted over her, Carlisle realized that he would have to continue to keep a very close eye on the Dubceks. A close eye indeed. She and her husband were at the center of one of his most ambitious and potentially lucrative gambling schemes. It would take the same finesse and behind-the-scenes manipulations that the Super Bowl champions upset had entailed; however, this time the sport would be basketball. Basketball on an international level.

Jack Carlisle continued to sip cold vodka and ponder the upcoming 2004 Olympic Games.

Larry Cole parked his car in the garage beneath his building and rode up to the lobby to check his mail. After finding a bill and four pieces of junk mail, he crossed the lobby to the elevator bank. He was mulling over the events of the evening when the door to one of the elevators opened. Before he could board, a female punk rocker, with electric blue hair formed into three spikes on top her head, stepped out. She looked at Cole, smiled, and said with a heavy cockney accent, "Good evenin' to you, guvner."

Cole managed a "good evening" in response. Then he watched the bizarrely dressed woman cross the lobby and exit onto the street. With a shrug, he boarded the vacant car and rode up to his floor.

He entered his apartment to find Butch sitting on the living-room floor in front of the television. Cole smiled when he noticed that his teenage son had arranged himself in the same manner to watch TV that he'd been doing since he was barely old enough to walk. He also noticed that Butch was dressed in Cole's black terry cloth bathrobe and that his hair was wet.

"How was your date, Dad?" Butch said. He was watching one of the *Die Hard* movies.

"Not bad," Cole said. "Not bad at all." He slipped off his dinner jacket. "I even got a couple of compliments on my Michael Jordan Number Twenty-three."

"I knew you would."

Cole started for the bedroom. "Did Judy come by?"

"Yeah."

Cole entered the bedroom. "Did you play chess?"

"No."

He took off his bow tie and began removing the studs from his shirt. "So, what did you do?"

Silence.

Cole placed his studs and cuff links in a jewelry box on the dresser and returned to the living room. His son was engrossed in Bruce Willis dispatching bad guys on a snow-covered airport runway. Butch had turned up the sound.

"Butch!" he was forced to shout to be heard over the TV.

The boy jerked around. "Yeah, Dad."

"Would you turn that down?"

Dutifully, Butch activated the mute button on the remote control, and the sound ceased.

"I asked what you and Judy did tonight."

His son looked him dead in the eye. "We went out for a Coke."

"No pizza?"

"No, sir."

Butch looked back at the silent television screen.

For just an instant Cole thought his son was hiding something, but he quickly rejected this. After all, Judy had been with him.

"Well, I'm going to bed," Cole said. "See you in the morning."

"Good night, Dad."

As Cole returned to the bedroom, Butch hit the mute button and the sound returned; however, he played it at a much lower level. Cole didn't hear the sigh of relief his son emitted.

*   *   *

The Holy Name Mission was located on North Clark Street. Housed in a three-story brick building, the facility was open daily from 6 A.M. until 11 P.M. to serve the poor, the homeless, and the indigent. The main floor consisted of a kitchen, a dining room, and a chapel. The upper floors were where the sleeping areas were located. Each night every bed in the men's and women's quarters was filled. Now the mission's capacity had been reached and the facility's administrator, Brother Steven Pasco of the Carmelite order, was about to lock up for the night. Brother Steve, as he was called by the regulars at the mission, was a short, stocky middle-aged man. He was passing the chapel when he saw someone kneeling in front of the plain wooden altar on which a single red votive candle burned.

Brother Steve entered the chapel with the intention of politely, but forcefully, ejecting whoever was there when he noticed that the kneeling man was a priest. A priest who was crying.

"Father?" Brother Steve said to get the man's attention.

The priest turned a tear-streaked face toward the brown-robed man. "I have failed in my mission and must atone."

The brother placed a hand on the priest's shoulder. "I'm certain that the Lord will forgive you, Father."

"But only if I do penance and complete the task which has been set for me."

"Perhaps you would like to sit down for a moment and talk things over? I could make some coffee and perhaps you would like something to eat. There are cold cuts and fresh bread in the kitchen."

The priest nodded his silent acceptance of the brother's invitation.

A short time later they sat drinking coffee in the mission's kitchen. Brother Steve had locked the doors and the building was quiet. The two men were alone. A bologna-and-cheese sandwich on white bread was on the table in front of the priest. So far he had consumed half of it.

"Are you feeling better, Father?"

The priest managed a weak smile. "I'm feeling much better. Thank you, Brother."

Brother Steve hesitated a moment before saying, "Perhaps you'd like to talk about what's troubling you. I might be able to help."

The priest smiled. "I think I can work things out, but I appreciate your offer." He looked around before adding, "This is an interesting place. I was able to see it from a hotel-room window not far from here. How did you come to serve in this particular ministry?"

Brother Steve smiled. "When I started out with the order I planned to be a scholar. I came here from Detroit seven years ago to study for a degree in philosophy at Loyola. I was put up at Saint Thaddeus Parish on Diversey while I was in school. On weekends I started working at the mission and the rest is history."

The priest leaned toward Brother Steve. "Please, go on."

2

"Now Who Are You Really,
Ms. Syriac?"
Jack Carlisle

CHAPTER 20

The Human Development Institute was located at the far southeast edge of the University of Chicago campus. In fact, although it was physically on the grounds of the U of C, it had no direct or official connection with the prestigious midwestern institution of higher learning. The Institute, as it was called, was funded by a private, confidential source, and its accountability had often been questioned by the local and national media. *Eye of the Public*, a national TV newsmagazine program, had once devoted a half hour to the Institute, focusing particularly on its nefarious activities, its secret funding, and its reputed ties to the CIA, which were denied by spokesmen for both the Institute and the Agency. A former Institute employee appeared on the program with his face electronically masked and told stories of the Institute attempting to fix elections, engaging in political chicanery and dirty tricks, and manipulating organizations, both political and private, by placing their own handpicked personnel to head them.

The disguised former Institute employee stated that its aims were accomplished with blackmail, political pressure, and dirty tricks. Although murder was never mentioned, it was hinted at, and investigators for the TV news program uncovered some startling, although unverifiable, information.

According to an unnamed source, the Institute had become interested in who was to become the new chairman of the board at IBM. The odds-on favorite for the post was not the

candidate that the Institute preferred. Suddenly, forty-eight
hours before the IBM board was to vote, the candidate inexplicably resigned and went into seclusion. A similar situation occurred involving a Supreme Court nominee. Before
being appointed, the justice nominated committed suicide. A
deputy director's position became open in the FBI, but this
time the number one candidate was killed in a mysterious
hit-and-run auto accident involving a Mack truck.

The *Eye of the Public* story drew a great deal of viewer
interest. Separate stories about the Institute were run in the
*Washington Post, New York Times, Wall Street Journal, Chi-
cago Tribune, Sun-Times*, and *Times-Herald*. All of the network news programs also launched investigations into the
goings-on inside the glass-and-metal structure on the South
Side of the city. Then the Human Development Institute
counterattacked.

Initially, a lawsuit was filed on behalf of the Institute by
one of the more high-profile law firms in Chicago. The news
program's attorneys were prepared to wage war based on the
First Amendment issues involved, but they never got the
chance. A memo came down from the president of the network the *Eye of the Public* show was carried on ordering the
executive producer to drop any further investigations of the
Human Development Institute and to remove the original
program from the summer rerun schedule. A short time later
the *Chicago Times-Herald* ran a five-part exposé of the *Eye
of the Public* news program, which alleged that a number of
stories they had run recently, including the one about the
Human Development Institute, were based on rumor, half-
truths, or outright falsifications. As the fall season began, the
formerly popular news program was pitted against the best
shows the rival networks could come up with. *Eye of the
Public*'s ratings plummeted. In a move to bolster the news
program's numbers, the executive producer and three of its
top reporters, including the one who had pursued the story
about the Human Development Institute, were fired. The Institute had successfully survived the assault on its internal
operations and secrets.

But what was the Human Development Institute? Primarily, it was a vehicle for gathering information. A place where facts were compiled. Since the end of the Second World War, the Institute had been engaged in studying the American condition. Some individuals, with liberal leanings and a firm belief that the Constitution should be the law of the land in reality, would call the "studying" the Institute was engaged in "spying." The population growths of minority groups, the unique operations of model communities such as Diggstown, Mississippi, and the examination and monitoring of the careers of high-profile cops like Larry Cole were just a few of the "studies" the Institute pursued. However, shortly after it was founded, the Institute moved from mere surveillance to action. On the morning of June 14, 2004, it was discovered that one of these actions had gone very wrong.

Dr. Gilbert Goldman, Ph.D., was the current director of the Human Development Institute. He was sixty-three years old, totally bald, and had been born with one leg shorter than the other. He walked with the aid of a gold-headed cane and had all his suits tailor-made. He drove a Lincoln Town Car, which he replaced each September with a new model. Dr. Goldman was not a very attractive man, but there was a quality about him which the majority of those he came in contact with found interesting. He had an IQ above 160 and an eidetic memory. He was a man who enjoyed his work and was single-mindedly dedicated to the Institute. He believed in the work he was doing with the devotion of the fanatic and he was very, very good at what he did.

On this late-spring morning he parked his Town Car in the designated parking spot for the HDI director at the rear of the building. It took him almost a full minute to extricate himself from the vehicle. Slowly, he made his way to the rear door. A palm sensor was located beside the entrance and Goldman placed his hand on it and waited for the dull click signaling the door unlocking. He entered.

The interior of the four-story building was clean, ultramodern, and as secure as the White House. Although Dr. Goldman had access to the entire complex, he was forced to stop three times en route to his office. Once was to sign his name on a log at the security station just inside the entrance, a second time was to be identified on a closed-circuit television camera before he could board the elevator, and the last time was at the locked double glass doors leading to the executive fourth-floor wing of the complex. The doctor did not mind these security procedures; in fact, he had put them in place himself when he had taken over from his predecessor. In the 150-year history of the Human Development Institute there had been a number of directors, and Dr. Gilbert Goldman had occupied the position for the past 23 years.

When he finally reached his corner office overlooking Jackson Park with the National Science and Space Museum visible off in the distance, his secretary was already at her desk. Her name was Virginia Daley. She was fiftyish, severe looking, and efficient to a fault. Before he was completely through the door, she was pouring him a cup of tea, which he preferred over coffee, and prepared to begin her morning report. She had begun compiling this report at 6:45 A.M., when she arrived for a day which would not conclude before 6:00 P.M. Virginia Daley was as fanatical about the Institute as her boss.

He walked behind his desk. She placed the teacup beside his desk blotter, took a seat across from him, and opened her notebook. She waited for him to take a sip of the steaming liquid and nod his approval before she began.

"From all indications, the information concerning the election of the vice president of Local 610 of the Teamsters Union is accurate. We can anticipate his selection by a substantial margin in September."

Dr. Goldman again nodded. "That is as we anticipated; however, let's continue to keep a close eye on his opposition in case there's a switch in the forecast for victory."

"And if there is?" she inquired with a raised eyebrow.

He graced her with a look of exasperation. "It is imperative that our candidate be the next Teamsters local VP. We must take whatever steps necessary to insure that his election occurs exactly as planned."

"I understand," she said. And she understood all too well. What he was communicating to her, without saying it plainly, was that any means necessary, both legal or illegal, were to be employed to achieve the Institute's, or more appropriately, Dr. Gilbert Goldman's, objectives. She knew that he did not operate independently, but took orders from someone or an authority which she never was provided any information about. As the *Eye of the Public* TV newsmagazine had implied, the Human Development Institute's master could have been the CIA, the National Security Agency, a secret arm of one of the political parties, the White House, or perhaps simply a very powerful, extremely rich individual. But to Virginia Daley, whomever Dr. Goldman received his directions from didn't matter. She had long ago realized that the work of the Human Development Institute was important to the safety, security, and continued good fortune of the true ruling class of this Great American Society.

She went on to the next item on this morning's agenda. "The Clinton bill is going to be up for another vote soon. It has been amended and there is a strong possibility that it will pass this time around."

Goldman began drumming his fingers on the desk blotter. The Clinton bill, named for the former president and first lady who had sponsored it, was legislation aimed at the decriminalization of illegal narcotics. This was something that the Institute was definitely against. In a position paper authored by Gilbert Goldman, Ph.D., personally, strong opposition was voiced against the passage of the Clinton bill. In the seven-page piece, published in the monthly *Journal of the Human Development Institute (JHDI)*, Goldman stated quite eloquently that the decriminalization of illegal narcotics was not only immoral, but a "cowardly act of surrender to the criminal drug culture and underworld in the United States."

But there was nothing moral at all about the Institute's opposition to the Clinton bill. The drug trade in the United States was a mega-multibillion-dollar business with profits that went into the pockets of not only drug dealers, but politicians, financial institutions, and corporate entities. To take the profit out of the drug trade would do some very serious damage to a number of Institute backers. The crime and violent-death rates that the Clinton bill would help lower were of no importance to Dr. Gilbert Goldman, Virginia Daley, or the Human Development Institute.

"We need to contact our people in the Senate and remind them of our feelings on this issue," Goldman said.

"Yes, sir." She had been given all the information that she needed to deal with this situation. She knew whom to contact and how to contact them. She went on to the next item. "It seems that there is still no trace of Thomas Kelly."

Now the director of the Human Development Institute sat up a bit straighter and a frown creased his features. "Then we don't know why he didn't complete the mission he took over from the James Lochran operative?"

She placed her notebook on her lap and stared across at him. "Three days ago we sent Kelly to check on the priest impersonator we had arranged to give the invocation at the PAC dinner. We were certain that no one in attendance had ever come in contact with the impersonator or had any knowledge of the extensive background we had set up for the Father James Lochran operative. We did realize that our operative was becoming unreliable because of a recently revealed tendency toward excessive drinking prior to operations. Kelly found him at the Lincoln Park Days Inn Motel. The operative was apparently quite drunk, and instead of having him removed before taking his place, Kelly sanctioned him."

Goldman listened patiently without commenting or otherwise revealing what was going on inside that genius-level-IQ mind.

Virginia Daley continued. "Of course Kelly has been authorized to sanction personnel for the Institute in the past; however, it was my understanding that this authority had been revoked by you some time ago."

Dr. Gilbert Goldman got up from behind his desk and, leaning heavily on his cane, went over to look out the windows at the spring greenery of Jackson Park on a beautiful day. However, the HDI director's mood was not very bright. Not very bright at all.

His secretary continued her report in crisply professional, unemotional tones. "Kelly called for a cleanup crew to remove the impersonator's body. He then took his place and accompanied Operative Silk to the Navy Pier rotunda. Silk placed the explosive beneath table thirty and left the remote detonator with Kelly, who was now posing as Father James Lochran." She paused a moment to study Goldman's back before concluding with, "Something happened during the affair and Lochran collapsed before he could detonate the explosive. He was removed by a Chicago Fire Department ambulance and taken to University Hospital. Before he could be treated he walked out. Operative Silk was dispatched to the rotunda early on the morning of the twelfth to retrieve the explosive, but it had been removed. Our sources in law enforcement have assured us that no local, state, or federal agency has it, so apparently Lochran-Kelly does."

Now Goldman spoke. "How much explosive?"

Virginia Daley did not have to consult her notebook as she said from memory, "Eight ounces of CX-22 plastique."

Goldman shuddered. For a long time he didn't speak. Finally he said, "Thomas is sick. I want as many of our resources as we can spare employed in the search for him." Now he turned to look at her. "But I want discretion and extreme restraint utilized. I don't want him sanctioned unless . . ." Dr. Goldman couldn't bring himself to say the words.

But with Virginia Daley the HDI director didn't need words.

"May I make a suggestion, sir?"

He returned to staring sightlessly out the window. "Go on."

"We could let the CPD handle this as a routine missing-persons case."

"No!" he said sharply. "Thomas hasn't been . . . well lately. If they do find him, someone could get hurt."

"Yes, sir. I'll handle it as you've instructed."

He remained at the window. "Is there anything else we need to cover this morning?"

"Yes, sir," she said. "We're monitoring the operation PAC has set up for later this morning."

Goldman allowed himself a brief smile. "Political terrorism doesn't strike me as Philo Coffey's thing, but I guess nowadays anything goes." After a moment he added, "Is that all?"

"For the moment, yes," she said.

"Keep me posted on the search and Mr. Coffey's operation."

She stood. "I will, sir." She let herself out.

For a long time after she was gone Dr. Gilbert Goldman remained at the window leaning on his gold-headed cane. Finally, he sighed and said, "God help you, Thomas, wherever you are."

CHAPTER 21

JUNE 14, 2004
8:57 A.M.

Gino Allegretti was seventy-two years old and had been a member of the Chicago Mob for over fifty of those years. He was a made wise guy and enjoyed the protection and cooperation of La Cosa Nostra from coast to coast. He was a powerful man who enjoyed the respect of his peers and the soldiers manning the army of the Chicago underworld. He had survived gang wars, indictments, and two assassination attempts by ambitious rivals.

Despite his age, he was a well-preserved man with a head of thick white hair he combed straight back from a high forehead and profile that both admirer and foe often compared to that of actor Cesar Romero. It was an image he enjoyed and cultivated, although at times he appeared a bit foppish and had taken to wearing garish, pastel-colored suits with matching accessories.

Although Allegretti had his fingers in a number of illegal pies, including truck hijacking, loan-sharking, and stolen-property fencing, primarily he was a pimp. He controlled most of the prostitution in the Chicagoland and northern Indiana area. Anyone, male or female, who placed his or her body on the open market for sex either belonged to Allegretti or paid him an exorbitant street tax, making the fine for independence impossible to pay. Freelancers were warned once. A second time more drastic and brutal methods of persuasion were employed. Miscreants never survived a third infraction.

Gino Allegretti was a very successful criminal; however, as was the case with all successful men, he had periodic business problems. Primary among these was that a rival pimp, sponsored by a South Side black street gang, was making a move on his organized crime operation. This had Allegretti concerned, but not overly alarmed. After all, he had been in this business for a very long time.

In keeping with his lavish lifestyle, the Mafia pimp enjoyed good food. As such, despite a spreading midsection and expanding double chin, Allegretti attempted to make every meal a feast. He was known to dine for breakfast, lunch, and dinner at some of the more exclusive restaurants in the city. Today, for breakfast, he was going to Carlo's, a Loop restaurant.

Carlo's had been on the same corner for over twenty years. The restaurant catered to the politicians and lobbyists from city hall and the banking institutions a few blocks north. However, the owner of Carlo's, a second-generation Italian of Neapolitan stock, realized that nefarious types like Allegretti gave the place an air of mystery. That is, as long as the mobsters didn't show up too frequently and in groups of more than four.

The breakfast rush was beginning to ebb when Allegretti's chauffeur-driven black Mercedes pulled up in front of Carlo's. A heavyset man with broad shoulders leaped from the front passenger seat and scanned the street for any signs of trouble or potential threats before he opened the back door. Gino Allegretti, dressed in a canary yellow suit with

matching shoes, socks, and tie, came out of the car, followed
by a beautiful black woman who stood at least a foot taller
than the pimp. As the chauffeur drove away, Allegretti and
the woman, followed by the bodyguard, entered the restaurant.

The maître d' on the day shift at Carlo's looked more like
a mobster than either Allegretti or his bodyguard. He also
spoke with a raspy voice that made him sound like a refugee
from one of the *Godfather* movies.

"How's it going, Mr. Allegretti?" The maître d's voice
came out a barely audible croak. "Your other guests have
already arrived."

The mobster's aging matinee-idol features twisted into a
frown. "Ain't got no guests for breakfast." Allegretti's Taylor
Street accent and lack of formal education were evident.

The maître d' shrugged. "I guess you can straighten it out
with them."

Allegretti, the woman, and the bodyguard followed the
rotund maître d' to a table near the back of the restaurant.
When the table came into view, the pimp halted. His entou-
rage stopped as well. There, seated at the mobster's designated table waiting for him, were Lieutenant Blackie Silvestri
and Sergeant Manny Sherlock.

"This is a private table, Silvestri," Allegretti said, attempting to control a nervous twitch that had developed below his
left eye.

Blackie finished chewing on a buttered croissant, chased
it with a swallow of coffee, and said a cheerful, "Hello, Gino.
Good to see you again."

"I said . . . ," the pimp started to repeat his statement, and
the bodyguard assumed a menacing stance as if he was preparing to forcibly eject the intruders.

Blackie and Manny fixed the bodyguard with cold stares,
which froze him in place. To keep the broad-shouldered man
from making a serious mistake, Blackie said, "Gino, why
don't you and your companions sit down before this little
meeting turns into a trip for someone to the nearest emergency room?"

Allegretti thought about this for a moment before motioning for the bodyguard to cool it. Then he stepped forward and held a vacant chair for the woman. The bodyguard retreated a short distance to a vacant table and sat down. He never took his eyes off the cops.

The maître d' with the raspy voice was joined by a white-jacketed waiter.

Allegretti made a show of unfolding a linen napkin and sticking it under his chin before saying to the waiter, "Give us the scrambled eggs and peppers with white toast for me and my *invited* guests along with orange juice and coffee all around. Now what do you cops want?"

Blackie smiled. "You ever heard of a guy by the name of Chester Collins?"

With an exaggerated gesture, Allegretti swung his eyes up to stare at the ceiling. Then he scratched his chin, looked at his beautiful companion, and asked, "Chester Collins? Chester Collins? Does that name ring a bell with you, baby?"

"He's talking about Chet the Jet, Gino," she said.

Allegretti slapped the surface of the table with his palm, making the silverware and china jump. "Chet the Jet! Sure I know him. Was even in business with him a few years back. Nice fellow. Of course I haven't see him in a while."

"But you have been having problems with him lately?" Manny said.

"Problems? Why would I be having problems with Chet?" Allegretti was such a bad actor it was nauseating.

"Could it be because you and Chet have become business rivals?" Blackie said.

"Business rivals? C'mon Blackie. I don't have no business rivals."

"What about business losses?" Manny asked with a hard edge in his voice.

Allegretti shrugged and held up his hands in a helpless gesture. "Everybody has business losses, Sergeant Sherlock. Even you cops."

"But your business losses entail the deaths of some of your people and Chet the Jet's," Sherlock responded. "Two girls working for you on North Lincoln Avenue and one of his pimps on the West Side. The women were knifed and the pimp shot to death."

Allegretti laughed. "I know you boys don't work vice, so that's why I'm talking so freely to you about my perceived business. Now I don't know what kind of game Chet the Jet is playing now, but I'm in the industrial laundry trade, which my income tax return will verify. Since you say Chet's a business rival I guess he's doing sheets, towels, and table-cloths for big hotels. Girls getting killed up on Lincoln Avenue sounds like you're talking about prostitutes, and a pimp on the West Side speaks for itself. Why you'd think I'd have anything to do with any of that is beyond me. But I'll just say this, I'm from the streets, just like you are, Silvestri, so you know it's tough out there, especially if you're in a hazardous line of work."

When Allegretti finished Blackie clapped. "That was really an eloquent speech for you, Gino." Then he leaned toward the pimp. "Now let me tell you something. You and Chet the Jet are fighting your little territorial war by killing off each other's street workers. If it keeps going like it is now, the body count will continue to rise, which the good citizens of this fair city won't like." Blackie and Manny stood up.

Towering over the pimp, the lieutenant concluded with, "Now if one more pimp or prostitute is killed because you and your competition can't get together on who owns what turf, then I guarantee you that two things are going to happen. One is that the Prostitution Unit of the Organized Crime Division is going to be beefed up and sent out to make sure that no whorehouse, streetwalker, or call operation is allowed to operate within a hundred miles of Chicago. That's what's known as a proactive way of dealing with our murder rate. And number two, I will personally make sure that you and Chester 'Chet the Jet' Collins get rousted for every crime you've ever been suspected of dating back to the day you were born. Have a nice day, Gino."

With that Blackie and Manny walked out of the restaurant.

When they were gone Gino said to his breakfast companion, "I always hated that fucking cop."

CHAPTER 22

Blessing was combing Orga's hair. They were in the master bedroom of the Syriac condo on Lake Shore Drive and Orga was preparing for her first day as a television newscaster. Throughout the morning Blessing had watched her mistress closely in order to detect any signs of nervousness, but also any problems with her maintaining her current appearance. There had been no emotional or physical difficulties, and Orga was more radiant than Blessing had ever seen her before.

"There," Blessing said. "I don't think that I or anyone else can improve on the way you look."

Orga gave her reflection a final inspection and stood up. She was dressed in a blue suit with a white ruffled blouse and black medium-heeled shoes. In the flesh she looked fantastic, but Blessing wondered how her appearance would hold up under the unrelenting gaze of the television camera.

"Larry should be here any minute," Orga said.

"It was nice of him to offer to take you to the station on your first day," Blessing said. "In that way you won't feel so alone."

Orga looked at her companion with an expression that held just the slightest hint of sadness. "I understand that he knows the news director, and I've been alone all of my life, Blessing."

Blessing placed a hand on Orga's shoulder and said with compassion, "Today will be different."

Orga managed a smile. "We shall see."

They left the bedroom and walked into the living room.

"Would you like a cup of coffee before Mr. Cole arrives?"

Orga shook her head. "No. I think I'll wait for him down-stairs. The fresh air will help calm my nerves."

Blessing bowed to her mistress and waited until she had let herself out. Then the woman with the face of a Nubian princess went to the prayer rug in her quarters, knelt on it, and began to pray. She was praying not only for the beautiful woman she served so faithfully, but also for the she-devil she could transform herself into at will.

Once outside her condo Orga Syriac did not proceed to the elevators, but instead to the south stairwell, which was under repair. At the door she found a wooden horse to which was taped a sign reading: *Danger—Do Not Enter!!!*

Without hesitation, but being careful not to get any plaster dust on her clothing, she reached down and moved the wooden barricade aside. Then she opened the stairwell door.

The tenth-floor landing was still in place, but the railings and the stairs were missing from the roof of the fifty-story structure down to the fifth floor. Orga stepped to the edge of the landing and looked down. Far below she could see men in hard hats working. Since she'd moved in, Orga had care-fully monitored their progress. It was taking them about two weeks to complete one staircase. At this rate it would be three months before they reached the tenth floor and over a year before the project could be completed.

She had casually inquired of the building manager why it was taking so long to complete the work. He had explained that the company hired had submitted the lowest bid for the project, which had been accepted at a meeting of the joint tenant council before Orga and Blessing had moved in.

However, Orga Syriac was not inspecting the stairwell construction because she was a concerned tenant. Instead she was looking for a quick way for the entity known as the Abo-Yorba to get in and out of the building. Now she studied the area beneath her with an eye toward climbing down and back up with ease. At least it would be easy for the she-devil.

Larry Cole was on vacation for a week. That morning Cole and Butch had gotten up at 7 A.M and gone to the police gym at Thirty-fifth and Normal. After changing into shorts and T-shirts they'd gone for a five-mile run. Returning to the gym, they'd lifted weights before spending some time in the sauna, showering, and changing back into their street clothes. They had breakfast at a restaurant not far from Comiskey Park and were now on their way to pick up Orga.

"You must really like this lady, Dad," Butch said as they sped south on Lake Shore Drive from Thirty-fifth Street.

Cole smiled. "I've only known her for three days, Butch. She's nice, but I think it will be awhile before we become anything more than just friends."

"Why? You like her and I'm sure she's crazy about you."

"How do you know that?"

"I could tell by the way she talked when she called yesterday."

"What did she say?"

"She just asked to speak to you, but it wasn't so much what she said as how she said it."

"I see," Cole said with a grin.

"And, Dad, she's really got a fantastic voice. She'll be great on TV."

"Let's see what you think of the rest of her." They pulled up in front of Orga's condo building. "That's her in the blue suit."

At the sight of Orga Syriac, Butch was stunned speechless. Cole got out of the car and came around to open the door for her. "All set for your first day on the job?"

She raised her arms to shoulder level. "I'm ready, but are they ready for me?"

"They're ready." He opened the door to find Butch still seated in the front seat staring at Orga. "Orga Syriac, this is my son, Larry Cole Jr., but to keep down confusion we call him Butch."

"Hello, Butch," she said, extending her hand.

It was at that instant that Butch realized he was still sitting in the car. Attempting to leap to his feet he banged his head hard on the doorframe. When he managed to extricate himself from the car he was seeing stars and a lump was forming on his head.

"Take it easy, son," Cole said, reaching out and grabbing the boy's arm to steady him.

"Did you hurt yourself, Butch?" Orga asked, reaching out and gently grasping his chin.

He managed to smile through his pain. "No, I'm fine, ma'am. It is a real pleasure to meet you."

Butch held the door while she got in the front seat. He then got in the back as his father returned to the driver's side of the car. He never took his eyes off her on the ride north to the WGN studios. Butch Cole was in love.

Sven-Erik Voman was the director of news programming at the WGN superstation in Chicago. As his name denoted, he was a six-foot six-inch Swede with a head of blond hair, going rapidly to gray, which he wore shoulder length. He also sported a beard, making him look very much like one of the legendary Vikings.

Sven ran one of the best local news programs in the country and enjoyed a healthy share of the Chicago area ratings for news shows. It was to him that Orga Syriac had sent her news audition videotape. In his eighteen-year career at WGN Sven-Erik Voman had hired and fired many newscasters and electronic-media reporters. Generally, newscasters were hired from other stations, fresh from journalism schools, or after working their way up through the ranks to the news desk. But Sven had never hired anyone on the basis of an introductory letter and a videotape.

When Sven received the package in the mail two months ago he had opened it in the course of answering his daily correspondence. When he read the letter accompanying the videotape his initial reaction was anger. He started to toss the letters, the tape, and the envelope they had come in into the trash can. Then his anger turned to amusement. He had to admit that this Orga Syriac had brass. He put the tape aside, planning to get rid of it later, but something about it kept nagging at him to the point that he was unable to complete much of the volume of paperwork which came with being a major television station's news director. Finally, with a whispered, "To hell with it," Sven shoved the tape into the video recorder beside his desk and sat back to watch what he expected to be a joke.

Orga Syriac's videotape was seven minutes and twenty-eight second's long. She was seated at a desk with her hands folded in front of her on the desktop. She narrated four stories that were in the news that week: one national, one local, one entertainment, and one sports. She had memorized each piece because she spoke without referring to notes and he didn't believe that she'd gone to the expense of purchasing a TelePrompTer. When the tape ended he played it again, and then a third time. To say the least Sven-Erik Voman was stunned.

In his entire life he had never seen anyone come across a television set with more impact than this woman. He couldn't actually believe what he was seeing. After watching the tape for the fourth time he yelled for his secretary to get the president of the company on the telephone and make an emergency appointment for him. Then, with tape in hand, he rushed out of his office to set in motion the events that would hire for WGN in Chicago the woman that Voman was certain would be the next Oprah Winfrey.

Now Sven-Erik Voman sat in his cluttered office waiting for his new star to arrive. Running a hand through his thick blond hair he wondered for perhaps the fiftieth time if the woman he had hired would be as good with on-the-fly spot news reporting as she'd been on the tape. He had only seen her in the flesh once, and she was even more stunning in person than she was on tape. But over the years he'd spent in the TV news business he had seen many pretty faces known as "talking heads," who could only read from a prepared script. If a breaking story developed while they were on the air some "talking heads" would become flustered. They were totally unable to take the gist of a breaking news story and transform it into a concise verbal narrative without having it put down on paper for them.

Sven-Erik sighed. He'd just have to wait and see how good Orga Syriac was.

His intercom buzzed.

"Yes?"

"Ms. Syriac is here," the receptionist at the front desk said before adding, "Chief of Detectives Larry Cole is with her."

Sven-Erik's thick eyebrows went up. Either his pretty reporter had some very impressive friends or she was in a great deal of trouble.

"Send Ms. Syriac and Chief Cole in."

At that moment across the city at 121 North LaSalle Street, the mayor of the city of Chicago was leaving his fifth-floor office for a luncheon at the McCormick Place convention center on the lakefront. Accompanying the mayor were four bodyguards from the Chicago Police Department and his female press secretary. There were a number of people in the fifth-floor corridor, and the bodyguards, who had been trained by the United States Secret Service, scrutinized everyone and noticed no overt threats.

The party proceeded to a key-operated elevator manned by a uniformed cop. They descended to the lobby and headed for the exit doors leading onto LaSalle Street.

The mayor was a politician, so he shook hands with a number of people as he moved along. A young blond woman carrying a straw shoulder bag entered City Hall from LaSalle Street and began walking in the direction of the mayoral party. At the same time two casually dressed black men carrying attaché cases began walking down the staircase at the south end of the lobby. The bodyguards were keeping a careful eye out for trouble and each cop had an "area" or "zone" to watch. They were attempting to protect their charge from everyone, so they were unaware of the threat they faced until it was too late.

"Your Honor," the blond woman called.

They stopped. The mayor flashed a smile as she walked up to him. The bodyguards were alert and watchful, but there was simply too much for them to take in at once. The woman extended her hand to Chicago's chief executive. In turn he raised his hand to shake hers. Then things began to happen very, very fast. The black men reached into their attaché cases and removed two semiautomatic handguns. Before they could bring them to bear on the mayor, the bodyguards reacted by pulling their weapons and opening fire. The two men were dead before they hit the marble floor of the City Hall lobby. The gunshots resulted in bedlam erupting, with people running for the exits in an attempt to get away from the source of the danger. The bodyguards hesitated only scant seconds before their training asserted itself and they began moving to protect their principal. By then it was too late.

The blond woman reached the mayor at the exact moment that the two soon to be dead men reached for their weapons. As the bodyguards reacted, the woman moved with amazing speed to pull a four-inch-barreled .357 magnum from her shoulder bag and jam it beneath the mayor's chin. By the time the bodyguards became aware of what had happened, she had spun the mayor around and was using him as a shield.

"If one of you moves, I'll kill him!" she screamed, and she began backing toward the LaSalle Street exit with her captive in front of her.

One of the bodyguards decided to attempt to rescue the mayor by rushing the kidnapper. Before he got two feet she shot him in the head and once more jammed the barrel of the smoking gun against the mayor's neck.

"The next one of you who tries anything will get this man killed and I mean that!" To emphasize her threat she pressed the gun into the mayor's flesh hard enough to make him grimace from the pain.

A second bodyguard, the supervisor of the team, took a step toward them, but the press secretary shouted, "Don't do anything! She means what she says!"

Then the chief municipal executive of Chicago and his kidnapper were through the door out onto LaSalle Street. This galvanized the bodyguards, who rushed to the door and out onto the street behind them. By the time they reached the sidewalk the woman was forcing the mayor into a black Jeep Cherokee with tinted windows. The bodyguard realized that these windows would make it difficult for them to see the driver or identify the vehicle's occupants. This would make it impossible to mount a surgical sniper attack to take out the kidnappers. But he wasn't about to let the black vehicle out of his sight. As he ran for an unmarked police car parked at the curb in front of City Hall, he shouted to the two surviving guards, "Get on the air and alert all police cars on citywide that the mayor's been kidnapped! Have them broadcast a description of the vehicle, but instruct them not to attempt to stop it. I'm going to follow them and broadcast their location."

Then he jumped in the car, executed a tire-screeching U-turn in the center of LaSalle Street, and took off after the Jeep.

CHAPTER 23

JUNE 14, 2004
10:27 A.M.

Deandra Priest was the senior anchorperson at WGN. She had been with the station almost as long as Sven-Erik Voman and was considered something of an institution on the electronic-media news beat in the Windy City. Deandra, or Dede as she liked to be called, could be described as a "talking head." She was more concerned about her makeup, hair, and voice than any of the stories she "read" off the TelePrompTers at noon, 3, and 6 P.M. Monday through Friday. She had been known to display the same pleasant smile while narrating in syrupy sweet tones the scalding of babies, the death toll from a plane crash, or the events surrounding a bombing in which hundreds were killed. During an interview some years ago at the Chicago Press Club, Dede Priest had carelessly disclosed to a room full of fellow journalists that she didn't consider herself a "newsperson," but rather a TV "personality." She went on to state, to the mounting horror of her colleagues, that she thought of herself as closer to Oprah and Jay Leno than to Dan Rather and Ted Koppel. But despite this professional faux pas, Dede had managed to survive at WGN.

But in order for her to have lasted for over a decade in this highly competitive field, Dede Priest had learned not only to cover her behind, but also to be viciously deceitful when it was necessary. She, like everyone else at the station; was aware of the "new girl" coming to work today. Dede had even managed to obtain a copy of Orga Syriac's audition video. And what the veteran "talking head" saw frightened her senseless.

If the newcomer came off only half as good on television as she had on the tape then there was no doubt in Dede's mind that this Syriac woman would be assigned to the noon, 3, and 6 P.M. news desk. These were Dede's spots, and the veteran was certain that Sven-Erik Voman would keep her on the air. However, she dreaded having to share her time on the tube with Orga Syriac. The reason for this was because the looks, which Dede Priest had felt were her greatest asset, were starting to desert her.

Dede was sitting in front of the mirror applying makeup. She was distracted by the pattern of tiny wrinkles beginning to form at the corners of her eyes and at the edges of her mouth. She religiously applied moisturizers and ointments that were touted by the pharmaceutical companies as guaranteed to make these scars of age vanish, but nothing ever really worked. At least not for long.

Dede was forty-five years old and still a very attractive woman. She had her hair washed and set by the studio hairdresser every day, and the studio makeup artist had done her face only a short time ago. But Dede wasn't satisfied. Not with Orga Syriac reporting for work today.

The interstation telephone on her makeup table rang. Picking it up, Dede snapped, "What?!" into the receiver.

It was her producer, who had been monitoring the police city-wide frequency in the newsroom. As she listened to the news story currently breaking in the Chicago Loop, Dede's face began changing. From one of worry, her expression became transformed to one of shock and then devious cunning.

Deandra "Dede" Priest had found a way to eliminate the threat that Orga Syriac presented.

"We're getting ready for the noon news report," Sven-Erik Voman was saying as he took Orga, Cole, and Butch on a tour of WGN studios. "You'll be doing the weather and sports along with Dede Priest, who is a station veteran."

Butch stopped at a studio that was semidark and empty. "This is where they do the *Bozo the Clown Show*. I remember watching it when I was a kid. But I always thought it was bigger."

Cole walked over and put his hand on his son's shoulder. "Maybe you're the one who got bigger."

Sven-Erik and Orga smiled.

They were just turning to resume the tour when two things happened at once. A young man sporting shoulder-length hair and a beard came running down the corridor toward them, and Cole's beeper went off. This surprised the chief of detectives because he was on furlough and Deputy Chief Martin was serving in an acting capacity.

"I've got to talk to you right away, Sven," the young man said breathlessly when he reached them. He eyed the news director's guests warily. "Alone."

"Could I use the phone in your office?" Cole asked Voman.

"Help yourself," he said, excusing himself from Orga and Butch before retreating a short distance and conducting a whispered conversation with the young man.

"I wonder what's going on," Butch said.

"Trouble," Orga responded.

Then Butch noticed that something about her had changed. He couldn't put his finger on it, but she was definitely different. He recalled that when he was a child, before his mother and father had split up, his dad would get calls to report to work. At such times Larry Cole Sr. would go through a change similar to what Butch was seeing, or more appropriately sensing, from Orga. But Cole's transformation was nothing as dramatic as Orga's. In fact, Butch was certain that the beautiful reporter had changed physically, but when he studied her he could find nothing different about her. Then, realizing his confusion, she turned to look at him.

For a brief instant terror gripped Butch with a ferocity the likes of which he'd never experienced before. It was as if he had suddenly been thrust into the presence of something extremely dangerous. A being more deadly and menacing than Margo DeWitt, who had kidnapped Butch Cole in the past.

The young man's heart began beating faster and he was preparing to run when Orga smiled at him. In that instant his terror evaporated and a feeling of safety and well-being came over him. He managed to smile back. Then Voman returned.

He was grim with tension. "We're getting word that the mayor's been kidnapped. The police are in visual contact with the kidnap vehicle and we're monitoring them so we know where they are. I need to send a camera crew out in a mobile van to cover this and we're going to get our chopper up. We've got a van out now, but it's in Indiana on a follow-up story and it would take them too long to get back into the city. So . . ."

"Why not send me out?" Orga said.

Voman studied her for a moment. "Dede Priest has already recommended that. I would send her, but we need someone here to coordinate everything. This is probably going to be the story of the year. Perhaps the decade."

Orga stepped forward and placed her hand on his arm. "Don't worry, I can handle it. Show me where to go and I'll make you proud of me."

It was obvious to both Orga and Butch that the news director was indeed reluctant to send the totally inexperienced reporter out to cover such an important story. They also realized that he didn't have any choice.

Finally, "Okay, you've got it. Come with me."

As they hurried down the corridor, Orga called to Butch, "Tell your father I'll call him later."

Remaining behind, Butch Cole crossed his fingers and wished his father's new friend good luck.

CHAPTER 24

JUNE 14, 2004
10:40 A.M.

Although the deputy chief of detective division administration, Theophilus Martin, was in charge in Cole's absence, Lieutenant Blackie Silvestri was really running things. Blackie did all the paperwork, reviewed all the cases, and made most of the decisions after first running them by Deputy Chief Martin to obtain his tacit approval. It wasn't so much that the deputy chief was lazy as that he was within six months of retirement and had been rewarded with the administrative post in the detective division after spending fifteen years as the commander of the Gang Crimes Section. So when Blackie heard about the mayor being kidnapped he made the decision to beep Larry Cole.

Now Blackie sat at his desk waiting expectantly for the phone to ring. Manny was sitting in a chair across from Blackie, and Judy was perched on the edge of the desk. There was tension in the air, but not the type born of worry; rather, it was that of a sprinter in the starting block waiting for the race to begin. After they got the word from Cole they would launch themselves into an investigation which would be aimed at rescuing the mayor and arresting whoever was responsible for his abduction.

The direct-line telephone on Blackie's desk rang. He only let it do so once.

"Silvestri."

Cole was on the other end calling from the WGN studios. Blackie explained what had happened before providing the latest information. "The black Jeep Cherokee went southbound on LaSalle to Madison then traveled westbound on Madison to the Dan Ryan Expressway and headed south. Right now patrol units have been dispatched to clear a path in front of the kidnappers' vehicle and there's a squadron of marked cars behind it. The state police have got a helicopter on the way. This thing is shaping up to look like the O. J. Simpson Bronco ride back in ninety-four."

Blackie paused to listen.

"No, boss, we have no idea where they're headed nor who is responsible. If they can contact us, they haven't."

Again he listened.

Nodding, he said, "Okay, we're on the way." Hanging up, he turned to Judy and Manny. "Let's go."

The mayor was scared. In fact, he'd never been more afraid in his life. With a stunning swiftness he had been snatched from his hectic daily political routine into an unimaginable nightmare. And with each passing second his feeling of impending doom increased.

The Windy City's chief executive realized that his abductors were not bungling amateurs, but cold-bloodedly efficient. They handled the kidnapping like it was a military operation. Now, as they sped south on the Dan Ryan Expressway, he could see that they had no concern for the phalanx of police cars following them or the cop cars clearing a path in front of the Jeep. He could also tell that they had a particular destination in mind; however, no words had passed between the kidnappers since he'd been shoved into this vehicle back at City Hall.

There were three of them: a man, who was the driver; a black kid who couldn't have been a day over sixteen; and the blond woman. When the woman had forced him into the back of the Jeep at gun-point, the mayor had initially attempted to issue a hollow warning that what they were doing was a capital offense, which could result in them receiving the death penalty. The black youth held a gun trained shakily on the chief executive while the woman taped his hands together and his mouth shut. As she worked he noticed that she displayed a detached efficiency. Every action was proficient and totally devoid of emotion. It was as if she'd been practicing what she was doing now for a very long time.

The mayor studied the driver, who was as Nordic in appearance as the woman. He also displayed a total lack of feeling and operated the Jeep with the casual regard of a man out for a drive in the country.

The teenager was different. The mayor could tell that he was badly frightened. Had the woman not entrusted the kid with the gun to hold on him while she taped his hands and mouth, the mayor would have certainly considered the possibility that this young man had also been kidnapped. No, he was a member of this little band of criminals, the mayor surmised, and possibly one that he could exploit to his advantage. But the mayor would have to be patient, which would be difficult as with each passing second his situation worsened.

Then, in an abrupt maneuver that took the army of police cars following them by surprise, the black Jeep Cherokee swung abruptly across three express lanes of the expressway to enter the local lanes. A number of the police cars following the kidnap vehicle were unable to duplicate the sudden turn without colliding with one another and causing a major chain-reaction accident, and so they continued on in the express lanes. They had been very effectively eliminated from the pursuit.

The kidnap vehicle made another unexpected move. It exited the Dan Ryan Expressway at Fifty-first Street. It was at this exit that the Area One Police Center was located, which was one of the largest and most heavily staffed law enforcement facilities in the city.

*   *   *

Cole and Butch were stuck in traffic on the Dan Ryan Expressway a mile north when the kidnap vehicle made the unexpected maneuver and rocketed up the Fifty-first Street exit ramp. All of the cars assigned to the kidnapping had switched to a special frequency and were ordered to keep voice traffic to a minimal level except for emergencies. The kidnap vehicle leaving the expressway was an emergency. The frequency erupted in bedlam.

The police car driven by the supervisor of the mayoral bodyguard detail had maintained contact with the kidnap vehicle since they'd left City Hall. After clearing the special frequency the detail used, he had methodically broadcast the Jeep's position block by block. The other units in the pursuit were placed on a separate frequency. The dispatcher had kept them posted on the kidnap vehicle's progress.

Chief of Detectives Larry Cole had access to both frequencies. Now he flicked a switch on his dash-mounted communications console to pick up the bodyguard's frequency.

". . . just crossed the overpass. We're proceeding eastbound on Fifty-first Street passing the Area One Police Center. We're under the railroad viaduct. They're making a right turn onto Federal Street."

"They're going someplace specific," Cole said more to himself than to his son.

Butch, who was enjoying the greatest adventure of his life despite his trip to the Dragon's Lair with Judy, said, "But what's around there other than those old abandoned project buildings?"

"That's it!" Cole's shout made Butch jump. Cole snatched the telephone from the console and punched in Blackie's number. The Lieutenant answered instantly. "Blackie, they're going to one of the abandoned project buildings. I don't know which one, but there are only a few left standing. Where are you now? Okay, I'm stuck in traffic. Get over there and liaison with the patrol commander on the scene. Seal off the area and make sure they initiate a Hostage Incident Plan. I'll be there as quickly as I can."

Cole stared out through the windshield and chewed on his lower lip. "What in the hell are they up to?"

Obediently, Butch replied, "I don't know, Dad, but I'm pretty sure we're going to find out soon."

The ABC Chicago station managed to get its helicopter up first and pick up the kidnap vehicle along with the pursuing police cars while they were still on the expressway. The images broadcast from 1,500 feet above the ground were of the black Jeep Cherokee being followed by a single unmarked police car, from the mayor's bodyguard detail, flanked by ten marked Chicago police cars. Occasionally the cars would pass a lone civilian vehicle that had been forced over to the side of the road by the city or state police. However, from the camera in the ABC helicopter, most of coverage was of a virtually empty expressway with the black Jeep traveling alone at the posted speed limit.

On the ground, less than fifty feet behind the last police car, was the WGN minicam van. Miraculously it had managed to slip through midday traffic and join in the pursuit before trailing cop cars slowed traffic on the expressway behind them, which had also trapped Cole's car. Jammed into the back with computers, minicams, TV monitors, and microphones of all sizes was Orga Syriac. Her producer was driving the van while the cameraman attempted to get pictures of the rear of the pursuit from ground level. The cameraman was belted in and had his minicam strapped to his shoulder. He was leaning out the window recording everything that had happened so far, but the feed being transmitted back to Sven-Erik Voman in the studio was so bad that the news director refused to transmit it.

Now in the back of the minicam van Orga had one of the monitors switched to the ABC station and was about to do her first on-the-air reporting. She paused a moment to look at the back of her hand. She watched it change momentarily from a five-fingered appendage to one with three fingers tipped with two-inch curved talons.

"I don't have time for this now," she whispered.

The hand reverted back to its human shape. Then she took a deep breath, keyed her mike, and said, "Sven, I'm ready."

From an overhead speaker he replied, "Okay, Orga, on my mark. One . . . two . . . three . . . You're on."

"This is Orga Syriac for WGN News in Chicago. Right now I'm in a van on the Dan Ryan Expressway behind a squadron of police cars, which are . . ."

WGN broadcast a photograph of the mayor to accompany Orga's voice. Although ABC was broadcasting the black kidnap vehicle's progress, the WGN feed had a viewer share twice that of the other stations covering the event.

"They've stopped," the mayor's bodyguard said.

"What is your location?" the dispatcher inquired.

"We're in the fifty-three hundred block of South Federal behind one of the last abandoned CHA high rises."

"What are they doing?"

After a pause the bodyguard replied, "Nothing."

Utilizing his siren and the shoulders of the expressway, Cole managed to make some progress and was fast approaching the Fifty-first Street exit ramp. Butch was sitting rigidly in the passenger seat with his eyes bulging from the thrill of this experience. If he'd ever had any doubts in the past, they were now erased. As soon as he was old enough he planned to become a cop just like his father.

The telephone on the communications console rang. Cole snatched it up and said, "Go, Blackie."

"This isn't Lieutenant Silvestri," a woman said. "I am the one who kidnapped your precious mayor, Chief Cole. I am now prepared to dictate my terms, but there is one preliminary requirement I have before we begin negotiations."

"And that is?" Cole said, gripping the telephone receiver tightly.

Our Lady of Peace Catholic Church was located approximately two miles from the abandoned project building where the kidnap vehicle had stopped. As school was out and the summer session had yet to begin, Sister Mary Louise Stallings, the lone nun assigned to the parish, was in the rectory watching television when the news story concerning the mayor's abduction broke. She crossed herself and said a prayer for his safety.

Sister Mary Louise, a pretty woman with blue eyes and a heart-shaped face, was alone. Father Philip Cisco, the thirty-two-year-old pastor of Our Lady of Peace, was out in the school yard playing basketball with a group of boys from the Washington Park Boulevard area. The Boulevard, as it was called, was recovering slowly from being one of the most impoverished, gang-infested slums in the country. However, due to the efforts of Father Phil and his predecessor, Father Ken Smith, Our Lady had become the source of a resurgence on and around the Boulevard area that was truly phenomenal.

She was about to go out and tell Father Phil what had happened when the rectory doorbell rang. The housekeeper had gone grocery shopping so there was no one to answer it but the nun.

She left the study and walked down the hall past the dining room to the front door. Even though the Boulevard area had improved, it was still not the type of neighborhood in which people opened doors without first checking to see who was outside. Sister Mary Louise looked through the peephole and what she saw surprised her to say the least.

There was a priest standing outside on the porch. Although Our Lady of Peace was a Catholic church, seldom were Father Phil and Sister Mary Louise visited by other priests or nuns. She opened the door.

"Good day to you, Sister," the silver-haired cleric said with a thick Irish brogue. "I'm Father James Lochran."

She managed a smile. "How do you do, Father? I'm Sister Mary Louise Stallings."

They stood there for a moment before he said, "Father Lochran from Detroit? You were expecting me, weren't you?"

"I don't. . . ." Sister Mary Louise's confusion was evident. Then she remembered her manners. "Won't you come in, Father?"

"Thank you," he said; carrying a valise in one hand and utilizing his cane, he limped into the rectory.

"Why don't you have a seat in the study while I go and get Father Cisco, the pastor?"

She led him to the study, where the TV was still on. Before leaving him she asked, "Can I get you a cup of coffee or perhaps a cold drink?"

The priest emitted a heavy sigh.. "It is quite a hot day and I was forced to take public transportation from the train station. A cold glass of water would be quite refreshing."

Something about him began bothering the nun. In her lifetime she had experienced her own share of problems and was not about to take anyone or anything for granted. "Did you come far?"

"All the way from Detroit," he said, sinking wearily into the armchair that Sister Mary Louise had been seated in only moments ago. "I'll be attending a seminar on contemporary theology at the University of Chicago. I'll be living here with you and Father Cisco until September."

"Oh," she said with genuine surprise. Sister Mary Louise had been at Our Lady of Peace for fourteen years and this priest would be the first guest they had ever had. The Boulevard area was not one that many people wanted to visit. Managing to conceal her shock she said, "I'll get you a glass of water before I go for Father Phil."

In something of a preoccupied daze she went to the kitchen and got him a glass of ice water. When she returned he was mopping his face with a handkerchief. She set the glass down on the table beside his chair. "I'll be back in a minute. Oh, by the way, Father, there's a bit of an emergency going on in Chicago right now. Our mayor has been kidnapped."

"Saints preserve us," he said making the sign of the cross.

"It's on the news now." Then she left.

The priest impersonator gulped down the glass of cold water. He looked around the rectory study. It was ancient, but comfortable. This would be a good home base for him to operate out of on his ministry of atonement. Brother Steve at the mission had given him the idea. It had been a simple matter to produce a forged letter from the archbishop of Detroit to this Father Philip Cisco requesting that Father James Lochran be allowed to stay at Our Lady of Peace for the next three months. According to Brother Steve, seldom would such a request be challenged or even checked. The man who had once been known as Thomas Kelly fit the mold perfectly of an aging Irish priest.

He took another sip of his water before placing the glass back on the table. He looked at the television set for the first time since he'd entered the rectory. The story concerning the mayor's kidnapping still occupied all of the public news channels. The set in Our Lady of Peace rectory was turned to WGN. The still photograph of the mayor was on the screen. Then the priest heard the commentator's voice.

Initially, he felt no more than a strange uneasiness. The picture of the mayor dissolved, to be replaced by the reporter whose voice he'd been hearing. She was standing in front of a building with vacant windows. Seeing her again caused him to emit a gasp before his paralysis of three days ago returned.

CHAPTER 25

JUNE 14, 2004
11:00 A.M.

The female kidnapper was a very cool, calculating killer. With a shudder, the mayor remembered how she had murdered one of his bodyguards back in the City Hall lobby.

He watched her use a cellular telephone to call Larry Cole. This was the first ray of hope for a possible rescue that the mayor had experienced. Despite his kidnappers' efficiency, if these people were intentionally taking on Chief Cole they were making a very bad mistake. Then when the mayor heard the kidnappers' initial requirements he was dumbfounded. They wanted safe passage into the building and a television news crew and commentator so they could make their demands for his release to the world.

When she hung up, the man looked at her and said, "Do you think Cole will go for it?"

The woman smiled, looked from the driver to the mayor, and said, "I'm counting on it. If he doesn't, Your Honor, then you're going to be a very dead man." Then she looked at a square gold wristwatch on her left arm. "Cole has seven minutes."

Cole arrived on the scene with headlights flashing and siren blaring. Yelling for Butch to stay in the car, he headed for the area where the news media were being sequestered. Manny Sherlock fell in step with the chief.

"Talk to me, Manny," Cole said without breaking stride.

Manny read from a pocket notebook. "The two men the bodyguards took out at City Hall have been identified as Carl Banister, aka Mustafa Ali, and Hezekiah Moore, aka Muhammad Rahim. They are, or should I say were, both members of the Twenty-first Century Black Nationalist Movement, which is reputedly a front for the Disciples street gang."

Cole frowned. "Why would the Disciples want to kidnap the mayor?"

"Maybe they didn't, boss. The kidnapper is a white female. Banister and Moore were low-ranking members of the Disciples. The Gang Crimes Section said that they have minor records for disorderly conduct and some gang violence, but are nowhere near sophisticated enough to pull this off."

They reached the press area. Cole stopped and turned to Manny. "The woman who called me knows what she's doing and I'd be willing to bet that she's not only educated but also smart and very deadly."

"What does she want?" Manny asked.

Cole turned to look at the cordoned-off press area, where the WGN van was still the lone news unit to have arrived.

Outside the van, Orga Syriac stood in front of a man holding a minicam. She was talking into a microphone with the abandoned sixteen-story project building behind her.

In response to Manny's question, Cole said, "Publicity." Then he walked over to the WGN van.

Cole quickly explained the situation to Orga. Almost before the last word was out of his mouth, she said, "I'll do it."

"This isn't your average news story, Orga," he explained urgently. "These people are not only ruthless but also extremely dangerous."

She smiled. "Larry, this is my first assignment on my first day as a reporter. I wouldn't know what an 'average assignment' is, but you don't have much more time to deliberate on this, so I'm going to have to be your girl."

Cole looked away from her. He had sent people into deadly situations before; however, he'd been fortunate that no one had ever been killed. He searched his brain feverishly for an alternative to this situation, but with the time constraints imposed by the kidnappers he had no choice.

Exhaling a deep sigh he said, "Okay, Orga, you and your cameraman are it." He turned to the cameraman, a slender man named Dave Spurgeon, who was clad in jeans and a worn Chicago Cubs T-shirt. "Keep your camera on them at all times. We'll need the tape later as evidence."

The cameraman nodded. Although Spurgeon knew who Cole was from previous news stories he'd covered, things had developed so fast he hadn't gotten a chance to formally meet the woman he'd be accompanying into the abandoned project building. Then he looked at the reporter.

Realizing that they were waiting for her to give the word, Orga said, "Okay, let's go."

Cole accompanied them from the press area, across the outer perimeter, to the edge of the inner perimeter.

Cole held the barrier tape up for Orga and Spurgeon. They slipped beneath it and began walking quickly toward the black Jeep. As they did so, Spurgeon raised the camera to his shoulder and turned it on. Orga Syriac's image flashed on television screens around the world.

CHAPTER 26

The blond kidnapper saw the approaching camera crew. She turned and leaned so close to the mayor that he could feel the pressure of her breath against his face. "Listen closely, Your Honor. You, this young man"—she nodded her head toward the black kid—"that woman, and her cameraman are going to form a shield around me and my driver." She lifter the revolver and waved it under his nose. "If Chief Cole or any of the other cops make one move, then you're going to instantly become the ex-mayor of Chicago."

Orga and Spurgeon reached the back door of the kidnap vehicle.

"Open it," she snapped at the black kid.

He jumped to do her bidding. It took him two tries to activate the door release. When the door opened, she shoved two black hoods at Orga and Spurgeon. "Put these on," she instructed, "and don't point that camera at us until I tell you to."

The newspeople complied, discovering that there were eyeholes in the black hoods, which reminded them of executioners' garb. Inside the van the three kidnappers were also wearing hoods, and one had been placed over the mayor's head. The abducted chief executive was having difficulty breathing with his mouth taped shut. The female kidnapper patted his bound wrists and said a far from soothing, "You won't have to wear that long, Your Honor. We're not going far."

She turned to Orga and Spurgeon. "You two and the mayor are going to form a shield around us. You will arrange yourselves in a circle and we will be inside that circle. If the cops try anything, then I guarantee that you and the Mayor will be the first to die. Do you understand?"

Now masked, the newspeople nodded. Something about the female began bothering the blond kidnapper. Reaching out she snatched the hood up to look into Orga's face. "I've never seen you on television before."

"This is my first assignment," Orga said.

The kidnapper stared at her for a long time. "Okay, but don't get cute and make it your last."

From the edge of the inner-perimeter barrier tape, Cole watched what was going on at the kidnap vehicle. When Orga and Spurgeon put the hoods over their heads, the chief of detectives was able to guess with fair accuracy what was going to happen next. A few moments later the kidnappers, who were also masked, came out of the van with the mayor. Slowly, using the newspeople and the mayor as shields, they began making their way toward the project building.

This was the moment of greatest tension for Larry Cole. Although he had ordered every cop assigned to this hostage incident to hold his fire, there was always a hot dog or loose cannon who would figure he had the skill to end it all with a few well-placed shots. But, despite there being over a hundred officers surrounding the kidnap vehicle, no attempt was made to interfere. The six people now making up the kidnap party crossed the cracked pavement to the boarded-up entrance to the project building without incident.

"Take off the hoods," the woman ordered when they were inside the main lobby of the building.

The mayor snatched off his hood and took in as much air through his nose as he could. The stench made him gag. After removing her own mask, Orga stepped forward and removed the tape from his mouth. The kidnap victim gasped before becoming violently ill. As Orga held him upright, the female kidnapper stepped behind her and placed the barrel

of a revolver against the base of her skull. "If you do anything like that again without asking for permission first, your
broadcast career is going to be over real fast."

Although Orga did not flinch, she said a contrite, "I'm
sorry, but he looked like he was going to have a heart attack
if I didn't remove the tape."

Still holding the gun to Orga's head, the kidnapper said,
"I would worry more about my own health if I were you,
sweet face."

The mayor managed to straighten up. Removing his
breast-pocket handkerchief, he wiped his face. He was pale
and his eyes were weary with fear, but he managed to say a
strong, "I don't see what you hope to gain by this. The police
have this place surrounded, so there's no way you can escape."

The blond kidnapper smiled. "We shall see, Your Honor.
We shall see." She turned to Spurgeon. "Get ready to film
sweet face here interviewing me." She said to Orga, "Are
you ready for the interview of your life?"

The reporter didn't respond immediately, but simply stared
at the hooded woman. Her mind was back in the past outside
a town called Diggstown, Mississippi.

"Don't look at me like that!" the kidnapper screamed from
beneath her hood. She raised her pistol and pointed it in
Orga's face. "I made no guarantees to Cole that you would
make it out of this alive."

Orga lowered her eyes and said softly, "I didn't mean to
upset you."

The male kidnapper looked from the reporter to his companion. He couldn't figure out what was going on between
these two. He decided it was some kind of woman's thing
and left it at that. The air was barely breathable as the stench
of decay and a nearby open sewer were strong, but the hood
helped cut the smell.

Spurgeon hefted the camera to his shoulder, peered
through the lens, switched on the light, and said, "Are you
ready?"

She nodded.

"Okay, one . . . two . . . three . . . We're transmitting."

"This is Orga Syriac for WGN News in Chicago. I am currently . . ."

Cole waited until the kidnappers and hostages had entered the building before he retreated from the edge of the outer perimeter back to the WGN van. There a monitor had been set up which picked up the direct feed from the cameraman. For a few moments the screen was blank. Then Orga's face appeared. The shot expanded to take in the hooded kidnapper.

As Orga began her introduction, a female police sergeant in uniform stepped up beside Cole. He merely glanced at her, taking in long black hair swept back into a ponytail and a blouse displaying a fairly decent figure, before he turned back to the screen. Then he heard his son say, "Do you think the kidnappers will hurt Orga or the mayor, Dad?"

Cole spun around. "I thought I told you to stay in the car?"

"It was hot in there, Dad, and Judy said I could stay with her so I won't be in the way."

"So where is Judy?" Cole said as some of his anger started to ebb.

"Right here, boss," the sergeant said. "Sometimes the obvious is the most effective disguise."

However, at that moment Cole's attention became focused on the television monitor as the hooded female kidnapper began her statement.

The lobby of the abandoned building was hot, musty, and dark. The light on Spurgeon's minicam provided the only illumination with the exception of cracks in the wooden panels boarding up the entrance through which they had entered. In the cone of light, like actors on a stage, stood Orga flanked by the kidnappers and the mayor. After completing her introduction, Orga said to the hooded female, "Would you care to identify yourself?"

"No," came the curt reply.

"Do you have a particular political affiliation?"

"We stand for oppressed people everywhere. We need no name or slogan to carry on our fight against tyranny."

"Is there a particular cause that the kidnapping of the mayor of Chicago will aid?"

The kidnapper's eyes flared. "I don't have time to answer your nonsensical questions. The world is waiting for the culmination of this mission against the forces of political injustice. But before that is done I want to say that . . ."

Outside, Cole's eyes were glued to the monitor. When the kidnapper mentioned the "culmination of the mission" his jaw muscles rippled.

"Has Sergeant Cappetto of the Special Weapons Unit arrived yet?" he asked Judy.

"Yes, sir. His team is over at the edge of the inner perimeter."

"Tell them to get in position for an assault right now. I think that woman is planning to kill the mayor."

Judy turned away, removed a walkie-talkie from her Sam Browne belt, and broadcast the message.

At the edge of the inner perimeter a muscular man with receding gray hair responded to the radio message from the Mistress of Disguise/High Priestess of Mayhem. Sergeant Cappetto, dressed in black combat fatigues and carrying a special assault weapon (SAW), turned to his assault team— three men and a woman—and said, "Let's move into position."

With well-trained efficiency, they trotted away from the inner perimeter and spread out as they approached the boarded-up entrance to the project building. They flattened themselves against the wall and flanked the doors leading inside. They were close enough to see the illumination from the minicam and hear the voices of Orga Syriac and the kidnapper.

After taking their positions, the Special Weapons Unit prepared to assault the building.

In his law office on South LaSalle Street, Philo Coffey watched the events taking place in the abandoned project building with rapt attention. He was alone, but had there been anyone there to observe him, they would have noticed a look of such anticipation on his face that it was almost sexual in intensity. As the kidnapper droned on about political tyranny, racism, and the exploitation of the poor, Coffey ground his teeth and said, "Would you get on with it?"

Today was payback time for the PAC chairman and he planned to enjoy every second.

The kidnapper's diatribe against society was becoming lengthy. She droned on about political injustice and protecting the rights of the oppressed. Finally, she came to a conclusion by saying, "Now we are going to strike a blow for justice and equality by . . ."

She began to raise the revolver she'd been holding down at her side. She was bringing it up to point at the mayor. Dave Spurgeon was staring in horror through the camera lens at the event he was recording for posterity. He had narrowed the focus to take in only the kidnapper and the man she planned to kill. He knew where Orga was in proximity to the others, but she was not in the shot.

Suddenly, there was a blur across his lens and his spotlight exploded, plunging the area into darkness. Something slammed into him and he was knocked backward with such force he felt as if he had been hit by a truck. His camera fell to the floor and shattered. It took a moment for his eyes to adjust. He could make out the shapes of the kidnappers and the mayor. Then there was another figure. He was certain that his eyes were playing tricks on him in the dark. Then whatever it was moved with an unbelievable swiftness.

The female kidnapper knew what she had to do. After killing the mayor, the cameraman, and the reporter she and her companions would set off a low-yield explosive that would slow down the assault team that Cole would certainly be sending to the rescue. Then they'd utilize the preplanned sewer escape route that, although filthy and foul-smelling, would enable them to elude the legion of cops surrounding the area.

She had to admit that she'd gotten carried away with her speech about tyranny and oppression. What she was doing had nothing to do with justice, but was instead about money.

The money she was being paid for this job. But even though she was masked and the world would never know who she was, this would be her moment of fame. Within hours she would be out of the country, leaving the black kid behind as the cops' only lead. Of course he would be dead, like his comrades back at City Hall; however, they would forge a link to the Disciples street gang. The outcry would be so great that the entire governmental apparatus would be set in motion to destroy them. Neat. Very neat.

Now she finished her speech and was about to carry out the assassination for the millions of people out there in TV land when the sweet-faced reporter moved. This was fine with the kidnapper, as killing her first really didn't matter. The mayor would be next and then the cameraman.

The kidnapper turned to execute the deed when the light went out and the cameraman was knocked to the ground. The reporter, or what had been the reporter, was again beside the kidnapper.

Even in the darkness the hooded woman was able to take in a sight that frightened her rigid. There was a creature here with her now. It had the eyes of a reptile, two rows of razor-sharp teeth set in a mouth that looked as large as an alligator's, and what appeared to be horns protruding from either side of a scaly, oblong head.

The kidnapper attempted to fire the gun, but the monster reached out, grabbed her hand, and ripped the weapon away with a paw tipped by two-inch-long talons. Before the woman could scream, she was snatched off her feet and dragged deeper into the shadows of the abandoned building. The kidnapper attempted to scream, but terror had frozen her vocal cords.

CHAPTER 27

JUNE 14, 2004
11:15 A.M.

Cole was studying the monitor in the WGN van when the screen blurred before the transmission was interrupted.

"What happened?" he asked the producer, who was seated at a console inside the van.

The white-haired, liver-spotted man who was a year short of his seventieth birthday, said, "Everything here is fine. There must be a problem at the source of the transmission."

Cole again turned to Judy. "Tell Cappetto's people to get ready for the assault, but I want them to wait until I get over there before they enter the building."

With that Cole ran toward the building entrance. Judy raised her walkie-talkie and transmitted Cole's message to the Special Weapons Unit as Butch took everything in with wide-eyed fascination.

Father Philip Cisco had the face of a poet beneath a head of thick brown hair. He had been a track star in the one-hundred- and two-hundred yard dashes at Quigley South Seminary. He could still move very fast and was in excellent shape, which the teenagers the priest had been playing basketball with could attest to.

Now Sister Mary Louise was forced to virtually run to keep up with him as they crossed the courtyard connecting the school grounds with the rectory. He bounded up the steps, entered the kitchen through the back door, and crossed the dining room. He walked into the study to find the white-haired priest sitting in front of a blank television screen. Puzzled, Father Phil crossed the study. Then a silent message was broadcast on the screen: "We are experiencing technical difficulties. Please stand by."

The newcomer turned around. "Good day to you, Father Cisco. I am Father James Lochran from Detroit."

Father Phil took the offered hand. He noticed that it was ice cold and that the priest possessed an unusually pale complexion. The pastor of Our Lady of Peace started to ask his visitor if he was ill; however, before he got the chance, the priest stood up.

Leaning heavily on his cane, he said, "From the good sister's reaction"—he nodded toward Sister Mary Louise, who had followed Father Phil into the study—"you were not aware of my coming."

"I'm sorry, Father," Father Phil responded, "but this is the first I've heard of it."

"No matter." He removed an envelope from his inside pocket and handed it to Father Phil. "I brought a copy with me in case there is some problem with the mail."

Sister Mary Louise read the letter over Father Phil's shoulder. As the man who had identified himself as Father James Lochran looked on, Father Phil read the forged communication from the archbishop of Detroit.

Looking up at Father Lochran, the pastor said, "Welcome to Our Lady of Peace."

The television blinked back on. "This is Dede Priest in the WGN newsroom. We have lost our feed from Orga Syriac, who is on the scene and in contact with the kidnappers of Chicago's mayor. However, we have received information that the police, under the command of Chief of Detectives Larry Cole, are currently assaulting the building."

The three people in Our Lady of Peace rectory turned to watch the television set.

Cole, Blackie, Manny, and Judy met with Sergeant Cappetto and his Special Weapons Unit at the entrance to the abandoned building.

"We've lost the television transmission," Cole said, donning a bullet-proof vest that Blackie had retrieved from the trunk of Cole's car. "We have no way of knowing what's going on inside."

Cappetto frowned and said, "We were able to see a light in there until a couple of minutes ago. Then everything went dark."

"Okay, we're going in," Cole said. "Judy alert the other units."

Cappetto's people trained daily, so he didn't have to tell them what to do. Two officers flanked the entrance while another pair positioned themselves directly in front of the boarded-up doors. Cappetto took up a position behind his officers. Cole and his crew stood off to one side, well out of the way. They would not be able to enter the building until after the Special Weapons Unit personnel had made their initial assault.

Cappetto spoke softly, "One . . . two . . . three . . ." Then he shouted, "Go, go, *go*!"

The officers flanking the doors rushed the entrance with their SAW rifles raised. They hit the doors with powerful flashlights switched on. These lights were attached above the telescopic scopes. As soon as they were inside, the second team followed them, with Sergeant Cappetto bringing up the rear.

For what seemed an eternity, but was in actuality less than forty-five seconds, Cole waited. Then Judy's walkie-talkie crackled to life. Sergeant Cappetto said, "The area is secure and we have the mayor."

"Manny and Judy, stay here and keep everyone out," Cole ordered. "I want this building treated just like any other crime scene. C'mon Blackie."

The lights from the Special Weapons Unit rifles illuminated the squalor of the abandoned high-rise with a daylight glow. Cappetto and one of his officers supported a frightened, but unhurt, mayor between them. Another team had two of the kidnappers, both males, spread-eagled against a wall. Dave Spurgeon, the WGN cameraman, remained sitting on the floor beside his damaged camera. Cole and Blackie helped Spurgeon to his feet. Both cops noticed that the cameraman was badly shaken.

"What happened here?" Blackie asked, indicating the smashed camera.

But Cole stepped forward with a more insistent question. "Where are Orga and the female kidnapper?!"

"I don't know," Spurgeon managed. "But there was . . . something . . . here . . . that . . ." He took in a deep breath before he was able to say, "It knocked me down."

"What kind of 'something'?" Blackie demanded.

The cameraman grimaced, shook his head, and squinted at Blackie before saying, "I know it doesn't make sense, but it was a monster or demon of some type. It looked like the devil."

At that instant a high-pitched scream, which was more the roar of a predatory beast, echoed from the upper floors of the building.

"Holy Mother of God!" the mayor said. "What was that?"

"I want you and one of your men to get the mayor out of here, Cappetto," Cole ordered. "Make sure the security of the area is maintained. I'm taking Blackie and the rest of your unit with me to search for the newscaster, the kidnapper, and"—Cole paused to look up at the ceiling of the abandoned main floor of the sixteen-story building before adding—"whatever made that noise."

Then a figure appeared standing in the shadows at the far side of the lobby. The guns of every cop present came to bear on it. The lights from the SAW rifles illuminated Orga, forcing her to put up her hand to deflect the glare.

"Are you okay?" Cole asked with concern.

Orga managed to smile at him and say, "I'm fine, Larry."

"Where's the woman?"

She looked away from him into the darkness of the abandoned building. "I think she's up there somewhere."

She started to walk past him, but he reached out and grasped her arm. "Orga, what happened here?"

She turned to look at him with a gaze that made him remove his hand. "I don't know what happened after the light went out. Now that the mayor's been rescued I need to get back on the air. Would you please excuse me?"

She walked over to Dave Spurgeon, who was picking up what was left of his smashed camera. Although he had another minicam unit in the van, he looked far from happy. After conferring briefly, they left the building.

"I thought you two were friends," Blackie said.

"I thought so too," Cole responded. "Let's go find our lady kidnapper and whatever made that noise."

A few minutes later they found the kidnapper. She was on the second-floor landing of the abandoned building. The only way that Cole, Blackie, and the Special Weapons officers accompanying them could characterize what her body looked like was to compare it to a broken doll. Her neck had been snapped with such force that her head had been rotated 180 degrees on her shoulders. Her back had been broken with the force that only the use of a medieval rack could have accomplished. The kidnapper's mask and gun were lying beside her.

"What do you suppose did that to her, boss?" Blackie asked.

"I don't know," Cole responded. "But I'm going to find out."

CHAPTER 28

JUNE 14, 2004
11:32 A.M.

Orga was on the air. "The mayor is unhurt, but shaken up after his ordeal at the hands of a band of kidnappers. Due to the efforts of the Chicago Police Department under the command of Chief of Detectives Larry Cole, the mayor, my cameraman Dave Spurgeon, and this reporter were snatched from the very grip of death. I am certain that the female kidnapper was planning to kill all of us when luckily our camera malfunctioned allowing the police to come to our rescue."

In her town house in the Hyde Park neighborhood of Chicago, Kate Ford was watching Orga on WGN. The investigative journalist was seated at her desk in front of a computer on which she was writing the book on African legends. She had taken a break from the work and switched on the television after Barbara Zorin telephoned to tell her about the mayor's kidnapping. Prior to the call, Kate had been transcribing the notes she had made so far using obscure reference works, ancient folktales, and in-person interviews with the few people still alive who claimed to have had direct contact with the myth she was investigating. She had learned a great deal about the being known in some quarters as the Abo-Esu. Kate had also entered into her notes Orga Syriac's reference to the mythical she-devil as an Abo-Yorba.

In an anthology of African folktales compiled in the late nineteenth century there was a story in which a griot (African storyteller) related to a group of children around a campfire the tale of the Abo-Esu. The fable followed the same pattern of the accounts Kate had discovered about the she-devil. In each tale, someone or a group was in danger of suffering from oppression and a beautiful black woman appeared. The oppressors either took the woman for granted or attempted to also take advantage of her when suddenly she transformed herself.

Only moments before Barbara called, Kate was silently musing that the entity the woman shape-shifted into was variously referred to as a demon, devil, beast, or monster. However, that was from the standpoint of those whose evil she fought. Those whom the she-devil helped always spoke of her as an angel. But there was never any doubt that the woman changed into a being whose appearance was truly terrifying to both friend and foe.

Television coverage of ongoing disasters is morbidly fascinating to the American public. The Kennedy assassination, Lee Harvey Oswald's murder, and the O. J. Simpson Los Angeles freeway ride all drew millions of viewers. The mayor's kidnapping qualified as such an event.

So Kate Ford, along with countless others, waited expectantly as the Jeep Cherokee raced down the Dan Ryan Expressway to its destination at the rear of the abandoned project building. The tension mounted as Orga and the cameraman entered the building with the kidnappers. When the hooded female finished her speech and started to raise the gun, Kate knew that she was about to witness a murder. Then the transmission was abruptly terminated.

"I don't believe this," Kate whispered.

When the broadcast resumed a few moments later it was all over. The kidnappers were either dead or in custody, the mayor had been rescued, and Larry Cole was again a hero. Kate had taped the program, and she ran it back to the moment Orga began interviewing the kidnapper.

"Would you care to identify yourself?" Orga said, holding a microphone in front of the hooded female.

"No."

"Do you have a particular political affiliation?"

Kate continued to watch the replay. The kidnapper raised the weapon and the screen went blank, followed a few seconds later by the caption across the bottom of the screen, "We are experiencing technical difficulties. Please stand by."

Kate noticed that the images had blurred for a split second just before the transmission stopped. She rewound the tape again and played it in slow motion. Frame by frame the tape approached the point when the screen went blank. Two frames prior to that point the blur appeared, but Kate could tell that the camera was still focused. She squinted at the screen. The distortion was caused by something moving rapidly in front of the lens.

Kate again rewound the tape, played it slowly once more, and then freeze-framed the blurred image. She was unable to accurately identify what was filling the screen, but she was able to tell that it possessed a regular shape and, if Kate Ford wasn't mistaken, there was an eye and what could have been a mouth in the caption. The more she stared at the image, the more she became aware that what she was viewing was not simply a camera distortion, but a physical entity. A physical entity that was not human.

At Our Lady of Peace Parish rectory, Father Phil and Sister Mary Louise were watching their new guest almost as closely as they were Orga Syriac's broadcast. Father Lochran was again seated in the armchair in front of the television. His head rested on the back of the chair; his eyes were shut and his face bathed in sweat. The pastor and nun exchanged puzzled looks. Could the Irish priest be having a heart attack or some type of seizure?

Before summoning medical assistance, Father Phil leaned down and said softly, "Father Lochran, are you feeling okay?"

The elderly priest's bloodshot eyes snapped open and he looked at the younger man as if seeing him for the first time. "Thank you, Father, I'm fine. Simply a bit of fatigue after a long journey." He stood up. "If you could show me someplace where I could rest awhile, I would be most appreciative."

Although he still questioned his guest's health, Father Phil said, "I'll show you to your room."

Father Lochran looked back at the screen. Orga Syriac's image had been replaced by Dede Priest in the newsroom. Then he said to Father Phil and Sister Mary Louise, "Why don't we say a prayer of thanks to Our Lord for saving your mayor?"

Taken by surprise at this suggestion, they mumbled a joint agreement. They joined hands and Father Lochran began, "Our Father, who are in Heaven . . ."

In his office in the Dragon's Lair, Jack Carlisle had also watched the coverage of the mayor's kidnapping. He was particularly drawn to WGN because of Orga Syriac. While he watched the drama unfold and then conclude on the South Side, the fixer opened a folder that Sonny Balfour had given

him when Carlisle arrived at the club that morning. He was
surprised that there was only a single page of data on the
beautiful newscaster. Initially, the fixer had thought that the
expug had simply failed to carry out his assignment effi-
ciently. Then, when Carlisle studied the information, or
rather lack of information, he realized that something was
very wrong here and it had nothing to do with Sonny Balfour's incompetence.

The new WGN newscaster was a mystery. She had a
name, an address, a telephone number, and a Social Security
number. She possessed an investment account with a balance
of over $3 million at the Northern Trust Bank on LaSalle.
Street. She also owned a South Lake Shore Drive condominium with a value of $1,936,457. An impressive financial
portfolio.

This intrigued Jack Carlisle. Orga Syriac had a net worth
of $5 million, yet there was no indication as to where that
money came from. The sources Balfour had used were also
unable to find any prior work history for her. She had apparently never been married or divorced, and she possessed
no credit history. She paid cash for her condominium. There
was no available educational background on her and she had
given no former address when she moved into the 5050
South Lake Shore Drive building. Balfour hadn't even been
able to obtain a birth date for her. It was as if she'd simply
dropped out of the sky and become an overnight sensation
in one of the largest media markets in the country.

When the WGN feed switched to Dede Priest in the studio,
Carlisle activated the remote control and switched off the set.
He reviewed his single page of data on the newscaster once
more before tossing the folder back on his desk.

Leaning back in his chair, he said into the emptiness of
his office, "Now who are you really, Ms. Syriac?"

CHAPTER 29

"Carl and Zeke told me to meet the woman in the black Jeep at the corner of Thirty-ninth and State at nine o'clock this morning," said the sixteen-year-old who had been part of the kidnap band. He had identified himself as Charlie Grubbs. He lived with his mother and three sisters in the new low-rise Brownsville apartment complex and was a self-admitted member of the Gangster Disciples street gang. "Her and the white guy picked me up. She pulled a gun and told me to do exactly what she said or she would kill me. Then she said that if all went well, I would make a lot of money for my family and the Disciples."

Judy Daniels, still in uniform, was conducting the interrogation. They were in Cole's conference room on the fifth floor of police headquarters. Present were Cole; a youth officer, who specialized in juvenile crime but was there primarily for the protection of the young kidnapper; a Cook County state's attorney; and the obligatory court reporter.

"Did you know what Carl and Zeke were going to do?" Judy asked, referring to the two men the bodyguards had killed at City Hall.

He shook his head in the negative.

"Charlie, I need you to answer yes or no," Judy said.

"No," he said abruptly. Then he looked down at the table. "They just told me to meet the woman in the black Jeep and to do what she said."

"Did the woman tell you her name?"

"No," Charlie said. "They didn't tell me anything. I just did what she told me."

"Did you know they were going to kill the mayor?"

He shook his head again before remembering to say "No." He paused a moment. "But I knew she was going to do something just before . . ."

Judy waited, and when he didn't respond she asked, "Just before what, Charlie?"

"Before that shadow appeared and snatched her into the dark."

Cole interrogated the Jeep driver. The youth officer had been replaced by an attorney from the Cook County public defender's office. After being allowed to consult with the public defender, the man was led into the conference room by Blackie and Manny. The beefy kidnapper was handcuffed.

He sat down at the opposite end of the ten-seat conference table from Cole. After advising him of his constitutional rights, Cole said, "Do you want to tell me about your involvement in what happened this morning?"

The man's face was drawn. When he spoke his voice was tight with fear. "I'll tell you anything you want, but first you've got to tell me what grabbed Tisha in that building."

Cole suppressed a look of triumph. Another piece of the puzzle fell into place. He picked up a computerized printout from his desk. On it were the results of the fingerprint check, which had identified the kidnapper as retired master sergeant John Webster of the United States Army's Special Forces. He had retired in 1999 after spending twenty-five years in uniform fighting in every hellhole from Grenada to Beirut. He had received three Purple Hearts and the Silver Star. What Webster had been doing for the past five years was a mystery. But Cole planned to solve that mystery, as well as find out what happened inside that project building earlier.

Cole looked down the table at the former master sergeant. "I've never known a Special Forces NCO to be afraid of things that go bump in the dark."

The glare the kidnapper fixed Cole with revealed a building insanity. The former Green Beret's voice cracked with emotion as he said, "I've soldiered all over the world and I've killed my share of men. I've seen things that have driven others mad, but I've never seen anything like what was in that building today."

Cole believed him.

Tisha Vander Muller was identified as the dead female kidnapper. She was thirty-seven years old and had been born in Cape Town, South Africa. After the defeat of apartheid, her family had taken a fortune in diamonds and moved to Zurich, Switzerland. The Vander Mullers lived a life of wealth, affluence, and privilege for ten years until an investment gone bad bankrupted them. At the time, Tisha Vander Muller was twenty years old, and she became the sole support for her aging mother and father. To maintain them in a style to which they had become accustomed, Tisha turned to crime.

Seated in his office, Cole reviewed her criminal record. Embezzlement, burglary, armed robbery, espionage, and kidnapping on an international scale had been just a few of the crimes she had reputedly been involved in, according to the Interpol file Cole had obtained on her. Yet she had only been arrested twice and had never been convicted. Tisha Vander Muller was a professional criminal, not a political terrorist. This told Cole that, despite her long-winded speech about oppression of the weak, she had been paid for the abduction and planned murder of Chicago's chief executive.

The autopsy results had come back from the medical examiner's office. The kidnapper's neck and back were broken, as Cole and Blackie were clearly able to see when they discovered the body. There were also scratch marks found on her ankles and neck. Cole had examined these wounds and agreed with the pathologist who had performed the autopsy; they had been made by the claws of an animal. A very large animal.

But there was no sign of any type of animal, other than small vermin, in that building. The police had searched the sixteen-story edifice from top to bottom. Nothing. But what kind of animal could have broken a human being's back?

Possibly a gorilla or an orangutan? But this was Chicago, not the Congo.

The police were receiving full credit from the news media for the rescue, which Cole knew would not have been the case if something had happened to the mayor. A few minutes one way or the other and the cops would have been forced to kill Tisha Vander Muller. But they hadn't, and Larry Cole wanted to know who or what had.

It was getting on to midafternoon and he still had no answers. Cole wanted to talk to the mayor; however, he was still being treated at University Hospital and the prognosis was that he'd be held overnight for observation. Cole wouldn't be able to interview him until tomorrow. He didn't think this would pose any critical problems for the investigation. At least he hoped not. He also planned to conduct extensive interviews with Orga Syriac and Dave Spurgeon. As they were still tied up with the media coverage being given to the kidnapping, he decided that the interviews could also wait. For some reason he didn't feel the pretty newscaster and the cameraman would be able to provide him with much more information than he already had, which wasn't much. It wasn't much at all.

There was a knock on his office door.

"Come in."

It was Butch. In all the commotion Cole had forgotten about his son. The last time Cole had seen him, he was with Judy behind the project building. Right now he and Butch were supposed to be at a White Sox—Yankees game that had started at one o'clock.

"I'm sorry, Butch. We can still catch the late innings."

The young man came into the office with an undeniable look of excitement on his face. "Forget the game, Dad. Judy's had me helping her coordinate reports on the kidnapping."

Cole raised an eyebrow, as he didn't know whether this was such a good idea or not. However, he didn't think that his son would ever become a security risk for the department.

Smiling, Cole said, "So what do you think?"

Butch flopped down in one of the office chairs. With a

note of authority, he said, "The kidnapping is an open-and-shut case, but there are going to be a lot of unanswered questions until we come up with who iced the broad."

"Butch, where did you get that from?"

"What?"

" 'Who iced the broad'?"

He hesitated a moment before responding, "I heard Blackie talking to Manny a little while ago."

Cole leaned his elbows on the desk. "Blackie's right. I was working on that same problem when you knocked."

A few moments later they were preparing to leave the office when Cole's private line rang. It was Kate Ford. Cole immediately noticed the excitement in her voice.

"I've got something to show you that might shed some light on what happened inside that project building this morning."

Cole looked at Butch. He knew that his son would be just as intrigued by this information as he was.

"Where are you? Okay, Butch and I will be there in a few minutes." After hanging up, he said, "C'mon, we've got a hot lead on the case."

"Cool," Butch said, following his father out of the office.

CHAPTER 30

JUNE 14, 2004
4:45 P.M.

Father James Lochran awoke from a nightmare with a start. For a moment the unfamiliar surroundings of the room on the second floor of Our Lady of Peace rectory were totally alien to him. Then, slowly, where he was and why came back.

He sat up in the huge bed and looked around. He was in a big room containing lots of old, heavy wooden furniture. There were paintings of Jesus Christ, the Blessed Virgin, and a number of cardinals dressed in their official robes lining the walls. There was a window air conditioner blowing cool air into the room, but it wasn't nearly enough to keep the huge area comfortable, and the priest impersonator was drenched in sweat.

Clad only in his underwear, he got out of bed and crossed to the private washroom. After relieving himself, he took a cool shower, which made him feel better. He dressed and was about to leave the room when the nightmare he'd just had came back to him. It was always the same; however, it never lacked in intensity. He was being pursued through a forest by the she-devil. She trapped him in a clearing and was approaching slowly. He stepped back just as she reached for him with a clawed hand. He fell into the darkness. Always, at this point in the dream, he awoke.

Now that he was fully awake the pain in his leg reminded him that his dream had a basis in a reality of long ago. Making the sign of the cross, he let himself out.

In his lawbook-lined office on LaSalle Street, Philo Coffey was numb from the shock of his failure. He couldn't figure out what had gone wrong with his assassination plot—a plot that had cost him a fortune and taken almost a year to plan. With the aid of the beautiful but deadly Tisha Vander Muller, he had planned for every contingency. The shock effect of the death of the mayor of Chicago would reverberate throughout the entire municipal government structure. Residual fallout would occur in Springfield and even Washington, D.C. This would forge an opening for Philo Coffey and his Political Action Committee during the chaos that would follow the assassination. But the plan had failed and Tisha Vander Muller, who had charged him a million dollars for the job, was dead.

This worried Coffey. Dead assassins tell no tales, but that

cop Larry Cole was handling the case and he would not only have identified Tisha Vander Muller by now, but would probably be checking everyone she'd ever come in contact with dating back to the day she was born. Coffey had had no dealings with her accomplices, so he was not concerned about them. But Cole could come looking for the attorney eventually.

Coffey decided that he needed to relax and clear his mind. Ordering his chauffeur to pick him up in front of the building, he left his thirtieth-floor office. In the Mercedes a few moments later he directed the driver to take him to the members-only Barristers' Club on Plymouth Court.

As a Chicago lawyer of some note, Philo Coffey was well known at the club. He went first to the Bar of Justice, a tavern on the third level, which was furnished like an Old English court. He was greeted by a couple of fellow attorneys and joined them at one of the tables shaped like a judge's bench. They spent an hour over drinks discussing the mayor's abduction and rescue.

Philo Coffey was usually a two-scotch-maximum man. On this summer evening he had four, which surprised his colleagues, as they'd never seen him drink so much in such a short period of time. The usually straitlaced attorney was even becoming a bit tipsy.

"You know, from a purely hypothetical standpoint," Coffey was saying to the veteran divorce lawyer whose offices were in the same building as the PAC chairman's, "if hizzoner had died, things might not have been so bad in this town." Coffey's words were slightly slurred.

The other two lawyers exchanged tolerant smiles. This was a private club and all its members were professionals. Indiscreet remarks had been exchanged in the Bar of Justice before. What Coffey was saying would never go beyond these walls; however, the attorneys realized that their inebriated colleague's remarks were in extremely poor taste. A few moments later they excused themselves, leaving Philo Coffey to drink alone.

Coffey ordered another scotch, but was smart enough to realize that he was losing control. He was the type of man

who strived to always be in control. Shoving the drink away
from him, he decided on going to the dining room for an
early supper. Then he would get a massage and spend some
time in the sauna.

On the Dearborn Street side of the Barristers' Club a taxi
pulled to the curb. After paying the driver, an octogenarian
member of the club struggled out of the backseat. He was
bald with only a couple of wispy strands of white hair sticking out above his ears. He was wearing an old but expensive
suit, and his shoes had a mirror shine. He had once been a
prominent criminal attorney, but had retired from active practice over twenty years ago.

Now, arthritic knees and a bad hip forced him to walk
barely faster than a crawl toward the revolving door. Then
the white-haired priest, who walked with a cane, stepped up
beside him.

"Can I be of some assistance to you, sir?"

The Irish brogue made the elderly man smile. His mother
had come from county Cork in the late nineteenth century.
He had also been born and raised a Catholic.

"Thank you, Father. I don't move as fast as I used to," he
said, taking the priest's arm.

"None of us move as fast as we once did."

Slowly, they made it across the sidewalk, through the
door, and into the lobby of the Barristers' Club. The receptionist, stationed at a desk in the center of the carpeted lobby,
recognized the aging attorney, and seeing the priest supporting him, figured that they were together. She didn't give a
moment's thought to the cleric being a trespasser. After all,
he was a priest.

The pair proceeded to the elevators at the south end of the
lobby. The receptionist watched them board an elevator together. Then she quickly forgot them.

After dinner and a massage, Philo Coffey, still feeling some
of the effects of the scotch he'd consumed earlier, headed
for the steam bath. With a towel wrapped around his lower
body, he entered the cloudy room. It was empty. Sitting

down on one of the porcelain-tile ledges, he felt the heat settle over him and open his pores. As the sweat began to flow, his mind returned to his earlier problem.

The money Coffey had paid Tisha Vander Muller was deposited directly into a numbered Swiss bank account, which even a cop as smart and innovative as Larry Cole would be unable to gain access to. The Vander Muller woman had had three face-to-face meetings with Coffey in his LaSalle office. Cole could find out about those, but if the chief of detectives came calling, the lawyer would claim attorney-client privilege and there wouldn't be a thing that Cole or anyone else could do about it. Coffey was turning his legal mind to the question of motive when the glass door to the steam bath opened and a white-haired man leaning heavily on a cane limped in. He also had a towel wrapped around his middle.

Through the haze Coffey gave the newcomer no more than a glance. He had seen this man before, but couldn't remember where or when. There were a lot of members of the Barristers' Club. The attorney had more important matters on his mind. Then something about the white-haired man made Coffey give him a second look. It was Father James Lochran, the priest who had collapsed at the Navy Pier PAC affair the other night. But what was the priest doing here now?

Coffey was about to ask this question when Lochran stepped directly in front of him and raised his cane. There was no one close enough to the steam bath to hear the lawyer's scream.

The attendant came into the locker room and began picking up the towels left by the guests. The gym area of the Barristers' Club was nearly deserted at this hour of the evening since most of the facility's users came in during the day. He had his arms full of damp white towels and was heading for a laundry bin to dump them when a priest stepped from behind a row of lockers. The attendant had thought the locker room was empty, and the sudden appearance of the man in black startled him.

"Hello, Father," the attendant managed.

"Good evening, my son," the priest said, walking past him with the aid of a cane.

The attendant noticed the priest's hair was wet and that he was sweating. The attendant started to recommend that the priest remain in the locker room for a while so that he could cool off. However, the priest had already reached the locker-room door and was exiting into the air-conditioned corridor beyond.

The attendant had only been in the United States a couple of years and had worked at the Barristers' Club for four months. It was not his job to check the credentials of club members and guests. This was the job of the receptionist downstairs. Even if the assignment had been given to him, he would not have questioned a priest. To do so would be tantamount to sacrilege.

The attendant had just dumped his load of towels and was about to mop the locker-room floor when he heard a high-pitched whistle coming from the steam bath.

With a frown of concern he went to the glass door and peered inside. The whistling noise was becoming so shrill that it was starting to make the attendant's ears ache. He couldn't see anything inside the steam bath because the steam billowing inside was too dense. He grabbed the handle but was forced to jerk his hand away because it was scalding hot.

This frightened the attendant. Something here was very wrong. The whistling noise was increasing in intensity. He needed to let someone know that something in the locker room was broken. He decided to call the female receptionist down at the front desk. Although she was snotty and had never even given the attendant the time of day, she was someone in authority.

He crossed to the wall-mounted house phone next to the shower stalls. He discovered that the receiver was slick with moisture coming from the steam bath, which was beginning to turn the locker room into a living hell. The attendant dialed the receptionist's intercom number.

*   *   *

"Good night, Father," the receptionist said to the white-haired priest, who was crossing the lobby in the direction of the Dearborn Street exit. He waved at her, but didn't stop. She noticed that he was moving much faster than he had been when he entered. In fact, she couldn't help but get the impression that he was in a great hurry. She wondered what had happened to the elderly member whom the priest had come in with.

Her intercom phone's ringing distracted her. "Front desk."

At first she was able to hear nothing coming over the line but a high-pitched whistling sound. Someone who didn't speak English very well was yelling.

"Stop shouting and speak more slowly," she demanded.

At that instant the three ounces of explosive that the priest impersonator had applied to a pipe in the steam room exploded. After placing the explosive the priest had disabled the steam-bath safeguard controls, causing the high-pitched whistling noise, as the steam began increasing to produce unbearable heat. The body of Philo Coffey, whose skull had been crushed, was left to cook.

The resulting explosion, amplified by the explosive, took out the locker room, the gymnasium, the Bar of Justice tavern, and half the main dining room. Twenty-seven Barristers' Club members and four employees were killed, including six judges, a former United States attorney, the elderly retired lawyer whom the priest impersonator had helped into the club, the two attorneys Philo Coffey had had drinks with earlier, and the locker-room attendant.

Father James Lochran had begun his mission of atonement.

CHAPTER 31

Sven-Erik Voman was in a state of intense excitement. He had covered his share of big stories in the past and had even won a couple of prestigious awards for news coverage. But he had never, *never* experienced anything in his career like he was now in the aftermath of Orga Syriac's coverage of the mayor's kidnapping and rescue.

In his office at WGN, Sven-Erik considered the *mysterious* aspect of what had occurred in that abandoned project building. Orga had broadcast that Larry Cole had carried out the rescue, yet the chief of detectives was being strangely noncommittal about what had occurred after Spurgeon's camera had malfunctioned. Sven-Erik frowned. Spurgeon's camera hadn't malfunctioned; it had been destroyed. One hundred thousand dollars down the drain. However, under the circumstances, this was of little note.

A media frenzy within a media frenzy was raging all around him. Every television station, radio outlet, and daily newspaper in the Chicagoland area was demanding interviews with his new star commentator. On top of that *60 Minutes, Eye of the Public, 20/20, The New York Times,* the *Washington Post, Time* and *Newsweek* were all clamoring for exclusive interviews with the woman who had "faced death to get the interview of the century."

Sven-Erik smiled at this quote. It was actually his. He had written it and forced a subdued Dede Priest to read it on the air. The veteran newscaster had expected Orga to botch the mayoral kidnapping coverage. When she hadn't, and had been propelled to superstardom, Dede became morose. On camera she managed to maintain her professionalism, but with a cool detachment which Sven-Erik realized was her petulance shining through.

So WGN and Sven-Erik Voman had a new superstar. But all was not well in this media paradise. Despite the awesome success of her first story, Orga refused to be interviewed by the other media outlets.

"But why, Orga?" he had asked, after telling the producer of the *Eye of the Public* news program that he would get back to him with an interview time and date for WGN's new star.

She was seated across from the news director. He couldn't help but be stunned by her appearance. She was radiant, and it was Sven-Erik's understanding that she hadn't been near a makeup table since she'd walked in the studio door that morning.

"I'm not the story, Sven," she said with amusement. "The mayor and Larry Cole are."

"But you provided the exclusive coverage of the most important event to happen in this town since the Chicago Fire."

She remained adamant. "If I start getting in the way of the stories I cover I won't be doing my job properly."

Sven-Erik Voman had heard this argument before. He had often made it himself to some of the talking heads who passed through WGN on their way to another news beat. Personally, the news director abhorred reporters who hogged the camera instead of telling the developing news story to a waiting public. Dede Priest came to mind. However, in Sven-Erik's estimation, this case was different. Orga Syriac and Dave Spurgeon were as much a part of the mayor's kidnapping as the mayor and Larry Cole.

Sven-Erik was about to voice this opinion to Orga when his intercom buzzed. There had been an explosion at the Barristers' Club in the Loop and a number of the prestigious legal organization's members were dead. Before he could get the assignment out of his mouth, Orga was out the door and on her way to the scene with Dave Spurgeon.

Left alone in his office, Sven-Erik had to give it to Orga Syriac; she was not only good, but also aggressive and smart. Very smart.

When Cole and Butch arrived at Kate Ford's Hyde Park town house they found Barbara Zorin and Jamal Garth were already there. Garth had hooked up a laptop computer to Kate's video recorder.

The greetings over, Cole turned to the blond investigative reporter. "So what have you got for me?"

Kate looked at Barbara and Jamal. "Maybe I have something and then again it might be nothing."

"Come again?" Cole said with confusion.

"Maybe I can explain," Jamal interjected, going over to sit at his laptop. Cole, Kate, Butch, and Barbara moved over to look over his shoulder. "Kate taped the mayor's kidnapping right up to the point that the transmission was interrupted."

"The camera was smashed in a rather mysterious fashion," Cole volunteered.

"It does fit," Barbara said.

"Fit what?" Cole asked.

"Okay," Garth said, "watch this."

He typed a command on his keyboard and Kate's television began playing the videotape. Simultaneously, what was on the screen began playing on Garth's computer screen. They only had to watch for a few seconds before the transmission was stopped and the screen went blank. Garth typed in another command and the tape began slowly rewinding. The tape stopped just an instant before the images of the mayor and the masked female kidnapper were erased by a blur. Then the computer screen became filled with the blurred image.

"This is what got Kate's attention initially," Garth said. "What does it look like to you, Larry?"

Cole starred at the screen for several seconds. He could almost make out something there, but then he couldn't tell if this was simply his imagination working overtime. He shrugged. "I don't know. There could be something or it could be nothing."

Butch was standing beside his father. Stepping closer to the monitor, he pointed at a reddish circle. "That looks like an eye, and down here"—he pointed to a pair of grayish lines—"could be teeth."

Kate placed her hand on the young man's shoulder. "That's what I thought I saw too, Butch, but with Jamal's help we can see it much better."

On cue, Garth typed in more commands and the image they were watching began to slowly alter. The lines became more distinct and the image came into focus. Butch emitted an audible gasp and Cole tensed. "What in the hell is that?"

Kate Ford went over to her desk and picked up a book with a worn cover. Returning, she opened it to an artist's drawing. "Does this look familiar?" Kate said, handing him the book.

The likeness between the drawing and the computer-enhanced image on the screen was startling. Cole read the caption under the sketch: "The African she-devil known as an Abo-Yorba."

The WGN mobile van completed their live broadcast from the site of the Barristers' Club explosion. They had just packed up their gear in preparation for returning to the studio. Dave Spurgeon had the police scanner on, but it was turned low and he wasn't paying it any attention. This had been one of the strangest and most exciting days of his long career in television. The coverage of the mayor's kidnapping, the mysterious events which had occurred inside that abandoned building, and the debut of Orga Syriac, who was one of the best on-the-spot news commentators he had ever worked with. However, he was still puzzled over what had caused the destruction of his camera and knocked him to the floor back in the project building. He had seen something, but he'd revised his earlier account that what he had seen was some type of demon. Such things didn't exist, he rationalized, did they?

Spurgeon took a seat in the back of the cramped van next to Orga. "So what do you think of your first day on the job?"

She smiled. "I hope every day is like this. I've always wanted to live an exciting life."

"What did you do before you came to work for WGN?"

"Not much of anything," she responded.

He waited for her to say more. When she didn't, he started to ask her a more direct question when she said, "Did you hear that last police call?" She pointed at the scanner.

"No. I wasn't paying attention."

"They reported a female homicide victim in a vacant lot at Five-thirty-three East Forty-third Street."

Spurgeon appeared a trifle apprehensive. "Sven usually likes to give us assignments from the studio and that area is kind of rough."

Something changed in her face. "Then why do we have the scanner?" she asked plaintively.

All he could do by way of reply was shrug.

"Let's take a look, Dave," she said, smiling. "There may be a story there. Don't worry, I'll protect you."

There were two police cars and a police wagon on the scene when the WGN van arrived. The cops were surprised to see the news crew. This was a crime-infested ghetto area of the worst type. At times the cops themselves didn't feel safe down here. When the pretty reporter who had covered the mayor's kidnapping earlier got out of the van, the cops were dumbfounded.

The sergeant-in-charge at the scene was a fifteen-year veteran of the war on crime in Chicago and had never been interviewed by the press, either print or electronic. The reporter walked up to him, extended her hand, and said, "Good evening, Sergeant. I'm Orga Syriac from WGN. Would you mind filling me in on what happened here?"

As Dave Spurgeon reluctantly began setting up for a shot, a flattered, hard working Chicago Police Department field supervisor began telling the tale of another dead prostitute on the South Side of the city.

The interview went well. By phone, Sven-Erik Voman had informed his mobile crew that he was very pleased with the additional story that had been covered on Forty-third Street. After the interview with the sergeant, Dave Spurgeon quickly packed up his equipment and was ready to get the hell out of this dark, menacing place. He was about to get into the van when he noticed that Orga was still on the street. In fact, she was on the other side of the barrier tape, standing over the rubber-sheet-covered corpse.

"Oh shit," the cameraman whispered under his breath when he saw her reach down and lift the edge of the sheet. Spurgeon had thought Orga knew better. She was an unauthorized civilian violating a crime scene. The cops could get real upset about things like this. He hurried across the sidewalk to the edge of the lot. He was about to shout a warning when he noticed that all the cops were staring at Orga and not one of them was making a move toward her.

Puzzled, Spurgeon turned to the sergeant they had just interviewed. "Uh, I'm sorry about her violating the crime scene, Sarge, but she's new."

The sergeant fixed the cameraman with a stare betraying annoyance. "She's not violatin' nothing, pal. I gave her permission. Ain't no dicks or crime-lab people coming out here tonight."

Properly chastised, Spurgeon retreated back to the van. He started to get back in, but instead he stood on the cracked ghetto sidewalk watching WGN's new star standing over the dead body of the streetwalker.

A few minutes later Orga turned away from the corpse. Outside the barrier tape she shook hands with the sergeant and all the cops still on the scene. Then she returned to the van. Spurgeon noticed that there were tears in her eyes.

They were silent for most of the way back to the studio. Finally, the cameraman got up the nerve to say, "That woman must have been messed up pretty bad."

When she looked at him her eyes were clear and she was as radiant as ever. However, there was nothing pretty about her words. "Whoever did that to her should be made to die a slow, very horrible death."

Dave Spurgeon felt a chill run up and down his spine.

CHAPTER 32

Jack Carlisle was hosting a private party at the Dragon's Lair. Most of the attendees were either professional athletes or affiliated with pro sports. Fuzzy and Pete Dubcek were in attendance.

The tall, dark-haired basketball star followed his wife around the private room like a frightened puppy. At one point she was becoming obviously annoyed with her husband's presence. Then she made eye contact with Carlisle. After that she became marginally attentive to her gangly spouse.

Two days ago gossip columns in the *Tribune* and *Sun-Times* had mentioned the spat the Dubceks had had outside the Dragon's Lair. The *Times-Herald*, which Carlisle considered little more than a daily scandal sheet, had carried a photograph of the basketball player standing outside the nightclub. There was blood running down his cheek and he appeared stunned. The caption under the photo read: "Discord in the Dubceks' Den? Wife scratches basketball star's face outside near north club."

The fixer was in his office when he saw the picture in the newspaper. At the time he'd remarked to the ever-present Sonny Balfour, "Fuzzy's lucky I didn't see this before I took that wet towel to her behind. The next time I'll use a coat hanger." Balfour laughed.

So Carlisle decided to throw a little party. This was not intended primarily to smooth things over with Pete and

Fuzzy, but to further one of the fixer's schemes.

Carlisle worked the room with his usual skill. He was talking to an assistant coach for the Indianapolis Colts when Paige Albritton walked in. The tall blond caused the eye of every male in the place to swing in her direction. Even Carlisle was impressed. She was wearing a tight, low-cut black dress, which cut off at midthigh. The fixer had ordered and paid for her to have her hair done at the exclusive Heidi's hair salon on the sixth level of DeWitt Plaza on North Michigan Avenue. The only jewelry she wore was a diamond pendant, which Carlisle knew had been a gift from the Albritton woman's dead cop fiancé. She was indeed dressed to kill, but she was not here simply to brighten the festivities. Carlisle definitely had plans for her. Plans for her and Pete Dubcek.

"Excuse me," the fixer said to the Colts assistant as he moved across the room to intercept Paige.

"You're looking good, baby," he said, coming up to her, placing his arm around her waist, and planting a kiss on her cheek. "And you smell delicious. New perfume?"

She nodded, but didn't comment. Her face was as emotionless as stone.

"You could smile, Paige," the fixer said. "It's not as if you've never done anything like this before."

She fixed Carlisle with a cold stare. There could have been more than just a hint of hatred in her eyes, but it was effectively masked. When she spoke her tone was neutral. "You're right, Jack. I have done this before."

Then she disengaged herself from his grasp and crossed the room in the direction of the Dubceks. Carlisle motioned for Sonny Balfour. The black man was at the fixer's side instantly.

"Go over there with Paige. When you see an opening, get Fuzzy away from Pete so he'll be alone with Paige. Take her out front and let her dance her brains out. Just keep her away from him for a while."

Silently, Balfour acknowledged the order.

Then Jack Carlisle found a strategic vantage point from

which to watch Paige Albritton attempt to seduce Pete Dubcek.

Father Philip Cisco was completing a check of Our Lady of Peace grounds for the night. He started at the youth center, checking to make sure all the doors and windows were locked. The center, constructed in 1992, had been the target of burglars three times due to the sports equipment stored there. Father Phil's predecessor, Father Kenneth Smith, had an alarm installed, but the last burglar had bypassed the system and stolen over six thousand dollars' worth of equipment. Now, satisfied that the youth center was as secure as was humanly possible, Father Phil moved on to the church.

The young priest loved his parish and at the core of that affection was his love of God and of God's house in the Washington Park Boulevard area. He entered through the side door, which was always left open during the day. Despite the problems that the youth center had had, no one in the long history of Our Lady of Peace had ever attempted to steal anything from the church. In order to not tempt fate, Father Phil checked the interior of the church before locking the door. He headed for the convent.

He rang the bell and waited. A few moments later Sister Mary Louise Stallings opened the door.

"Good evening, Father," she said. "Locking up for the night?"

He nodded. "Everything is secure. I guess things in this town have quieted down after all the excitement this morning."

She stepped out onto the porch. It was still warm, but a cool breeze blew off the lake. "I guess we had our own share of excitement around here today."

For a moment he wasn't following her. Finally, he caught on. "Oh, you mean Father Lochran. I guess he does vary our routine a bit."

She looked up and down Washington Park Boulevard. Then she turned to the pastor. "Don't you think it would be"—she paused for a moment to select the right words—"more convenient for Father Lochran to stay at Saint Thomas the Apostle Parish with Father Jack Fary instead of here at Our Lady of Peace."

"I'm not following you, Sister."

She wrapped her arms around herself. She knew she possessed a slightly suspicious nature, and with good cause. Prior to her becoming a nun she had been stalked by a madman, who had even invaded the church to get at her. It was an effort for her to see people in an objective light instead of imagining that they had some dark ulterior motive behind every action. But she had prayed for God to help her and he had. That is until today, when the aging Irish priest had arrived unannounced.

Sister Mary Louise explained her misgivings to Father Phil as best as she could. "Well, he is taking a theology course at the U of C and being at Saint Thomas would have placed him in walking distance of the campus."

The young priest smiled. "I must say that I had the same thought, but perhaps there's another reason why he chose Our Lady of Peace."

"Such as?"

He thought for a moment. "At one time this was the largest church in the Chicago archdiocese. There was even a monsignor assigned here."

"So?" the nun questioned.

"Maybe Father Lochran heard about Our Lady of Peace in Detroit and selected it at random." She could see that he was struggling to explain it to himself.

They lapsed into silence for a time. Then he said, "What ulterior motive could Father Lochran have for coming here anyway?"

She dropped her hands to her sides, shrugged, and said a resigned, "I don't know, but somehow it just doesn't feel right."

"Well sleep on it, Sister, and we'll talk about it some more tomorrow."

A short time later he crossed the courtyard between the convent and the rectory. There were no lights in this area and it was dark. Father Phil climbed the back steps. He was about to let himself into the rectory when he heard a noise behind him. Startled, he spun around.

Father James Lochran stepped from the shadows. "I'm sorry, Father, but I didn't have a key. I was waiting for you to let me in."

Father Phil had been badly frightened by his guest. He managed to catch his breath and say, "I didn't know that you'd gone out."

"I had some business to attend to," Lochran said, leaning on his cane as he crossed the porch. "I must say that all was concluded well, but I have so much still to do."

Father Phil unlocked the door, and he and Father Lochran entered the rectory.

Chester "Chet the Jet" Collins was a pimp and a member of the Disciples street gang. In dated popular fiction, pimps have generally been depicted as slimy but charismatic creatures who entice women into selling their bodies. Chet the Jet was indeed slimy; however, there was nothing at all charismatic about him. He was a mean-faced man with brutal features on a shaved, bullet-shaped head. An obese black man who weighed over three hundred pounds, Chet had learned his business from Mafia pimp Gino Allegretti, who was now not only a rival but also a bitter enemy. The black pimp had gotten the nickname "Chet the Jet" from Allegretti because Collins moved with an awkward slowness due to his obesity. However, he was a very powerful man who could actually move very fast when he wanted to, and he was given to fits of extreme violence. Now he was about to indulge himself in another act of violence.

Chet's car was a champagne-colored Lincoln Town Car. It was a well-known vehicle on the South Side and Chet drove it when he went out to check on his people. He employed both male and female prostitutes. So did Gino Allegretti. Chet had begun muscling in on the Mafia pimp's operation some time ago. Allegretti struck against Chet's operation by killing a local pimp working for the Disciples. Chet retaliated by brutally murdering two of Allegretti's female streetwalkers. In the interim, the CPD became aware of the pimp war, which resulted in Blackie Silvestri and Manny Sherlock visiting Allegretti at breakfast that morning. The cops had also planned a visit to Chet the Jet, but the mayor's kidnapping caused a postponement.

But Collins and Allegretti weren't about to stop their war because of a few threats from the cops. Earlier that night Chet had sliced up one of Allegretti's streetwalkers up on Forty-third Street. Now the Jet was out looking for another of the Mafia pimp's people in order to send a double message to his nemesis.

Allegretti had maintained virtual control of the area bordered by Thirty-ninth Street on the north, Fifty-first Street on the south, Indiana Avenue on the west, and Washington Park Boulevard on the east. The Mafia pimp had a couple of gorilla pimps named Jerry and Jojo watching out for his people, but they usually stayed up on Forty-seventh Street idling their time away in a Dunkin' Donuts restaurant beneath the El station. However, the two pimps spent most of their time drinking coffee and eating doughnuts. The girls were supposed to check in with them after each trick, but the security arrangement was far from efficient.

Now Chet turned onto a darkened side street and searched the shadows for the furtive, self-conscious movements of the streetwalker. He cruised for a couple of hundred feet before he spotted a woman on the street. Chet pulled to the curb and got out. He figured that Allegretti's people would have been alerted to the threat the black pimp presented and the type of car he drove. The woman he was approaching was dressed in a full-length black cape, and a hood obscured her face in shadow. He had expected her to make a run for it, but she stood her ground and waited for him. Chet hesitated for a moment, feeling a wave of apprehension wash over him. He smelled a trap. He paused for a moment and the woman still didn't move. This angered him. She was either stupid or crazy, and he planned to do things to her that would send a message to Allegretti that he would never forget.

Chet moved more rapidly, pulling a straight razor from his pocket as he did so. He flicked the weapon open and the woman raised her head. The nearest working streetlight was a hundred feet away and provided very poor illumination on the dark ghetto street. Now the black pimp was able to see the woman's face. Her beauty stunned him. Gino was really putting some lookers out here. Chet would have put this woman in one of his call operations and charged the johns a thousand dollars a trick. He was actually considering making a play for her to leave Gino and join his stable when something about her changed. Chet stopped again and squinted into the shadows at her. Then terror set in.

The black pimp began to quickly retrace his steps and then turned to run back to his car. He was grabbed from behind.

Chet's scream of terror and pain carried all the way to the Forty-seventh Street Dunkin' Donuts restaurant where Allegretti's gangster pimps Jerry and Jojo had stationed themselves. They briefly considered going to investigate what had made the terrible sound they'd heard, but they figured by the time they got there it would be too late. They were right.

3

"Larry, This Is Scaring Me to Death."
Kate Ford

CHAPTER 33

The gray unmarked police car pulled off of Forty-seventh Street and drove down Calumet. The location of the crime scene was easily identifiable by the knot of police cars lined up at the curb between the vacant lot and an abandoned building. The gray car parked behind a marked unit and Sergeants Judy Daniels and Manny Sherlock got out. There was also a Lincoln parked at the curb.

Today Judy had adopted her Whoopi Goldberg dreadlock look, with black-painted lips and an enormous pair of gold earrings dangling from her ears. She was wearing loose-fitting black jeans and a Superman T-shirt. To make sure there wouldn't be any confusion with the other cops, she had her sergeant's star clipped to her gun belt next to her holstered Beretta. She kept her identification card in her wallet because the photograph rarely matched her appearance.

Manny Sherlock, all six feet four inches of him with the horn-rimmed glasses that gave him a scholarly look, was dressed in the standard conservative business attire of the contemporary police detective: cotton shirt, dark tie, blue blazer, and gray slacks. He carried a .357 magnum nickle-plated snub-nosed Python revolver and three speed loaders containing .38 caliber ammunition on his gun belt beside his five-pointed Chicago police sergeant's star.

They crossed the cracked pavement and entered a garbage-strewn vacant lot. They proceeded along the north wall of the abandoned building. The morning was overcast with a threat of rain in the air. The sky's grayness and this desolate section of the urban landscape added additional menace.

Judy and Manny found the crime scene in what had once been the backyard of the abandoned building. The area was cordoned off by yellow barrier tape bearing the printed legend in black block letters, "Crime Scene—Do Not Enter." Four police officers in uniform stood outside the tape, while a crime-lab crew was inside the cordoned-off area processing the murder scene.

The cops outside the area saw the badges and guns on the plainclothes cops and allowed them to approach the edge of the crime scene. Manny and Judy knew better than to cross the barrier tape before the crime lab finished; however, they could see quite clearly what had happened here.

The body of a black male was suspended upside down by ropes from the second-floor porch, which looked in imminent danger of collapse. The corpse was nude and looked to have been ritualistically mutilated in a very brutal fashion.

By the time the crime-lab technicians finished processing the scene and the cops lowered the body to the ground, a slight drizzle had started to fall. Before the body could be removed the medical examiner arrived.

The ME, a middle-aged, gray-haired man, started to give the body a cursory examination, but something about the wounds caused him to give them closer scrutiny. Judy and Manny stood by watching him work. When the rain had started falling, Judy had produced an umbrella from the oversized shoulder bag she carried. Now Manny held the portable covering over both of them.

When the ME finished he stood up. The two detective sergeants noticed the quizzical expression on his face.

"Something wrong, Doc?" Manny inquired.

The ME's frown did not alter as he turned to face them. The rain was starting to plaster his thinning hair to his skull.

"This man has obviously been tortured," he said. "My initial examination reveals that whoever did this, besides hoisting him up there, opened up his arteries with a near surgical precision and let him exsanguinate."

"Exsanguinate?" Manny said with a curious frown.

"Bleed to death, Manny," Judy said, before asking the medical examiner, "But something's bothering you about the wounds?"

He looked back at the body. "Like I said, those wounds were made with surgical precision with the obvious intent of killing him very slowly. The only thing that I can't figure is that those cuts look like they were made by the claws of an animal. A very large animal."

Judy and Manny looked first at each other, then back at the ME, and finally down at the dead body of former pimp Chester "Chet the Jet" Collins.

CHAPTER 34

JUNE 15, 2004
6:21 A.M.

Virginia Daley entered her office at the Human Development Institute and checked her computer for all of the events in the past twenty-four hours that could be of any interest to the Institute or her boss, Dr. Gilbert Goldman. She was shocked when she saw that Philo Coffey had died in a mysterious explosion at the Barristers' Club the previous night. Coffey's death solved a major problem for the Institute, but there was something about his demise that began bothering the executive secretary.

The report had been compiled by the Institute's night duty officer utilizing every available source of information available, including police reports, government briefing papers, and news accounts. The HDI summary stated that the police suspected arson in the Barristers' club explosion. The CPD's

Bomb and Arson Unit had been sifting through the debris all night.

Virginia looked away from the screen and stared out the window at the overcast Chicago morning. The search for Thomas Kelly was still in progress. She punched some keys on her computer and a lengthy program on the missing Institute operative began to scroll across the screen. The Human Development Institute had thousands of sources to call on in the pursuit of Kelly. If he checked into a hotel using his own name, the name of Father James Lochran, which he had assumed before he disappeared, or any of the other names he had employed during his many years with the Institute, they would know instantly. If he contacted or was observed by anyone connected with the Institute they would be notified immediately. If he was fingerprinted by any municipal, state, or federal agency they would know. And if his body turned up in any morgue, Dr. Gilbert Goldman would be notified as his next of kin.

The HDI executive secretary spent some time reviewing Thomas Kelly's personal history. It was as strange as the events surrounding his disappearance.

As a six-day-old infant, Kelly had been left in the vestibule of a southwest side Chicago church. He had been raised in a Catholic orphanage, as he was never fortunate enough to be adopted. When he was fifteen years old, the then HDI director had begun putting together research teams to gather data around the country. Dr. Gilbert Goldman's predecessor had the foresight to give such teams the innocent appearance of vacationing American families. However, such teams were trained to be very deadly when they had to be. From that point on the Human Development Institute had become Thomas Kelly's family. Then Virginia Daley came across the incident that had occurred in Diggstown, Mississippi, in 1956.

The HDI executive secretary had heard the story about the problem that the Institute's research team had had nearly a half century before in the southern town. However, she had never read the official account of the incident which had been stored in the archives. Of the team of three that had gone into the South to investigate Negro myths, only the sixteen-year-old Thomas Kelly had survived. Kelly had been found badly injured by a farmer whose farm was five miles from the site of the town, which was now considered mythical. The Mississippi State Police had investigated the injuries sustained by the young operative. The location where Diggstown was rumored to be was also examined. No one was found there and only a few burned-out buildings remained. The Institute had spent a great deal of money attempting to find out what had occurred on that night so long ago, but little was uncovered. Kelly was unable to provide much information. He remained in the hospital for six months and was in a nearly comatose state for most of that time. After intensive therapy, Kelly was only able to tell the psychiatrist that he had been attacked by a she-devil.

Virginia Daley shook her head. From some of the vague accounts the Institute managed to obtain from the reclusive residents of the area, this "she-devil" was some kind of myth associated with Diggstown. In one report, from a self-admitted member of the Ku Klux Klan, this being was capable of shape-shifting from a beautiful Negress into a monster.

The HDI executive secretary shook her head. She considered this story no more than a fable made up by a backward, uneducated people. She turned her attention to examining the methods which Thomas Kelly had used to sanction targets during his long history with the Institute. She noticed that he had utilized explosives applied to steam pipes three times. The explosion at the Barristers' Club had reportedly originated in the steam room and Philo Coffey had been killed. This could be their first lead to Kelly. Virginia Daley placed this item at the top of her morning briefing list for Dr. Gilbert Goldman.

Blessing completed her morning prayers and stood up. She went to the drapes in her room and opened them. She emitted a heavy sigh when she saw the rain streaking the windows. The forecast was for the rain to last all day and into tomorrow. Where the pretty black woman came from, it only rained all day during the very short, mild winter season.

It was a few minutes after seven when she left her room and walked down the hall to her mistress's bedroom. She knocked softly before opening the door and going inside. The room was dark. Blessing stood at the entrance and waited for her eyes to adjust to the shadows. She could hear Orga Syriac's soft breathing across the room. Blessing did not want to startle her mistress awake. To do so could be very dangerous.

Blessing started to let herself out and return later. Then the rhythmic sound of Orga Syriac's breathing stopped. Blessing stood stock-still and said evenly, "Good morning, madam."

A figure rose from the bed across the room. It remained motionless for nearly a full minute. Then the outline of the shape softened and the melodious voice of Orga Syriac answered, "Good morning to you, Blessing. What time is it?"

"A little after seven."

There was movement between the bed and the windows. Orga opened the thick curtains and the room was flooded with light. The new television star, clad only in a black silk nightgown, stood there, her black hair cascading down to her shoulders. Even though she had just awakened, she looked radiant.

"I shouldn't have slept so late," Orga said. "I have a great deal to do today. We don't have much time left."

"Yes, madam," Blessing responded. "What would you like for breakfast?"

Orga was crossing to her private bathroom. She said over her shoulder, "Coffee, fresh fruit, and a small steak."

When her mistress closed the bathroom door, Blessing headed for the kitchen. The companion realized that Orga Syriac would consume the fresh fruit and coffee; the Abo-Yorba, the raw steak.

CHAPTER 35

Larry and Butch Cole entered the Museum of Natural History in Museum Park at 1200 South Lake Shore Drive. Although Butch didn't comment when his father announced where they were going after their daily run and breakfast this morning, he had been more intrigued than disappointed. After they left the museum they were planning to spend the balance of the day sailing on Lake Michigan with Kate Ford on her forty-five-foot sailboat.

Cole proceeded to the information desk and requested to see Dr. Silvernail Smith.

"Do you have an appointment?" the severe-looking Oriental woman inquired in a less than cordial tone of voice.

"Yes, I do," Cole replied with a smile.

The woman seemed far from pleased at this revelation as she picked up a phone and dialed a two-digit number. After announcing Cole she hung up the phone and said, "He'll be right out."

A few minutes later a tall, handsome man with long gray hair combed back off his forehead and bound into a ponytail came out to meet them. He was dressed in a denim shirt and trousers and wore a pair of worn moccasins. Butch noticed the graceful way he moved on the balls of his feet. It was obvious to the younger Cole that the older man could move very fast and in virtual silence. He was the perfect picture of the Native American hunter from a bygone era.

"Larry," he said in a deep voice, "it has been a long time."

"Yes it has, Doctor. How have you been?" Cole said, taking the proffered hand.

Dr. Silvernail turned and smiled at Butch. "And it doesn't take any great feat of deductive reasoning to tell me who this young man is. You're exactly like your father."

The gray-haired man's eyes narrowed a bit and Butch felt an odd, but not uncomfortable, chill. It was as if Dr. Silvernail had peered into his soul. Silvernail repeated, "Exactly like your father."

A few moments later Silvernail was leading the Coles across the museum rotunda into a side corridor in which a number of stuffed animals were exhibited. At the display of the giant gorilla Bushman, Cole stopped. Silvernail and Butch had proceeded a few feet farther before they realized that he was no longer with them. They also stopped.

After staring at the gorilla for a moment, Cole rejoined his companions.

Dr. Silvernail's office was located beyond a door which was virtually unnoticeable between two ten-foot-tall display cases containing Native American artifacts. The historian's office was modern, with the usual accoutrements, including a computer, fax machine, and copier. The walls were lined with photographs, oil paintings, and charcoal sketches. There were also a number of Native American artifacts, such as bows, arrows, spears, and knives. Butch was drawn to them like a moth to a flame.

"Butch," Cole cautioned.

"Oh, it's all right, Larry," Dr. Silvernail said. "As long as he's careful with some of these weapons, which are razor sharp."

"I'll be careful," Butch promised.

The cop and the historian settled down on a couch across the office, while Butch began examining the artifacts from early America.

"What can you tell me about African legends, Doctor?"

Silvernail shrugged. "I'm no expert, but I know a thing or two. You must remember that Africa is an immense continent with a myriad of nations with a rich multicultural background."

"I'm only interested in one particular legend. It's something called an Abo-Yorba."

Silvernail's eyes widened. "The she-devil."

"You know of it?"

Silvernail stood up, plunged his hands into his pockets, and began pacing across the oriental rug covering his office floor. "It, or more appropriately she, is a shape-shifter. One moment she appears as a very beautiful woman and the next she becomes something which can only be described as demonic."

Cole smiled. He had come to the right place. The policeman opened the black leather portfolio he carried and removed Kate Ford's book of African folktales and a reproduction of the computer-enhanced image Jamal Garth had taken from Kate's videotape. He handed them to Silvernail and said, "Kate Ford has been doing research for a book on African legends, but most of what she's been able to learn so far comes from legends and folktales."

Silvernail studied the photograph. "Where did you get this?"

Cole told him.

The historian sat back down. "Where was the woman before this"—he paused a moment—"appeared?"

"She was killed during the kidnapping and attempted murder of the mayor."

Silvernail shook his head. "I'm not talking about the kidnapper. There was another woman there."

"Didn't you see the live coverage?"

Silvernail smiled. "I'm much too busy to watch television." He could see that something was troubling Cole. "What is it, Larry?"

"The only other woman in the place where this thing appeared," Cole said, tapping the enhanced photo Silvernail was holding, "was the news commentator, "Orga Syriac.""

"If she's on television then she must be very attractive."

"Outrageously so," Cole volunteered.

Again the historian got back to his feet and resumed his pacing. "You must remember that what I'm telling you is not based on empirical scientific data, but on information consisting of little more than myth. When you're talking about shape-shifting from humanoid into demonic form, you're in the realm of ghosts, goblins, and werewolves. As a scientist and a historian I'm not supposed to have anything to do with such hackneyed superstition." Now Silvernail stopped pacing and stared down at Cole. "But the longer I live on this earth, the more I realize how much we've still got to learn about this fascinating universe we live in.

"However, in every story I've ever heard about this African she-devil, which is not a lot, there are three things that are consistent in each account. One is that she always appears first as a beautiful woman. Second, the she-devil always fights for the poor and the oppressed. And third, she is extremely cunning and equally dangerous."

Cole thought for a moment. "If the newscaster is the she-devil then she must be capable of moving extremely fast and is also very strong."

Silvernail nodded. "Legends, especially over the span of a millennium or two, have a tendency to become exaggerated, but if what has been captured in this picture is the storied Abo-Yorba then you have a bona fide monster on your hands."

Cole looked back at the computer-enhanced photo; however, he wasn't seeing the image of a so-called monster, but that of the beautiful newscaster Orga Syriac.

CHAPTER 36

Sister Mary Louise Stallings had been working in the Our Lady of Peace school preparing for the summer session. She was drawing up the class schedules, but was having difficulty concentrating on the task at hand. She looked up from the yellow legal pad she'd been writing on and gazed out the window. It was raining heavily now and it looked more like fall than summer.

She and Father Phil had eaten breakfast in the rectory at 7:30 A.M. Following the meal the priest had left for a meeting at Holy Name Cathedral and would not be back at Our Lady of Peace before midafternoon. This had left Sister Mary Louise and the housekeeper, Mrs. Turner, alone with Father Lochran. Their guest had still been asleep and did not come down for breakfast. After Father Phil was gone Sister Mary Louise had grabbed an umbrella, crossed the courtyard behind the church, and entered the school. Now, two hours later, her mind wandered from her work.

Their guest had been on her mind when she went to bed last night and he was the first person she thought of that morning. Something about the elderly man was bothering her. It was more instinct than anything she could put her finger on, but she trusted her intuition, as it had served her well in the past.

Deciding on taking a break from her labors, she got up from her desk and headed for the rectory. She let herself in the back door and found Mrs. Turner in the kitchen preparing lunch. The housekeeper was a woman with a somewhat severe outward manner who possessed a heart of gold.

"Could I get you a cup of coffee, Sister?"

"Thank you, Mrs. Turner. That would be nice," she responded, taking a seat at the kitchen table. "Has Father Lochran come down yet?"

The housekeeper set a coffee cup down in front of the nun and returned to her lunch preparations. "Ain't seen him. Must still be up in his room. Father Phil was telling me that the old priest wasn't feeling too well yesterday." She turned around to look at the nun. "I would have gone up there and checked on him myself, but I didn't think it was my place to do so."

The nun took the hint. A few moments later she was walking down the second-floor corridor approaching the former monsignor's room. As she walked up to the door she heard moaning coming from inside. She stopped. The door was heavy, which made it virtually soundproof. However, the sound she heard was clearly audible out in the hall. It was obvious that Father Lochran was in a great deal of pain. Sister Mary Louise knocked on the door, but the moaning continued. She knocked again before stepping forward and opening the door.

The priest was lying on his back in the canopied bed. He was clad only in shorts and a sleeveless T-shirt. His face and flabby body were drenched with sweat, which caused his skin to gleam in the gray light filtering through the bedroom window. His features were contorted into a grimace and his continuous groaning indicated that he was in intense distress. His limbs were spasming rigid as he fought the images in his dream.

Sister Mary Louise stood a few feet away staring at the man locked in the anguish of a nightmare. She started to wake him up and even took a step toward the bed. Then she noticed the smell.

It was a chemical odor, which reminded her of gunpowder, although it was more pronounced. She looked around and saw a number of small plastic pouches on top of the dresser. They contained a thick, pale yellow substance and were obviously the source of the odd odor. It didn't take any great feat of the imagination for her to guess that this was an explosive.

"Sister?"

Startled, she spun back toward the bed.

Father Lochran was sitting up staring at her with a curious expression. He appeared more puzzled than surprised.

"I heard you moaning in your sleep and came in to see if you were all right," she managed with a nervous voice.

"I'm fine," he said, pulling up the sheet to cover his body.

She blushed and looked away. "If you'd like I can have Mrs. Turner fix you some breakfast and bring it up on a tray."

He smiled and his brogue deepened as he said, "I haven't been feeling well, Sister. That's why I slept so late this morning. I'm fine now and will be down to take my meal in the dining room."

She hesitated a moment longer before heading for the door. Once more her eyes strayed to the plastic packages on the dresser.

"Sister Mary Louise," the priest called from behind her.

She stopped, but did not turn around. "Yes, Father."

"Thank you."

"You're welcome," she said, stepping out into the corridor and closing the door behind her.

CHAPTER 37

The rain was still falling when Larry Cole pulled into the parking lot of Belmont Harbor, where Kate Ford kept her sailboat. He got out of the car and pulled up the hood of his nylon windbreaker. He walked through the rain toward slip 19, which was about a quarter of a mile from the parking lot. Cole trudged along feeling a bit stupid. Butch had opted out of this foray onto the lake because of the rain and a temperature that had dropped below seventy degrees. Instead he was visiting with some of his friends he had gone to grammar school with. Cole had attempted to call Kate at her home, but all he got was her answering service with the message that she was going sailing. So, feeling obligated, Cole was out here in the rain.

He finally reached slip 19. The sailboat—*Kate's Folly*—was lashed securely to the dock, although it was bobbing up and down with the motion of the waves slamming into the harbor from the lake. There were no signs of life on the craft, and for a moment he thought that Kate had reconsidered this foolhardy idea on such a wretched day. Then he saw movement on the deck, and she appeared wearing a knee length yellow raincoat. She had on black canvas shoes and her legs were bare.

She spied Cole and said, "Well, hello there, sailor. Where's the rest of your crew?"

Cole bounded onto the deck and told her about Butch after requesting the obligatory permission to come aboard.

"You're already aboard, but permission granted anyway."

The deck was slippery and he found it difficult maintaining his balance.

"It will probably take you a while to get your sea legs," she explained.

"You're not seriously considering going out today, are you?"

She looked out at the windswept lake. "The wind is going to die down by noon and the rain will let up later. Then we can go out. In the meantime come on down to the galley and I'll fix you a cup of tea."

Cole was glad to get out of the bad weather. Below deck Kate led him into a small but well-appointed combination galley and sleeping area. The walls and floor were of highly varnished wood. The room held the faint aroma of Kate's perfume. It was also warm, for which Cole was grateful.

"Take off that wet windbreaker and hang it behind the door," she said. Then she took off her raincoat. Cole turned around to find her bending over a small electric stove. His jaw muscles rippled when he saw that she was wearing a pair of very short white cutoff jeans and a low-cut halter top. Kate Ford was a five-foot two-inch blonde with a very good figure, which was definitely enhanced by her makeshift sailor's outfit. She straightened up from the stove and noticed him staring at her. Her cheeks colored slightly.

An awkward moment of silence ensued. Finally, Cole cleared his throat and said, "I brought your book back." He removed it from the pocket of his windbreaker. "I took it over to the museum and let Dr. Silvernail take a look at it and the photo."

She crossed the small galley area and took the book from him. "What did he say about them?"

As Cole began to explain she remained standing close to him. He was very much aware of her proximity. So much so that he was having difficulty concentrating. When he finished she remained in the same position. She was looking up at him. "Could you tell me something, Larry?"

He stared down at her. "Sure."

"Why haven't you ever made a pass at me?"

"I didn't know that you wanted me to."

She reached out and placed her hands beneath his knit shirt. Her palms were cold against his bare flesh; however, rather than causing discomfort, the chill heightened the excitement of the moment. She ran her palms up across his flat stomach to caress his pectoral muscles. At the same time she pressed her body against his. She emitted a slight gasp when she felt his erection through the clothing separating them.

"Are you going to make me do all the work?" she said in a husky voice.

"I wouldn't dream of it," he whispered back as he wrapped his arms around her and crushed her against him.

Kate Ford and Larry Cole had known each other for five years. During that time they had maintained a close friendship beneath which there had always been a lingering sexual tension. Perhaps it was the roles which society had forced each to play—she an investigative journalist and he a high-ranking cop—that had caused them to move slowly in the direction of an amorous liaison. More than once they had separately speculated what it would be like to make love, but for the most part they had maintained a professional friendship. That is until a rainy summer afternoon when they found themselves alone in the cozy cabin of *Kate's Folly*.

They moved with exquisite slowness. Cole disrobed Kate and gently massaged her breasts until her pink nipples hardened under his touch. She undid his belt buckle and assisted him in slipping out of his jeans and shorts. They fondled, kissed, and nibbled gently at the most sensitive spots of each other's body until their mutual excitement caused their breathing to come in sharp rasps. Finally, Cole lifted her off her feet and carried her over to the bed. He laid her down on it before straddling her. He supported himself on his arms as he lowered himself slowly between her legs. When he penetrated her she rose up to completely envelop him. Then they began.

Outside, the rise and fall of the waves rocked the sailboat *Kate's Folly* in slip 19.

*   *   *

Paige Albritton entered the Dragon's Lair nightclub. It was approaching noon and the place wouldn't be open for business until three. She proceeded straight to Jack Carlisle's office. The fixer and the ever-present Sonny Balfour were waiting for her.

Today Paige had reverted from her glamour girl look of last night back to her casual, near slovenly, appearance of before. This drew a frown from Carlisle.

"How did it go last night?" the fixer asked.

She sat down in a chair across from him and said, "It didn't. I tried everything I could to seduce Pete Dubcek except coming right out and saying, 'Let's fuck.' But no matter what I did he kept looking around for his sweet little wife."

Carlisle graced Paige with a chilly smile. "That's why I had Sonny get Fuzzy away from him."

"Well with her or without her, he's still not going to go to bed with me. Face it, Jack, our star basketball player is one of a vanishing breed known as a faithful husband."

The fixer stood up. "You're selling yourself too cheaply. No red-blooded male can turn you down. At least not for long. Maybe you should give it another try."

Her shoulders drooped and she ran a hand through her hair. "It won't work, Jack. I get any more obvious with my play than I did last night and Dubcek will know something's up. You'll just have to figure out another way to blackmail him."

Carlisle's smile broadened. He walked around the desk and stood in front of her. She tensed when he reached down and gently grasped her chin. He lifted her face up. She looked at him with eyes lidded by fear. His voice was soothing as he said, "I want you to try with Pete again for me. Okay, Paige?"

She maintained eye contact with him, but she was definitely frightened. "I'll try again, Jack."

He released her chin and reached down and took her left hand in his. He patted it gently. "You wait and see. Pete Dubcek will fall into your arms so fast you won't believe it, but"—his tone changed from soothing to harsh as he twisted her fingers back, making her cry out—"the reason why I

want Pete Dubcek to screw you is none of your damned
business!"

Carlisle maintained the pressure on her fingers until tears
began running down her face. His voice adopted its soothing
tone once more, but he still didn't release her hand. "You
just follow my orders from now on and don't go around
using words like 'blackmail.' Am I making myself clear,
babe?"

Her eyes were shut against the pain, but she managed to
nod.

He increased the pressure on her hand, but his voice didn't
change. "I can't hear you, Paige."

"I . . . understand."

Finally, he let her go. As she slumped in the chair, clutching her aching fingers with her free hand, he walked back
behind his desk and sat down. "Sonny, take Paige out front
and get her some ice for those fingers."

The ex-boxer moved across the room and helped Paige to
her feet. She was barely able to walk as they left the office.
A slight smile played across the fixer's face as he watched
them go.

CHAPTER 38

JUNE 15, 2004
Noon

Orga Syriac had spent the morning completing the tour
of the WGN studio which she had begun the day before. She had met the people she would be working with and
had received a number of compliments about her coverage
of the kidnapping of the mayor. There were also positive

comments about the Barristers' Club explosion and dead prostitute coverage. Even Dede Priest seemed to thaw a bit when Orga expressed a desire to remain with the mobile news van and cover stories in the field. As lunchtime approached she headed for Sven-Erik Voman's office.

Today she was wearing a burgundy suit with a diamond-studded pin in the shape of a lion over her left breast. Walking through the halls of the television studio, there was a smile on her face. Things were going very well for her and she expected them to get better. Everything was working out exactly as she had planned. Now it was just a matter of time before she moved on her primary target. In the meantime she would do something about the victimization of the street-walkers.

She knocked before opening the door and entering the news director's office. The big Swede was at his desk going over his usual heavy volume of paperwork. He looked up over the top of his wire-frame glasses at her. Orga was sensitive enough to be aware that something was bothering her new boss. She would give him time to get it out. Then she had her own agenda to pursue with him.

"Sit down, Orga. I'll be with you in a minute."

She took the seat and waited. She noticed her single-page bio on Sven-Erik's cluttered desk blotter. She had submitted it with the job application she was forced to fill out when she was hired. Orga and Blessing had carefully constructed the items contained on that page. Her birthplace was listed as Diggstown, Mississippi, which no longer existed. The places where she had received her degrees from were in Europe and Africa; however, none of those institutions were still in existence. She knew that the fiction of her background wouldn't stand up under prolonged scrutiny, but it wasn't supposed to. Yesterday's events would speed up the deception's eventual discovery, but Orga was confident it would hold up until her mission was completed.

Sven-Erik put his pen down, removed his glasses, and rubbed his eyes. "I make a New Year's resolution every year that I'm going to ease up, get more rest, eat healthier, and get more exercise. But by January second my resolve is gone and I revert back to my old ways, which in the long run will shorten my life."

Orga smiled. "You have a long life ahead of you, Sven. I can tell about such things."

"I love your optimism, Orga." He picked up an envelope which was lying beneath her bio. "We've received some calls from viewers who taped the mayor's kidnapping story. Maybe five or six people claim they were able to see some type of strange image appear on the screen before Spurgeon's camera was destroyed. They're saying that it resembled a monster or some type of demon."

Orga was sitting very still.

The news director continued. "I ran the tape myself this morning and did notice something strange right before the screen went blank. I had the frame computer-enhanced and this is what it showed." He removed a photo from the envelope and placed it on the desk in front of her.

Slowly, she reached out and picked it up. She studied it a moment before looking back at the news director. "Do you know what this is, Sven?"

Something about her voice and the way she looked made him so uneasy that he was actually starting to become frightened. "No, I don't know what it is, Orga. Since you were there I was hoping that maybe you could tell me."

She continued to stare at him. "I wasn't the only one there. Have you talked to Dave?"

Sven was becoming increasingly nervous. He couldn't understand how she was doing this to him and it was making him angry. His face darkened and he snapped, "Either you know what it is or you don't! How it got there is a mystery right now, but you can bet that this is going to get out, and when it does we'd better have some type of explanation."

She placed the photograph back on his desk. "I think the source of that image is fairly obvious."

He waited, his anger and fear ebbing away.

"When the camera was damaged an image from another transmission in the area became superimposed on our feed. Whatever it was became distorted, which resulted in this." She gestured toward the photo with her hand.

"I've never heard of anything like that happening before," he said stubbornly.

"I don't see how you or anyone else can explain what was picked up by Dave's camera. That doesn't even appear to be human, and those of us who were there, including the mayor, didn't report seeing anything like this at all."

He took a moment to digest what she had said. Finally, "I guess I can go along with that. At least for the time being."

Her face lit up with a smile, which actually made her glow. "So now that we've got the ghost image out of the way I'd like to discuss some projects with you."

"Such as?"

"I want to do a couple of investigative pieces in connection with my duties as a field reporter for WGN."

Sven-Erik Voman raised a skeptical eyebrow. "Do you think you have the experience to take on something like that?"

"You underestimate me, Sven. I may not have done this before, but I'm a personal friend of Kate Ford, who is one of the best investigative journalists in the country. I'm sure she can give me some pointers."

"So what do you want to investigate?"

Orga sat forward on the edge of her seat. "Two things. One will be on the streetwalker and pimp murders which have occurred in Chicago recently. It was on the wire this morning that a pimp was found brutally murdered."

"But what would you be investigating?"

"That fact that these murders aren't random acts of street violence, but a war between two organized-crime factions."

The news director nodded. "There has been some talk about friction between the Mafia and the Disciples street gang. But messing around with them could be dangerous."

Her smile never altered. "Isn't uncovering the truth part of our job despite the danger, Sven?"

She had him there. "Okay, you can do your investigation of this prostitution war. What else do you want to do a feature on?"

Orga Syriac replied evenly, "Something called the Human Development Institute."

CHAPTER 39

"Can I get you anything else, Father?" Mrs. Turner asked the Irish priest, who was finishing up a meal consisting of a chicken-fried steak, eggs, hash browns, and toast. He was on his second cup of coffee and was leaning back in one of the rectory dining-room chairs with a contented expression on his face.

"Thank you, Mrs. Turner, but I don't think I could put another morsel in this ample midsection of mine if my life depended on it. And I must say, madam, that you are a wonderful cook. A wonderful cook indeed."

The severe Mrs. Turner smiled in spite of herself as she began clearing the table.

"I saw a computer in Father Cisco's office. I wonder if he would mind if I used it?"

"Ain't my place to say, Father," she replied. "But Father Phil's still downtown and Sister Mary Louise is back over to the school. I guess as long as you don't go busting it up, I don't see no problem with you using it."

He remained in the dining room until he heard her washing the dishes through the closed kitchen door. Then he rose from the table and crossed the main hall to the pastor's office. The computer was on a desk next to a window that overlooked the courtyard surrounded by the church, school, rectory, and convent. He could see the school entrance he had seen the nun enter earlier from his second-floor room. If she left the school before he finished he would have ample warning.

The computer was a fairly new IBM model equipped with a modem and printer. It would serve him well for what he needed to accomplish. First he would perform the less complicated task before moving on to the more complex. Turning the computer on, he interfaced with a computer in the downtown law offices of Coffey, Cox, and Davenport, the firm in which the late Philo Coffey had been the senior partner. The law firm's computer required a password to enter. Former HDI operative Thomas Kelly had stolen this password over a week ago, when he'd planned the PAC affair disaster. Now, as the priest impersonator Father James Lochran, he typed the word "Litigation" to gain access to the law firm's main directory. He scrolled down the list until he came to the entry "PAC Affair—compiled 5 May 2004." Under the "Comments" section was the entry "Guest List."

The priest impersonator called the list up on the screen and reviewed it briefly. The name, address, telephone number, and zip code of each of the people who had purchased tickets to the affair were listed. He activated the printer and made himself a copy of the list. Exiting the law firm's computer, he was now prepared to move on to a more difficult task. He was going to sneak into the computer files of the Human Development Institute. He realized that the HDI computer was infinitely more difficult to break into than the Coffey, Cox, and Davenport law firm's computer. However, the man who called himself Father James Lochran had an ace up his sleeve. He possessed the computer access code of the Institute's director, Dr. Gilbert Goldman.

The code was a series of letters, numbers, and signs that had to be entered correctly in the proper sequence or not only would access be denied, but HDI security would be alerted to the intrusion. On numerous occasions in the past Goldman had blundered while attempting to enter his code, necessitating a call to security to warn them of the mistake. If the priest impersonator failed to enter the code properly there would be no call to security and HDI would be aware that a very real attempt was being made for an unauthorized interface with their computer system. Father Lochran knew that it wouldn't take them long to figure out that he was the intruder, and steps would be taken to prevent him from doing it again.

Tension began building inside him, because the success of his mission of atonement depended on him gaining access to the Institute's records. There was no place else in the world he could go to get what he needed.

Feeling sweat form on his forehead, he clenched and un-clenched his fingers. He began to type. The HDI logo appeared on the screen above the words "Enter Access Code."

Carefully he typed 321A4G;///417G1@. The screen went momentarily blank before "Please Stand By" appeared. He chewed his bottom lip to the point of coming close to drawing blood. He almost cried out with relief when a menu of services appeared on the screen. His fingers now began to fly over the keys, as he began gathering the information he needed. There was a smile on his aging features and a gleam in his blue eyes as he worked.

CHAPTER 40

JUNE 15, 2004
2:00 P.M.

The two priests walked behind the rectory to the garage where Father Phil kept his car. They were dressed in civilian sports shirts and jackets.

"This is most kind of you, Father Cisco," Father Lochran said as the priest handed him the keys to a 1999 low-mileage Chevy Blazer. "I'll return it to you filled with gas and in the same shape as it is now." Father Lochran carried a black attaché case with him.

The rain had turned to a slight drizzle, but it had warmed up a bit. With his hands thrust into his pockets, Father Phil said, "Do you think we could dispense with all the formality? Since you'll be staying with us for a while, wouldn't first names make things easier all around?"

The older man looked away. Father Phil could detect an odd nervousness or apprehension in his guest. For a moment the pastor of Our Lady of Peace thought he had offended Father Lochran.

"That would be most kind of you, Phil. And of course you can call me James. But perhaps I could ask you something?"

"Sure."

"I notice that you maintain a certain formality with Sister Mary Louise. I also have noticed that she doesn't seem very friendly toward me."

Now it was the younger priest's turn to display apprehension. "It's kind of a difficult thing to explain, but Sister Mary Louise hasn't had the easiest life. I'm sure she doesn't mean anything by her manner. It's just that we're not used to visitors here at Our Lady. If you'd like I could speak to her."

"Oh no, no. Perish the thought, Phil. I understand perfectly. This is a pretty rough place you practice your ministry in and I understand that the good sister's been here awhile. That would make anyone a bit uneasy around strangers. Give me a couple days and me and Sister Mary Louise will be the best of friends."

Then the man Phil Cisco knew as James Lochran climbed into the Blazer and drove from the rectory garage. As he passed the school, Sister Mary Louise Stallings was standing at her office window. There was a frown of curiosity and suspicion etched on her face.

Traffic on the Kennedy Expressway was backed up for miles from the site of a multivehicle chain-reaction collision. Four trucks and eleven cars were involved. Seven people were dead and eighteen seriously injured. Police vehicles, ambulances, and a huge crane were attempting to bring some order out of this scene of ultimate chaos.

On the Lawrence Avenue overpass Orga Syriac stood on the sidewalk with the scene of the accident down on the expressway behind her. Off in the distance the skyscrapers of the Windy City were visible.

Orga finished her narration of the events of the accident, which was believed to have been caused by the wet pavement. She waited until Dave Spurgeon gave her the sign that they were off the air before she retreated out of the drizzle into the back of the van.

When they had settled in she said, "Tell Steve to head for the Riteway Laundry Company at Fifty-one-twelve West Douglas Boulevard."

Spurgeon was cleaning a camera lens. "We doing a story there?"

"In a way," she replied. "We're interviewing the laundry's proprietor. A gentleman by the name of Gino Allegretti."

The cameraman went pale. "Orga, Allegretti's hooked up with the Chicago Mob."

She smiled. "I know."

Ronnie Skyles pulled his canary yellow Corvette convertible into a reserved parking space in the private parking lot of the Riteway Laundry Company on West Douglas Boulevard. Skyles, a pimp in the Allegretti organization, was a man of medium height with sandy-colored hair and a perpetual tan. He had startling hazel eyes under girlishly long lashes and matinee-idol features. He wore a white denim suit and a black silk shirt with the top three buttons undone to expose a hairy chest. He had a thick gold chain around his neck and had doused himself with an expensive cologne that enveloped him like a personal cloud. He carried a tan attaché case and walked with the confident saunter of a man who was very satisfied with his life.

He entered the laundry through a door marked "Authorized Personnel Only." On the other side of the door, seated at a desk reading that day's edition of the *Times-Herald*, was a 250-pound black slab of muscle with a shaved head. The

black man's eyes swung up from the paper. When he recognized Skyles his face split in a grin and he said, "My main
man," and extended his palm.

"What's happening, Brother Buck?" Skyles responded,
slapping the hand. Then he proceeded past Buck to a flight
of stairs leading up to the plant's administrative offices.

The smell of detergent and starch was strong, and the
washing machines and dryers produced not only excessive
heat but a continuous din. Skyles walked down a balcony,
stopped at a door, and knocked. The gravelly voice of Gino
Allegretti called from inside, "C'mon in, Ronnie."

The office was plush to the point of being garish. There
were three overstuffed red sofas and a couple of orange ve-
lour chairs. The carpet was a thick white shag that most
visitors' shoes disappeared in when they walked across it.
There were no desks, file cabinets, or office paraphernalia in
evidence. Other than the furniture, there was a bar along one
wall and a large glass cocktail table in the center of the room.
Four paintings of nude women lined the walls. Each pose
could be considered nothing less than obscene. It was a totally tasteless room, which mirrored its owner, clad in a kelly
green silk robe, reclined on one of the sofas.

"How's it going, Gino?" Skyles said, crossing the office
and placing his attaché case on the cocktail table.

"Life's a bitch, but I manage," the Mafia pimp said. "What
have you got for me?"

Skyles opened the case. Inside were rubber-band-bound
bundles of greenbacks. The bills were worn, and ranged in
denominations from fives to hundreds. The sum represented
the previous night's take from Allegretti's prostitution operation in the city and suburbs.

"How much is there?" Allegretti asked without moving
from the sofa.

"Two hundred and thirty-eight thousand dollars and
change."

"Not bad," Allegretti said, swinging his bare feet to the
floor and sitting up.

The door to the adjoining bathroom opened and the tall,
stunningly built black woman who had accompanied the

pimp to breakfast the previous morning walked in. She was
clad in nothing but a sheer black negligee. The view was not
wasted on Ronnie Skyles. However, he managed to keep his
mind on business.

"Did you hear about Chet the Jet?" Skyles asked.

The mention of the black pimp's name got the attention
of both Allegretti and his shapely companion. "What about
him?" the woman asked.

"Somebody did a real number on him. Tied him upside
down from the second-floor porch of an abandoned building
on Calumet, opened up his arteries, and bled him dry."

"No shit," Allegretti said with awe. "Serves the bastard
right. He sliced up one of my girls with a razor over on
Forty-third Street last night. Do they know who got him?"

Skyles raised a questioning eyebrow. "Don't you know?"

"Haven't the slightest idea." Allegretti collapsed back on
the sofa. "But you can bet one thing for sure, those fucking
cops Cole and Silvestri will be climbing up my asshole about
it before long."

The telephone on the cocktail table rang. The woman
walked over and picked it up. Placing her hand over the
mouthpiece, she said to Allegretti, "Buck says that Jack Carlisle and Sonny Balfour are downstairs to see you."

"Tell Buck to send them up," he said. Then he asked Ronnie Skyles, "What do you think the fixer wants?"

"Probably a woman," the pimp said.

A few minutes later Carlisle was seated in one of the orange chairs, while Sonny Balfour lounged against the wall
next to the painting of a woman with her legs splayed open.

As Skyles had guessed, Carlisle was indeed looking for a
woman. A particular type of woman.

"I need her to speak German and know something about
German culture. She should be tall and athletic. I'd prefer a
blonde, but a redhead or brunette will do just as well. And
she's got to know how to do what she's told and keep her
mouth shut."

Gino looked at Skyles, who said, "Except for the German
part, Paige Albritton fits the bill pretty good."

The fixer gave the pimp a chilly glance before turning his

attention back to Allegretti. "I'll pay whatever finder's fee you quote, but I haven't got a lot of time for this."

Allegretti said to his scantily clad companion, "Get me a stogie, babe."

She went to the bar and removed a cigar from a wooden box. Carrying a gold table lighter, she walked over to the Mafia pimp. She held the lighter until he got the cigar going and a thick cloud of smoke rose up to momentarily obscure his face. He didn't offer his guests cigars or any other form of refreshment. He removed the cigar from his mouth, examined the glowing tip, and said, "I'll probably have to contact the West Coast to get a broad like that. Sounds like you need an actress who does some hooking on the side. How soon do you need her?"

"Yesterday," Carlisle responded.

Allegretti stuck the cigar in the corner of his mouth and said, "It'll cost you twenty grand and that's just my finder's fee. Then we'll talk price."

The fixer snapped his fingers and Balfour came off the wall. He removed two sealed white envelopes from his inside jacket pocket and handed them to Carlisle. He tossed the envelopes on the cocktail table and stood up.

"I expect to hear from you very soon, Gino, so don't let me down." There was no mistaking the underlying threat in the fixer's voice.

"Have I ever?" Allegretti said, getting to his feet. "Let me walk you out."

Carlisle looked at the pimp's garish robe and shrugged. With Balfour and Ronnie Skyles in tow, they left the office and walked down the steps to the main floor, where the muscular Buck was still reading the paper while keeping half an eye on the door.

As they moved slowly along, Allegretti and Carlisle made idle chitchat about business. Balfour and Skyles walked behind them. They stepped out onto the loading dock. The rain had stopped, but it was still an unseasonably cool summer afternoon. Allegretti pulled his green robe closer around him and was about to say good-bye to the fixer when he saw the woman in the burgundy suit walking rapidly across the parking lot toward them. When the Mafia pimp saw the man with the camera accompanying her, his mouth dropped open and he said, "What the fuck is this?"

It didn't take Ronnie Skyles long to size up the situation. Turning, he shouted back inside the laundry, "Buck!"

The big bodyguard appeared instantly. Orga Syriac reached the bottom of the stairs and raised a microphone. "Are you Gino Allegretti, the owner and operator of the Rite-way Laundry Company?"

"This is private property, lady, and . . . ," Allegretti began.

Dave Spurgeon flicked on the camera strobe light, bathing the five men on the loading dock in a bright glare.

"Are you also the Gino Allegretti who was indicted in December of 2002 on twenty-seven counts of pimping, pandering, and racketeering?"

Jack Carlisle and Sonny Balfour were viewing this event with amusement. The fixer had never been a man who shied away from the limelight. Carlisle was also enjoying the shock and confusion exhibited by the Mafia pimp. However, the fixer could tell that things were going to get very ugly real soon.

"Look," Allegretti spluttered, his face turning crimson, "I told you this was private property. Now you and your cameraman get out of here before—"

Orga cut Allegretti off. "Are you aware that prostitutes and pimps are being killed in a very violent street war? A war that is reputedly being fought between you and the Disciples street gang for control of prostitution in Chicago?"

Allegretti opened his mouth, but no sound came out. Ronnie Skyles decided to step in. "This is your last warning, sweetheart. If you're not off the premises in five seconds then Buck here is going to have to eject you forcibly."

This didn't faze the pretty reporter at all. She even took another step up toward them and asked, "Do you have any comment about the street war, Mr. Allegretti?"

Buck charged. The big man leaped down the steps. He had worked in the Allegretti organization for a number of years and was known to get his kicks out of abusing women. Even though they were on camera, Buck was intent on hurting the pretty reporter very badly. Then he would deal with the nosy cameraman.

The fixer, Sonny Balfour, and the two pimps watched the violence unfold. Then something happened that none of them would be able to explain later.

Buck's body obscured the woman momentarily. The camera picked up nothing but her back as the big man charged her. He reached her and suddenly spun away. It appeared as if he had lost his balance and fallen. He screamed and clutched his right arm as he landed hard on the asphalt surface of the parking lot.

Orga Syriac remained standing on the steps looking down at the injured man. Then she turned to look up at the men standing on the loading dock. "Do you have any further comment, Mr. Allegretti?"

Stunned speechless, the pimp was unable to respond. Ronnie Skyles stepped forward and pulled Allegretti back inside the laundry. Carlisle and Balfour remained in place for a moment before starting down the stairs.

When they passed Orga she stuck her microphone under the fixer's chin. "Perhaps you have some comment for us, Mr. Carlisle?"

The fixer smiled. "Not today, Ms. Syriac. Not today."

Then he and Sonny Balfour descended to the bottom of the stairs, walked past the still-prone bodyguard, and proceeded to Carlisle's Cadillac.

"Can we summon medical assistance for you, sir?" Orga asked Buck.

With agony contorting his face into a scowl, he struggled to his feet, still clutching his arm. "Get away from me, bitch!" he hissed, as he made his way back inside the building.

Dave Spurgeon, the WGN cameraman, had recorded it all.

CHAPTER 41

Larry Cole and Kate Ford were lying in the small but comfortable bunk in the cabin of *Kate's Folly*. Because the bed was so narrow they were huddled together with Kate lying on her side with one leg draped over Cole and one arm cradled beneath her head. She used her free hand to trace a line from his sternum to his navel.

He sighed. "If you keep doing that you're going to get into trouble."

She moved slightly so she could get herself in position to bite one of his nipples, making him flinch. "Am I in trouble yet?"

"Definitely."

A half hour later they were once more lying intertwined; however, a thin film of perspiration covered Cole's chest and Kate's face was still flushed as a result of their recently spent passion.

"Can we talk business now?" she said.

"Business?"

"What you found out from Dr. Silvernail."

He raised his head and looked into her face. "I told you when I came in."

She smiled. "I guess I wasn't paying attention."

"Okay," he said. "Silvernail pretty much agreed with what you've found out so far about this Abo-Yorba. He did emphasize that everything known about this shape-shifter is based on folktales and myth. But there was one thing he said that was interesting."

"What?"

"If the Abo-Yorba was responsible for rescuing the mayor, then Silvernail believes that Orga Syriac is the shape-shifter."

Kate sat up so quickly she almost fell off the bed. Cole's arm saved her. "That's crazy, Larry. Orga's no monster."

Cole stared at her.

She looked away, shaking her head in confusion.

"Kate, it was you who first told us about this Abo-Yorba changing from a beautiful woman into a demon, and, if you recall, Orga became visibly uneasy at the PAC dinner when you were talking about it."

She shivered and Cole felt goose bumps form on her bare flesh. He pulled her against him and arranged the blanket to cover her. She began shivering so violently that her teeth chattered.

Holding her close against his body, he asked, "Kate, are you okay?"

She continued to shiver, but managed to say, "Larry, this is scaring me to death."

Joseph Silk was an operative for the Human Development Institute. He had accompanied Thomas Kelly to plant explosives at the PAC dinner. Silk was an emotionless man who generally sported a two-to-three-day growth of beard and said very little. He had been recruited by the HDI from the CIA. Basically, he was a technician, a man who could repair firearms, make bombs, and invent other infernal machines of mayhem. And he was very good at what he did.

Because Dr. Gilbert Goldman did not want explosives on the Institute grounds, Silk was barred from the HDI "campus." So he worked out of the garage at the rear of his north suburban home. The garage's exterior was of red brick and neatly trimmed with white aluminum siding; however, the windows were secured inside by steel shutters and the garage doors were steel-reinforced and alarmed, which would make unauthorized entry very difficult.

Now, as the day wound down toward evening, Silk exited

his house through the back door and headed for the garage. He was dressed in stained coveralls and a Chicago Cubs baseball cap. As he sauntered along, he chewed on a tuna fish sandwich.

With the remains of the sandwich in one hand, he removed a remote control device from his coverall pocket, turned off the alarm, and unlocked the side door. He was about to step inside when he saw the Chevy Blazer parked in the alley. He frowned. He had never seen this vehicle before. Then the man he knew as Thomas Kelly got out of the Blazer.

"Good day to you, Mr. Silk," the white-haired man said, leaning heavily on his cane as he limped toward Silk.

The technician's face remained as impassive as ever. He realized he would have to inform the Institute that he had made contact with Kelly. But, as they were seasoned professionals, he would wait to see what the old man had to say.

Twenty minutes later the Blazer pulled out of the alley behind Silk's suburban home. It had traveled less than a mile when a massive explosion rocked the area. The blast knocked out all the windows in every house on the block where the HDI technician had lived and completely obliterated the brick garage and Joseph Silk.

The Cook County state's attorney was hosting a fund-raiser at Willie's Tavern on West Madison, a few blocks from the United Center, where the Chicago Bulls and Blackhawks played. Willie's was not what its name signified. It was more of a trendy saloon in which one could purchase hot dogs, hamburgers, and french fries along with draft beer to cleanse the less-sophisticated palate. There were also steak, lobster, and gourmet foods on the menu, which were available to be consumed at bare wooden tables jammed into a large room with walls of raw brick and sawdust-covered floors. Arranged around the room were movie screen-sized television monitors on which were continuously shown sporting events featuring Chicago teams. The main adult beverage at Willie's was draft beer; however, hard booze was available to be purchased by the shot, carafe, or even fifth. Wine was not served at all. The proprietors, George and Willie Stanponopolous, who had started their business from a portable hot-dog stand on South Halsted, were broad-minded enough to permit vino lovers to bring their own bottles and purchase setups for a minimal service charge.

The primary stated objective of tonight's affair was to raise money for the reelection of the current Cook County state's attorney. The underlying reason was to mend fences between the beleaguered prosecutor's office and the Chicago Police Department. This rift had developed following a series of well-publicized prosecutions of cops for engaging in excessive force. One trial had focused on an allegation that a police lieutenant had murdered his wife and gotten his cop buddies to cover up his involvement and make it look like a burglary gone bad.

The Chicago Police Department, as is the case with the majority of the departments across the nation, would never sanction a murder by one of its members or, for that matter, anyone else. The superintendent's office ensured that the CPD cooperated fully in each prosecution. The state's attorney, a lifelong Chicago Democratic machine functionary who had never actually conducted a criminal trial during his legal career, had zealously held daily press conferences on the progress of his "cop cases." This brought charges of "grandstanding" and "publicity seeking" from the state's attorney's rivals and critics. At the time, the county's chief prosecutor hadn't cared. He planned to waltz to reelection and he didn't care what his rivals or the Chicago Police Department thought about it. The problem was that each of the accused cops was acquitted.

Every cop organization in the city not only failed to endorse the incumbent, but instead endorsed his opponent. In each of the pre-election polls he was lagging behind by no less than ten percentage points, and the margin was increasing. So he had decided on this little soiree to which he extended invitations to the city's fifteen-thousand CPD employees. Ten showed up.

The first deputy superintendent, three of the four deputy superintendents, two assistant deputy superintendents, and four deputy chiefs were in attendance. Coincidentally, they were the same police department representatives, minus Larry Cole, who had been in attendance at the PAC dinner. They went to a number of affairs such as the state's attorney's fund-raiser. Many members of the GPD, including Chief Cole, considered these members of the upper command structure of the department to be more politicians than cops. They consistently played both sides to ensure that whoever happened to end up with the political power would be friendly toward them. They didn't consider the correctness or morality of their position, as they believed that what they were engaged in was basic survival in a political town like Chicago. They also thought of cops like Larry Cole as anachronisms and, to some extent, threatening.

So tonight they circulated among the fund-raiser attendees engaging in small talk and making sure they were seen by the "right" people. And they were noticed, particularly by a white-haired gentleman who was standing at the bar sipping a beer and munching on complimentary peanuts.

The bartender, a pretty young woman wearing a bow tie and red plaid vest over a white shirt, came down the bar to check on him. He reminded her of a dead uncle.

"Can I top that off for you, sir?"

He turned from his scrutiny of the room, smiled, and replied, "Thank you, darlin'. I could use another, if you don't mind."

As she refilled his mug from a Budweiser tap behind the bar, she said, "This one's on the house." Setting the mug down on a coaster in front of him, she added, "You a supporter of the state's attorney?"

He took a healthy swallow of his beer and grinned. "I'm a supporter of all mankind, which includes the fair sex as well."

"Boy, did you kiss the Blarney Stone."

He lifted his mug in a salute to her. "I have to plead guilty on that point."

She walked away to wait on someone else, and Thomas Kelly, aka Father James Lochran, turned around to survey the room once more. The cops were circulating like ward heelers. There were about 250 people in the restaurant. He closed his eyes and said a silent prayer for them. What was about to happen was God's will. He was only the instrument of that will. The only problem was that Cole wasn't here. But the priest impersonator would work that out later.

He drained off the rest of his beer, waved to the pretty bartender, and went to the door. At the exit he allowed a heavyset woman to pin a red-and-white "Reelect the State's Attorney" campaign button on his jacket lapel. Out on the street he proceeded to the self-park lot where he had left Father Phil's Blazer. The bored lot attendant, who had collected the priest impersonator's ten-dollar fee when he drove in, barely looked up from a girlie magazine as Lochran limped by.

At the Blazer he looked around to make sure there was no one to observe him before he opened the back door. His attaché case was on the floor. He opened it up on the backseat. There were a number of the late Joseph Silk's infernal devices inside. They came in various sizes and shapes, from that of a ballpoint pen to a four-hundred-page hard-cover novel. Lochran selected three flat-cylindrical devices made of gray metal and a cheap digital chronometer. He carefully slipped the cylinders into his jacket pockets and strapped the watch to his left wrist. Then he returned to Willie's; however, he did not go inside.

Slowly, he made his way around the outside of the building. The structure was new and had been constructed on a vacant lot with no other buildings within a distance of two hundred feet. The entrance to Willie's faced south. The priest impersonator walked slowly around the building and placed one of the magnetized cylindrical devices on the north, east, and west walls. While he worked, he kept an eye out for anyone who might be watching him, but all the activity was focused on the comings and goings at the south entrance.

His work completed, he returned to the parking lot and drove the Blazer onto the next block and positioned the vehicle so that he had an unobstructed view of the front of Willie's Tavern. He examined the watch. There were four buttons surrounding the dial. He pushed the first one and said, "In the name of the Father . . ." He pushed the second button ". . . and the Son . . . ," then the third button, ". . . and the Holy Spirit." He looked out the windshield at the front of the saloon. Tears welled up in his eyes. With a deep sob, he murmured, "Lord, your will be done, amen!" Then he pushed the last button.

The deafening blast, caused by the three explosives going off simultaneously, was blinding. Debris was hurled hundreds of feet, and everyone inside Willie's at the time of the explosion was killed instantly. As flames leaped into the air and thick black smoke clouded the sky, the man known as Father James Lochran of the Detroit Archdiocese put the borrowed Chevy Blazer in gear and drove away.

CHAPTER 42

JUNE 15, 2004
5:45 P.M.

Ronnie Skyles drove Buck back to the Riteway Laundry Company from the hospital. The pimp was dumbfounded when the big bodyguard told him that he had sustained a broken wrist and a fractured forearm. What further astounded Skyles was that Buck also told him that he had not sustained the injuries as a result of the fall, but that the pretty reporter had done the damage when she grabbed him.

After parking the Corvette, Skyles came around and helped the scowling bodyguard out of the car. Buck's right arm was covered with a cast, which extended from his knuckles to his elbow, and the entire arm was held immobile in a sling. The big black man was obviously in a great deal of pain, but he was also very angry. On the drive from the hospital, Buck had called Orga Syriac every name in the book and threatened to do everything to her from flaying her alive to crushing every bone in her body.

The pimp had remained silent, but he figured that if the reporter had busted up his arm with a move that none of them saw, Buck's best bet would be to stay as far away from her as he could.

They entered the laundry and headed for Allegretti's office. The late shift was getting off and the huge washers and dryers were being shut down, eliminating the noise, which was soon replaced by an eerie silence. The pimp and body-guard entered the office, which was furnished à la cathouse, to find Allegretti, clad in an electric blue suit, seated on one of the sofas. He had a cigar going and a martini with two olives in his hand. His long-legged, shapely companion was clad in a white evening gown. The Mafia pimp and his lady were about to leave the plant for the day and go out on the town.

"How's the arm?" Allegretti asked.

"Fucked up," Buck said, going to the bar and opening a metal box from which he removed a cellophane envelope containing cocaine. With his injured arm hampering him, he was having a difficult time opening the packet. The woman walked over, took the packet, and spilled its contents onto the surface of the bar. She handed him a straw. Buck's un-injured hand trembled as he bent to inhale the narcotic.

"I don't get it," Allegretti said. "You've taken worse falls than that when you were playing pro football and didn't even get a scratch."

"He thinks that news broad did it," Skyles said, going to the bar and pouring himself a glass of grapefruit juice.

"She did," Buck spat, stifling a sneeze.

Allegretti frowned and was about to say something when a noise came from down in the plant.

"Did you lock the door when you came in?" the mobster asked.

"That's the plant manager's job," Buck said, concentrating on his cocaine.

Allegretti sneered. "Lay off the nose candy, Buck, go downstairs and do your job."

The bodyguard slammed the straw down on top the bar and, with his jaw muscles rippling in anger, stormed to the door. Before he could exit, Allegretti's voice stopped him. "And watch that arm."

Without turning around, the big man continued down into the plant.

"So what are you going to do about the reporter?" Skyles asked.

Allegretti shrugged. "Right now, nothing. But I'm gonna talk to my lawyer tomorrow, have him go to court and get an—"

Buck's scream caused the pimp's words to stick in his throat. For a moment no one moved. Then Allegretti jumped up and ran across the room with an impressive speed. He pressed a switch at the corner of one of the nude paintings and the frame swung away from the wall on hinges. Inside there was a secret compartment containing weapons. The pimp pulled out two Uzis and an AK-47 assault rifle. He handed the Uzis to Skyles and the woman, keeping the assault weapon for himself. They were ready to fight a war and also prepared to kill anything that moved.

Allegretti motioned the woman to go through the door first, followed by Skyles. The Mafia pimp brought up the rear.

The area, where the laundry machines were located beneath the walkway, was in semidarkness. Like soldiers in enemy territory, the trio moved to the top of the steps.

"Buck!" Allegretti shouted.

There was no answer from below.

"What do you think happened to him?" the woman whispered.

"Maybe it's some of Chet the Jet's friends come to pay us a visit?" Skyles said with a voice that trembled.

"Whoever it is," Allegretti said, "they'd better be ready to die."

Slowly, they descended to the main floor. They could detect nothing moving in the huge building. Then they found Buck.

The sight of the muscular bodyguard stunned them into immobility. He was lying on the floor twenty feet inside the loading-bay door, which stood open. His injured arm was still in its cast and the cast was suspended in the sling. However, the rest of him looked to have been broken up with a methodical efficiency that denied explanation. His head was tilted at an odd angle, indicating that his neck had been broken. His previously uninjured left arm was bent backward at the elbow and both legs were twisted like those of a child's doll which had been run over by a truck. In death, Buck's eyes and mouth remained open, telling the tale of the horror he had experienced in the final seconds of his life.

"We'd better get the hell out of here," Ronnie Skyles said in a voice muted to a whisper by terror.

Gino Allegretti, who didn't possess an ounce more intestinal fortitude than his fellow pimp, was about to argue when the creature known as an Abo-Yorba in African myth leaped out of the shadows and grabbed the mobster. In vain, he attempted to defend himself and fired the assault rifle, accidentally stitching his black female companion with bullets. She was dead before she hit the floor.

The she-devil lifted the Mafia pimp off his feet and held him with one three-fingered hand as easily as a child toying with a puppet. She glared at him for a moment before using the razor-sharp talons of her other hand to rip his stomach open. Throwing him to the floor, she was turning to her remaining prey when she noticed the dead woman lying on the floor. The she-devil stopped.

Shocked by what he had just witnessed during a time period lasting no longer than the blink of an eye, Ronnie Skyles was unable to move. The thing that had killed Allegretti began to change into the beautiful reporter who had been there earlier. She stood over the dead woman and a tear ran down her cheek to land on the stone floor. The single drop of liquid became mixed with the dead woman's blood. A deep sigh rocked the shape-shifter's body. Then she turned toward Ronnie Skyles.

The pimp didn't hesitate. He dropped the Uzi he had been unable to fire and ran. He didn't look back as he charged through the open door out onto the loading dock. He leaped onto the parking lot surface while fumbling in his pocket for the remote control device which would unlock the doors to the Corvette and simultaneously start the engine. Yanking open the door, he stopped to see if he was being pursued.

The she-devil was just emerging from the building and was seventy-five feet away from Skyles. For a moment she hesitated, searching for him. When she saw him she unleashed a roar, which chilled the pimp to the marrow, and leaped off the loading dock toward him.

He jumped behind the wheel and yanked the sports car in gear. Flooring the accelerator, he peeled rubber, and the car bounded across the parking lot onto the deserted industrial street running behind the laundry. He fishtailed wildly when he hit the asphalt surface and struggled to bring the car back under control. He looked into his rearview mirror. His heart became trapped in his throat when the image of the she-devil filled the reflection.

Skyles pushed his foot to the floor with such force that his knee ached. The car rocketed down the street at a dangerously high speed. He expected a truck to pull from one of the driveways in the industrial area and abruptly end his escape. However, no obstructions appeared, and a quarter of a mile later, when he forced himself to look into his rearview mirror once more, the she-devil was gone.

Ronnie Skyles kept driving, but slowed down to a less suicidal speed. He kept looking back the way he had come, but there was nothing behind him but empty streets. Finally, some of the terror that had gripped him began to ebb, but he was still badly frightened. He began trembling violently and was having trouble controlling the car. But he wasn't about to stop until he'd put a lot more distance between himself and the horror he'd just left back at the Riteway Laundry.

CHAPTER 43

Larry Cole and Kate Ford were in Cole's car en route to the New Sandy's Jazz Club on Fifty-third Street in Hyde Park when the car phone rang.

"It's probably Butch checking up on me," Cole said, picking up the dash receiver.

She smiled. "Do you think he would approve of the way that his father spent the afternoon?"

Cole laughed. "I hope not." Then he added, "At least not yet."

Blackie was on the line, and it had been a long time since the chief of detectives had heard his old friend sound so grim.

"Boss, there's been an explosion at Willie's Tavern over on West Madison."

As Cole listened to the lieutenant narrate the scene of carnage and death, Kate watched the veins and muscles of her new lover's forearm bulge with tension.

"Tell the superintendent I'm on the way, Blackie," Cole said before hanging up the phone. His face was bloodless, and to Kate it was obvious that he was badly shaken by what he'd just heard.

She reached out her hand and touched his shoulder. He glanced at her and managed a smile which came out as more of a grimace. His voice was hoarse as he told her about the explosion at the state's attorney's fund-raiser. When he mentioned the names of the cops who had died, she frowned.

"Weren't they the same ones who were seated at the police table at the PAC dinner the other night?"

Cole thought for a moment. "Yeah. They were. Every cop who was there died tonight." Then a thought struck him that made him shudder. "Every cop, that is, except me."

"And yesterday Philo Coffey was killed in a mysterious explosion."

He focused his attention back on his driving. "It could be just coincidence or there might be something to it, but one thing's for sure, I'm going to find out."

"I thought you were on vacation."

He sighed. "As of five minutes ago the superintendent ordered me back to work. He wants me over at the scene of the explosion as soon as I can get there. Do you want me to drop you at Sandy's?"

"No," she responded. "Take me home. I've had enough stimulation for one day."

Jack Carlisle was in his Dragons' Lair office watching a videotape of a basketball game played that previous March between the Chicago Bulls and the New York Knicks in Madison Square Garden. The tape was being run on one of the eight full-color security monitors behind the fixer's desk. The other seven were hooked up to cameras which continuously scanned activity in the busy nightclub. Sonny Balfour sat across from Carlisle. The ex-boxer was keeping more of an eye on the security monitors than he was on the game. This was not only because it was his job to do so, but also because Carlisle had rerun this game at least twenty times since it was originally broadcast.

"Here it comes," the fixer said with the same excitement he'd displayed during each previous replay of the game.

Balfour managed to stifle a yawn and look considerably more attentive than he felt. Carlisle was riveted to the screen.

The Bulls were dressed in their black-and-red pin-striped road uniforms, the Knicks in the white of the home team. There were eight black players and two white players on the floor. Both of the white players—seven-foot three-inch Greg McDermott, the backup center, and Pete Dubcek—played for the Chicago team. Balfour had a sneaking suspicion that the Bulls' racial complement in this game was one of the main reasons why Carlisle was so fond of it. The fourth quarter was three minutes and twenty-two seconds old. The Bulls trailed by thirteen points. The New York team, considered to be superior to the Bulls, due to preseason sportswriters' rankings and their current won-loss record, was expected to coast to an easy victory. Then Pete Dubcek went into action.

On the television screen, in the midst of the giants surrounding him, the German player appeared of below average height despite his six-foot six-inch frame. His baby face and perpetual expression of innocence made him look like a kid who had been permitted to play with adults. But Dubcek was as fast and skilled on the court as any player in NBA history.

Dubcek began his run by stealing the ball from the Knicks' all-pro starting guard. Dribbling the length of the court with three Knicks in pursuit, the superstar took flight from the free throw line and jammed the ball into the hoop with one hand.

Viewing the replay, Carlisle said to Balfour, "Have you ever seen anything like that in your life?"

Sonny Balfour had been asked this same question by the fixer many times before, and each time he'd responded with a polite negative. However, the ex-pug had seen dunks like the one Dubcek had just made on the videotape a number of times in the past. Such feats had been routinely performed by the likes of Michael Jordan, Charles Barkley, Reggie Miller, and Shaquille O'Neal.

During the remaining minutes of the game, Dubcek put on such a show of offensive and defensive basketball skill that it became the subject of the Chicago ball club's advertising highlight film for the remainder of the season. The Knicks were unable to stop Dubcek and totally incapable of scoring points against him. The next time Jack Carlisle uttered a superlative concerning the play of the star guard was when Dubcek, standing eight inches shorter than the Knicks' center, rejected the bigger man's layup. The fixer muttered more to himself than Balfour that on this play Pete Dubcek seemed to hang in the air as if he were suspended from wires anchored to the ceiling.

Then Balfour interrupted: "Something's happening."

"You're damn right something is happening," Carlisle said. "Pete Dubcek is single-handedly kicking New York's ass!"

On the monitor screen, to emphasize Carlisle's words, Dubcek hit a three-point jump shot while being triple-teamed by the Knicks.

"No," Balfour insisted. "I'm talking about downstairs in the club."

Reluctantly, Carlisle tore his eyes away from the game to examine the monitors. On the one covering the entrance, he saw a highly agitated Ronnie Skyles struggling with two Dragon's Lair security guards. Turning his attention back to the March Bulls-Knicks game replay, the fixer said to Balfour, "Go down there and see what's wrong with the pimp."

A few minutes later Ronnie Skyles was sitting in a chair across the desk from Jack Carlisle. The fixer would have ordered the pimp to remain silent until he finished watching the basketball game replay. However, when Balfour brought him into the office, it was obvious that Skyles was so badly frightened he was very close to going into shock.

Shutting off the basketball game, Carlisle said to Balfour, "You'd better pour our friend here a shot of Rémy Martin before he goes completely to pieces on us."

When the ex-fighter handed the pimp a half-full brandy snifter, Skyles's hands shook so violently that he spilled most of it on his trousers and the carpet. But he did manage to get some down, and after a refill, he began to regain some control.

"So, what happened to you, Ronnie?" Carlisle asked pointedly. The fixer didn't like Mob types hanging around the Dragon's Lair. Having it labeled a Mafia hangout would be a perfect excuse for the city to revoke his very expensive licenses.

Skyles swallowed more brandy before placing the glass down on Carlisle's desk. Balfour moved forward to give him more, but the fixer stopped his assistant with an upraised palm. Then they waited.

Skyles started shaking again and was forced to place his hands between his legs and clamp his knees tightly shut to keep himself from vibrating out of the chair. His mouth opened and he attempted to speak, but no words came out. He snapped his jaws together and ground his teeth so violently that the sickening sound was quite clearly audible in the office.

"Are you on something, Skyles?" the fixer demanded.

The pimp shook his head violently from side to side and once more opened his mouth to speak. This time he managed to say, "A . . . thing got . . . into the plant . . . tonight. Gino, Buck, and the girl . . . are. . . ." Tears formed in Skyles's eyes and began running freely down his face.

Carlisle's interest was heightened considerably. Leaning forward, he asked, "Is Gino dead, Ronnie?"

The pimp began shaking again and was starting to sob. The fixer jumped up, charged around the desk, and backhanded Skyles hard across the face. This forced the pimp to pull himself together a bit faster than he'd been able to so far and say a halting, "Yes. They're . . . all . . . dead."

Skyles motioned to the empty brandy glass. Carlisle nodded to Balfour, who came forward with the cognac bottle. But the fixer only allowed the pimp one swallow before taking the liquor away from him and saying, "Ronnie, tell me about this 'thing' that killed Gino."

It took him a while, but Ronnie Skyles told Jack Carlisle and Sonny Balfour everything that he knew.

CHAPTER 44

Larry Cole watched the flames spew from the remains of the building which had once been the trendy tavern known as Willie's. The fire department had twelve pieces of equipment clogging Madison Street. They were pouring continuous streams of water from six different locations onto the conflagration. The water was turning to steam when it hit the flames, imposing a sauna-like atmosphere on the area. Slowly, the fire was being brought under control. A team of Bomb and Arson investigators were standing by preparing to sift through the wreckage when the fire was finally struck. Blackie Silvestri and Manny Sherlock had been conferring with the Bomb and Arson personnel. Now they disengaged themselves and walked over to Cole.

"This remind you of anything, boss?" Blackie asked, chewing on the tip of an unlit cigar.

"Yeah. Hell on earth," he replied.

"The Temple of Allah, Chief," Manny Sherlock volunteered. "It was one of the first cases I ever worked under your command at Area One."

Cole looked back at what was left of the burning building, which wasn't much. The memory came back to him quickly. Steven Zalkin had destroyed the former gang hangout over on Washington Park Boulevard using powerful explosives stolen from a military research facility. As Manny had said, the result of that blast looked amazingly similar to what Cole was now viewing. He waited for them to give him the rest of it.

"The arson dicks don't want to go too far out on a limb until they get a chance to sift through the debris," Blackie said, "but this definitely looks like an arson using something very similar to the stuff Zalkin used on Abdul Ali Malik and company back in ninety-one."

The parcel of land on which Willie's had been in operation only a short time before was now a blackened mass of smoldering debris. The investigators would soon be moving in to look for clues. But there was more than one type of evidence.

"Do we have a motive yet?" Cole asked.

"No," Blackie said, "but we've got a witness."

A short time later Blackie escorted the parking lot attendant, a thin pockmark-faced man named Joey Varnado, to Cole's car and placed him in the backseat. Blackie took a seat up front. Cole was behind the wheel.

After making the introductions the lieutenant said, "Joey, you want to tell the chief what you told me and Sergeant Sherlock a little while ago?"

"Sure," the attendant said in a high-pitched, almost feminine voice. "There was this guy who parked his car in the lot and went into Willie's. I remember him because he looked something like Senator Kennedy. You know the dead president's only surviving brother."

"We know, Joey," Blackie said patiently.

"Well, he was driving a Blazer and used a cane to walk. When he paid, he spoke with a thick Irish brogue that I thought was a put-on. He went into Willie's and was in there maybe thirty or forty minutes. Then he came out and went to his car. I thought he was leaving, but a few minutes later he returned to the front of the tavern, but he didn't go inside. I saw him walking around the outside of the building. Then he came back into the lot and picked up his car. He left and that was the last I saw of him. A few minutes later Willie's blew up."

Cole was impressed by the lot attendant's powers of observation. He told him this.

Varnado looked out the window and said, "I was on the job for three years, Chief. I got addicted to cocaine and was fired. Now I've got my act together, more or less."

A moment of silence ensued and then Blackie asked, "You didn't happen to get his license plate number, did you, Joey?"

"Sorry, Lieutenant, I sure didn't."

After Varnado got out of the car Blackie asked, "So what do you think, boss?"

Cole stared through the windshield at the disaster area. A joint police-fire operation had commenced to remove the bodies from the wreckage.

"First there was Philo Coffey getting blown up in the steam room of the Barristers' Club. Now this, and we know for a fact that ten high-ranking department members, who were also at the PAC affair the other night, were in Willie's at the time of the explosion. Then . . ." His voice trailed off.

"What is it?" Blackie asked.

Cole rubbed his chin. "The parking lot attendant's description of the man who was acting suspiciously fits that of the priest who was supposed to give the invocation that night before he collapsed. He was taken to the hospital, where he mysteriously vanished before he could be treated."

Now it was Blackie's turn to react. "Did you say a priest?"

"I think his name was Father Lochran. Why?"

"Right before the blast at the Barristers' Club, a white-haired priest who walked with a cane was seen hurriedly leaving the building. Coincidence?"

"Somehow I don't think it is, Blackie."

Manny hurried over to the car. Cole rolled his window down. "It just came over the wire," the sergeant said breathlessly. "Gino Allegretti was found with his gut ripped open. His girlfriend and one of his bodyguards were with him. They're also dead. Judy's over there now and she told me the pimp's wounds look a lot like the ones this morning on Chet the Jet. The medical examiner on the scene agrees with the ME who examined Collins this morning. The wounds in both cases were made by the claws of a large animal. A very large, vicious animal."

CHAPTER 45

Sven-Erik Voman was livid. Veins stood out on his forehead and neck as he screamed into the telephone, "What do you mean you don't know where she is, Dave?!"

Two big stories were breaking at the same time and his best reporter had vanished. Voman took a moment to compose himself and then said, "Okay, start with the tavern explosion and then go over to the laundry. Shoot both scenes and we'll have a studio voice-over for the nine o'clock news."

Then Dave Spurgeon said something that made the news director's night. "You've got Allegretti and his bodyguard on camera?! Forget the explosion and get in here as fast as you can. We'll be able to scoop every news beat in town with this."

Butch Cole got out of a cab in front of Paige Albritton's apartment building in Rogers Park. After paying the driver he entered the courtyard and proceeded to her second-floor apartment. Climbing the stairs, he looked down at the pool. He recalled that when he was a child he had promised his mother that he wouldn't go near it alone. Now he was a star on the varsity swimming team at the Shrine of the Little Flower High School in Detroit.

He reached the door to Paige's apartment and knocked. For a long time there was no response. Then he heard a muffled sound coming from inside.

Stepping forward, he said, "Paige, it's Butch Cole."

There came a protracted silence. Finally, the door was unlocked to open into a darkened apartment. Butch was unable to see anyone inside. He took a tentative step forward.

Once inside he heard Paige say a hoarse, "Shut the door." He still couldn't see her.

With the door closed the apartment was plunged into total darkness. He waited.

"What do you want?" she asked.

He was surprised at her harsh tone, but he had come here to check on her and he wasn't about to leave until he'd accomplished his task.

"I came to see if you were okay."

"I'm fine."

"Then why are you sitting here in the dark?"

A sigh came from the shadows in front of him, followed by a table lamp beside a sofa being switched on. Paige was sitting on the sofa. Her right hand was wrapped in a towel. She kept her head down, and her hair partially obscured her face.

Slowly, he crossed the room to stand over her. She refused to look up. He knelt down. "What happened to your hand?"

She didn't respond.

"Let me see it."

She didn't move.

He reached out and touched the towel, which was wet from the moisture of melting ice cubes. She resisted at first, but not much. He unwrapped the towel, cradling the vestiges of ice in the cloth as he placed it on the floor. When he saw her three middle fingers, he gasped. They were swollen to twice their normal size and one of them looked broken.

"Paige," he said softly, "we've got to have a doctor look at this."

Her head finally came up and she looked at him with eyes so filled with pain and anguish it tore his heart open.

He started to get to his feet, but she stopped him.

"Butch." She reached out her uninjured hand for one of his. "Could you just hold me for a moment before we go?"

"Sure," he said, finding that his own eyes were beginning to fill with tears.

He sat down on the couch and placed his arms around her. They remained like that for a long time. Finally, she said, "I like you better without green hair."

After the incident at the Riteway Laundry Company, Orga wandered aimlessly. For her attack against Chet the Jet Collins last night, and today's against Gino Allegretti, she had worn her black hooded cape. Now, walking the streets with a steady summer rain falling, she felt an agonizing remorse at the loss of her sister's life, which had been so violently snuffed out because of the Abo-Yorba's mistake.

In a park on the West Side of the city, she stopped in a deserted athletic field. Alone, she stared at the heavens through the falling rain. The sky above her was dark. The tears of the part woman/part demon mixed with nature's moisture.

Despite what she was—a being whom those she fought to protect thought of as a monster—she loved all humanity. Even those who did evil.

The Abo-Yorba were a species which had evolved aeons ago to correct an imbalance in the ecosystem in the cradle of civilization known today as the continent of Africa. Basically, nothing more was required than the survival of the fittest. Then the weaker animals began to be hunted to extinction.

Ten millennia before the dawn of mankind's recorded history, the Abo-Yorba sustained and protected a small tribe of defenseless but extraordinarily intelligent monkeys. The enemies of these apes were predators who roamed the African plains and forests then, as they do now. Their ferocity went unchallenged, and the monkeys, which would evolve into the species Homo sapiens, were easy prey. The Abo-Yorba began defending them, at no little risk to the protectors.

The two species coexisted together for thousands of years. During this evolutionary period, they progressed and, in some instances, interbred. Only female children of the Abo-Yorba species survived these occasional unions. Then mankind became more sophisticated and learned to construct devastating instruments of death to kill not only their enemies, but also themselves.

As the last of her kind, the African shape-shifter stood in the rain and came to the realization that humans didn't need her anymore. Another disturbing thought occurred to her: Perhaps she still needed them.

She was distracted by something approaching her. A number of animals were coming fast from several different directions. They were closing in rapidly to surround her.

Flipping back her hood, Orga opened her robe and permitted the image of the Abo-Yorba to descend on her.

The pack of wild dogs rushed toward her. They had detected her female scent and were attracted to it. At a distance of twenty feet they stopped and stared at her warily. There were some whimpers and a single growl, but not one of them barked. Fear washed over the pack, and they were about to flee when she extended her being to them. This essence, which she and her kind had used since the dawn of time, succeeded in communicating with them telepathically and transmitting that they had nothing to fear from her.

She reverted to her human form and walked through them and out of the park. On a rain-swept boulevard running beside the park, she flagged a passing taxi and gave the driver her address. She was going home.

CHAPTER 46

Larry Cole awoke with a start. He swung his feet to the floor and looked around frantically for any sign of the demon that had been pursuing him in the nightmare he'd been experiencing. The familiarity of his bedroom overlooking Grant Park brought him back to reality.

Slowly, he got to his feet and made his way to the bathroom. He splashed cold water on his face and examined his reflection in the mirror above the sink. "You don't look like you're coming back from a well-deserved, restful furlough."

Going back into the bedroom, he donned his robe and went into the living room. His son was asleep on the couch. Cole suppressed a frown. Paige Albritton was in the spare bedroom. Butch had brought her home after he'd taken her to the hospital. It had been necessary for the doctor who examined her to place a cast on her injured fingers.

They had been waiting for him when he walked in the door shortly after midnight. Despite her affiliation with Jack Carlisle, there was no way he could turn her away. Cole and Paige's dead fiancé, Clarence "Mack" McKinnis, had been friends in high school. Cole would have been the best man at their wedding if Mack hadn't been the victim of a serial killer. Cole would work out what they were going to do with Paige later. Right now he had a number of more pressing problems on his mind.

Going into the kitchen, Cole spooned coffee into the percolator and sat down at the table to wait for it to brew. The view from the kitchen window was east over the lake, and the sun was already coming up on what promised to be a hot, sunny day in Chicago. After the rain of yesterday, Cole was looking forward to the sunshine.

But the chief of detectives did not expect this to be a very sunny day for him personally at all.

He had handled complicated cases before. In fact, there had been a number of very involved investigations. And he'd seen it all: mass murderers, serial killers, mad scientists, monsters, maniacs, and all manner of crazies. They'd used guns, knives, explosions, flame throwers, and even electronically animated carcasses which were capable of killing human beings. Each case was as uniquely bizarre as it was different. But he'd never had two strange cases going simultaneously.

The coffee finished percolating and Cole got up, poured himself a cup, and returned to his seat with the view of the sun coming up over the lake.

He had kicked this around with Blackie last night while they were driving from Willie's to the murder scene at the Riteway Laundry. It was a long shot, but Blackie agreed with Cole that there was a definite possibility that the murder of Philo Coffey and the explosion at the fund-raiser could be connected. Coffey's death had been classified as a homicide when an autopsy revealed that the prominent attorney had died from a crushed skull before the explosion at the Barristers' Club. The presence of the white-haired Ted Kennedy look-alike at both locations indicated his possible involvement. Then everything appeared to originate at the PAC dinner. Although they were unable to come up with a motive, Cole and Blackie knew that they had to find the white-haired priest who spoke with the thick Irish brogue.

Cole sipped his coffee. Besides the mysterious explosions he also had to deal with the possibility that there was a bona fide shape-shifting monster roaming the streets of Chicago. A monster who had killed Tricia Vander Muller, Chester Collins, and Gino Allegretti in a very brutal fashion. It didn't matter to Cole that all of the victims so far were criminals. He still had the responsibility of stopping the Abo-Yorba before it could kill again. This would not be easy to do, because there was every indication that Orga Syriac was the entity he was hunting. Her being a media celebrity would make things infinitely more complicated.

Then there was Paige Albritton staying in his apartment. Cole had heard that she'd gone to work for Jack Carlisle, who was not considered a career criminal, but was a man with a less than stellar reputation, who definitely possessed criminal tendencies. First Cole would make sure that Paige severed all contact with the fixer. Then Cole would deal with Carlisle personally.

Rubbing sleep from his eyes, Butch came into the kitchen. "Morning, Dad."

"Good morning," Cole said, smiling at his son. He was proud that the young man possessed the strength of character to help Paige.

As his son shuffled to the refrigerator and removed a carton of orange juice, Cole pushed his professional problems to the back of his mind, for the time being.

Pete Dubcek was lifting weights in the basement of his north suburban home. He was booked on an 11 A.M. charter flight to Atlanta, where the 2004 American Olympic basketball team would begin training. As all the members were NBA veterans, there would only be two practices before "the Dream Team for the Third Millennium," as they had been dubbed by a sportswriter for *The New York Times*, played their first game. As Dubcek completed his sixth set of ten biceps curls with seventy-five-pound dumbbells, he remembered that the USA team's first opponent would be Italy. The Italians would field a pretty good team and would win their share of Olympic games. However, they would be no match for the Americans. Although Pete never gambled, his wife had told him that the Dream Team was favored to beat the Italians by forty-five points.

His workout completed, the star basketball player headed for the shower. Before going into the bathroom, he checked on Fuzzy. She was still asleep. He knew she wouldn't get out of bed until well after his plane was airborne en route to

Atlanta. They'd had a mild argument last night when he
asked her to come to the airport and see him off.

*"Why, Pete? Can't you find the frigging airport by your-
self?"*

But they had made love; the one area of their marriage in
which they were completely compatible. After the shower
and a shave, Pete fixed boiled eggs, toast, and coffee. He
consumed his meal alone in the kitchen of the suburban
ranch-style home, which had come with an $850,000 price
tag. As he ate he thought about Fuzzy. While he was gone
he probably wouldn't hear from her at all. Even if he called,
he'd be lucky to find her at home. She would spend most of
her time at that nightclub Jack Carlisle owned. Pete had only
been there twice. Carlisle was a gambler and Dubcek knew
that being around him would only cause trouble. He touched
his cheek where Fuzzy had scratched him in front of the
Dragon's Lair. It was almost healed. He always recovered
quickly from injuries. At least as far as his body went. His
heart was another story. But he was learning fast.

It hadn't taken long after his marriage to Fuzzy for Pete
to realize that he had made a very bad mistake. As a party
girl out on the streets having a good time, Fuzzy had no
peer. As a wife, other than the time they spent in bed, she
was a disaster. He had long ago come to the realization that
she was slowly destroying him.

His play on the basketball court had never been better. In
fact, lately, when Fuzzy pulled some stunt like staying out
all night or ridiculing him in public, he turned into a terror.
Zipping up and down the hardwood floors of the teams of
the National Basketball Association like a man possessed, he
felt that he could do anything he wanted with the roundball.

Last March, after Fuzzy had been gone from home for two
days and he'd been unable to find her, the team had a road
game in New York's Madison Square Garden. For the first
three quarters, Pete's play had been lackluster.

The coach pulled him out of the game and screamed on
national television, "Pete, what in the hell is wrong with
you?!"

Dejected and ashamed, Dubcek took a seat on the bench.

The game proceeded without him and the Knicks opened up a sizable lead. He happened to look up into the stands behind the Bulls' bench and saw a woman who looked a lot like Fuzzy. The resemblance was extraordinary, but he was certain that it was not his wife. She was seated with a man, who had his arm around her. Her head rested on his shoulder. For what seemed an eternity, Pete Dubcek was unable to take his eyes off this couple. Despite being aware that the woman was not Fuzzy, he couldn't get the image out of his head of his wife in an intimate position with another man. Suddenly, he became very, very angry.

"Dubcek!"

The coach's shout brought the star guard back to reality.

"Get back in there and let's play some ball."

What occurred in the next few minutes made history and, unbeknownst to Pete Dubcek, got Jack Carlisle extremely interested in him.

Dubcek finished eating and washed the dishes. Fuzzy didn't do housework in any form. If it wasn't for a cleaning woman coming in once a week, their luxury home would resemble a pigsty.

Starting for the front closet, where he'd placed his bags last night, he remembered that after the March game in Madison Square Garden, he was besieged by the media. But he refused to give any interviews and rushed into the visitors' locker room. Somewhat surprised at his star player's reaction after such a stellar performance, the head coach stood in for him. No explanation was given for Dubcek's refusal to meet the press. Had the truth been known, the reason the Bulls' star couldn't face the media was because he was in a rage. It was anger that had fed the frenzy he had unleashed on the court against the Knicks. His fury had not abated after the game, and he sat stonily in front of his locker staring off into space. His teammates gave him a wide berth until he calmed down.

However, for the remaining weeks of the season, Dubcek's rage returned during each game. The anger never led to fights with members of opposing teams, but resulted in him averaging a phenomenal forty-two points a game. Performances which made Piotr Dubcek, originally of Heidelberg, Germany, a living American sports legend. And it was all because of his wife.

Finally, he decided to confide the motivation for his frenzied play to his coach and a select few of his teammates. Their reaction was predictable. If the anger he felt toward Fuzzy was the reason for his exceptional play, then he needed to stay mad at her as long as he could, or at least until the end of the season.

Pete was about to let himself out of the house when he stopped for a moment and looked toward the rear of the expensive home, where Fuzzy was still sleeping. Bit by bit the love he had felt for her since the moment they met was turning to hatred. Yes, she fueled the white-hot intensity of his play on the basketball court. He only hoped that the anger he felt would never be directed at her. If it did, he would certainly kill her.

Pete Dubcek let himself out and headed for Atlanta.

CHAPTER 47

JUNE 16, 2004
8:00 A.M.

Kate Ford had difficulty falling asleep and finally gave up at about 2 A.M. Going to her study, she turned on her computer and called up the data she had accumulated on the she-devil. She wrapped her wool robe closer around her when she recalled what Larry had said about Orga Syriac being the Abo-Yorba. However, this had yet to be proven despite the computer-enhanced image and the respected Dr. Silvernail's opinion.

She read through all the data in the, to date, 150-page manuscript. As Barbara Zorin had said a few days ago, researching African myths was not Kate's usual line of investigative inquiry. She had gotten the idea from Sandra Devereaux, the owner of the New Sandy's Jazz Club.

It was the end of January and snowing heavily. On a Friday night, after the last show in which Kate had indulged her second love of blues singing Chicago style, she and Sandy were seated at one of the tables sipping brandy as the last customers drifted out into the cold night. It was at such times that the light-complexioned, voluptuous black woman, who had to be in her seventies but didn't look a day over forty, would tell strange stories. Some such tales dealt with voodoo and the occult. Sandra Devereaux was believed by many to be a voodooiene, who was capable of casting spells and "fixing" her enemies. Of one thing Kate was certain: The jazz club owner could tell a story with the skill of the most gifted novelist.

This winter night's tale was not about voodoo or Sandy's life in New Orleans before she came to Chicago in the mid-sixties, but of a small southern town called Diggstown, Mississippi, a settlement founded by Sandy's great-grandfather Isaac Diggs, a man who had lived to be 110 years old. The town, which was self-sufficient and had prospered as an almost exclusively African American settlement in the midst of one of the most bigoted societies in history, was protected by a beautiful woman who could turn herself into a demon, called an Abo-Yorba, at will.

"Diggstown was started by Isaac Diggs before the Second World War," Sandy told Kate. "At that time, in most parts of the South, black folks were living in conditions which were only a shade better than had been the case during slavery. There were few, if any, educational or economic opportunities for us. Most were sharecroppers working white-owned farms for a pittance. So Isaac founded Diggstown."

Benny, Sandy's bartender and ex-husband, let the last customer out and turned off the marquee and the window lights in front of the club. Sandy's had been reconstructed as a replica of Rick's Café Americain from the Humphrey Bogart movie *Casablanca*. This remodeling job was necessitated after Jonathan Gault destroyed the former Sandy's five years before. Sandra Devereaux walked with a stiff gait due to her legs being broken during Gault's attack.

"At first, nobody thought the small settlement could make it, but Isaac, who had been born a slave, was intelligent, innovative, and refused to accept anything less than excellence for any aspect of the town's development. And slowly, from what had once been a swamp, rose the phenomenon of Diggstown."

Sandy's eyes glistened with tears of pride as she continued. "It had paved streets at a time when most back roads in the South were of dirt or gravel. It had its own school and church, and every building was electrically powered from an independent plant. Isaac had taught himself horticulture and animal husbandry. He made sure the crops were properly rotated and the livestock were fed an appropriate diet. They made money and prospered. New buildings went up and the town began expanding. They were paid a visit by the county sheriff followed by the Klan. Then the she-devil came to help them."

Kate decided to take a break from her labors and went into the kitchen of her town house to make a cup of tea. After placing the kettle on the stove to boil, she went to the window and looked out on what promised to be a beautiful summer day. There was a garden growing in the backyard, and after yesterday's rain, her roses were beginning to bloom. Making sure the flame under the teapot wasn't too high, she walked outside.

The day was perfect and the air particularly fresh after yesterday's rain. She smiled when she remembered how she'd spent her afternoon with Larry Cole on *Kate's Folly*. She hoped he would call her today, but she'd understand if he didn't. Being called back to duty at such a critical time would undoubtedly keep him very busy.

Kate knelt on the grass and examined the bulbs of her roses. They were coming along beautifully. She noticed the sharp thorns protruding from the stalks. They reminded her of the Abo-Yorba. Beauty and the beast coexisting in the same entity.

The gate to her yard opened behind her. Casually, she turned around to see who was there. Her heart raced and fear froze her motionless when Orga Syriac closed the gate behind her, smiled, and said, "Good morning, Kate. I'd like to talk to you."

Orga could immediately sense Kate's fear. The she-devil allowed a feeling of goodwill to descend over her. She then extended this feeling to the woman kneeling on the other side of the garden. Kate remained rigid with terror. Orga realized that Kate knew what she was and that possession of such knowledge effectively blocked the she-devil's attempt to telepathically alleviate her fear. The investigative journalist's intellect and willpower were too strong for the Abo-Yorba's psychic influence. But if she couldn't appeal to Kate's emotions, the she-devil could achieve her objective by appealing to the thing that made Kate Ford what she was: curiosity.

"Are you still investigating the African myth known as the Abo-Yorba?" Orga asked.

Kate didn't answer, but remained in the same rigid pose she'd been in since she first set eyes on her visitor.

Orga did not advance toward Kate for fear of further frightening her. In a soft voice the shape-shifter said, "I didn't come here to harm you, Kate. I actually need your help. In exchange for your assistance in helping me destroy an evil organization, I will tell you everything there is about the Abo-Yorba."

Kate still didn't move; however, something in her face changed. There was a slight knitting of her eyebrows and her lids narrowed slightly.

Now Orga chanced a step forward. Kate tensed, but still didn't move. The shape-shifter took another step. Kate relaxed a bit, but there was still tension in her posture.

Orga came within arm's reach of her and said, "I can hear your teapot whistling. Shall we go inside?"

Slowly, Kate got to her feet, turned around, and led the
she-devil into her town house.

Sonny Balfour picked the lock on the front door of Paige
Albritton's apartment and let himself in. He had rung the
bell repeatedly and knocked for five minutes without receiving any answer. Once inside he remained by the front door
and called her name. It wouldn't be smart to go roaming
around the blonde's apartment without being announced. She
still had a couple of her dead fiancé's guns.

Balfour waited awhile longer before starting a careful
search of the one-bedroom apartment. A few minutes later
he returned to the living room and picked up the telephone
extension on an end table. He spied a towel on the floor and
picked it up. It was still slightly damp. As he waited for Jack
Carlisle to answer, the ex-boxer put his foot up on the beige
brocade couch and polished his shoe.

"Hello," the fixer answered.

"She's gone."

"Maybe she just stepped out."

Balfour put the other foot up and began working on that
shoe. He ignored the stain he was leaving on the fabric.

"Yeah, but I don't think she'll be coming back soon. There
are no toiletries or toothbrush in the bathroom, and a couple
of the drawers in the bedroom were pulled out and empty. I
also checked the locked drawer where she keeps her guns.
Although the padlock was on it, I was able to open it. It's
also empty. I'd say we won't be seeing her again for some
time."

There was no immediate response from the fixer. Finally,
he said, "With Allegretti dead, I won't be able to find the
woman I need in time. Now that Paige is gone, I'll have to
change my plans completely." Carlisle paused. "Okay, get
back here as soon as you can. We need to get in touch with
Fuzzy."

Tossing the dirty towel back on the floor, Balfour took a
final look around before leaving.

CHAPTER 48

Sister Mary Louise Stallings was making out an invoice for textbooks for Our Lady of Peace School. She remembered that Father Phil also wanted her to order replacement hymnbooks for the church. That meant she would have to make a count of how many serviceable hymnbooks they still had on hand. For that she would have to go over to the church.

She exited the school and crossed the courtyard. She entered the side door of the church and was crossing to the hymnal closet when she heard sobbing. She stopped.

The lights were out, and the sunlight filtering through the stained-glass windows cast the interior of the cathedral-sized building in shadow. She squinted and managed to see Father Lochran kneeling at the altar rail. He was the source of the crying she had heard. Slowly, she moved down the center aisle toward him.

The priest's head was cradled in his folded arms and his back was bowed into a curl. While he cried, his shoulders shook. Sister Mary Louise stopped twenty feet behind him. She didn't know what to do.

Father Lochran's head came up and he stared at the altar through eyes blurred by tears. His voice shook with emotion as he said, "Lord, I know your will must be done and that I am your servant. But the road on which you have placed my feet is rugged and filled with thorns and briars which rend the flesh of my soul."

Sister Mary Louise was impressed by the poetry and fervor of the older man's prayer, but she was concerned that he was in such agony. But she didn't feel it would be right to interrupt his communication with the Almighty. Then something bizarre occurred.

"Yes, Lord," the crying man said. "I understand." He paused. "But do all of them have to die?"

Sister Mary Louise Stallings's blood ran cold. Slowly, and as quietly as she could, she began backing down the center aisle away from him.

"Of course, Lord," he continued. "I was told by your emissary many years ago that you had something important for me to do." He again paused. "Yes, yes. I understand completely. You can count on me." Then, he wiped the tears from his face with the back of his hand, chuckled softly, and said to the empty altar in front of him, "Thank you. I will try to live up to the standards I have maintained in the past."

Sister Mary Louise reached the side door of the church and attempted to let herself out as quietly as possible. But the church door was heavy, and when she attempted to close it she lost control. Although the door didn't bang shut, it made a loud enough noise to attract the kneeling man's attention. By the time he turned around, the nun was gone; however, he had a sneaking suspicion who had been there. Been there spying on him.

Larry Cole and Blackie Silvestri pulled into the parking lot of the Human Development Institute. As they got out of the car they noticed a closed-circuit television camera tracking their movements. They walked to the entrance, where an intercom was positioned beside locked glass doors. Blackie pushed the red button on the intercom panel and waited.

"Welcome to the Human Development Institute," an artificial-sounding female voice said cordially. "May I help you?"

"I'm Chief Cole and this is Lieutenant Silvestri of the

Chicago Police Department. We have an appointment to see Dr. Gilbert Goldman."

"Please come in."

The door clicked open and they entered. After passing through the second security checkpoint they were being escorted to Dr. Goldman's office by an armed security guard when Blackie quipped to Cole, "What are they guarding in this joint, the crown jewels?"

They entered the office to find the doctor and his severe-mannered executive secretary, Virginia Daley, waiting for them. The policemen were offered coffee, tea, or water, which they declined. Cole and Blackie waited for the director of the Human Development Institute to get down to cases.

When Cole had arrived at his office earlier there was a message waiting for him from the superintendent stating that this Dr. Gilbert Goldman of HDI possessed information believed to be vital to investigations currently being conducted by the CPD into the explosions at the Barristers' Club and Willie's Tavern. Cole had never heard of this Human Development Institute, but if the superintendent wanted him to talk to Goldman then he would. Now Cole and Blackie were about to find out what the HDI director had to tell them.

"I'd like to thank you gentlemen for responding so promptly," Goldman began solemnly. "I have asked Ms. Daley to sit in with us not only for the purpose of providing a record of this meeting, but also in case there might be something that she can add to the information I am about to disclose to you."

Cole and Blackie didn't comment. They noticed that Virginia Daley had opened a notebook and written down Goldman's comments in shorthand for the purpose of "providing a record" of the meeting.

Goldman cleared his throat, straightened his glasses, and continued. "A few days ago one of our researchers mysteriously disappeared. He's been acting strange lately and developed an odd fixation. He has delusions of being a Catholic priest."

Larry Cole and Blackie Silvestri displayed no visible reaction to this revelation. Dr. Goldman was obviously disconcerted by the flat, unemotional stares of the two cops. Virginia Daley decided to step in and assist her boss.

"Doctor, perhaps if I provided the officers with a bit more information concerning our operative's background they might understand our dilemma a bit better."

Dr. Goldman, appearing a bit perplexed, nodded his approval. Blackie Silvestri removed a small notebook from his pocket, opened it, and wrote on a blank page the words "priest" and "operative." Behind each he placed exaggerated question marks.

"Our operative's name is Thomas Kelly," she began in crisply efficient tones. "He has been employed by the Human Development Institute for all of his adult life. Some years ago he was seriously injured while engaged in a research project in the Deep South. This injury resulted in his not only being forced to walk with a cane for the rest of his life, but also having periodic mental problems."

Cole and Blackie still made no comment; however, the lieutenant placed a second question mark behind the word "operative" in his notebook.

"Mr. Kelly has always been deeply religious," she continued. "Possibly this was because he was raised in a Catholic orphanage and never knew his parents. At times he was fanatic about his faith, and he has been known to impersonate clerics in the past."

Blackie added the word "impersonate" to his list.

Dr. Goldman interrupted Virginia Daley and said impatiently, "We have good reason to believe that Thomas Kelly posed as a Catholic priest named James Lochran at the PAC dinner the other night. We also have reason to believe that Thomas Kelly, assuming the identity of this Father Lochran, was directly responsible for the explosion at the Barristers' Club and the state's attorney's fund-raiser last night. We are willing to provide you with information to assist you in apprehending Thomas before there is any further loss of life."

Cole finally responded. "I appreciate the information you've given us so far. It fits with what we've already uncovered concerning the explosions. But there are a couple of things Lieutenant Silvestri and I would like to clear up."

Goldman and Virginia Daley exchanged glances.

"Perhaps you could tell us what it is that the Human Development Institute actually does?"

Goldman graced Cole with a chilly smile. "We do a number of things, Chief Cole. Primarily, our mission is to study the human condition worldwide and come up with ways to improve that condition for all humanity."

"And Thomas Kelly conducted such studies?"

"Let us say that he assisted in them," Goldman replied. "Our research personnel are professionals with advanced degrees in history, anthropology, sociology, and political science to name just a few. Our work has been studied at prestigious academic institutions around the world, and the United States government has incorporated our recommendations into a number of public programs."

"Could you tell us exactly what Thomas Kelly's area of expertise is?" Cole questioned.

Goldman looked at his secretary, who responded, "Mr. Kelly pursued a number of academic disciplines and has earned advanced degrees in several of them, including a master's in theology from Notre Dame."

"Did he spend any time in the military?"

"No," Goldman said. "His crippled leg exempted him from service."

"So where did he learn so much about explosives?" Cole asked.

Without flinching, Goldman said, "I have no idea."

"Then why do you think he had anything to do with what occurred at the Barristers' Club and Willie's?"

Goldman locked eyes with Cole. "Kelly fits the description of the man suspected in both bombings."

Cole smiled. "How do you know that, Dr. Goldman? We haven't released the description of the suspect to the press."

Goldman sighed and said with annoyance, "Chief Cole, the Human Development Institute has many sources of information. We also have any number of resources we can call upon for support, including your police superintendent, the mayor, and, if necessary, the president."

Cole's smile never altered. "Then we have something in

common Doctor, as I can call on those same resources myself."

"Excuse me, gentlemen," Virginia Daley interrupted, "but
I don't think that this is getting us anywhere." She removed
a manila envelope from the attaché case beside her chair and
handed it to Cole. "In there you will find all the pertinent
information we have on Thomas Kelly."

Cole opened the envelope. There was a single page of data
containing nothing more than Kelly's vital statistics. No date
of birth was listed. On the reverse side of the page was a
composite sketch, which vaguely resembled Senator Ted
Kennedy.

"You don't have a photograph of Kelly in your personnel
files?" Cole asked.

"No," Goldman replied smugly. "One of Thomas's pho-
bias is that he is extremely camera shy."

"Could you tell us what he was working on for the Institute before he had his breakdown and started killing people?"

"I don't think that will be of any relevance to your case."

"Why don't you let us be the judge of that?" Cole said.

"I'm sorry," Goldman pronounced, "but that information
is confidential."

Cole looked at Blackie, who rolled his eyes in exasperation. The two cops got to their feet. "Thank you for your
time, Doctor. And a good day to you, Ms. Daley."

"There's one more thing," Goldman said. "We need to be
notified of the progress of your investigation in the search
for Thomas Kelly. Ms. Daley will give you a number to
call."

"That won't be necessary, Doctor," Cole said, heading for
the door. "That information is confidential."

When the two cops were gone, Virginia Daley said to her
boss, "Were you surprised by his arrogance?"

"Not at all. Cole is everything he's reported to be. He'll
find Thomas for us. Then we'll take him away from our
esteemed chief of detectives."

CHAPTER 49

This is monstrous," Kate Ford said with a mixture of disbelief and fascination as Orga Syriac told her about the Human Development Institute's sordid history.

"The concept of HDI," Orga explained, "goes back to pre-Civil War days, when it was known as the American Investment and Security Consortium. The Consortium was a privately funded company founded by a group of wealthy men who wanted to maintain a certain status quo in the United States. At the time, this country was radically split over the issue of slavery. The Consortium examined the situation and decided that the continuation of forced Negro servitude would serve the best interests of the businessmen they represented. Based on the information they possessed at the time, which was primitive and grossly inaccurate by today's standards, they opposed the election of Abraham Lincoln and backed the secessionist movement in the South. When the Civil War began, they supported the Confederacy, which resulted in nearly destroying the Consortium and all of its backers.

"After the war, the organization which had been known as the American Investment and Security Consortium went underground, but it was rumored that John Wilkes Booth was one of their operatives. Booth probably knew very little, if anything, about his superiors.

"In the post–Civil War world they rebuilt their operational

apparatus. Having learned from their mistakes of the past, they became a great deal more intelligence-minded. That led them into the world of academia."

Kate got up from the kitchen table, where she and Orga were seated. Going to the stove, she picked up the teapot and refilled their cups. Returning to her seat, she realized that she was no longer afraid of Orga Syriac. She was also aware that she was in no danger from the entity known as the Abo-Yorba.

Orga continued her story. "By the turn of the century the consortium was headquartered in a brownstone near Gramercy Park in New York. They initiated studies into the contemporary political, economic, racial, social, and educational conditions in America and began making predictions on where the country was going based on where it had been. As a purely academic pursuit it had merit; however, the Consortium decided to act directly on the information they had obtained. They began to manipulate the future. To change it for the benefit of the rich, elite few who supported them."

With ever-increasing horror and the realization that what her guest was telling her was true, Kate listened. This Consortium, which became the Human Development Institute after World War II, not only manipulated governments all over the world, but also nurtured conflicts leading to war. However, what Kate found most abhorrent about the operation of the HDI was its interference in and manipulation of the lives of not only individuals, but entire societies and races of people.

This interference was the reason the entity known as the Abo-Yorba had come to Chicago. She was going to destroy the Human Development Institute.

Kate looked away for a moment. She thought furiously and then said, "How can I help you?"

"I need to get inside the Institute," Orga said. "I can use my job at WGN to do that, but they can put me off indefinitely. However, I have an idea."

Kate listened. When Orga finished, the investigative journalist admitted to herself that her new friend's plan had merit and might just work.

"When do you want to start?" Kate asked.

"Today. Within a few days Dr. Goldman will be eager for an audience. Then he'll let me inside and lead me right to the place where I can destroy the evil that has caused so much anguish and pain in this world."

"I have one request to make of you," Kate said.

"What?"

"Could you show me the Abo-Yorba?"

Orga smiled. "If you wish."

The image of the beautiful black woman intensified and appeared to glow momentarily before darkening and being replaced by the she-devil. Kate was fascinated by what she was witnessing. The Abo-Yorba remained for only a moment and then was gone, replaced once more by Orga Syriac.

Now Kate Ford understood.

Jack Carlisle and Sonny Balfour entered Orga Syriac's condominium building on South Lake Shore Drive. The doorman on duty looked up from watching a twelve-inch portable television. His face was a mass of scar tissue and his nose was crooked from having been repeatedly broken. When he saw Balfour he grinned and said, "Look what the cat drug in. How's it going, Sonny?"

"Pretty good, Flipper. How've you been?"

The doorman raised his arms in a gesture intended to encompass the spacious lobby and answered, "Welcome to paradise. At least it keeps me in beer and cigarettes."

Balfour nodded. "This is my boss. Jack Carlisle, meet Karl 'Flipper' McBride. Was a pretty good middleweight in his day. How many fights did you have, Flip?"

"Seventy-five," the doorman said, eyeing Balfour's companion warily. The fixer's reputation had preceded him.

"I've got a little proposition for you, Flipper," Balfour said. The ex-boxer was obviously punchy. His brain was too bruised to accept an offer from the fixer. For his trouble, Jack Carlisle might end up with a broken jaw. But Sonny Balfour was an old friend of the boxer turned doorman.

"What kind of proposition?" Flipper asked suspiciously.

"Isn't there someplace we can go and talk?" Balfour said.

"Not while I'm on duty. I gotta watch the lobby."

Carlisle flashed his characteristic grin. "Why don't I wait in the car and let you two guys renew old acquaintances?" Turning, he headed for the exit. Stopping at the revolving doors leading out to the street, Carlisle paused and said, "It was nice meeting you, Flipper. I'm sure we'll meet again."

Balfour remained in the lobby with Flipper McBride less than ten minutes. When he came out, he slid into the driver's seat of the fixer's Cadillac and said, "He'll do it for a couple of hundred bucks. He's got a crush on this Syriac woman and turned me down flat at first, but I convinced him."

"Can he be trusted?" Carlisle asked.

Balfour put the car in gear. "Not really, but Flipper and I go back a lot of years. He'll play ball, as long as he gets his money."

"Good," the fixer said.

CHAPTER 50

JUNE 16, 2004
11:02 A.M.

Larry Cole and Blackie Silvestri left the mayor's office on the fifth floor of City Hall and returned to their police car, parked on the west side of the building. They didn't comment about their meeting with the Windy City's chief executive until they were in the car rolling north on LaSalle Street.

"That didn't give us much more to go on than we already have," Blackie said. The lieutenant was driving the car and had remained silent during their interview with the mayor.

Cole was looking out the passenger-side window at the

sites of the Chicago Loop. "You're an optimist, Blackie. Actually, the mayor didn't give us anything. He doesn't know what happened to Spurgeon's camera after the strobe light went out, he didn't see what happened to Tisha Vander Muller, and he couldn't tell us anything about Orga's movements inside the building at all."

"At least we're all going to get awards for what we did."

"Great," Cole responded with a pronounced lack of enthusiasm. "Head up to the WGN studios. Now is as good a time as any to interview our star reporter."

"That was good coverage of the prostitute murder on Forty-third Street, and it looks like Orga Syriac was the last reporter who ever interviewed the late Gino Allegretti," Cole said to Sven-Erik Voman.

The chief of detectives and Blackie were seated in the news director's office. Initially, the giant Swede had been happy to see the cops and even talkative about the success of his new reporter. But he'd been in the information-gathering business too long not to come to the quick realization that the two cops weren't here to simply pay a social call. They were after something.

Guardedly, Voman said, "I think that what happened with Orga was simply beginner's luck. She was at the right place at the right time to get that last interview with the mobster. It was too bad she wasn't around later after he was killed. We could have hooked the two segments together into quite an exclusive."

To keep the conversational tone of the meeting going, Blackie asked, "I was thinking the same thing, Sven. What did she do, go off duty or something?"

Voman smiled at the lieutenant. "Yeah, Blackie. Or something."

The cops could tell that this wasn't going to be as easy as they had thought. They decided to press on without making it official. At least not yet.

"Could you tell us how Orga Syriac managed to select Allegretti to interview, Sven?" Cole said.

The news director was about to provide another evasive response when he looked out his office window and saw his star personality crossing the parking lot. "Tell you what, Larry," Voman said, "why don't you ask her yourself?"

Cole and Blackie followed Sven's gaze to see Orga Syriac approaching the entrance to the studio. Cole was surprised to see Kate Ford with her. Behind them a large truck pulled into the lot.

The Mack truck had been stolen from a roadside diner parking lot in Calumet City, Illinois, off of Interstate 94, an hour before. It contained loads of chilled strawberries and lettuce intended for the supermarkets of the city. The only thing that the bewildered truck driver had been able to tell the Illinois state trooper dispatched to investigate the theft was that he had stopped for a late breakfast, and when he returned, the truck and trailer were gone.

The trooper asked if anything out of the ordinary had happened after the driver parked his rig or while he was in the diner. He thought for a moment and then said, "Well, there was this white-haired guy with an Irish accent who was leaving just as I was going in the diner. He said something about what a beauty my truck was. I thought he was joking, because there's nothing at all pretty about my rig. It's a big, ugly truck with a humongous grille. It's more of a tank than a road vehicle. Could probably knock a building down without too much trouble."

The trooper thought about what the driver said before deciding that it had no relevance to the truck theft. He left any mention of the white-haired man with the Irish accent out of his report.

Now the giant truck and connected trailer were parked at the edge of the WGN studio parking lot. Its engine was running and through the windshield the driver, wearing dark glasses, was visible. He was in his sixties and had white hair. He was waiting. Waiting for Orga Syriac—the woman he knew to be the she-devil—and Kate Ford to enter the building and join Larry Cole. Then the man impersonating Father James Lochran planned to ram the building.

As the driver from whom this massive vehicle was stolen had told the state police, the truck had the power of a tank.

That factor, along with one of Joseph Silk's infernal devices rigged to explode on contact attached to the truck's bumper, would effectively turn the stolen vehicle into a guided missile on wheels.

Now the priest impersonator made the sign of the cross, said a silent prayer for the souls of the lives he was about to take, and put the truck in gear. Slowly, it began to roll across the parking lot toward the windows where Sven-Erik Voman's office was located.

When the two women entered the office, Larry Cole took one look at Kate Ford's face and knew that she was hiding something. He looked at Orga, whose expression was non-committal. A bond had been established between the two women. Cole didn't like this development at all.

"Come in, ladies," Sven-Erik said, getting to his feet. "We were just discussing something which you both might find interesting." The news director looked at Cole. Both the chief of detectives and Blackie had gotten to their feet when the ladies entered. Now Voman added, "Wouldn't you agree with what I said about them finding it interesting, Larry?"

Cole managed a smile, but made no comment. He again glanced in Kate's direction. She looked away. He looked at Orga once more. The gaze she gave him chilled him to the marrow. Voman stepped in to play host.

"Ms. Ford, I haven't had the opportunity to meet you, but your reputation in journalism circles is quite stellar. I understand that you and Orga will be working on a project together."

They took seats; however, Orga remained standing. Turning, she looked out the windows of Voman's office. Cole was the first to realize that the beautiful reporter was still standing. He turned to see what she was staring at just as she shouted, "Everybody get out of here now!"

The priest impersonator locked the wheel in place with an antitheft device. Using a snow brush he'd found in the rear storage compartment of the truck cab, he depressed the pedal partway to the floor and shifted into second gear. The gigantic vehicle continued to roll toward the building. When it reached ten miles an hour, the white-haired man opened the door and stepped onto the running board. Displaying amazing agility for a man with a bad leg, he leaped to the ground, landed on his good leg, and managed to remain on his feet. The trailer swept past him, continuing to accelerate toward the studio building.

Without stopping to admire his handiwork, he limped away.

The occupants of the office began moving the instant they recognized the rapidly approaching danger. Orga was the first and the quickest. She grabbed a stunned Kate Ford by the shoulders and shoved her backward through Sven-Erik Voman's open office door. The investigative journalist was propelled across the wide external corridor to land hard against the opposite wall. She struck her back against the flat surface, knocking the wind out of her. Dazed, Kate slid down into a sitting position.

Cole, Blackie, and Sven-Erik Voman were rushing toward the door as fast as they could. Orga stood beside the exit, reaching to assist the news director, then the police lieutenant out in much the same violent manner that she had done with Kate Ford. But the truck reaching the point of impact was imminent and there was simply no more time.

Cole reached Orga just as the truck made contact with the building and the device that Father James Lochran had attached to the front bumper detonated.

The antitheft device keeping the truck on course was not intended for the task which Father Lochran had employed it for. The dynamic pressure of the steering mechanism loosened the device's hold on the wheel, which forced the huge vehicle off target. The truck did strike the building; however, the main force of the explosive was directed to another area of the brick structure, inside of which an empty studio was located. The building was severely damaged by the collision and resulting blast, but Larry Cole's and Orga Syriac's lives were spared.

*   *   *

Cole found himself floating in a black void, where there was
no light, sound, gravity, or substance. He couldn't remember
how he'd gotten there, but he realized that only a short time
ago, which could be measured in nanoseconds or aeons, he
had been someplace else. A place where he belonged. A
place he wanted desperately to return to.

Somewhere in the back of his mind the realization dawned
that if he stayed in this place an instant longer he would
remain there forever. He began struggling to free himself.

The office was covered with debris. The acoustical tile ceiling had been blown to pieces, the bookshelves and the books
they contained had been wrenched from the walls, and the
windows, curtains, and blinds had imploded into the room.
The television studio, at the point where Sven-Erik Voman's
office and the vacant, damaged studio were located, was open
to the sky. The door from the office into the corridor, through
which Kate Ford, Blackie Silvestri, and the news director had
managed to escape, was completely blocked with plastic and
heavy cinder blocks.

As sirens became audible signaling the approach of emergency vehicles, there was movement in the destroyed office.
A figure rose from the wreckage. It moved quickly to the
spot where Larry Cole's body was covered with the detritus
from the explosion. With a pair of immensely strong appendages sporting three taloned fingers, the Abo-Yorba
reached down and pulled the policeman from his makeshift
grave.

Cole was still unconscious as she cradled him in her arms.
Then she carried him through the breach in the wall out onto
the lawn surrounding the studio. She staggered slightly as
she laid him on the ground. A wave of dizziness swept over
her, her knees buckled, and she almost passed out. Two police cars and an ambulance screamed into the WGN lot. The
she-devil knew she had to get out of sight before they saw
her. She started back toward the large hole in the studio wall
when Cole's voice stopped her.

"Orga, wait."

The she-devil turned to look at him. Their eyes—his human, hers belonging to a near extinct species—locked. Then she went back into the studio just as the police cars and the ambulance skidded to a stop.

CHAPTER 51

JUNE 16, 2004
1:50 P.M.

Sister Mary Louise Stallings was drinking coffee in the rectory dining room. The television set was on, but she wasn't paying it the slightest attention. Instead, she was staring at a statue of Our Lady of Peace that was mounted on a pedestal in the alcove. In a sense she was praying, but not in a traditional manner. She was silently communicating with the image of the Blessed Virgin, attempting to decide what she was going to do about Father James Lochran.

It would be a great deal simpler if she could come out and confide her misgivings to Father Phil. But she had nothing of any substance to tell him, and the pastor of Our Lady of Peace was the type of man who rarely saw the bad in others. This was not to imply that the nun thought Phil Cisco to be weak or indecisive, because he certainly was not. Perhaps the youth center director, a good-natured, immensely strong man of seventy-four named Jim Patton, had best characterized him when he called the pastor "Mr. See No Evil." This nickname was applied after the priest had permitted members of the Insane Lords street gang to use the center despite the fact that they terrorized the Washington Park Boulevard area with their violence. However, the nun had to admit that this display of tolerance by Father Phil had yielded positive results. Although the Insane Lords still postured and wore their gang colors in the community, they spent the majority of their time engaged in sporting activities at the youth center, and Father Phil had even gotten a few of them to attend occasional Sunday masses.

Sister Mary Louise was proud of the young pastor's success with the street gang, but she realized that they were only a bunch of kids attempting to survive in an urban cesspool. She was sure that the opportunity Father Phil had given them and the genuine kindness he displayed were something extremely rare in their lives. Father James Lochran was another story.

The nun finished her coffee but did not take her eyes off the statue of Our Lady of Peace. With each encounter she had with the elderly priest, the more uneasy he made her. But what did she have that she could take to Father Phil without making it appear that she'd been spying on their guest?

First she had entered his room while he was asleep, and then she'd eavesdropped on his prayers. Despite her belief that he possessed explosives in the rectory and that in his prayers he talked about people dying, she knew that Father Phil would find a way to either explain away her fears or dismiss them altogether.

The situation comedy rerun that was playing on the dining-room television was interrupted and an off-screen announcer's voice said, "Please stand by for a special news bulletin."

Sister Mary Louise turned to look at the screen just as a thin young man with dark hair was shown. A black plume of smoke billowed into the sky behind him. The nun sighed. Another disaster had struck the Windy City.

"In a freak accident, which occurred only moments ago, a stolen truck rammed into the WGN studio building on the city's North Side," the reporter began. "No one was seriously injured and the driver escaped. Chicago police chief of detectives Larry Cole and lieutenant Blackie Silvestri were in the building at the time of the accident."

The scene switched to take in a tall black man walking

slowly toward a fire department ambulance. The nun experienced a momentary despair when she recognized Larry Cole, whom she had known for years and who had once helped her when she was in a great deal of trouble. Her anguish eased when she noticed that the bruised and battered cop was able to walk without assistance.

As the announcer continued the narrative of the strange accident, Sister Mary Louise suddenly realized what she could do about her dilemma concerning Father James Lochran. With Cole having been involved in the accident she would wait a day or two. Then she would pay him a condolence call, during which she would bring up Our Lady of Peace's strange houseguest.

Larry Cole, Blackie Silvestri, Kate Ford, and Sven-Erik Voman were treated at Illinois Masonic Hospital for minor bumps and bruises before being released. To everyone's amazement, with the exception of Cole and Kate Ford, Orga Syriac had required no treatment at all despite her being trapped in a room that had been completely destroyed in the catastrophic incident. As of 5:00 P.M. on the sixteenth of June, 2004, the Chicago Police Department had classified what had occurred at the WGN studio as a traffic accident, although the evidence indicated otherwise.

In the hospital waiting room Butch Cole, Paige Albritton, Manny Sherlock, and Judy Daniels stood by exhibiting noticeable anxiety. They were relieved when their injured friends ambled slowly out of the treatment area.

Butch rushed up to his father and embraced him.

"How's it going, champ?" Cole said. "Shouldn't you be out enjoying your summer vacation instead of hanging around here?"

Paige stood behind Butch. Now she moved forward and said, "What happened today, Larry?"

"I'm not sure. One minute we were sitting in the news director's office and the next the building came down on top of us."

"We've found out a thing or two while you were being treated, boss," Judy said. "The truck was stolen from

Calumet City. Manny talked to the driver, who lives out in South Chicago. He wasn't able to tell us much that wasn't contained in the state police report. We located a cable repair truck driver who was working near the studio and saw the truck pull into the parking lot. He noticed it because the trailer was a refrigeration unit and he couldn't figure out what could be delivered to a TV studio cold. He managed to catch a glimpse of the driver." She flipped open the pocket note-book she held in her hand. "He had thick white hair, a fleshy face, and was wearing sunglasses. The cable repairman couldn't tell us much at all about what he was wearing."

Cole turned to look at Blackie, who was standing nearby. The driver Judy described fit the general description of the man who was missing from the Human Development Insti-tute. Blackie's only reaction was a raised eyebrow.

Judy concluded her report. "The cable man didn't see any-thing else until he heard the truck crash into the building. This was followed by an explosion. We're still sifting through the wreckage, but there's not a lot of the truck left. From the looks of that place you guys are lucky to be alive."

"Okay," Cole said with a fatigued sigh. "There's not a lot more we can do tonight. We'll take a closer look at every-thing tomorrow."

Slowly, the survivors of the WGN studio disaster walked out of the hospital.

Activity at the Dragon's Lair nightclub was at its usual fre-netic, crowded level. Fuzzy Dubcek, dressed in a sleeveless blouse with a plunging neckline and skintight slacks, had arrived at four o'clock. Now it was after five and she hadn't left the dance floor in over an hour. She had worn out two partners and was now taking a third to the limits of exhaus-tion.

Up in his office Jack Carlisle, accompanied by Sonny Bal-four, watched the star basketball player's wife's frantic gy-rations with interest.

"Have you ever seen anyone dance like her?" the fixer said.

"No," Balfour responded, "but if she ever really learned

how to dance and did anything else than jump around like somebody stuck a live wire up her ass, she'd be dangerous."

The fixer laughed. "What are you saying, Sonny? White folks can't dance?"

Without blinking an eye the ex-boxer responded, "Sure they can. Travolta and that chick that stood in for Jennifer Beals in *Flashdance* prove that." Balfour pointed at the monitor, where Fuzzy was visible doing her thing with a fourth partner. "I don't know what Fuzzy's doing, but it sure as shit ain't dancing."

"You've got a point," the fixer said more to himself than his companion. "Well, she won't be doing much dancing for a while anyway. Do you know what to do?"

"Yeah."

Carlisle hesitated a moment longer, continuing to stare at the monitor screen. There was a cold feeling in the pit of his gut. The fixer was frightened. If he hadn't been in complete control of his emotions, the building terror would have taken over. However, he liked it like this. The bigger the game the higher the stakes; the higher the stakes the greater the risk. And Carlisle wouldn't have it any other way.

"Okay," the fixer said, "we've got to make sure that nobody can connect her disappearance to us or the club."

"I've got all that covered," Balfour said. "Our little funky chicken down there is going to get very drunk tonight, thanks to a little added something that will be placed in her drinks. When she starts falling down all over the place, a couple of our girls are going to put her in a taxi out front. No one will be around to later tell the cops anything except that it was an unmarked, dark-colored Ford with livery plates. When Fuzzy wakes up she'll be out on the Indiana farm with our friend Ronnie Skyles. She'll be held incommunicado until you say different."

Carlisle never took his eyes off the monitor. He had considered asking Fuzzy to cooperate in his plot to fix the USA-Italy Olympic basketball game. However, that would add an unreliable element to his scheme. So he decided it would be best to actually kidnap her. If all went well she would be released unharmed. If not . . .

Abruptly, he turned from the monitor console and snapped, "Okay, let's do it."

With a nod, Balfour let himself out. Carlisle went over and sat down behind his desk. In less than forty-eight hours it would begin, and he would be ready.

4

"All We Can Do Is Wait to Die."
Jamal Garth

CHAPTER 52

Virginia Daley arrived at the Human Development Institute building on the expansive University of Chicago campus. By 6:32 she was at her desk booting up the computer to review yesterday's events. As the screen brightened, her eyes glistened with anticipation. Had anyone been present, they would have observed a look of erotic anticipation on her face.

The material she was reviewing was not of a sexual or suggestive nature; however, Virginia Daley was a woman who got her kicks out of invading the privacy of others. It was the HDI executive secretary's work, avocation, and hobby to be a snoop. And she enjoyed it immensely.

First, she checked to see if Cole had made any progress in the search for Thomas Kelly. Finding that there was none, she moved on to other events.

The accident at the WGN studio in which Cole, Kate Ford, Blackie Silvestri, and Orga Syriac had almost been killed was contained in the summary. The official version was that the driver of the stolen truck had lost control of the vehicle and rammed it into the building. A police spokesman had said that, although the driver had escaped, the police had strong leads as to his identity.

She moved on to the rest of the world, finding that the usual wars, maimings, and conflicts raged unchecked. She idly wondered what chances mankind would have of surviving without the guidance of the Human Development Institute.

She took a quick glance at local news items, finding little of any interest to the Institute. That is until she got to the summary of an article that would appear in that morning's edition of the *Chicago Times-Herald*. The HDI synopsis read:

> Investigative journalist Kate Ford reportedly has evidence that the Human Development Institute on the University of Chicago's campus, a social research organization, is actually a secret intelligence operation. Ms. Ford claims that not only is the funding for HDI questionable, but that it engages in illegal spying and overt acts of domestic sabotage against innocent United States citizens. Ms. Ford has scheduled a press conference for noon today outside the Human Development Institute building, located on the Midway Plaisance.

Virginia Daley stared at the computer screen until her vision blurred. Finally, she looked away and glanced out the window. After a moment of contemplation, she snatched up the telephone. Although it was not yet seven o'clock, she planned to wake up Dr. Gilbert Goldman.

The U.S. Olympic team completed the final practice prior to their game with the Italians at seven o'clock that evening. Pete Dubcek had enjoyed the workout, one of the best practices of his career. The star player from Chicago liked Atlanta. Although it was a bit warm for the European immigrant's tastes, he took to the atmosphere of the genteel southern city. He had even temporarily forgotten about his marital troubles. In fact, at a press conference held at the downtown Atlanta Radisson Hotel the previous night, he'd had a mild flirtation with a reporter for *USA Today* who was from Germany. Although nothing serious developed, it had shown Dubcek that he could have a love life after Fuzzy.

But he wasn't ready to face the issue of how he was going to extricate himself from a bad marriage.

The players filed off the court into the locker room. Dubcek went to his locker and began taking off his practice uniform. When he reached onto the top shelf for a towel he noticed a miniature tape recorder, which had not been there before practice. There was a white envelope lying beneath the recorder. It hadn't been there before practice either. His name was typewritten across the front of the envelope, and he studied it momentarily before finally shrugging and ripping it open. Inside he found a single sheet of white notepaper. The message "Play the tape immediately!" was written in the same block print that was on the envelope.

Pete Dubcek played the tape.

Larry and Butch Cole jogged around the south end of the McCormick Place annex and turned north on Lake Shore Drive, heading back to Cole's condominium building. The chief of detectives was exerting himself for the first time since the incident at the television studio. He had spent most of the previous day either in bed or lounging around the apartment. With each passing hour he'd discovered another ache or pain and an additional bump or bruise. The highlight of the evening was Paige fixing the Coles the best southern fried chicken dinner they'd ever eaten.

When he had awakened that morning Cole had been so stiff he could barely get out of bed. Never being one for taking pills, he had decided to work out the kinks with exercise.

He had got Butch up and together they'd gone for a morning run. At first Cole found the effort difficult, but after the first mile his body warmed up and the aches and pains vanished.

Now, as they started the last leg of the five-mile run, Cole picked up the pace. Butch kept up with his father easily; however, he realized that they were running faster than they ever had before. By the time they slowed to a walk in front of the condo building, they were both breathing heavily and sweating profusely.

"Wow, Dad," Butch gasped, "you sure made a quick recovery."

Cole smiled and mopped sweat from his brow with a towel he carried in the pocket of his sweatpants. "That," he said, motioning to the route they'd just run, "was just what the doctor ordered."

After cooling down they went inside the building. They entered the apartment and were greeted by the aroma of frying bacon. Paige was in the kitchen fixing breakfast. She was not alone.

Larry and Butch were surprised to see Sister Mary Louise Stallings seated at the kitchen table.

"Hello, Sister," Cole said. "It's been a long time."

"How are you, Larry, and how have you been, Butch?"

"Hi, Sister," Butch said.

"You all get cleaned up," Paige said. "As soon as you're ready, I'll start the eggs."

Walking to the back of the apartment, Cole and Butch exchanged puzzled looks. It was unusual for the nun to visit them. Of course, she was always welcome.

Larry Cole, Butch, Paige, and Sister Mary Louise consumed a breakfast of freshly sliced cantaloupe with strawberries, bacon, scrambled eggs, grits, biscuits, coffee, and orange juice. After their run, the men were famished and ate everything that was put in front of them with relish. Paige and the nun ate enough to ensure there were no leftovers.

Cole, with Butch's acquiescence, demanded that the men wash the dishes. The nun and Paige went into the living room. After rendering the kitchen spick-and-span, the Coles joined them.

It didn't take Larry long to realize that Sister Mary Louise's visit wasn't purely of a social nature and that there was something on her mind. After exchanging a few pleasantries and catching up on what had been going on in their lives since they'd last seen each other, the nun fell silent.

"Weren't you and Butch going over to your place to pick up some of your things?" Cole asked Paige.

Somewhat surprised, it took Paige a moment to catch on.

Then she said, "Right. Uh, Judy's going to meet us there. We'd, uh, better get started, Butch."

Looking as confused as Paige, Butch got to his feet and followed her out the door.

When they were alone, Cole said, "You want to tell me what's troubling you, Louise?"

Larry Cole and Louise Stallings had known each other for close to thirty years. His first case, as a tactical officer assigned to the old Nineteenth District, had involved a madman named Martin Zykus. A madman who had returned fifteen years later and attempted to get revenge on both Cole and Sister Mary Louise Stallings. Now, she apparently needed his help again.

Before beginning her story Louise looked down at her clasped hands and said a silent prayer. Then she began.

"A few days ago a priest from Detroit came to stay with Father Phil Cisco at Our Lady of Peace rectory. He's an elderly white-haired man who walks with a cane. He looks a lot like Senator Ted Kennedy or maybe the actor Brian Dennehy."

She paused for a moment. If she wasn't mistaken, Cole had gotten very still and was staring at her with a near frightening intensity. The nun continued.

"Well, he's been acting strange since he arrived. He goes out at all hours of the day and night, and I think he has some type of explosive in plastic pouches in his room. Then this morning I borrowed Father Phil's Blazer to come here and I found this on the floor."

She removed a red-and-white button from the black leather shoulder bag she carried and handed it to Cole. He examined the dead state's attorney's reelection campaign button.

In a gesture of weariness, she placed her hand to her forehead. "I just don't know, Larry. Maybe my suspicious imagination is working overtime and I see the ghost of Martin Zykus in every stranger I meet."

Cole smiled. "No, Louise, you aren't seeing ghosts. As a matter of fact, I've been looking for Father James Lochran."

Sister Mary Louise Stallings was shocked speechless.

CHAPTER 53

Father Phil Cisco was hanging freshly dry-cleaned vestments in a closet in the sacristy of Our Lady of Peace Church. He checked the mass supplies in the wooden cabinets and was about to return to the rectory when he heard a noise coming from the church proper. He listened for a moment and was able to identify the sound of someone sobbing. Quickly, he moved over to the sacristy door and opened it. He peered out across the altar and saw Father Jim kneeling at the marble railing. He was crying. Without hesitating Phil Cisco rushed over to assist him.

When the young priest approached, the older man's head came up with a jerk and he got quickly to his feet. Snatching a handkerchief from his back pocket, he wiped his tear-streaked face and blew his nose. By the time the pastor reached him he had managed to compose himself.

"Are you okay, Father?" the young priest asked.

The imposter managed a smile. "I'm fine, Phil. I sometimes get overwhelmed when I'm inside a church."

The two men turned and started for the side exit.

"I haven't brought this up before," the pastor said, "but if you'd like you could say the eleven o'clock mass on Sunday."

The older man stopped. The priest turned to face him, noticing the shock on his face. "Is there something wrong, Jim?"

The imposter looked down at the floor. "That's nice of

you, Phil, but I'll be tied up all day Sunday over on the campus."

The pastor shrugged. "Whatever you say. Maybe next week."

"Maybe," was the only comment.

The two men continued to walk slowly from the church.

The press and curious onlookers began gathering on the Midway Plaisance, parallel to Sixtieth Street in front of the Human Development Institute, an hour before Kate Ford's scheduled press conference. There was an air of anticipation running through the assemblage. They were aware that something quite extraordinary was about to happen here, and each of them wanted to be a part of it in whatever way that he or she could.

Calling a press conference was not an unusual occurrence in the Windy City. In fact, they happened almost daily. However, the number attending these events varied depending on who was covering them and the subject matter under discussion. What was taking place on the spacious Midway Plaisance, which was bordered on both sides by the stately buildings of the University of Chicago campus, would qualify as a definite success even before it began. This was due to two contributing factors. One was that Kate Ford, despite being a relatively young woman, had an outstanding reputation in journalism circles nationally. The other element was that she was taking on the Human Development Institute, which was shrouded in as much mystery as any secret organization in history.

Standing at the window of his office, overlooking the gathering below, stood Dr. Gilbert Goldman. Behind him, seated in her usual chair in front of the HDI director's desk, was Virginia Daley.

"Couldn't we do anything to stop this?" Goldman demanded.

"Kate Ford is a freelance writer," the executive secretary answered. "Unlike the last media problem we had with the *Eye of the Public* program, we have nothing we can use for leverage against her. Her record is quite impressive and her reputation is spotless. I don't know what she has or claims to have, but we could experience some problems or, at the least, be placed in a delicate position if forced to respond to any allegations."

"What about having our legal people get an injunction against her?"

"We'll have to wait until we find out what she's got to say. However, I would advise against legal action unless we have ample grounds. Actually, a lawsuit would give Ms. Ford a larger audience because of the controversy that would accompany it."

Goldman turned around and sat down behind his desk. In frustration the HDI director slammed his fist down on the desk blotter. "There's got to be something we can do!"

"Of course there is, Doctor," she said without losing one iota of her composure. "We have a number of options. Since Ms. Ford is using the media, we can also employ them to tell our side of whatever scenario she unfolds down there today. We can also put some of our people to work on discrediting her. Take a very close look into her background. I'm sure we'll find something that she won't want disclosed. Then there is the more extreme measure."

Goldman stared at her for a moment as if he couldn't fathom what she meant. But he knew. He knew all too well.

"Let's first see what unfolds at her press conference. Then we'll decide what to do about Kate Ford."

"Whatever you say, sir," Virginia Daley said, opening up the ever-present notebook on her lap. "Have you been using the Institute's computer system lately?"

"I haven't for a while."

"What about in the last two or three days?"

"No. Why?"

"Someone using your pass code logged on and obtained information from the system about Philo Coffey, the ten cops attending the PAC dinner the night Thomas Kelly vanished, Larry Cole, Kate Ford, Orga Syriac, Jamal Garth, and Barbara Schurla Zorin."

Goldman's eyes narrowed as if he were in pain. The only person other than himself and Virginia Daley who knew his computer access code was the missing Thomas Kelly. "What do you think he's doing?"

"Collecting information about his potential victims," she said matter-of-factly. "It's too bad he wasn't successful with Cole and Kate Ford at the WGN studio. It would have made things much easier for us."

Goldman turned his chair around to look out the window. Kate Ford was getting out of a taxi down on the street. The press conference would soon begin.

"So Thomas is also responsible for the explosion that killed our operative Mr. Silk," he said flatly.

"We can assume that, sir."

The HDI director sighed. "So, after he kills, or attempts to kill, everyone of prominence who attended that dinner, what will he do?"

Virginia Daley stood up. "I have no idea, Doctor. But if he logs on to our system using your pass code again, I'll be able to locate him. Then it will be a simple matter to send a team out to snatch him up. Now I want to see what Kate Ford has to say about us."

Before she reached the door he called to her, "I don't want Thomas hurt."

She turned and stared at the back of his head. She said an emotionless, "I wouldn't dream of it."

Then she let herself out.

Orga Syriac did not cover Kate Ford's press conference. This was by design. Sven-Erik Voman, working in an empty studio on the opposite end of the WGN complex while his office was being repaired, was livid. That was until she explained that she was covering the same story as Kate Ford, only from a different angle. All the giant Swede could do was shrug his massive shoulders.

But as Kate Ford stood on the grass of the Midway Plaisance reciting a litany of charges against the Human Development Institute for doing everything from spying on innocent American citizens to political assassinations, Orga was a short distance away. Seated in her black Lexus sedan at the rear of the Institute building, the entity known as the

Abo-Yorba allowed the visage of the she-devil to come over her. This heightened her perception remarkably, to the point that she could hear Kate's comments over a hundred yards away. She could also make out the images behind the glass in the third-floor window of the gray stone building where Dr. Gilbert Goldman's office was located.

It had taken her half a century to find the source of the evil that had caused the destruction of the model community of Diggstown, Mississippi, in 1956. She had done all that she could to keep the town from being destroyed, but the three operatives had been too formidable for even an Abo-Yorba. They had even come close to killing her with their weapons. For that she had disposed of them, but with some difficulty.

She had been severely wounded and bleeding heavily when she pursued the boy into the woods. Had she been at peak efficiency she could have caught him easily. As it was, she barely managed to corner him on that cliff before he fell. She was certain that he was dead and she gave him no more thought as she dragged herself away. She had never been more close to death than she was that night. However, she vowed that her existence would not end before she destroyed whoever or whatever had sent those people to Diggstown.

And now she was here and her plan to get inside the structure was proceeding as planned. She did not expect to survive the confrontation beyond the walls of the building she was examining. But her death wouldn't matter.

She flexed her taloned appendages into fists and then returned to her human form. It was time for her to report back to the studio. As she put the car in gear and drove away from the Institute, she once more went over the attempt the other day to kill her, Larry Cole, and Kate Ford. As she hunted, someone was hunting her, and she had a good idea who it was.

Now it had come full circle. From Diggstown of the past to the Human Development Institute today. And if the man who had been a boy on that long-ago night got in the she-devil's way, she would indeed kill him as she had intended to do in the past.

CHAPTER 54

Father James Lochran was seated at Father Phil Cisco's computer. He was once more accessing the files of the Human Development Institute. He was unaware that his intrusion had been discovered and that Virginia Daley was currently supervising a trace in an attempt to locate him.

The priest impersonator retrieved the information he needed and decided to make a printout of it. As the data was being transferred from computer to paper, the white-haired man began whistling "When Irish Eyes Are Smiling."

He was dressed in full clerical garb, and after his accidental meeting this morning with Father Phil, he'd had his hair cut by a barber over on Fifty-third Street near the University of Chicago campus. Now he was ready to move on to another phase of his mission. He refused to dwell on the fact that the previous operation against Cole, Kate Ford, and the demon in human form had failed. It was the Lord's will that they were still alive; however, he planned to fulfill his mission of atonement against them even if it was the last thing he ever did. This afternoon he had other things to occupy his time.

The printout completed, he tore the paper from the spindle, folded it, and placed it in his inside jacket pocket. He was still whistling as he left the study and crossed the hall to the dining room. A woman in a nun's habit was sitting at the dining-room table reading a book. He assumed that it was Sister Mary Louise.

"Oh, I didn't mean to disturb you, Sister," he said.

He was startled when she turned around and revealed that it wasn't Sister Mary Louise at all. He had never set eyes on the woman in the light blue habit before.

"Good afternoon, Father," she said in a voice possessing an Irish accent almost as pronounced as his own. "I'm Sister Mary Bridgit O'Farrell from Saint Columbanus." She got to her feet and extended her hand. "I just came over to visit with Father Phil and Sister Mary Louise. You must be Father James Lochran from Detroit."

"Yes, I am," he responded warily. "It's a pleasure to meet you."

Something about this woman disturbed the former HDI operative. Initially, he couldn't discern what it was, but he didn't have the time to dwell on it right now.

"Well, I've got to be going, Sister . . . uh . . ."

The nun graced him with a sweet smile. "Sister Mary Bridgit. Will you be back for supper?"

He was unable to suppress his suspicion. "Why? Will you be staying?"

The nun's friendly manner didn't alter. "As a matter of fact I am, Father. After dinner I was looking forward to spending some time with you. Sister Mary Louise told me that you're studying advanced theology at the U of C. I'm studying the same subject in the undergrad program at Loyola. Besides you being from Ireland, I'm certain we could have a very interesting little talk."

"That depends on what time I get back, Sister. Of course, I'd be delighted to talk to you."

But as the man posing as Father James Lochran let himself out of the Our Lady of Peace rectory, he was not smiling. Despite his phony piety and the bogus religious front he maintained with such zeal, his espionage training and instincts had not diminished. And at this moment he was very, very suspicious of the woman calling herself Sister Mary Bridgit O'Farrell.

When the front door shut behind Father Lochran, the pleasant expression on the face of the young nun with the sparkling blue eyes and peaches-and-cream complexion dissolved to be replaced by one which was nearly as cynical as that of the imposter who had just left. From a pocket in her habit she removed a compact walkie-talkie that fit snugly in the palm of her hand.

"Did you get all that, boss?" Judy Daniels asked.

"Yes," Cole responded. "But he sounded suspicious."

"One thing's for sure, he's hiding something."

"Okay, we're on him. Oh, Judy."

"Yeah."

"You need to work on your Irish accent."

Unkeying the mike, she said into the emptiness of the spacious rectory dining room, "Everyone's a critic nowadays."

The Yellow taxi cruised slowly down Washington Park Boulevard. The priest, leaning heavily on his cane and carrying a black attaché case, flagged it down and got in.

"Where to, Father?" asked the heavyset white driver with the receding hairline.

The passenger hesitated a moment before saying, "Midway Airport. The main passenger terminal."

"Sure thing," the driver responded, pulling the flag down and picking up a clipboard to record the point of origin and the destination of his fare.

The driver made a sharp U-turn and headed back the way he had come. "I was gonna take Fifty-fifth Street, if that's okay?"

"It's up to you."

The driver was wearing dark glasses, and the look he gave his fare was noncommittal, which masked his curiosity. The man dressed as a priest had not spoken with an Irish accent.

Lieutenant Blackie Silvestri, playing the role of a taxi driver, was behind the wheel of the Yellow cab. Chief of Detectives Larry Cole and three teams of detectives in four separate vehicles had taken up alternate routes to follow the taxi.

*   *   *

Thomas Kelly, in his disguise as Father James Lochran, sat
back and willed himself to relax. Something was very wrong.
First there was the strange nun back at the Our Lady of Peace
rectory. Then this cabdriver.

The imposter hadn't been certain about the nun because
she appeared to be legitimate. However, Father Phil had
made it a point of saying on more than one occasion that
they rarely, if ever, had visitors at Our Lady of Peace. It
could have possibly been an oversight that the young priest
had failed to mention Sister Mary Bridgit O'Farrell from
someplace called Saint Columbanus Parish. However, Thomas Kelly, during his many years as an HDI operative, had
learned to be extremely wary of such accidental omissions.

Kelly now realized that his Father Lochran disguise was
blown. This was because of the cabdriver. He was white and
in the Washington Park Boulevard area, which was a black
ghetto of the worst variety. The cab he drove was brand-
new. Kelly leaned forward and checked the mileage. Less
than five hundred.

The imposter considered the possibility that the driver
could have gotten a fare whom he had been forced to drop
in the ghetto. Chicago taxis were not allowed to decline fares
no matter what part of the city the passenger wanted to be
taken to. The taxi being new wasn't impossible to explain,
as even the most dilapidated jalopy on the street started out
new. But new cab or not, the driver didn't fit.

Most of the problem Kelly had with the heavyset man was
instinctive. He just didn't *feel* right. Then there had been the
business with the flag and the clipboard. A veteran cabbie
would never have dropped the flag first before entering the
destination on his trip log. To do so could draw a protest
from the fare.

There were too many coincidences for him to ignore. That
meant Father James Lochran would have to vanish, and the
disappearance would have to be carried out right under the
noses of whoever was watching him. This saddened the imposter, who had been given the name Thomas Kelly in an
orphanage by a nun when he was still an infant. The persona
of Father Lochran had become as important to him as his

faith in his mission for the Almighty. Yet, despite having to abandon his clerical identity, he would never abandon his mission.

He sighed.

"You say something, Father?" the driver asked.

"No." The priest stared at the bald spot at the back of the other impersonator's head. "I didn't say a word, my son."

CHAPTER 55

JUNE 18, 2004
2:41 P.M.

Bradley "Buster" Quint and his wife, Joy, were rich. Buster had started out at the age of twenty-one as an editorial assistant for a New York pulp fiction publishing firm. Within five years he had risen to editor in chief. During the next ten years he had acquired a number of name-brand authors for the house, which many in the publishing industry had once thought of as a joke. In 1985 he was made a partner. By 1995 he had bought out the other partners and become the sole operator of the firm, which he renamed Buster Quint and Associates. Two of his best-selling authors were Barbara Zorin and Jamal Garth.

Joy Malone Quint was fifteen years her husband's junior. She had been a Hollywood actress of some prominence. One of her most noteworthy roles was portraying the heroine in the movie version of Barbara Zorin's novel *Evil Places*. Joy had become famous portraying the Zorin character Chicago police undercover officer Esmeralda Lacy, who was modeled closely after Judy Daniels—the Mistress of Disguise/High Priestess of Mayhem. Judy had served as a consultant on the film. She and the then Joy Malone had gotten along famously. Then Joy met publisher Buster Quint and fell in love.

On this summer afternoon the Quints, who still considered themselves newlyweds after five years of marriage, were preparing to fly from Chicago to Denver on Buster Quint and Associates business. Buster had been an Air Force fighter pilot during the Vietnam War and had just purchased a new Gulfstream twin-engine jet plane. Painted with the gold-and-blue color scheme of the Buster Quint and Associates Publishing Company and named the *Lady Joy*, the jet was being serviced at the Midway Airport charter hangar. The private flight number 200 Zebra was scheduled to take off at 3:30 P.M. It would be piloted by Buster, and three passengers would be aboard the ten-passenger Gulfstream: Joy Quint, who would also serve as copilot, Barbara Zorin, and Jamal Garth. This information had been filed by Quint when he submitted his flight plan. The Human Development Institute monitored the points of origin, destinations, and passenger lists of flights all over the world. The assassin, posing as a priest, had retrieved the information on Flight 200Z from the HDI computer. He wasn't interested in the Quints, but he was in their passengers, who had attended the PAC dinner.

The Yellow cab bearing Father James Lochran crossed Kedzie Avenue at Fifty-fifth Street. There had been no conversation between the driver and the passenger since they'd left the Washington Park Boulevard area. The priest had rolled the window down and, as far as appearances went, was casually observing the passing scene. The driver kept his eyes on the traffic. The Yellow cab was not remarkable in any way and did not attract the slightest interest from anyone they passed. However, the vehicle was being closely scrutinized by the network of police vehicles tailing it.

In the front passenger seat of a green Jeep Cherokee which was in reality an undercover police vehicle, Larry Cole monitored Blackie's progress on an illuminated screen displaying a map of city streets. An electronic homing device in the trunk of the cab broadcast its location block by block. Cole also had the other vehicles on the surveillance—a battered pickup truck, a U.S. Mail truck, and a black Lincoln Town Car—periodically making visual contact with the taxi.

Cole suspected that the passenger in the cab was a deranged mass murderer. The chief of detectives had agonized over letting Blackie drive the undercover vehicle and had even hoped that the man in clerical dress who had exited the Our Lady of Peace rectory would ignore the cruising cab. When the priest got into the taxi, Cole had nibbled at his bottom lip, crossed his fingers, and said a silent prayer for the safety of his oldest friend in the department. Then he settled in to command the multivehicle surveillance operation.

Manny Sherlock was driving the Jeep. Twice he and Cole had made visual contact with Blackie during the rolling surveillance. The young sergeant's palms were moist, making the steering wheel slippery. He had lost contact with the cops on operations like this before. The guy in the cab with Blackie was not only a suspected homicidal maniac, but obviously cunning and extremely dangerous. Manny had volunteered to drive the taxi. Blackie had overruled him.

"It's my turn to see what Judy finds so interesting about this undercover business, kid."

Manny smiled in spite of the anxiety that was making him sick to his stomach. Blackie had been his immediate supervisor since Manny was a rookie detective right out of the academy. That was thirteen years ago. Yet Blackie still called him "kid."

"They're pulling onto the airport's main drive," Cole said, staring hard at the monitor screen. Picking up a walkie-talkie, which was set to the car-to-car frequency the rolling surveillance was operating on, Cole said, "This is Car Fifty. Fifty Boy, you are to follow this unit onto Midway Drive and maintain visual contact with Fifty Adam. Fifty Charlie and Fifty David, you are to take up positions on Cicero, which will enable you to back us up and respond immediately if there is a problem. Do you copy?"

All units responded in the affirmative.

"Stop right here!" came the sharp order from Blackie's passenger.

"Hey!" Blackie's voice held noticeable tension.

"Let's go!" Cole shouted at Manny.

The sergeant floored the Jeep's accelerator and the un-marked police vehicle leaped forward onto the airport drive. However, they were forced to slow down because of the dense traffic heading for the main terminal.

"I'm going in on foot," Cole said, opening the door.

"You guys listening?" Blackie said in a maddeningly calm tone. "Our suspect just jumped out of the cab at the southeast end of the terminal building. It's crowded over here so I didn't see which way he went, but with that limp and the priest get-up he should be easy to spot." Blackie paused. "Oh yeah. He dropped the fare on the front seat when he got out. He left me a five-dollar tip."

"Very funny, Blackie," Cole said. "Very funny."

The white Land Rover pulled up in front of the charter flight terminal adjacent to the commercial building, where the cops had lost the priest impersonator. Buster Quint, a broad-shouldered man with a narrow waist and thinning silver hair, got out first followed by his platinum blond wife, Joy. Barbara Zorin and Jamal Garth exited the backseat. A pair of stewards came forward to load the Quint party luggage on a trolley and valet-park the publisher's car. As this procedure was taking place, the pilot and passengers on Flight 200Z were standing on the sidewalk of Midway Drive.

Blackie was waiting for Cole and Manny in front of the commercial terminal when he saw the Quints and their guests in front of the charter terminal fifty yards from where he stood. He would have called a greeting to Jamal and Barbara, but he had more important things on his mind. Then Cole and the other cops arrived, and the lieutenant forgot about the authors as the cops began searching for the bogus priest.

*   *   *

The commercial terminal was crowded when the priest impersonator rushed in. He knew exactly where he was going and made steady, if not rapid, progress toward his destination. Although he had yet to see his pursuers, he knew they were there. In his current guise he would be easy to spot. However, the Institute had trained him to always be prepared.

He reached the end of the terminal. This was where the abandoned check-in counters for the now defunct Central Illinois Airline were located. The waiting area in front of the counters was also deserted. The imposter went to a door on the far side of Central Illinois Airline. It was marked "Authorized Personnel Only."

After first checking to make certain that he was unobserved, he tried the door. As he had expected, it was locked. After making another quick survey of the area for prying eyes, he removed a small square device from his trousers pocket. A pair of thin, ridged wires protruded from the end of this device. He inserted the wires into the lock and depressed a small black button. A soft buzzing noise became audible, followed by a sharp click. Removing the device, he grasped the knob and opened the door. He entered.

Larry Cole stood in the main commercial terminal. He was waiting for the CPD lieutenant in charge of the Midway detail to arrive. What had started out to be a routine surveillance and apprehension of a suspect was turning into a major operation. As he watched the crowd surging back and forth, rushing either from or to flights, Cole once more went over his rationale for approaching the investigation of James Lochran/Thomas Kelly in this manner.

Basically, it was because of Dr. Gilbert Goldman and his Human Development Institute. The clout Goldman had generated with the superintendent to obtain knowledge of the police investigations was enough to warn the chief of detectives of a potential problem. So when Sister Mary Louise had given him the tip as to where they could find the bogus, possibly homicidal priest, Cole had decided to adopt the rolling surveillance. His intention was to catch this Father Lochran or HDI operative Thomas Kelly actively engaged in one of his acts of destructive sabotage. Then it would take more weight than Goldman could ever come up with to get the killer away from Cole.

Blackie, accompanied by an attractive black female police lieutenant, came up to the chief of detectives. "Boss, this is Lieutenant Nora Smelser. She's in charge of the detail out here. I've briefed her on the guy that we're looking for."

The female lieutenant frowned. "You're after a white-haired Catholic priest in his sixties?"

"I know it's a bit out of the norm, Lieutenant," Cole said, "but believe me, this man is dangerous. Now, all I want your people to do is locate him. Then my people will move in for the arrest."

Lieutenant Smelser looked around the crowded main terminal.

"This place is a madhouse today, but he should be fairly easy to spot. Do you know what airline he's going out on?"

"We don't know if he's booked on a flight at all or has any intentions of purchasing a ticket," Cole said.

"Then why is he at the airport?" Smelser asked.

"We don't have the answer to that one either," the chief of detectives responded, "but I want to find out as soon as possible."

Aware of Cole's intensity, Lieutenant Smelser said, "Okay, all the officers on the airport detail will be alerted to be on the lookout for the priest. We'll also notify airline and maintenance personnel. If he's anywhere on the airport grounds we'll find him, sir."

"Good, Lieutenant," Cole said. "And it was nice meeting you."

"Same here, sir," she said, turning away and pulling a walkie-talkie from her belt.

When they were alone Blackie said, "If he's not catching a plane, what is he doing out here?"

"I don't know, Blackie. I don't know."

The immediate area beyond the door through which the man dressed as a priest had gone to leave the terminal had previously been the Central Illinois Airline administrative offices. Now all that remained of the former independent air carrier were a couple of rickety desks coated with dust and a few chairs. There was a door leading from the offices directly onto the tarmac. It was locked from the inside. He proceeded over to the closed, dust-laden blinds and peeped out.

Planes were being loaded and unloaded, and were taxiing from and taxiing onto the runway for takeoff. He remained at the window for some minutes studying the activity outside in an attempt to discern if there was anything going on which could pose a threat to him. Satisfied that there was not, he moved across the vacant office to a washroom, equipped with only a toilet and sink. The place had not been cleaned since Central Illinois Airline had gone bankrupt two months ago. Ignoring the filth, he placed his attaché case on top of the toilet tank and opened it. It was time for Father James Lochran to disappear forever.

CHAPTER 56

JUNE 18, 2004
2:55 P.M.

Sure we've got more independent distributors now than we had five years ago, but the market is still tight," Buster Quint was saying. "I remember when I took over the company in ninety-five I could easily ship four hundred new titles into the impulse-item market like the Target stores, Safeways, Oscos, and Dominicks supermarkets and maintain a high sales volume. That market collapsed with the consolidation of the independents in the late nineties. When that happened we had to drastically reduce what we shipped."

The publisher pointed at his two star authors, Barbara Zorin and Jamal Garth, "But you two have always been in demand, because you've achieved name-brand status."

Joy Quint was seated next to her husband, holding his arm. Now she rubbed his biceps and said, "Then you should pay them more money, Buster."

"Hear, hear," Jamal said with a grin.

"I'll drink to that," Barbara said, raising a plastic cup of Sprite.

A Hispanic ground attendant wearing blue coveralls approached the party. "It's time for the preflight check, Mr. Quint."

"Thank you, Matt," the publisher said, getting to his feet. "We can continue our talk on the plane. I've got to prepare for takeoff."

Quint followed the attendant out onto the runway, where the *Lady Joy* waited in all its needle-nosed blue-and-gold splendor. Joy Quint and the authors would remain in the VIP lounge until the flight was announced.

The Hispanic attendant went as far as the mobile staircase that had been rolled into place next to the twin-engine Gulfstream. He waited until the publisher boarded the plane before he retreated to the hangar where the *Lady Joy* had been serviced. The maintenance personnel who had worked on the plane had now moved on to other tasks in another area of the airport, and the building was deserted. The attendant pulled a marijuana cigarette from his pocket and lit it with a disposable lighter. He took a deep drag, held the smoke in for a moment, and then exhaled slowly. He felt the narcotic rush wash over him and he became light-headed.

He still had to load the passengers' luggage onto flight 200Z, but he knew it would take the millionaire publisher at least half an hour to go through the preflight check. He took another drag on the cigarette. He didn't particularly care for this job, but it kept him in tequila and pot. Basically all he had to do was load a few bags on a couple of private planes a few times a day.

The attendant heard a noise behind him. He quickly

cupped the illegal butt in his hand and placed the hand behind his back. He spun around to locate the source of the noise.

There was a man in the deserted hangar with him now. A white man with a ruddy complexion, thick red hair, and a red beard. He was wearing a filthy Central Illinois Airline jumpsuit that was too small for him. The attendant had never seen him before.

"How ya' doing, man?" the redhead said. "Mind if I take a hit?"

The attendant relaxed. This guy was a fellow pot head, which meant he wasn't a threat. He handed over the joint.

The redhead took it, drew deeply making the tip glow bright orange, held in the smoke, and exhaled. He handed the hand-rolled cigarette back and limped to the hangar entrance and looked out across the tarmac at the *Lady Joy*. "You loading that bird?"

The attendant had gone back to his marijuana. He managed a strangled, "Yeah." The smoke went down the wrong way. He gasped for breath, choked, and had managed to bring himself under control when he realized that something about this guy was wrong. He remembered that Central Illinois Airline was no longer in business, and he'd never seen a ground attendant walk with a cane.

He was about to raise these issues when the redhead spun around and raised his cane. The pot-smoking airport worker's reflexes were frozen by the narcotic and he was unable to defend himself. The sound the tip of the assassin's cane made on impact with the attendant's head sounded like a small-caliber pistol shot in the emptiness of the airport hangar. With the still-burning joint in his hand, the attendant collapsed to the floor. His skull had been crushed.

The redheaded man stood over him for a moment before lowering his head, making the sign of the cross, and saying a silent prayer for the soul of the dead man. Then he propped the murder weapon against the wall beside the entrance and went to the cart bearing the luggage for Charter Flight 200 Zebra.

* * *

They couldn't find him. The search of the terminal had turned up two Catholic priests, both under thirty years of age, a rabbi, and a Greek Orthodox minister. But there was no one in the religious habit resembling the man known as Father James Lochran or Thomas Kelly of the Human Development Institute.

Cole, Blackie, Manny, and Lieutenant Smelser retreated to an area beside a W. H. Smith newsstand. They examined their options.

"There is no way he could have gotten out of the terminal after he came in here," Blackie declared.

"Well, he's not here now," Lieutenant Smelser said. "We've checked every square inch of this terminal."

"Maybe he changed his appearance," Manny volunteered.

"That's possible," Smelser said. "He could have ducked into one of the washrooms and taken off his habit. That would have enabled him to blend in with the crowd quite easily."

"It doesn't fit," Cole interjected.

"What doesn't fit, boss?" Blackie asked.

"When he did the job on the Barristers' Club, he went in as a priest and came out as a priest. At the state's attorney's fund-raiser he was in civvies. When he came out here, he was again dressed as a priest and I bet he planned to do what he had to and leave as a priest."

"But suppose he made us, Chief?" Manny said. "He could have changed his appearance, like Lieutenant Smelser said, and caught a plane going anywhere in the country."

"Maybe he's not running, Manny," Cole argued. "He could be out here still engaged in his self-appointed mission of death. What we need to do is figure out who or what his target could be."

Blackie craved a cigar in the worst way, but the airport had been smoke free for years. He happened to glance at the book rack inside the newsstand. Then it hit him. Barbara Zorin and Jamal Garth, who had been at the PAC dinner, were also at the airport. He turned around to tell the other cops.

CHAPTER 57

"Flight 200 Zebra," the air traffic controller's voice came over Buster Quint's headset, "you are cleared for take-off."

The publisher's deep voice rumbled into the speaker, "Roger, Tower. We're rolling."

The *Lady Joy* rocketed down the runway and leaped into the air. Quint kept the nose elevated as he climbed to his twenty-five-thousand-feet cruising altitude for their flight to Denver.

"Are you going to set it on autopilot, honey?" Joy asked, as he leveled off.

"I think I'll keep it for a while," he responded. "Why don't you go back and see to our guests?"

She unfastened herself from the copilot's chair, removed her headset, and kissed her husband on the cheek before going back into the passenger cabin.

Barbara Zorin and Jamal Garth were seated in window seats on opposite sides of the aisle that bisected the private jet. They were both looking down at the smattering of clouds dotting the western Illinois sky beneath them.

"This is the only way to travel," Jamal said without taking his eyes off the landscape far below. "I've traveled first-class before, but having the entire plane is really living in the lap of luxury."

"I agree," Barbara said, smiling when she realized that she

was able to cross her legs in the spacious personal area of the cabin.

Joy Quint came in from the cockpit. "How about a drink before we have our in-flight snack?"

"Sounds good," the writers said together.

Jamal requested a glass of white zinfandel; Barbara, a light bourbon and water. Joy poured herself a glass of champagne in the galley behind the cockpit and returned with the drinks on a tray. Her husband would be unable to drink anything alcoholic during the flight and would only have a cup of black coffee when Joy served turkey sandwiches at about the midway point of their flight.

She turned one of the chairs around so that she could face her guests. They exchanged idle chitchat for a time, as the quiet hum of the powerful jet spiriting them on through the skies surrounded them in a cocoon of peaceful security.

"Did you manage to solve the problem you were having with the motivation of the villain in your new novel, Jamal?" Joy asked.

The black author frowned. "Yes and no. He's becoming increasingly more complex with each draft, but this time I think I'm close to what I want."

"Can we see it?" Barbara asked.

"Maybe we could give you a hand," Joy added.

Garth nodded. "You know, that might be just what the manuscript needs. A fresh viewpoint. Where are the bags?"

"In the—" Joy started to say, and stopped. Instead of being in the storage area behind the passenger compartment, they were piled on seats. And not too neatly at that. The former screen star planned to mention this to her husband. Buster would give the ground crew more than just a piece of his mind. However, playing the good host, Joy didn't mention this dereliction of duty and pointed out the luggage at the rear of the passenger compartment.

Garth unstrapped his seat belt and went to retrieve the laptop from his suitcase.

The marked police vehicle screamed across the tarmac and skidded to a stop at the entrance to the tower overlooking the runway. Cole, Blackie, and Lieutenant Smelser leaped out. They ran into the building and bolted up the steps to the Midway air traffic control center. The supervisor of the facility was waiting for them at the entrance. The ebony-skinned black man wearing silver wire-framed glasses had been alerted to their imminent arrival by Lieutenant Smelser via airport radio.

Breathlessly, she introduced Cole to the man in charge of the air traffic control center, whose name was Joe Ballard. She punctuated the introduction by saying in a voice barely above a whisper to keep anyone else in the area from overhearing her, "Joe, the chief strongly believes there's a bomb on a plane that just took off from here."

Ballard blanched and managed a strangled, "Which flight?"

Cole stepped forward. "Two hundred Zebra. A private plane belonging to publisher Buster Quint."

"Are you sure about this bomb?"

"No, I'm not, but we need to get that plane back on the ground as soon as possible!"

The supervisor shook his head. "I don't know. This is very irregular."

Cole was fast reaching the end of his patience. "Look," he said, towering over the smaller man, "I've got some very good friends on that plane and I'm trying to save their lives. Now, I'll take full responsibility for whatever you've got to do, but I want you to recall that plane right now!"

The policeman's words galvanized Supervisor Ballard and he said an urgent, "Come with me."

The three cops followed him across the air control center.

Jamal had been out of his seat long enough for Barbara and Joy to wonder what had become of him. When he finally did return from his venture to retrieve his computer from the luggage, there was a look of obvious strain on his face.

"Is there something wrong?" Joy asked her guest.

He sat down heavily in his seat but did not refasten his seat belt. They noticed that he was starting to sweat profusely despite the cool air blowing from vents throughout the luxury aircraft.

"Jamal, are you ill?" Barbara inquired.

He took a deep breath and steeled himself before saying, "Someone planted an explosive device in my bag. It's small, but if I'm not mistaken, extremely powerful. It's on a timer which looks to have about eight minutes left before it blows. I estimate that we're about twelve minutes out from Midway."

The women were momentarily stunned speechless. Then Joy Quint got up and walked rapidly to the cockpit door. She went inside.

"Isn't there anything we can do?" Barbara asked. "Like throw it out or disarm it?"

Garth measured his words carefully. "Once this device is activated it can't be stopped or disarmed. We also can't move it or it will detonate instantly. All we can do . . ." The words caught in his throat. He swallowed hard and managed to finish, ". . . is wait to die."

The situation was critical, but Buster Quint had been in critical situations before. When his wife told him what Garth had said, the publisher-pilot activated his headset microphone. "Mayday, Mayday, Mayday. This is Flight Two hundred Zebra declaring an emergency. Mayday, Mayday." His voice never rose above a conversational tone, but it didn't have to. The words themselves held sufficient urgency.

Air traffic control supervisor Joe Ballard had taken over the position monitoring the flight of 200 Zebra on radar. Cole, Blackie, and Lieutenant Smelser stood behind him. All eyes were glued to the illuminated green screen on which the logo 200Z was displayed.

After his initial anxiety when he was confronted by the cops and told they suspected that there was a bomb on 200 Zebra, Ballard had settled into the role of a cool professional. He was just about to contact the flight when Buster Quint's voice rumbled over the speaker announcing an in-flight emergency. Ballard acknowledged 200 Zebra and waited for the pilot to define the emergency.

"Midway Control," Quint said, "be advised that we have discovered a possible explosive device aboard the aircraft. It is strongly believed, I repeat, it is strongly believed that this device will detonate in less than eight minutes. Again, I repeat, less than eight minutes. Request instructions for a return to Midway and an emergency landing."

Depressing a foot pedal beneath the console, Ballard said, "All traffic is being cleared for your return to Midway. Execute an immediate one-hundred-eighty-degree turn to bring your aircraft to coordinates zero niner eight seven."

"Roger, Midway Control," Quint acknowledged. "Executing a one-hundred-eighty-degree turn now and headed your way."

On board the *Lady Joy*, Buster Quint turned to his wife. "Baby, go back and have Barbara and Jamal strap themselves in. I'm going to get us back to Chicago as fast as this bird will fly."

Joy managed a smile. "I know you will, honey." Then she got up and went back into the passenger compartment.

Alone in the cockpit, Buster Quint fingered a Saint Christopher medal he'd worn around his neck since Vietnam and said, "Okay, Chris, it's up to us now. Let's do it."

Then he took the *Lady Joy* into a wing-stressing 180-degree turn, accelerated to the jet's maximum air speed of six hundred miles per hour, and rocketed back toward Chicago.

In Jamal Garth's bag in the passenger compartment the explosive device reached the six-minute mark and continued to countdown to detonation.

CHAPTER 58

Manny Sherlock and two officers assigned to the airport detail found Matt, the ground attendant, in the hangar. How the deadly priest impersonator had gotten from the commercial terminal onto the airfield and managed to plant a bomb on Buster Quint's plane was still a mystery. But Manny realized that his job was not only to solve this mystery, but find the man calling himself Father James Lochran as soon as possible.

The sergeant was about to request more uniformed cops to assist him when one of the other officers conducting the terminal search discovered that an unauthorized entry had been made to the now defunct Central Illinois Airline office at the far end of the main terminal.

Manny Sherlock arrived at the runway entrance to the abandoned offices less than a minute after he'd received the call from the Midway detail cop. He found a couple of officers prowling around the interior of the small administrative area.

"Who made the call?" Sherlock asked.

"I did," said a grizzled older cop with a face seamed by wrinkles and wise eyes. He nodded at a door across the room. "And I think I know what happened to your white-haired priest, Sarge."

Manny, followed by the old veteran, crossed to the door and opened it. There, on the dirty floor, was a clerical collar and black bib. Then they saw what had been left on the sink.

The box read, "Vogue Instant Hair Color." The tint was red. A plastic bottle containing a reddish-hued liquid rested on the edge of the sink beside the box. The dye job had obviously been hastily carried out, as red stains liberally dotted the sink's dirty porcelain surface and the floor.

"I want to keep everyone out of here until the crime lab arrives," Manny said to the old cop.

"Done, Sarge."

Then Manny raised his walkie-talkie and began to revise the description of the wanted man from that of someone with white hair to that of a man with flaming red hair.

At the exact moment that Sergeant Manfred Wolfgang Sherlock was transmitting his message to the police units engaged in the hunt for the bogus Father James Lochran, the shuttle bus which transported passengers from the air terminal to the remote long-term parking lot west of the airfield pulled to a stop. Seven passengers got out on the island at the center of the lot. Six of them began moving in various directions in search of their cars. The seventh, a heavyset man wearing a black T-shirt bearing the Chicago White Sox baseball team logo and black slacks, sat down on the bench in the glass-enclosed shelter on the small island. The man had red hair and a beard that didn't quite match the hair color. However, no one, including the bus driver who made this run an average of ten times a day and his six weary fellow travelers on the shuttle, had noticed this minor discrepancy.

Casually, he looked around the long-term lot. It was now deserted. He knew that they would be expanding their search for him soon. Especially after what would soon happen to the Gulfstream aircraft bearing Barbara Zorin and Jamal Garth. But the man, who had now reverted to his original identity as Thomas Kelly and adopted the red hair color that had been his naturally on that long-ago night in 1956 when the she-devil had attempted to kill him, refused to panic. He was following his training and the instincts he'd developed during his many years as an HDI operative.

A car pulled into the parking lot. Kelly's eyes widened a bit when he saw that it was a fifteen-year-old, but fairly well maintained, blue Buick with Wisconsin plates. The thing about this car that particularly attracted Kelly was the driver. He was a heavyset white man of about fifty with reddish brown hair and a beard. That the driver's beard was turning white and was much more luxurious than the fake facial hairpiece the impostor was wearing didn't matter to Kelly.

The impostor got up and, leaning heavily on his cane and carrying his briefcase in the opposite hand, began moving toward the aisle the Buick with the Wisconsin plates had just entered. As the driver cruised slowly down the aisle looking for a parking space, the man with the dyed hair followed.

CHAPTER 59

JUNE 18, 2004
3:47 P.M.

Larry Cole, Blackie Silvestri, and Nora Smelser stood behind air traffic control supervisor Joe Ballard. They were looking over his shoulder as he monitored Flight 200 Zebra's progress as it returned to Chicago's Midway Airport. The three cops were frozen into a rigidity which made them resemble statues. Their eyes never left the blinking green signal indicating 200 Zebra's position. It was moving rapidly across the scope.

Cole broke his mannequinlike pose and glanced at his watch. 200 Zebra had three and a half minutes left before the bomb went off.

On board 200 Zebra Buster Quint was concentrating on flying. His face was set in a mask of intense fury. Had it not been for the dire straits in which he and his passengers found themselves, the publisher-pilot would have been enjoying himself immensely. He hadn't flown at these speeds and in this devil-may-care manner since Vietnam. But he derived no pleasure from his deft manipulation of the twin-engine Gulfstream. He had to get this bird and the people it was carrying back on the ground in the next three minutes. If Quint failed, then they were all dead.

He was pushing the Gulfstream to its maximum. A red light, indicating that one of the engines was beginning to overheat, began flashing on the control panel. He ignored it. The engine could continue to operate, despite the overheating, for another twenty minutes. Of course, it wouldn't have to, as they had only a fraction of that time left.

Quint was sweating. He wiped away the moisture dripping from his forehead down into his eyes. Clutching the yoke firmly, he concentrated every fiber of his being on flying. He intended to bring the *Lady Joy* in and successfully evacuate his passengers before that bomb blew, even if it was the last thing he ever did.

Quint managed a grim smile and said out loud into the lonely isolation of the *Lady Joy*'s cockpit, "Poor choice of words, Buster. Poor choice of words."

"How much time?" Supervisor Ballard asked as he continued his scrutiny of the radar screen.

"Two minutes and forty-five seconds," Cole responded.

"Okay," the air traffic controller mumbled, "he just might make it." Keying his microphone, Ballard said, "Two hundred Zebra, you may begin your approach, and good luck."

On board the *Lady Joy*, Buster Quint activated the intercom. "Okay, gang, we're going in. As soon as the aircraft stops rolling, I want you out the emergency exit. I'll be right behind you."

Then Buster Quint took the *Lady Joy* into a steep dive. There were two minutes left before detonation.

"I'm going out to the field," Cole said, turning from the radar screen. Blackie and Lieutenant Smelser followed him out of the control tower.

Without acknowledging their departure, Supervisor Ballard said into his microphone, "Flight Two hundred Zebra, you are cleared to land on Runway One Left."

"Two hundred Zebra, roger."

Visibility over the airfield was virtually limitless and the *Lady Joy* could be seen in the western sky while it was still some miles from Midway. Lieutenant Smelser pulled her marked police car up beside the emergency vehicles waiting for the plane to touch down. Cole got out and conferred with the airport fire chief.

"The main priority will be to get everyone off that plane as soon as it stops rolling. Then we need to clear an area of at least one hundred yards surrounding it."

The fireman nodded. "How much time do we have left?"

Cole glanced at his watch. "About ninety seconds."

One of the emergency ground crew members was standing a short distance away staring up into the sky at the rapidly approaching aircraft. She said loud enough for the cops and fire chief to hear, "He's going to make it to the field, but will he be able to stop, as fast as he's going?"

Everyone turned to watch the *Lady Joy* drop from the sky.

Buster was bringing her in hot. He was painfully aware that he was quickly approaching the one-minute mark before detonation. First he would make sure he got the plane down on the ground. Then he would have to stop it. With the runway in sight he began experiencing the first glimmer of hope that they would indeed make it.

In the passenger compartment of the *Lady Joy*, Barbara Zorin, Jamal Garth, and Joy Quint were strapped securely in their seats. Their chairs were turned so that they could stare at Garth's bag, which contained the deadly device. The expression on their faces was a mixture of horror and awe. The last few minutes had seemed to last an eternity for them. An eternity which could be over in a single flash of blinding light.

*   *   *

Cole, Blackie, and Lieutenant Smelser got in the marked police car and prepared to follow the *Lady Joy* down the runway after it touched down. The plan was for them and another police vehicle assigned to the airport detail to quickly drive up to the plane, load the passengers, and spirit them away before the bomb detonated.

Cole took off his wristwatch and handed it to Blackie. "We're coming up on one minute. Once we get there give me a countdown in ten-second increments."

"You got it, boss," Blackie said, taking the black-dialed Rolex Submariner.

The *Lady Joy* touched down with smoke spewing from its landing gear. Buster Quint reversed the engines and jammed on the brake pedals. He fought with the yoke to keep the plane from skidding off the runway.

The aircraft raced past the emergency vehicles seemingly without slowing a centimeter. The tires scorched, throwing up a back plume of smoke behind the plane. Then the *Lady Joy* slowed down.

"Fifty seconds," Blackie shouted to be heard over the wail of Lieutenant Smelser's siren as they raced after the *Lady Joy*.

The plane came to a halt and Quint cut the engines before unstrapping his seat belt and leaping for the door connecting the cockpit with the passenger cabin. His wife already had the starboard exit door open and Jamal Garth had jumped to the ground. He turned and assisted Barbara Zorin and then Joy Quint from the plane. Buster was right behind his wife.

The men grabbed the women by the hand and led them away from the gold-and-blue death trap. A hundred yards away, coming fast down the runway, were the Chicago police cars. The four people ran as fast as they could toward them.

Thomas Kelly drove the blue Buick with Wisconsin plates up to the fare booth of the long-term parking lot. The attendant took the ticket and frowned. "You just came in, sir."

Kelly shrugged and graced the young attendant with a
smile. "I left something back in the city that I really have to
get. I guess I'll just have to pay the going rate."

The attendant smiled back. "That's okay. I won't charge
you twenty dollars for fifteen minutes."

"Bless you, my son," The words were out of Kelly's
mouth before he realized what he was saying.

The attendant looked curiously at the heavyset, bearded
man in the old car, but before he could comment, the sound
of a massive explosion could be heard coming from the airport.

"Oh, my God," the attendant screamed, "a plane must have
crashed!"

But the man in the Buick was already driving away. There
were tears of anguish in his blue eyes.

CHAPTER 60

JUNE 18, 2004
4:07 P.M.

Judy Daniels, in her disguise as Sister Mary Bridgit
O'Farrell from Saint Columbanus Parish, accompanied by
Sister Mary Louise Stallings, was searching the former monsignor's bedroom in which Father James Lochran was staying. After learning that their houseguest was an impostor and
suspected of being a killer, Louise had dropped all pretenses
of propriety and had led Judy to the second floor of the
rectory. Then she stood by while the Mistress of Disguise/
High Priestess of Mayhem searched the room.

Sister Mary Louise watched Judy move from the closets,
to the bed, to the chest of drawers, to the washroom. Judy

wore latex gloves and carried a transparent plastic bag into which she placed various items as she moved along. The nun was weighted down by a sense of guilty triumph. She had managed to prove that Father Phil's houseguest was a fraud. However, she derived no joy from this. Now it would fall to her to tell the pastor how she'd gone to the police without telling him. By now the phony priest would be in custody. But she realized it was better to have uncovered the impostor before Father Phil got hurt.

Judy finished her examination of the room and walked over to the door where Louise was standing. "Okay, I'm finished. Let's go downstairs and we can take a look at what I've found."

The two women left the room and a few moments later were seated at the dining-room table. It was the house-keeper's day off, so they were alone in the rectory.

Judy emptied the plastic bag on top of the table. There wasn't much there: a few paper receipts, some clothing tags, and three empty plastic pouches that still held the aroma of an explosive.

"Our friend Mr. Lochran," Judy said, refusing to dignify the imposter with his phony religious title, "traveled real light. Everything up there in that room, from his underwear and socks to his civvies, is brand-new." She fingered the tags and receipts. "He paid cash for everything. I would say that marks him as a man on the run."

At that moment the front door of the rectory opened.

"That must be Father Phil," the nun whispered. "I'd like to talk to him alone about this."

Judy quickly shoved her evidence back into the plastic bag. "Who are you going to say I am?"

The priest's footsteps could be heard approaching the room. The two women got to their feet. Before Louise could answer Judy, Father Phil walked through the door.

The nun managed a smile and said, "Father Philip Cisco, I'd like to introduce you to Sister Mary Bridgit O'Farrell from Saint Columbanus."

The young priest managed a smile, but there was trouble clouding the pastor's usually cheerful features. After acknowledging the woman calling herself Sister Mary Bridgit, the priest said to Sister Mary Louise, "I put in a call to the Detroit Archdiocese regarding Father Lochran. A Monsignor Willendez in the archbishop's office checked their roster of priests and there is no Father James Lochran assigned there. Our houseguest is an impostor."

The relief the nun felt was so intense it made her giddy. She was about to explain what she and Judy had uncovered when the doorbell rang.

"I'll be right back," the priest said.

Sister Mary Louise sighed. "Judy, the Lord definitely had his hand in this. I was really worried about how Father Phil would take my snooping around."

"I need to let Chief Cole know what your pastor found out," Judy said, reaching into her pocket for the small walkie-talkie she had used to communicate with earlier.

But before she could do so, two broad-shouldered men in business suits walked into the dining room. The instant Judy laid eyes on them she knew they were trouble. Her initial impression was that they were feds. But there was something a little too smooth and too polished in their manner and dress.

"Good afternoon, Sisters," said one of them, a tall man with a toothpaste ad smile. "All you have to do is exactly what you're told and everything will be just fine."

Although they didn't know that they were too late, the operatives from the Human Development Institute had discovered Thomas Kelly's hideout.

The pilot and passengers on board the *Lady Joy* had been rescued before the plane was destroyed, but just barely. Had the two airport detail police cars not reached the Quints, Barbara Zorin, and Jamal Garth and gotten them inside the vehicles prior to the detonation, they would all surely have been killed. The concussion from the blast cracked terminal windowpanes hundreds of feet from the location on the runway where Buster Quint had managed to bring the twin-engine jet to a halt. The sound of the explosion was heard as far away as the Chicago Loop. As it was, after getting the Quints and the authors into the police cars, the cops raced away from the site of the anticipated explosion as fast as they could. However, they only made it a short distance before the plane blew up.

Both cars, weighing over three tons each, were lifted off the ground by the blast. One of them, in which the Quints were huddled alone in the backseat, came close to being flipped over. It rocked precariously on its suspension before the airport cop, driving the car, managed to regain control. The other car—containing Cole, Blackie, Lieutenant Smelser, and the recently rescued authors—fared a bit better. They were still battered unmercifully by the explosion, and all of them would experience continuous ringing in their ears for hours to come. But they survived.

The emergency ground crew had moved in to cover the ensuing conflagration with foam and then water until the location on Runway One Left resembled a charred bomb crater. Pieces of the *Lady Joy*'s blue-and-gold fuselage were spread over a wide area of the airfield. If there was anything that could be classified as of a positive nature about what had just occurred, it was the fact that there had been only one life lost in this incident. That was the ground attendant, whose skull had been crushed. Also, the airport was able to resume arrivals and departures thirty minutes after the explosion of Flight 200 Zebra.

The cars bearing the survivors of the explosion pulled up to the hanger where the *Lady Joy* had been serviced earlier. Manny Sherlock was waiting for them. He had to shout to be understood by the partially deafened Cole and Blackie.

"The priest impersonator took off his collar and bib, dyed his hair red, and managed to get over here, where he killed a ground attendant."

Buster Quint was standing a short distance away with his arms around his trembling wife. "Where is this attendant?"

Manny looked at Cole, who nodded his approval.

"This way, sir," the sergeant said.

Leaving his wife in Barbara Zorin's and Jamal Garth's care, Quint followed Manny inside the hangar. The publisher returned a few moments later. There was a grim expression on his face. "That was Matt. He was supposed to load our luggage on the plane. I assumed that he had done so and took off without personally checking."

"Don't blame yourself," Cole said. "The man responsible for this is very good. Much better than I anticipated." Cole turned to Manny. "How is the search for our man coming?"

Manny's shoulders sagged. "We haven't come up with anything on a guy with red hair fitting our intruder's description. But we're still looking. We did find a homicide victim in the long-term lot. Guy's a dairy farmer from Wisconsin."

"What does he look like, Manny?" Blackie asked.

The sergeant read the description he had scrawled in his notebook.

Cole turned to Blackie. "Kelly has managed to get off the airport grounds. He could be headed back to Our Lady of Peace. We need to let Judy know right away."

Blackie snatched a walkie-talkie from his pocket and spent the next five minutes attempting to contact the Mistress of Disguise/High Priestess of Mayhem without success. By that time Cole and the rolling surveillance detail he had used to follow the bogus priest were racing back across the city en route to Our Lady of Peace Catholic Church. Police units in the Second District, which patrolled the Our Lady of Peace complex, had been alerted and were waiting for the chief of detectives when he arrived. The rectory was deserted.

The two black Ford panel trucks pulled into what, from the street, appeared to be a sublevel loading-dock area beneath the Human Development Institute building. An overhead door was opened by remote control and the vans entered. Two men wearing tailored business suits stood inside the spacious loading-dock area. They both carried large-bore machine pistols containing multiround clips. The armed men kept the loading-dock doors covered until the trucks had entered. Once the doors were closed, the armed men escorted the vehicles over to a freight elevator large enough to accommodate both vans.

The vans were driven onto the elevator, and the freight car descended fifty feet below street level. The doors opened on a man-made subterranean cavern constructed of gray stone. The walls dripped with moisture due to the close proximity of Lake Michigan. One-hundred-watt lightbulbs, encased in plastic, were arranged at fifty-foot intervals along the walls. Despite the lights, the area still resembled a medieval dungeon.

Two more armed men in suits were waiting for the vans. There was also a woman present. Virginia Daley, the HDI executive secretary, waited as the vehicles drove off the elevator and pulled to a halt in the cavernous corridor.

The agent with the dazzling smile who had confronted Sister Mary Louise and Judy Daniels, disguised as Sister Mary Bridgit O'Farrell, back at Our Lady of Peace rectory got out of the lead van and walked over to the Daley woman.

"Did you get him?" she demanded.

"No, but—" he began to explain.

Ignoring him, she stormed over to the first van and opened the back door. Inside were two armed men clad in a similar fashion to the other armed HDI operatives. Father Phil Cisco, blindfolded with a black cloth and bound with plastic flex-cuffs, was also there.

Virginia Daley went to the other van and discovered the two nuns guarded, blindfolded, and bound in the exact same manner as the priest. Spinning around, she stomped back to the man with the perfect smile.

"Who are they?!" she screamed.

His smiled vanished and his complexion turned a shade or two paler. He whispered, "Kelly wasn't there, but they were. They probably know where—"

The HDI executive secretary's right palm came up with a blur and she slapped the man hard across the face. He reeled backward from the blow, but made no attempt to defend himself or retaliate. The Human Development Institute sanctioned the physical punishment of its employees even to an extreme. And no one in the service of this clandestine organization over the many years of its nefarious existence had ever complained. At least not for long.

"Your stupidity borders on the criminal," Virginia Daley snarled. "I'll have to take this up with the director."

She walked rapidly toward a passenger elevator next to the freight lift.

The agent, whose left cheek had turned bright red, called after her, "What should I do with them?"

She stopped and turned around. Her eyes, behind dark-framed glasses, studied the occupants of the two black vans. The words "Kill them" were on the tip of her tongue. Then she took a deep breath and said, "Confine them. I'll let the director decide." Then she was gone.

CHAPTER 61

JUNE 18, 2004
6:12 P.M.

In his office at the Dragon's Lair nightclub, Jack Carlisle sat alone. He had shut off the closed-circuit television monitors and most of the lights. As there were no windows in the room, the office was cast in semidarkness. The fixer looked at the wall clock. In forty-eight minutes the USA-Italy Olympic basketball game would begin. The game would be televised on a cable sports channel and would probably receive a decent, if not overwhelming, share of the viewing audience. This was no Super Bowl, World Series game, or NBA Finals contest. By rights there shouldn't have been any professionals playing tonight at all. Because of this the Americans were favored to win by forty points, which was the last spread the Las Vegas book had quoted Carlisle. "The Dream Team for the Twenty-first Century" was simply too good, and there was no team from any country in the world which would be able to compete with them. At least there wasn't supposed to be.

Finally, Carlisle picked up the telephone. He punched an automatic dial button and waited. The phone rang only once before it was answered.

"Hello." The man spoke in a low voice barely above a whisper.

"I'd like some action on tonight's Olympic basketball game between the Americans and Italians."

"How much?"

"Two million."

"On the USA team?"

"No. On the Italians."

There was a brief pause from the other end. "The odds are one hundred to one against the Eye-ties and the spread is thirty-seven points."

"It was forty a couple of hours ago."

"That was then, this is now. I don't think it will matter in the long run. Pete Dubcek's playing for the Americans."

For the first time in quite a while Jack Carlisle managed to smile. "I know."

There was another pause from the other end of the line. Then, "Okay, Mr. Carlisle, you've got two million on the Italian team with a point spread of thirty-seven at one hundred to one odds. If the USA loses or fails to cover the spread, you will win two hundred million dollars. Have a nice day."

"You do the same," Carlisle said before hanging up the phone. Now the fixer was going to find out how much Pete Dubcek loved his sweet little wife.

ATLANTA, GEORGIA

The Dream Team completed their warm-up prior to the first Olympic basketball game. The Americans were clad in traditional red, white, and blue uniforms highlighted with stars. The Italians wore green and white. There were pregame interviews being conducted at various locations around the main court of the Atlanta Sports Center. Select members of both teams were targeted to respond to inane and at times stupid questions asked by the interviewers.

Gerald Sheppard, the star guard for the Indiana Pacers, was one of those being interviewed. Sheppard was scheduled to start the game beside Pete Dubcek. A sports reporter with styled hair and a baritone voice that came out sounding like the reverberations from a kettle drum asked, "Do you think the Italian team has a chance against you guys tonight?"

Sheppard, a six-foot four-inch black man sporting a shaved head, goatee, and Fu Manchu mustache managed to smile. He was a popular player in the league with a following almost as large as Dubcek's. His nickname was Shazzam, due to a combination of his genie-like appearance and the way he could perform seemingly magical feats on the basketball court. In response to the question, Shazzam said, "They have an excellent team. Got some guys over there who could start for any team in the NBA right now. I'm sure they will acquit themselves admirably."

"But are any of the members on the Italian team capable of playing at the level of a Pete Dubcek or Shazzam?" the interviewer pressed.

Sheppard had reached the limit of his patience. "We'll just have to wait and see what transpires on the court tonight."

"By the way, Shazzam, I didn't see Dubcek come out for the warm-up. Is he okay?"

"Pete doesn't need a warm-up." With that Sheppard turned around and ran back to the Dream Team's dressing room.

Pete Dubcek sat in front of his locker staring at the small tape recorder that only a few hours ago had turned his world upside down. During that period he had experienced a plethora of emotions; fear, anger, remorse, and despair were just a few. He was also terribly confused and realized there was no place that he could go for help. The message on the tape had been quite explicit. If he didn't do exactly what the disembodied voice instructed, then his wife, Vanessa "Fuzzy" Dubcek, was going to die.

He picked up the tape recorder and rewound the short message. Glancing around to make sure none of his teammates were close enough to hear the message, Dubcek played the tape.

The voice was a computerized transmission. The artificial sound gave the threatening words even greater impact.

"Piotr Dubcek of the USA Olympic basketball team, on the night of June eighteenth, 2004, you will participate in a game against the Italian national team, which will be played in the Atlanta Sports Center. You are to utilize the formidable athletic skills you have displayed in the past to ensure that the Italians do not lose this game by more than ten points. If you fail to do what I have instructed, your wife will be killed. You are to tell no one of this message and you are not to go to the police. If you do so Fuzzy will die. To guarantee that you take this message with the sincerity with which it was intended I suggest that you listen to the following carefully."

There was a brief pause and then the computerized voice was replaced by a woman's. It was Fuzzy.

"Pete, you've got to do what they say. Please, Pete. They're going to hurt me if you don't. I love you, baby."

There was another pause and the computerized voice resumed. "You have been given your instructions, Piotr Dubcek. Don't let me or your pretty wife down."

The tape ended.

The first time Dubcek played the tape that morning he thought it was a joke. He even tried calling home, even though he doubted Fuzzy would be there. All he got for his trouble was their answering machine.

He played the tape at least a half dozen times more, and each time the impact of the threat hit him harder, until there was no longer any doubt in his mind that whoever had done this was in deadly earnest. And if he didn't do what they said, Fuzzy was going to be killed.

Slowly, the realization dawned as to exactly what was being demanded of him. They wanted him to alter the outcome of a basketball game by doing something that was not only unethical, but also illegal. The thought of doing such a thing was so abhorrent to Pete Dubcek that he became violently ill. He made it to the bathroom of his Radisson Inn hotel room in downtown Atlanta and emptied the contents of his stomach into the toilet bowl. He staggered back to the bedroom, collapsed on the bed, and curled himself into a fetal ball. He remained in that position for hours, until the desk called to notify him that a car was waiting to take him to the Sports Center.

During the ride Pete frantically searched for alternatives. He could tell the coach that he was ill and not play in the game at all. But the Dream Team was so good and possessed such a great degree of depth on the bench that Dubcek would hardly be missed. They could easily coast to a victory over the Italians without him. A victory with a margin greater than ten points. No, Pete Dubcek would have to play.

As he was escorted through a crowd of fans at the entrance to the Sports Center by a pair of uniformed cops, Pete considered informing the authorities about the tape recording and leaving it in their hands. Then the computerized words came back to him: *"You are to tell no one of this message and you are not to go to the police. If you do so your wife will die."*

In the locker room, Dubcek had undressed slowly and put on his uniform. Then he'd sat down in front of his locker. When the rest of the team went out for the warm-up, Pete had remained behind. Now, it was almost game time.

The replay of the threatening tape recording was almost over when Shazzam Sheppard came over to Dubcek's locker. The star player from Chicago jammed the off button with such force that he lost control of the device. The recorder fell to the tile floor and smashed into a number of pieces.

Sheppard stood over Dubcek looking down at the plastic and electronic parts lying in front of the locker. "That's junk, Petey. I'll buy you a good one after we go out there and hold up the USA's reputation in roundball."

The black basketball star turned away. Dubcek remained seated, staring down at the smashed tape recorder. When Shazzam noticed that Dubcek wasn't following him, he called, "C'mon, Pete. They're about to sing the anthems and announce the starting lineups."

Dubcek hesitated a moment and then got to his feet. Looking down at the remains of the recorder, he raised one of his size fourteen Nike All-Stars and stomped down on what was on the floor.

Then he followed Shazzam Sheppard out of the locker room.

CHAPTER 62

ATLANTA, GEORGIA
JUNE 18, 2004
7:30 P.M.

The first half came to an end. The USA team retreated to its locker room. The players and their coach appeared stunned to the point of confusion. The pro-American crowd had gone eerily quiet. The eyes of almost everyone present—both spectator and participant—were on Pete Dubcek. The star player had not only failed to play up to his potential, but had performed as if he didn't know anything at all about the game of basketball.

At this point the United States led the Italians, 50–46. Dubcek had scored no points, committed three fouls, and been responsible for four turnovers. For their part the Italians had risen to the occasion and, as a unit, played far above their level. They performed more like an NBA playoff team than an amateur European squad. Everyone watching the game could tell that there was something strange happening here.

CHICAGO, ILLINOIS

Cole left the Chicago police department superintendent's office and headed back to detective division headquarters at the other end of the police complex. The administrative area was dark at this time of night, which mirrored the chief of detective's mood. He had hoped that with the superintendent's assistance he could obtain an open-ended search warrant for the Human Development Institute complex. But when the superintendent called the chief judge of the Cook County Circuit Court to request the slightly illegal document, he'd been turned down flat. The reason, although not openly stated, was the Institute and its politically heavy director, Dr. Gilbert Goldman.

The chief judge had refused to listen to Cole's argument, delivered via the superintendent's speakerphone, that there was a strong possibility that Sister Mary Louise Stallings, Father Philip Cisco, and Judy Daniels had been kidnapped by Institute operatives and could be in danger. The judge had stated quite emphatically that the CPD and Larry Cole simply didn't have enough to go on. No search warrant would be forthcoming.

So Cole would have to figure out another way to get inside the heavily guarded building on the Midway Plaisance. He also realized that he would have to come up with something fast.

He was walking through a shadowy area of the police complex when he heard a noise behind him. Turning around he came face-to-face with the Abo-Yorba.

The shock of encountering the she-devil without warning frightened Cole into reaching for his gun. Then, less than six feet away from him, the image of the shape-shifter altered and Orga Syriac appeared.

Cole lowered the Beretta to his side and said a shaky, "How did you get in here?"

"I'm covering the explosion on Buster Quint's plane," she

THE LEFT HAND OF GOD 301

said. "We're taping a segment in the lobby inside the main entrance."

The main entrance was at Thirty-fifth and Michigan, which was two blocks from where they now stood. There were police officers posted at strategic locations of the headquarters complex, and sensitive areas were covered by closed-circuit TV cameras. Yet Orga had been able to elude all of the security measures and find Cole. He didn't know whether to be terrified or impressed.

"I don't have much time. I asked to use the washroom and slipped away. Someone will come looking for me if I don't get back soon. I think you and I can help each other."

"How?" Cole said, returning his gun to its holster.

"You need to get inside the Human Development Institute. So do I."

"How do you know that?"

"Kate Ford told me."

Cole had talked to Kate before he went in to see the superintendent. He had confided to her his suspicions as to what had happened at Our Lady of Peace after Thomas Kelly's escape. Had the investigative journalist shared this information with anyone else other than the woman standing before him now, Cole would have been more than a trifle irritated.

"Why do you need to get inside the Institute, Orga?"

"I've got a score to settle with them."

"Them?" Cole said with a raised eyebrow.

"I'll explain it all to you later, but we can help each other on this. You're going to have to force your way inside because you can't get a warrant. If we work together I can at least get the front door open for you."

"And once we're inside?"

"What I do does not concern you."

"Orga—" he began, but she cut him off.

"Someone's coming and I've got to get back. If you leave your friends in there with those people too long they're going to die. The Institute will do whatever it has to, including murder, to keep its secrets. I'll contact you later tonight."

Then, as Cole looked on, she returned to her Abo-Yorba

form and vanished back into the shadows. He was still staring at the spot where he'd last seen the she-devil when Blackie Silvestri approached from the opposite end of the corridor.

"How did it go, boss?" the lieutenant asked.

Cole recovered quickly and said, "We're not going to get the warrant, so we'll have to figure out something else."

"Like what?"

Cole looked off into the shadows of the darkened police complex. "I'm working on it."

ATLANTA, GEORGIA

In the locker room Pete Dubcek's teammates and even the coach ignored him. Dubcek went over to his locker and sat down. While the team had been out on the court the maintenance staff had come in and cleaned up the locker room. The smashed recorder and the blackmail tape were gone.

Dubcek stared blankly off into space. He had never felt like this before in his life. Basketball had meant everything to him for as far back as he could remember. He had begun playing with American GI's stationed at the United States Army European Command Hospital in Heidelberg. Although he was only twelve years old, the Americans, who were mostly black, would smuggle the German youth onto the base to play in their well-equipped gym. After that his life had never been the same.

Now all he had worked for was being destroyed. Destroyed because of his wife.

Although the tape was gone, he could still remember every word. Especially those spoken by his wife. *"I love you, baby."* It was strange that she would say such a thing even after she'd been kidnapped and in danger. On the day that they were married she'd never professed her love for him in such a manner. In fact, she had never voiced any love for him at all.

"I love you, baby."

"Pete?" the voice of Shazzam Sheppard came from behind him.

Dubcek didn't turn around. "What?"

"You want to tell me what's going on?"

"There's nothing going on."

Sheppard reached down and grabbed the German's arm. "That's bullshit! I've been playing against you for five years and I've never seen you, or a player of your caliber, fold up the way you're doing!"

Dubcek snatched his arm away and went back to his examination of the empty space in front of his locker.

The black player stood over his white counterpart for a moment longer and then turned away in disgust.

"I love you, baby," kept echoing through his head. *"I love you, baby."*

CHICAGO, ILLINOIS

In his office in the Dragon's Lair, Jack Carlisle was experiencing a building excitement. Everything was going according to plan. He was thirty playing minutes away from winning two hundred million dollars. Of course when the game was over there would be heat. A great deal of heat. In the fallout following tonight's game a lot of people would be looking into what happened. The media would have a field day, the Olympic committee would have a conniption, the Vegas Mob would be ready to outfit a few people in cement wet suits, and Pete Dubcek's basketball career would be over. But the fixer would get his money, and when he did it would be time to retire from serious sports gambling.

The announcer on the television was interviewing a game analyst, who was castigating Pete Dubcek for his first-half play. Carlisle muted the sound and punched a button on the communications console on his desk. A bartender working in the nonalcoholic side of the club answered.

"Send Sonny in here."

After hanging up, the fixer sat back to watch the remainder of the game that was going to make him a multimillionaire. However, first he would begin putting his insurance policy into effect.

CHAPTER 63

JUNE 18, 2004
8:36 P.M.

The cell was comfortable, but still a cell. There was a living-room area, individual sleeping rooms, a washroom, and a kitchen. The walls had been recently painted a rose color, and there was a brown-and-beige carpet on the floor. Sister Mary Louise, Father Phil, and Judy Daniels were together in the living-room area. Since they'd been forced from the Our Lady of Peace rectory at gunpoint, blindfolded, bound, and brought to this place, they had said very little. Father Phil and Sister Mary Louise displayed a combination of confusion and no little degree of fear. Judy was also feeling the same confusion and fear, but she was also experiencing another emotion—anger.

The Mistress of Disguise/High Priestess of Mayhem had been kidnapped before. The idea of someone exerting control over her by force made her furious. But she controlled her anger in order to not jeopardize the lives of her fellow captives. She planned to continue in her disguise as Sister Mary Bridgit O'Farrell so that her captors would continue to treat her in a nonthreatening fashion. So far things had gone well for the captives. Despite the high-tech weaponry and obvious sophistication of the men and the lone woman, whose voice they'd heard, the kidnappers had made a basic procedural error. They hadn't searched their prisoners.

When the well-dressed guards removed their blindfolds and flex-cuffs, Judy had expected a frisk despite all the guards being male. Had they indeed searched her, they would have discovered some very interesting items beneath the habit she wore. Besides her palm-sized walkie-talkie, she had her Chicago police badge, a photo ID card, and a nickel-plated .38 caliber snub-nosed revolver strapped to her inner thigh. However, the weapon was hardly a match for the guns their kidnappers carried. The time might come when Judy's pistol could come in very handy. She was prepared to wait for the right opportunity, if and when it arose, to make her move.

Now, as Sister Mary Louise explained to Father Phil what she and Judy had discovered about the phony priest, the Mistress of Disguise/High Priestess of Mayhem carefully examined their modernistic dungeon. For the most part it looked like a somewhat spartan, but clean, furnished apartment, with two major exceptions. There were no windows and the door was of reinforced steel. She checked for eavesdropping devices but was unable to discover any. At least none that could be detected with the naked eye.

Deciding not to take any chances, she went over to her fellow captives and whispered, "I'm going to try and contact Chief Cole, but I need your help to do so."

When Father Phil and Sister Mary Louise became aware of her low tone of voice, they looked warily around the cell.

"In case we are being observed we need to be doing something collectively that will appear to be innocent to anyone watching. Can we say a prayer?"

Father Phil nodded. "Because of the fix we're in I was going to recommend that anyway. Now it will serve a two-fold purpose."

They knelt down on the carpet. Carefully, Judy removed the walkie-talkie from her pocket. Holding it in her left palm, she clasped both hands together and lowered her head in a pose of reverence. With her thumb she depressed the transmit button.

"Sister," Father Phil said, "will you lead us in prayer?"

Sister Mary Louise began to recite the Our Father.

Judy whispered into the walkie-talkie, "Fifty Paul, emergency. Any unit picking up this message please respond. Fifty Paul, emergency." Releasing the key, she waited for a response. None came.

She was about to repeat the message when the cell door opened and two guards entered.

The buzzer sounded in Orga Syriac's Lake Shore Drive condominium. Blessing, the TV newscaster's companion, answered it.

Flipper McBride, the ex-boxer doorman, said over the intercom, "There's a delivery man down here with a package for Ms. Syriac."

"Send him up, Mr. McBride." Blessing said before going to open the door.

Atlanta, Georgia

"*I love you, baby*," continued to echo through Pete Dubcek's head. He was riding the American bench in the Sports Center gymnasium. The boos cascading down from the stands swirled around him, but his wife's tape-recorded voice blocked them out. However, the boos were not only directed at him. Now they included the entire USA team.

The Americans had collapsed. Even the supertalented Shazzam Sheppard had gone cold. It was as if Dubcek had cast a spell over his own team. They couldn't buy a basket and their play was so bad that one of the announcers made the statement that the Dream Team of the Twenty-first Century couldn't beat a "pickup squad of old ladies."

Dubcek sat alone. He had a warm-up jacket around his shoulders and his head was down. The phrase kept echoing through his head, "*I love you, baby.*"

Out on the court the USA had fallen ten points behind the Italian national team as they reached the midpoint of the second half. And things were getting progressively worse.

Then Shazzam Sheppard went up for a layup, which he missed, came down in an awkward position, and broke his right ankle.

The game was halted and a stretcher brought out to remove the injured player. The coach, his teammates, and the team doctor surrounded the prone player. Pete Dubcek remained on the bench.

"I love you, baby."

The words pounded against the inside of his skull like a runaway jackhammer. He slammed his hands over his ears, as if this act would block out the sound. But all it did was intensify the pain. Finally, the agony became too great and he leaped to his feet screaming, "No you don't!"

Shazzam had been removed and the coach had gathered the team in front of their bench. When Dubcek screamed they all turned to look at him. No one spoke. Then he noticed that the voice in his head was gone.

He joined the circle of players. "I'm ready to play some ball, guys."

The coach looked skeptically at him, but Pete Dubcek had a reputation for being a spectacular late-game player. And they sure as hell needed one now.

"Okay, Pete, you're the man. Cook, go in for Shazzam." Kevin Cook, a starting guard for the Phoenix Suns, had been playing in Dubcek's absence. "And let's look like a basketball team!"

CHICAGO, ILLINOIS

Paige Albritton was in the kitchen of Larry Cole's apartment when she heard Butch shout from the living room, "I don't believe this crap!"

Surprised at hearing the usually polite young man use such language, she went to see what was wrong.

He was in the living room, seated with his legs crossed in front of the television set. There was a basketball game being telecast. Paige had never been a great fan of this sport, preferring football, which her dead fiancé, Mack, had played at the high school, college, and professional levels.

"What's wrong, Butch?"

He turned from the set and said, "Pete Dubcek and the so-called Dream Team stink."

At the mention of the basketball player's name, Paige experienced a flash of unease. Jack Carlisle had wanted her to seduce Dubcek, and when she failed, the fixer had crushed her fingers, which were still in a cast.

Slowly, she crossed the living room and sat down on the couch. If something was wrong with Dubcek or his team, she strongly suspected that her crooked former boss was involved. She sat in silence and watched the TV screen.

In the detention area beneath the Human Development Institute, the guards stood at the door staring at the three kneeling people. Father Phil and Sister Mary Louise looked up. The woman posing as Sister Mary Bridgit O'Farrell remained in her prayerful pose. Father Phil got to his feet. He took a step toward the guards, moving imperceptibly to shield Judy Daniels from view.

"Why and by whose authority are you holding us here?" the priest demanded.

The well-dressed men, holding machine pistols, stared stonily back at the priest. They were so similar in appearance that they could have been clones. The only readily noticeable difference in their sameness was that one was wearing a blue double-breasted suit and the other an olive green single-breasted one.

The guard in the blue suit responded to the priest's question. "You'll be told in good time, Padre."

The other one raised a paper sack. It bore the McDonald's logo. In a voice that sounded amazingly similar to his partner's, olive green suit responded, "Sorry to interrupt your prayers, folks, but we brought you some food. Hope you like double cheeseburgers and vanilla milk shakes."

With that he placed the bag down on the floor and they backed out of the room. When they were gone the three captives breathed a sigh of relief. The nun and the priest resumed praying and Judy Daniels continued attempting to contact Larry Cole.

CHAPTER 64

The USA team rallied. Pete Dubcek led the charge by scoring eighteen points in a span of six minutes. As the game progressed, the Americans were up twelve points over the Italians, but Dubcek had only just begun.

The Dream Team was now playing an errorless game at both ends of the court. They were not only scoring points, but had virtually shut the Italian team down offensively. In a matter of scant moments, the crowd in the Atlantic Sports Center had gone from being hostile, to apathetic, to surprised, and finally hysterically exuberant. It was as if they were viewing a completely different game. It was a surprise to not only the people in Atlanta.

CHICAGO, ILLINOIS

Jack Carlisle stared at the television set with an emotionless gaze. Had anyone been capable of looking inside his heart they would have been shocked at the icy blackness it contained. The fixer had lost money before. In his line of work it was inevitable. He had lost vast sums of money in the past, but nothing close to two million dollars. But Carlisle would never make a bet he couldn't cover. Two million dollars was a lot of dough, but he would come up with it. The problem was that if the game continued as it was going now, he would not collect the two hundred million he'd planned to retire on. For that, someone would pay and pay very dearly.

The object of Carlisle's wrath appeared on the television screen flickering in front of him. As the fixer watched, Pete Dubcek pulled up from a distance of forty feet and fired a jump shot over three Italian defenders. The camera followed the arc of the ball as it rose above the court and began its descent to swish through the basket. The net snapped with a sound that carried easily over the television audio transmission.

The ten-point spread the fixer had quoted was arbitrary. Carlisle knew that, with the other Dream Team members participating, it would be difficult, if not impossible, to prevent them from beating the Italian team by a much larger margin. But with Dubcek out of the picture what the fixer had expected to happen had indeed occurred—the Americans became demoralized and played badly.

Now Dubcek was again performing like a man possessed and his teammates, minus the injured Shazzam Sheppard, had mounted an impressive comeback. With six minutes left in the game, the USA had taken a twenty-five-point lead. For every basket that the Italian national team managed to make, their opponents scored three. Jack Carlisle's thirty-seven-point cushion began evaporating rapidly, and as it did so the fixer's black heart turned meaner and colder.

Dubcek had been warned what would happen if he didn't "play ball" the fixer's way. That meant that Fuzzy would have to die and in a very horrible fashion. However, her husband would also experience some severe problems.

On the TV screen, Pete Dubcek performed a spectacular dunk to give the Americans a thirty-six-point lead with two minutes left in the game. Ten seconds later he hit another long-range jump shot to give the USA a thirty-nine-point advantage. The fixer was going down fast. The money he owed would be due tomorrow. The Vegas bookie would send a collector and crew around to see him. And Carlisle would pay. But so would Pete Dubcek.

*   *   *

Larry Cole had done all that he could tonight. He sat in his office in the Investigative Services wing of the police headquarters complex with Blackie. They had gone over everything they had on the investigations of the mysterious explosions, the Human Development Institute, Thomas Kelly/Father James Lochran, and the missing pastor of Our Lady of Peace, Sister Mary Louise Stallings, and Judy Daniels. Cole didn't mention to Blackie anything about Orga Syriac, what she was, or her offer to help him get inside the Human Development Institute.

It had been a long day for the cops and they could feel it. Rubbing his eyes, Cole said, "There's got to be something we missed."

Blackie stifled a yawn. "I don't know what we missed, boss, but our batting average is lousy today. Besides failing to nab Kelly, we lost Judy."

Cole had no answer for that one. "I think we should go home and get a few hours' sleep, Blackie. In the morning we'll try to get in to see Goldman again."

"You got a point about the sleep," the lieutenant said, getting wearily to his feet. Cole was about to rise as well when the telephone on his desk rang. It was his private line, the number to which only a select few possessed.

"Cole."

"Chief Cole, this is Dr. Gilbert Goldman."

Cole's frown got Blackie's attention. "What can I do for you, Doctor?"

"I'm still looking for Thomas Kelly."

"So are we."

"I understand that you had him earlier today and he managed to slip through your fingers."

Cole had a pretty good idea where he had obtained this information, but that wasn't the issue right now.

"I think we can be of mutual assistance to each other."

Cole's jaw muscles rippled. This was the second time tonight that someone had offered him unsolicited help.

"Are you still there?"

"I'm here. So, tell me, Doctor, how can we be of 'mutual assistance' to each other?"

"I want Thomas Kelly."

"So do I and I have a priority claim on him for multiple counts of murder and a few of attempted murder."

Goldman sighed noisily. "I know you have what you would call priorities, which I respect, but so do I."

"What kind of priority supersedes murder?"

"The lives of a priest and two nuns from Our Lady of Peace Catholic Church."

Cole stiffened. "If those people are harmed . . ."

"Cole, Cole, I must take umbrage with your accusing, or attempting to imply, that I or the Human Development Institute has committed any crime."

Fighting for control of his rage, Cole said, "Where are the priest and the nuns?"

"Where is Thomas Kelly?"

"We're still looking for him, Doctor, but I assure you we will find him."

"And when you do I want him brought to the Institute, not put in jail." Before Cole could interject, Goldman added, "While you are doing that I will move heaven and earth to locate your friends from the Christian community. I don't think that either of us has to stipulate in regards to the relative safety and well-being of our respective charges in this little, shall we call it, transaction?"

Cole couldn't stand it any longer. "Doctor, I've had some questions about you and your operation since the moment I heard of it. Now you've cleared everything up for me. You people are criminals. You have no little degree of political influence and I'm quite sure that you perceive yourselves as being invincible, but this time you're going to lose."

"Spare me your impassioned threats. You and your department mean nothing in the greater scheme of things, Cole, and I don't have time to explain political realities to you. Now I suggest that you do what you've been told and find Thomas Kelly. When you do, call me and we'll see about your friends. Good night."

When Cole hung up he was so angry he was forced to clench his hands tightly into fists to keep himself from exploding.

"I guess that tears it," Blackie said, having monitored this end of the conversation.

Cole exhaled slowly to relieve the tension and said, "At least we now know for a certainty where Judy is, and Goldman doesn't seem to be aware that she's a cop."

"Do you think he cares?"

"Maybe not, but their continuing to believe she's a nun could work to our advantage. You know Judy."

"Yeah. That disguise might just keep her breathing."

There was a knock on the office door followed by Manny Sherlock entering. "We have a lead on Thomas Kelly, boss,"

ATLANTA, GEORGIA

The USA Olympic team beat the Italian nationals by forty-eight points. When the game was over, Pete Dubcek, who had scored a game-high fifty-two points, didn't stop to give interviews or sign autographs. Instead he rushed into the locker room, where he showered, changed into civilian clothes, and requested the services of the Atlanta Police Department to get him from the Sports Center to the airport. Thirty-five minutes after the game ended, Pete Dubcek was on a charter flight bound for Chicago.

CHICAGO ILLINOIS

Orga Syriac entered her Lake Shore Drive condominium. The mail had been left on a marble table in the entrance alcove. She picked it up and was starting to flip through the bills and correspondence when she realized there was something wrong. Dropping the mail back on the table, she walked to the rear of the apartment and called, "Blessing?"

She was met by silence.

Orga went from room to room searching for her companion. The condo was empty. Puzzled, she went to Blessing's quarters in case her companion had left a message for her. She found nothing.

She allowed the visage of the Abo-Yorba to descend on her. This enhanced her physical and psychic perceptions immensely. She reached out for Blessing, and what came back weakened the she-devil to the point that she nearly collapsed. Her friend had been taken from this place by force. Then the rage set in.

She unleashed a scream of such intensity that it shook the very foundation of the fifty-story building.

The doorman, Flipper McBride, had gone along with Sonny Balfour.

At least so far. For a $250 advance he had agreed to let Balfour into the building by way of the rear service entrance. Then he watched the lobby while his former boxing pal and another guy, whom McBride had never seen before, went up to Ms. Syriac's condo. He didn't know what they did up there and he didn't want to know. He would get another $250 before they left. If anyone came asking, he hadn't seen or heard anything and he knew absolutely nothing. Then Balfour had thrown a monkey wrench into things.

McBride had given Balfour the keys to the freight elevator at the rear of the building. When he returned, the doorman noticed that the other ex-boxer's left cheek was bleeding from scratch marks. That was the first thing McBride didn't like about what was going on.

"Here's your money, Flip," Balfour said, handing him one of two envelopes. Then he extended the second envelope. "I need you to do one more thing for me."

McBride avoided the envelope like it was a live snake. "I ain't getting no deeper in this thing, Sonny."

Balfour pulled a handkerchief from his back pocket and dabbed at his cheek. The look he gave McBride was frightening. "Oh, you'll do it, Flipper, or Mrs. Cushing, the condo manager, will get a telephone call informing her of your involvement in what went down upstairs a few minutes ago."

McBride considered punching Balfour, but the doorman was giving away ten pounds to a man who had once been a contender. So he took the envelope, which Balfour told him to slip under Orga Syriac's door after the beautiful newscaster arrived home. It was addressed to "The Monster."

So Flipper McBride, whose brain had been so battered in the ring that he had a moron-level IQ, had waited for the newscaster to return home. Five minutes later he went up to the tenth floor. The corridor was carpeted, which muffled his footsteps as he approached the condominium. The task was simple. He did this kind of thing routinely with everything from packages to bouquets of flowers. At the door he squatted down and placed the envelope on the floor. Using the toe of his shoe, he pushed it slowly through the crack. His job done, he breathed a sigh of relief and was about to go back to his post when the door opened.

He was attempting to come up with a plausible lie that would absolve him of any culpability for whatever Balfour had done, when he was confronted by a beast. A beast that grabbed him and snatched him inside Orga Syriac's apartment.

CHAPTER 65

JUNE 18, 2004
8:45 P.M.

Brother Steven Pasco of the Holy Name Mission on Clark Street was calm, as far as outward appearances went. He seldom allowed himself to be affected by fear. At the location where he practiced his ministry, he'd learned to handle terror. During his years at the mission he'd been stabbed twice, beaten up six times—once so severely that he'd ended up in a coma—and shot at. Yet he'd returned each time and redoubled his efforts to help the less fortunate of God's hu-

man creations. But tonight he was frightened to the very
marrow of his being.

It had begun earlier that night, shortly after the evening
meal. He had been supervising a cleanup detail in the mess
hall when he noticed that one of the men present looked
familiar. Brother Steve couldn't place him immediately and
had simply relegated the stranger to the category of a former
mission visitor who hadn't been around in a while. The man
was sixtyish, bearded, heavyset, and walked with a cane. He
was wearing a dirty denim baseball cap over a head of flaming red hair and possessed a ruddy complexion. There was
nothing in the least bit extraordinary about him and he fit in
with the other homeless and impoverished types that fre-
quented the mission.

Then Brother Steve saw the redheaded man enter the
chapel. The administrator of the Holy Name Mission had
thought nothing of this, as access to the chapel was available
to anyone during the hours that the mission was open. Then
one of the regulars, who had been around as long as Brother
Steve had been there, told him that there was a man crying
in the chapel.

This was the first chord of memory struck in Brother
Steve's mind. He had gone to the chapel and peered in at
the man kneeling at the small, barren altar. And he was indeed crying. Then Brother Steve noticed his posture, the set
of his shoulders, and even the position in which he'd placed
his cane beside him. It took a moment to recall the priest's
name. Father Lochran. Father James Lochran.

At that instant Brother Steve's life took a fortunate turn.
Officer Bob Roselle walked a beat out of the Eighteenth District on Clark Street, where the mission was located. A con-
scientious, hardworking cop, Roselle had monitored a radio
transmission of a lookout for a man wanted for murder. A
wanted man who had dyed his hair red and previously im-
personated a priest. As Brother Steve Pasco stood peering
into the chapel, Officer Roselle walked in the front door.

"How's it going, Steve?" the veteran officer said. "What's
going on?"

Quietly, Brother Steve closed the chapel door to keep from disturbing his guest's tearful prayer and turned to the cop.

Thomas Kelly found himself in the depths of a depression possessing a weight so great that it threatened to crush his soul. He had heard on the car radio in the stolen Buick that his latest mission of atonement had also failed. Now his anguish threatened to rip him apart. Through the internal pain he was feeling and the sobs that racked his body, he managed to say, "Oh, Father, please forgive me. I have again failed in my mission of atonement. Perhaps . . ." The words caught in his throat. He swallowed hard. "Perhaps if you could give this poor servant some sign that my feet are on the path that you want me to tread, I will be renewed and able to better serve you."

There was a noise behind him. Slowly he turned around to find that two men had entered the chapel. He recognized them both. One was the cabdriver who had picked him up in front of the Our Lady of Peace rectory and driven him to the airport, a cabdriver whom Thomas Kelly suspected was an imposter. The other man was Larry Cole.

Cole and Blackie had the fugitive trapped. The building in which the Holy Name Mission was located had first been evacuated and then surrounded by cops. Larry Cole was not going to let Thomas Kelly escape again.

Cole and Blackie had slipped into the chapel and taken seats in the pews behind the sobbing murderer. With silent hand signals, Cole had communicated to his partner the location of the attaché case and cane, which were within arm's reach of the fugitive. Their mission was to keep him away from those items, which in the past he had employed with such deadly results.

Now that Kelly had become aware of them, the cops began putting their plan into effect.

"Mr. Kelly," Cole said quietly, "I want you to stand up and raise your hands."

Kelly didn't move.

In tandem, Cole and Blackie stood up. Both had guns in

their hands, although they had yet to point them at Kelly. Cole moved toward the center aisle, Blackie to one of the side aisles. They hoped to avoid killing him if they could.

"Thomas," Cole said, beginning to advance toward the mission chapel's altar, "I want you to stand up and raise your hands."

Without attempting to reach for his cane, Kelly struggled to his feet. He did not raise his hands.

Blackie reached the front of the chapel and had an unobstructed view of the wanted man. The lieutenant possessed above average competency with the four-inch-barreled .357 magnum Colt Python he carried. If he was forced to, he would first attempt a disabling shot; however, Blackie had little faith in such a maneuver. From long experience and his years on the department, he knew that such shots were rarely effective. He was also aware of Dr. Gilbert Goldman's demand that this fugitive be turned over to the HDI alive in exchange for Judy, Sister Mary Louise, and the Our Lady of Peace pastor.

Cole's voice held authority, but was nonthreatening, as he repeated, "Thomas, slowly raise your hands."

Kelly stared at Cole, but still did not comply with the cop's order.

Cole and Blackie were aware that with each passing second the situation was worsening. It was obvious that the deranged mass murderer had something on his mind that had nothing to do with surrendering to them.

The cops raised their guns. Simultaneously, Thomas Kelly brought his arms up to shoulder level.

Cole started forward with the intention of placing handcuffs on the man he now considered a prisoner. Blackie, viewing Kelly from a different angle than Cole, noticed that the murderer was holding something in his left hand. All the lieutenant was able to see was some type of small device connected to a black cord leading down the killer's arm to an area at the small of his back.

"Larry," he cautioned, before lining up the front and rear sights of his revolver on Kelly's left temple. Then he said to the murderer, "Whatever you're holding I want you to drop it right now."

Despite the tears that were still evident on Kelly's face, he smiled. In a lilting Irish brogue, he said, "What would you be intending to do if I don't, Mr. Cabdriver, shoot me?"

"Exactly," Blackie said, cocking the weapon and holding his arm dead steady.

"And if you do," Kelly added, "I'll release my thumb from the button on the device I'm holding and you gentlemen, me, and this building will instantly cease to exist."

Blackie's finger tightened on the trigger and for a moment he considered blowing Kelly's head off. Then Cole spoke.

"Don't, Blackie."

The lieutenant hesitated a moment before noisily decocking the weapon and lowering it once more to his side.

"What do you want, Kelly?" Cole demanded.

Kelly looked at Blackie. "Larry here called you Blackie. Would you be Irish, lad?"

"Not a chance," Blackie sneered.

"No matter. Me and Larry won't be requiring your presence any longer."

"I'm not going anywhere," Blackie snapped.

"Do what he says," Cole said.

"But, boss . . ."

"Blackie, do what he told you. That's an order!"

The lieutenant looked from his oldest friend on the department to the mass murderer and back again.

"Larry, I don't think you should stay in here alone with him."

"He really doesn't have a choice, Blackie," Kelly said. "But you do."

Still Blackie didn't move.

"Go now," Cole said in a near whisper. Then he added, "Please."

Blackie hesitated a moment longer and then headed for the chapel exit.

When they were alone, Cole repeated, "What do you want, Kelly?"

"It's not me, Chief Cole," Kelly said, dropping the Irish brogue. "It's what the Lord wants."

"The Lord, as in the Lord God?"

"Is there any other?"

"Are you saying that you've been committing murder in God's name?"

"I had to atone!" he shouted.

Cole returned the Beretta to its holster and sat down in one of the pews. "What did you have to atone for?"

The assassin's shoulders sagged and he lowered his head. "I failed in my mission."

"What mission?"

"I was sent to the PAC dinner on a mission and I failed to carry it out."

Cole leaned back in the pew and assumed a relaxed posture, although he was far from at ease. "Who gave you the mission?"

Kelly's head came up and he stared at the ceiling. He began crying again, but he didn't answer Cole.

"Was it God?" Cole asked.

Kelly remained silent.

"Or was it Dr. Gilbert Goldman of the Human Development Institute?"

Kelly lowered his head and looked directly at Cole. "Dr. Gilbert Goldman?"

"You work for him."

"I work for the Lord," Kelly wailed.

"Father James Lochran worked for the Lord," Cole said. "Thomas Kelly is an operative for the Human Development Institute."

"Both of us work for the Lord. We must destroy the she-devil."

Cole recalled the night of the PAC dinner when the priest collapsed after Orga entered the Navy Pier rotunda. There was a connection between them that Cole didn't understand, but that he would have to explore now in order to survive.

"Was it after you encountered the she-devil that you were given your mission?"

"The Lord came to me that night while I was in the hospital and told me what I had to do."

"And that was to kill everyone who had attended the dinner?"

"That was my mission before . . ." Kelly now became confused.

Cole got to his feet but maintained a nonthreatening posture. "Before you saw the she-devil?"

"Yes," Kelly whispered.

"Then who gave you the mission to kill everyone at the dinner?"

"I . . . don't . . . know!" Kelly screamed, tightening his grip on the device in his left hand.

Clark Street had been blocked off in front of the Holy Name Mission and vehicular traffic was being rerouted east into Lincoln Park or west to Halsted. Blackie stood across the street from the entrance to the mission. Officer Roselle, the Eighteenth District foot patrol cop, and Manny Sherlock stood beside him. The lieutenant and Roselle had known each other since Blackie and Cole had worked as tactical officers in the adjoining Ninetheenth District years ago.

"What in the hell is he doing in there, Blackie?" Roselle asked.

Blackie didn't answer right away. Finally he said, "I hope he's not trying to get himself killed, Bob. I hope he's not trying to get himself killed."

At any second Blackie expected the mission to disintegrate in a blast like the one that had destroyed Buster Quint's plane earlier. Then the front door of the mission opened and Cole, accompanied by a handcuffed Thomas Kelly, came out.

Blackie, Roselle, and Manny Sherlock rushed over to them.

"Are you okay, boss?" Blackie asked.

"I'm fine," Cole said. Turning to Manny, he added, "We need to have the Bomb and Arson people take a look at the device strapped to Mr. Kelly's waist."

Carefully, Manny took the prisoner from Cole and led him away.

When they were alone Blackie said, "How did you get him to surrender?"

Wearily, Cole replied, "I offered him something that he wants more than anything else in the world."

CHAPTER 66

The suburban home of Pete and Fuzzy Dubcek was dark. The ranch-style house, surrounded by a sloping, well-manicured lawn, was attractive, which its six-figure cost would attest to. However, something about this place was different tonight. There was a sinister atmosphere surrounding it. Something that was intangible, but somehow had developed an evil physicality of its own. A terrible event was about to take place here.

A paved alley ran behind the house. It was wide and well lighted. There were sporadic portable plastic garbage containers located beside the two-car garages in evidence. Only six houses were constructed on each block, and at this time of night the neighborhood was deserted. There were no vehicles or people walking to be seen on the streets. Most of the houses surrounding the Dubceks' were dark, as their occupants generally went to bed early. It was a peaceful, quiet neighborhood populated by well-to-do professionals. Tonight that tranquillity would be destroyed forever.

There was a white Ford Bronco with tinted windows parked in the alley behind the Dubcek house. It had been there for ten minutes. Five people were inside, three men and two women. The women were dead. One of the men was bound and gagged. The driver of the Bronco, who was clad all in black and wore a ski mask despite the heat of the summer night, got out. He walked to the gate behind the house and entered the deserted grounds. He was gone less than two minutes. When he returned he rapped sharply on the window. A second man, dressed identically with his companion, got out of the Bronco and went around to open the back door. Together they removed two bodies encased in zippered body bags from the storage compartment. Carrying the bags over their shoulders, they slipped back into the yard. The back of the Bronco was left open momentarily, making the captive Ronnie Skyles visible. The pimp was the bait, although the people setting up this trap did not want to catch anything.

The masked men returned to the alley. Closing the door on a terrified Ronnie Skyles, they got back inside the Bronco and settled in to wait. The Abo-Yorba came nine minutes later.

Pete Dubcek took a taxi from O'Hare Airport to his home. The driver was a young black man who was so impressed with the basketball star being a passenger in his cab that he missed two turnoffs along the route. For his part, Dubcek was polite, but said very little. When they pulled up in front of the dark house, Dubcek signed an autograph for the driver, paid the fare, and got out.

As the cab pulled away, Pete stood on the street staring at the building in which he had lived for the past year. He had never felt such a foreboding sense of impending doom before in his life. Slowly, he began walking toward the front door.

There was a row of evergreen trees separating the Dubcek property from their nearest neighbor twenty-five yards away. As Pete sauntered past them he caught movement out of the corner of his eye. Spinning around, he examined the area, but nothing was there. He continued on.

He reached the front door and was about to place his key in the lock when he discovered that it was open. Dropping his bag on the stoop, he stepped inside.

The entrance alcove was dark. Reaching out, he switched

on the living-room chandelier. The interior of the house was
bathed in light. Pete could see all the way from his front
door across the living room and dining room to the kitchen
entrance. He could tell that the cleaning woman had been in
recently, because the furniture was dusted and the rug had
been vacuumed. However, the relative cleanliness of the
house was something that he didn't dwell on for long, because there were two dead bodies lying in an ever-expanding
pool of blood on the living-room floor. They were both
women and one of them was Fuzzy.

Sonny Balfour drove the white Ford Bronco into the alley
behind the Dragon's Lair nightclub. He told the over-the-hill
boxer who had accompanied him to kidnap Orga Syriac's
companion and carry out the deeds at Pete Dubcek's place
to wait for him. Then he went inside to see Jack Carlisle.
   The fixer was alone in his office. The lights were out, but
the television was still turned to the sports channel station
on which the USA-Italy Olympic basketball game had been
telecast earlier. There was not even the hint of a smile on
Carlisle's usually gregarious face.
   "Everything's been taken care of, Jack," Balfour said, going to the bar and pouring himself a double shot of Chivas
Regal.
   "Did you do what I told you?"
   The ex-boxer downed a hefty swallow of scotch before
removing a videotape that he had stuck in the waistband of
his black trousers. He walked over and placed the tape on
Carlisle's desk. "I got it all right there. Used an infrared lens
to enhance the visual."
   The fixer placed the tape in the video recorder attached to
his television set. The screen went momentarily blank before
the transmission began.
   "Prepare yourself," Balfour said. "Everything Ronnie
Skyles said about this broad is true. She sure as shit is scary."
   The tape began. The view was of the rear of the Dubcek
house from the alley. Then Ronnie Skyles was shoved into
view. The pimp was obviously terrified. For an instant he
looked directly at the camera and then began backing away.

"I told that son of a bitch to get moving or I was going to kick his ass," Balfour commented, sipping scotch.

Carlisle stared silently at the screen.

Skyles moved slowly across the backyard. Then Pete Dubcek appeared. He shouted at the pimp, but Carlisle and Balfour couldn't hear him because the video recorder's audio was shut off. When Skyles saw Dubcek, he turned and ran back in the direction of the camera. The basketball player caught the pimp easily and threw him to the ground. There was a lot of blood visible on Dubcek's clothing. He had obviously found the nasty package Sonny had left for him inside the house. Then Dubcek began beating Skyles with his fists.

"I thought Pete was going to kill him the way he was pounding on Skyles," Balfour quipped.

Carlisle remained silent.

"The tape gets better real soon, Jack."

And, on cue, it did.

In front of the stand of trees to the left of the screen a shadow appeared. It began moving rapidly toward Dubcek and Skyles. Then it came into focus. The sight of the she-devil was enough to get even the laconic Jack Carlisle's full attention.

"My God," the fixer said with awe, "she is a monster."

As the tape continued to roll, Carlisle and Balfour watched the she-devil snatch Pete Dubcek off of Ronnie Skyles. Carlisle thought his eyes were playing tricks on him when the monster lifted the basketball player off his feet and easily held him dangling in front of her.

"What's she doing?" Carlisle asked.

"Checking him out. I could hear the snorting noise she made. She's searching for the scent of the blood from the woman she lived with."

The she-devil tossed Dubcek away from her and went after Skyles.

"The pimp has the black chick's blood all over him," Balfour said with a grin. "Now dig this."

And Carlisle watched in horrified amazement as the she-devil tore Ronnie Skyles to pieces. Then the tape ended.

"You want a drink, Jack?" Balfour asked, returning to the bar for a refill.

"No," the fixer responded, continuing to stare at the blank screen. "But tell me something, Sonny."

"Yeah."

"Who killed the woman who lived with Orga Syriac?"

Balfour turned around with a fresh drink in his hand and ran his fingers across the scratches on his cheek. "I did. When we went in to get her she started kicking and screaming. I hit her and . . ." He took another pull of his drink.

"Then you've got her blood on you too," Carlisle said.

Balfour shrugged. "I guess so."

Carlisle shut off the VCR and stood up. "Lay off the booze, Sonny. Go home, shower, and burn those clothes. Torch the Bronco. I'll buy you another one tomorrow."

The ex-boxer put down his half-full scotch glass and headed for the door. "See you in the morning, Jack."

Once alone Carlisle went back to brooding about his loss. But now he could bask in the satisfaction that his betrayer had been taken care of and would be the number one suspect in the triple murder.

The fixer was about to begin tallying up the assets he would have to liquidate tomorrow to cover his bet when he heard a strange noise. He listened for a moment, but only the silence of his office could be heard. He was about to go back to his list when he realized that he was no longer alone.

Orga Syriac was standing at the entrance to his office. He couldn't figure out how she had gotten in. She stood in shadow and all he could see of her was a silhouette. A silhouette that was human. The fixer tensed. There was a Colt .45 automatic in his center desk drawer. Slowly, he began inching his hand toward it.

She spoke. "I know you are responsible for what happened this evening, but I have not come here to deal with you. At least not yet, but you and I are far from finished."

Carlisle snatched the automatic from the drawer and fired at the woman, point-blank. She had been standing less than twenty-five feet away. He was certain that at this range he would hit her. But he didn't.

Orga Syriac had managed to get out of the line of fire. The .45 slug had zipped across the office to lodge in the wall behind the spot where she'd been standing.

Carlisle kept the gun pointed at the doorway. His heart was beating furiously and his gun hand shook so badly he was forced to use his other hand for support. He stood that way for a long time. Then, from somewhere very close by, he heard her say, "You and I are far from finished, Mr. Carlisle."

CHAPTER 67

JUNE 19, 2004
MIDNIGHT

Kate Ford had been working in her den since early evening. She was about to shut off her computer when the doorbell rang. When she looked through the peephole and saw who was there, she smiled. She opened the door to admit an exhausted Larry Cole.

"I was driving by and saw your lights on," he said, taking her in his arms. "Tonight I could use a little TLC."

"I'm your girl." She got up on her tiptoes and kissed him. She poured wine and broiled a steak while he called home. He listened patiently as Butch raved about Pete Dubcek's play during the earlier basketball game. When his son finished, Cole told him that he would be home in time for their morning run. Butch knew that his father was at Kate Ford's place, but was not about to pry into the older man's personal life. Before they terminated the conversation, Butch mentioned that Paige wanted to talk to him in the morning. Cole was too weary to speculate as to what she wanted to discuss.

After Cole ate, he and Kate Ford went to bed.

Blackie Silvestri finished brushing his teeth and stepped out of the bathroom of his southwest-side home. He was wearing his "Jackie Gleason" pajamas with the broad red and white stripes. His feet were in worn leather slippers that his married daughter Maureen had given him for Christmas five years ago. His wife, Maria, was already asleep, her thick silver hair splayed out across the pillow. It was at times like this that he found it hard to believe how fortunate he was to have a woman like her.

He sat down on the side of the bed and took off his wrist-watch. He left his wedding ring on. He never took it off. It would be removed from the third finger of his left hand on the day they buried him.

Blackie Silvestri took a moment to recap the past twenty-four hours. This would prepare him for what they had to face tomorrow. There had been some good and some bad, but they—Cole and the other cops he worked with—had a much better handle on things than they had had before. Although Judy Daniels was in a fix, they had Kelly, which would keep her safe for the time being. Larry had told Blackie that he had a plan to get inside the Human Development Institute, but the chief hadn't disclosed how. Blackie realized that this omission was Cole's prerogative, as he was the boss.

Tomorrow was another day, Blackie thought as he slipped off his house shoes and got into bed. He moved over until his hip rested against Maria's buttocks. He'd been sleeping in this exact same position every night for over thirty years. In less than a minute, he was snoring softly.

In their cell in the bowels of the Human Development Institute, Judy Daniels, Sister Mary Louise Stallings, and Father Phil Cisco were making the best of a bad situation. They had managed to eat the food that the guards had brought for them. Judy had initially considered mentioning the possibility that the burgers could be poisoned. However, she finally rationalized that if these people wanted to kill them they possessed much more efficient ways of doing so.

They had eaten, prayed again, and settled in for the night, with Father Phil taking one of the bedrooms, and Judy and Sister Mary Louise doubling up in another.

The Mistress of Disguise/High Priestess of Mayhem was forced to abandon her attempts to get help by using her radio. She was simply not getting through. She was also running the battery down on an instrument that just might save their lives later.

She took off her habit and got into bed clad only in her slip. Sister Mary Louise was sleeping in a similar fashion: Judy stared up at the tile ceiling. The radio was functioning, but the transmission was not being received. That meant something was blocking it. She recalled the blindfolded ride in the back of a truck. At their final destination they had remained stationary for some time before being placed in this cell. She could surmise with fair accuracy that they were below ground. Possibly far below ground.

With a sigh, Judy turned over and said, "Good night, Sister."

Lying in the dark a few feet away, Sister Mary Louise started to respond, "Good night, Judy." She managed to catch herself in time and say, "Good night to you, Sister Bridgit."

Then they slept.

The police car turned into the alley behind the Dubcek house. The lone male officer was on routine patrol in an area in which few calls for service were ever received. But there was always the possibility that a professional burglar would target one of these expensive residences, so the suburban force maintained its vigilance.

The young cop had eighteen months on the job. He had yet to make a felony arrest or handle a homicide. Now, within a matter of the next few minutes, he was going to do both and in spades.

He was cruising slowly past the Dubceks' back fence when he noticed that the gate was standing open. Stopping the patrol car, he shined his spotlight into the dark yard. The illumination enabled the cop to see the walkway that ran all the way out to the street. Then he noticed that there was something on the cement surface. Initially, it appeared to be a shadow, but the officer rejected this. Shadows didn't reflect light.

He decided to get out of the car, go through that gate, and investigate whatever was on the sidewalk. Before doing so he followed proper police procedure. He called the dispatcher, gave his location and the reason he was there, and asked for backup. Less than a minute later his supervisor, a female sergeant in her mid-thirties whom the young patrolman had a crush on, pulled into the alley and parked behind his squad car.

He quickly told the sergeant what he had found, and together they went through the gate. They discovered what was left of Ronnie Skyles lying on the grass in the backyard. More assistance was requested, and they proceeded to enter the house through the still-open front door. There they found Fuzzy Dubcek and a woman who would later be identified as Blessing, Orga Syriac's companion.

Finally, they found Pete Dubcek. The star basketball player was in the laundry room at the rear of the basement of the ranch-style home. He was curled into a fetal ball on the floor next to the washing machine. He was noisily sucking his thumb. His clothing was covered with blood.

The Midway Plaisance, which bisected the University of Chicago campus on the South Side, was deserted and dark. From the outside, the Human Development Institute appeared shuttered and secure. But inside the glass edifice the organization that spied, manipulated, and even killed to achieve its objectives was alive with activity.

Dr. Gilbert Goldman was staying in the building tonight. There were executive sleeping quarters on the third level of the Institute. They were much more luxurious and spacious than the area in which the captives from Our Lady of Peace were being held. As the early-morning hours passed, Goldman slept soundly in a four-poster bed.

On the level above him, Virginia Daley was in her office working. She planned to stay there all night. At that moment, the chief operatives of the HDI were as secure as any two beings on the earth could be.

There were twenty-two security people assigned in and around the Institute building. Five were assigned to internal physical security, five to external security, and the remainder to electronic monitoring.

The HDI electronic monitoring center was located two levels above the cell where Judy Daniels had attempted to call for help on her CPD walkie-talkie. There were two reasons why her transmissions had not been received outside Institute walls: One was due to her being too far below ground, which she had already surmised, and the other was the HDI electronic monitoring center.

As the wee small hours of the morning advanced, one of the monitoring center operatives manning a security console noticed movement on a motion detector scanning a tree-lined section of the Midway Plaisance. He switched to visual, but was unable to see anything except the trees blowing in a gentle wind. He switched to infrared, and what he saw shocked him out of his early-morning stupor.

He hit the silent emergency alarm, which sent a transmission to an external security unit and a monitoring center supervisor. The supervisor notified Virginia Daley of a possible intruder.

Less than a minute after the alarm was sounded, the HDI executive secretary stormed into the monitoring center. A male supervisor in shirtsleeves, but wearing a tie, was standing behind the operator who had activated the alarm.

"What is it?" she demanded.

"I saw something in those trees," the operator explained, pointing to his screen.

There was nothing visible there now.

"Something, like what?" she asked with an edge in her voice.

"I took a picture of it," he said in a voice that trembled noticeably. He pressed a button on the console and an eight-by-eleven-inch Polaroid photo rolled from a slot next to the screen.

Virginia Daley snatched the photo and studied it. "There's nothing here," she snapped.

The operator pointed to an area at the center of the picture. "I think you can see it right here."

For just a brief instant, the HDI executive secretary thought she could make out a figure with a head, legs, and arms, but it couldn't have been human. She quickly relegated it to the category of an optical illusion.

"What do the outside units report?" she asked.

The operator returned to his seat and picked up a microphone. "Unit H-three, come in."

"This is H-three," a female voice responded.

"Did you find anything in Sector Four?"

"Negative."

Virginia Daley fixed the operator with a cold stare. "Make sure you have something concrete before you go sounding the alarm again." Then she stomped from the monitoring center.

There had been something in the trees. The Abo-Yorba had been studying the exterior of the Human Development Institute. In a few hours she would be going inside. She would be invited to do so by none other than Dr. Gilbert Goldman.

CHAPTER 68

JUNE 19, 2004
6:07 A.M.

Larry Cole awoke from a sound sleep. For a brief moment he was disoriented, as he was in a strange bedroom. Then he became aware of Kate's warm body lying next to him. They had slept in the nude and he felt a familiar stirring. He placed his arms around her and pulled her closer to him. She awoke, emitted a sigh, threw the single sheet they had slept under to the floor, and climbed on top of him. They were both soon wide awake.

Kate was in the kitchen when Cole came downstairs an hour later. She was seated at the kitchen table. There was a small television set on the counter beside the sink. The morning news was on.

He poured himself a cup of coffee and turned around to notice that she was staring at the screen with wide-eyed shock. Before he could ask, she said, "Pete Dubcek, the basketball player, has been arrested for murdering his wife."

Cole had been a cop specializing in the investigation of homicide for too long to be shocked at what she'd said, but he was a bit surprised. Carrying his coffee, he sat down beside Kate to watch the news.

There was an on-scene reporter standing across the street from the expensive suburban ranch-style home. This segment had obviously been taped earlier, as it was still dark outside. The reporter narrated that the bodies of Vanessa Dubcek, the basketball player's wife, Ronald Skyles, an apparent acquaintance of his wife who had an arrest record; and an unidentified black female had been found at the Dubcek house. Each of the victims was brutally slain and a police spokesman speculated, pending an autopsy, that the murders were committed by a very strong person wielding a large knife. Pete Dubcek, covered with blood and in a state of shock, was currently being treated in the jail ward of Cook County Hospital.

As the newscast moved on to other stories, Kate refilled their coffee cups. Seated once more she said, "Do you think he did it?"

Cole shrugged. "I don't know. Husbands killing their wives and vice versa is not uncommon. There were other people killed too, and Ronnie Skyles's reputation precedes him."

"In what way?"

"I've never had any direct dealings with him, but he worked in the DeLisa and Allegretti pimping operations. At one time he ran Paige Albritton before she met Sergeant Mack McKinnis. The detectives assigned to the murders of Allegretti, his girlfriend, and one of his bodyguards at the Riteway Laundry a few days ago have been looking for Skyles."

"Was he a suspect?" Kate asked.

"Possibly, but one way or another we wanted to talk to him about what happened. We know that he was at the laundry on the day the mobster and the others were killed. That would be enough for us to bring him in, but he disappeared, and there was some speculation among the cops handling it that the pimp could already be dead."

"How did Allegretti die?"

Cole placed his coffee cup down and said, "I suspect that your Abo-Yorba had something to do with what happened at the Riteway Laundry Company and also the death of a pimp named Chester 'Chet the Jet' Collins."

Kate looked down at the table surface. Her cheeks colored slightly.

Cole reached over and took her hand. "You know what she is, don't you?"

Kate hesitated before nodding.

"I've been a cop for most of my life, Kate, and during that time I've always lived by a certain code. I never look the other way for any reason after a crime has been committed."

"Orga's not a criminal, Larry—she's actually a living legend."

"A legend that kills people," Cole countered. "And it doesn't matter to me who she's killed, Kate. She has still committed the crime of murder. Murders that appear to have been carried out with a sharp knife used with a near surgical precision. Or possibly very sharp claws."

"What are you going to do with her?" Kate asked.

Cole got to his feet. "Today I'm going to have to work with Orga on something else. When it's over I'm going to arrest her for murder."

Kate Ford watched him cross to her front door and let himself out.

Sven-Erik Voman was organizing WGN's coverage of the Pete Dubcek murder case. By three o'clock that afternoon, he wanted to run a thirty-minute special on Dubcek, his wife, the pimp, and the unknown black female found in the house. By seven, in a prime-time slot opposite a televised White Sox—Yankees baseball game, the station would air a one-hour segment on the murders, featuring interviews with friends, relatives, acquaintances, and former teammates of the star Bulls player along with any other cops or official types who would stand still long enough to have a microphone shoved under their chin. Right now Voman had a crew over at the Berto Center, the Chicago Bulls' headquarters, getting all the information available about Dubcek. He had the best freelance investigative reporters that he could find looking into the backgrounds of the murder victims, as well as the suspected murderer, and he had conned an additional half million dollars out of the network president to finance the media coverage. This was going to be the murder of the century, at least in Chicago, and Sven-Erik Voman vowed that the WGN superstation was going to be on the ground floor of the coverage.

Voman was about to pick up the phone to order a search of the WGN archives for any tape footage they possessed on the Dubceks, when Orga Syriac walked into his temporary office.

The TV studio the news director had commandeered was last used to televise a twenty-four-hour telethon. It was multitiered, with desks arranged on six levels. It was constructed in the form of a semi-amphitheater, and Voman's desk was at the bottom. Two entrance doors led out into the studio, and when the news director chanced to look up, his star newscaster was standing in one of them. He could see enough of Orga to recognize her, but he was unable to detect anything more.

"Come on in, Orga," he called to her from where he still had the phone to his ear. "I've got an assignment for you."

He went back to his call and made the connection. He was talking when he turned around and noticed that she still hadn't moved from the doorway. Too preoccupied to fathom why, he motioned for her once more. A short time later he hung up to find her standing right next to him. He was stunned by her appearance.

Orga Syriac looked as if she had aged ten years during the sixteen-hour period since Sven-Eric Voman had last seen her. There were dark circles under her eyes, her skin held an unhealthy pallor, and her hair wasn't combed.

"Are you ill, Orga?" he asked with concern.

Remaining on her feet, she responded, "I'm fine. After a cup of coffee and a trip to makeup, I'll be my usual self."

The news director nodded, but forced himself to look away. For just a moment he seriously considered sending her home or maybe to see the studio nurse, but with this Dubcek thing going on, he needed every warm body he could get.

"I want you and Dave Spurgeon to go out to the Dubcek house and do an update for me on the story. Tape at least three minutes in the neighborhood and another ninety seconds or so at the police station. I'd prefer you inside, if the cops don't make too much noise about it."

He took a quick glance at her. She hadn't moved, and whatever was wrong with her had gone beyond illness to be actually frightening.

"We'll make that a top priority, Sven," she said in a tired voice that sounded different from the melodious tones he'd heard from her in the past. Now she sounded strident, almost harsh. "But I'd like to work on another story as well," she added.

Voman concentrated on a list of things he had to make sure were done in connection with the Dubcek murder coverage. "You're going to be spending all of your time on this Dubcek thing until further notice, Orga." He tried to make it come out sounding like an order, but failed miserably.

"I want to do an interview with Dr. Gilbert Goldman at noon today in his office."

"What has Goldman got to do with Dubcek?"

She walked around in front of his desk and looked down

at him. "The story that I'm working on will be much bigger than Pete Dubcek. Especially when it comes out that he's innocent."

"What?!"

"Dubcek is innocent. I have evidence that he was framed and I know who did the framing."

The longer Sven-Erik Voman stared at his star reporter the more she appeared to be changing right before his eyes. The circles beneath her eyes faded, her complexion cleared, and her image softened to become that of the Orga he knew. It was as if she was accomplishing this by an act of her will. He would have been amazed by the transformation had it not been for the impact of what she had just told him. As always, the news came first.

"If you can prove that Dubcek is innocent, we'll have a story the likes of which this country has never seen or heard before."

"And I'll give it to you, Sven, but I must interview Goldman at noon."

He frowned. "You're not trying to blackmail me on this, are you?"

"I wouldn't dream of it," she said with that smile that could melt stone. "I'm about to give you two of the biggest scoops of your career and all I need from you is a little help."

"What kind of help?"

"How well do you know the president of the Tribune Company?" she said, referring to their corporate boss, whom Voman reported to every day.

CHAPTER 69

When the guards entered with their breakfast—bagels, cream cheese, coffee, and fresh fruit in a paper sack—Judy and Father Phil were alone in the sitting-room area of the cell. Sister Mary Louise was still in the bathroom.

The guards were the same in basic appearance as the ones they had seen before. However, there was one major difference. They were not carrying the formidable-looking machine pistols their predecessors had displayed.

One of them placed the bag down on the floor in the exact same spot where the captives' junk-food dinner had been left the night before. As they turned to leave, Judy Daniels watched them closely.

There was a nonchalance about them now, as opposed to the vigilance the others had displayed. This was what Judy had been waiting for. When they delivered lunch, the Mistress of Disguise/High Priestess of Mayhem would be ready.

Blackie Silvestri drove Cole's unmarked black Chevy police car into the parking lot of the Field Museum of Natural History in Museum Park at 1200 South Lake Shore Drive. In the backseat of the car, securely handcuffed, sat a subdued Thomas Kelly. In the Jeep Cherokee used on the surveillance the day before, Manny Sherlock followed.

"Wait here, Blackie," Cole said, getting out of the car. "And keep a close eye on our friend."

"Don't worry, boss," the lieutenant said, turning in his seat and glaring at their prisoner. "Mr. Kelly and I are going to get along just fine."

Cole entered the museum and proceeded to Dr. Silvernail Smith's office. The historian was waiting for him.

"I did the research that you asked me for, Larry, although I don't know if it will tell you much more than you're already aware of," Silvernail said as they took seats in his office. "The she-devil is very difficult to kill, but she's not invincible. You are aware that she can move amazingly fast and is immensely strong?"

"I've seen her in action."

Silvernail opened a book on his desk. The cover was of genuine leather and the pages were gilt-edged, but it was obviously very, very old. "There is also something else you should know."

Cole waited.

"There are a number of accounts of she-devils engaging in combat with both man and beast." He opened the book to a woodcut depicting an Abo-Yorba fighting with a lion. Cowering behind the shape-shifter was a woman holding two small children. Silvernail continued, "Members of their species have obviously suffered wounds in the past, but I couldn't find a single incident in which one of them was reported to have been killed."

Cole felt a sudden chill. "I thought you said she was vulnerable."

Silvernail shrugged. "She's flesh and blood. And these stories"—he patted the old book—"are nothing more than legends. But this being is not human, and the rules that apply to us, as far as the physical, objective universe goes, do not necessarily apply in the same way to her. We have no way of knowing what will indeed kill her. Or if she is injured, how long it will take her to recover. Or even what her life expectancy is in terms of years."

Cole thought for a moment. "So it might not be possible to use force, even deadly force, to arrest her?"

Silvernail stared at the cop. "It might not only be impossible, Larry, it could be extremely dangerous."

*   *   *

"Fine, fine," Dr. Goldman said into the telephone, "and give my best to the family."

After hanging up he used the intercom to summon his executive secretary. Virginia Daley came into the office a few minutes later.

"Yes, sir," she said, taking her usual seat and opening the ever-present notebook.

"Remember when we talked about countering any scrutiny which might be directed our way by the Kate Ford inquiry?"

She nodded.

"Well, I just talked to the president of the Tribune Company. He's an old friend of mine. That new reporter at WGN, the one that's been doing most of the field coverage lately, wants to interview me."

"Orga Syriac," Virginia Daley prompted.

"That's her. She's coming here at noon. I'll have the opportunity to tell our side of the story. If I handle this right it could make the dear Ms. Ford look quite ridiculous."

"Do you think it's wise having a TV crew come out here today? Especially with the guests we have staying with us?"

"I'm not going to take them underground, Virginia," he chided. "The priest and the nuns are my bargaining chip with Cole to exchange for Thomas. Then we'll decide how to handle it."

"Whatever you say, sir," the executive secretary said with a disapproving tone.

Orga Syriac finished the assignment Sven-Erik Voman had given her in connection with the Dubcek murder case and returned to the WGN van. Dave Spurgeon accompanied her carrying his new minicam unit over his shoulder. She stood on the asphalt surface of the police station parking lot until the cameraman had loaded his equipment. Stepping forward, she said, "Dave, what was the name of the police chief?"

The cameraman turned around. "Hayes. Maurice Hayes." He was aware that the reporter was standing very close to him. Despite her tremendous beauty, he felt an overwhelming sense of peril.

"What about the name of the lieutenant in charge of the Dubcek case?"

He shrugged. "Jeez, Orga, how would I know that?"

"Could you go back inside and find out for me?"

For just a brief instant Spurgeon started to refuse. He was a skilled technician, not a runner for talking heads. However, something about Orga made him realize that if he didn't do what she had requested he would be very sorry.

"Sure thing, Orga," he said, going back into the station.

Spurgeon was crossing the lobby a short time later when he saw the van driver standing at the entrance waiting for him.

"What do you want me to do, Dave?" asked the young man, who'd been a WGN employee only a week longer than Orga.

The cameraman frowned. "What are you talking about?"

"Orga said that you have something for me to do."

Spurgeon walked past the driver and out the front door of the police station. As he had expected, the van and their star television personality were gone.

The previous night had been one of the worst of Orga Syriac's long existence. She hadn't experienced a bloodlust like she had in the backyard of the Dubcek house in a long time. That last time was when she was protecting the residents of Diggstown, Mississippi, from the Ku Klux Klan nearly a half century ago. And this was with good reason.

An Abo-Yorba in a bloodlust was a very dangerous creature indeed, but a creature of emotion as opposed to intellect. More wild animal than human, the she-devil adopted the instincts of the African rain forests in which her species had originated. This caused the shape-shifter to lose her ability to reason. This could result in her striking out blindly, which could result in the death of an innocent. This was something she could not allow to happen. At least not again.

Last night she had been forced to stop herself after she killed the man she had chased from the Riteway Laundry and who had the scent of Blessing's blood on him. Through the red haze of her fury, the Abo-Yorba realized that if she didn't stop herself now, the bloodlust would take over and she would no longer be in control of her actions. This was why she had not killed Jack Carlisle, despite her intuitive abilities conveying to her quite clearly that he was responsible for Blessing's death. But she planned to deal with him later. She promised herself that.

Now the objective Orga had sworn to achieve fifty years ago in Mississippi was about to be accomplished. She drove the WGN van north on the Dan Ryan Expressway. At Garfield Boulevard she exited and drove east toward the University of Chicago campus. She was less than five minutes away from the Human Development Institute.

CHAPTER 70

JUNE 19, 2004
11:47 A.M.

The cops, with the handcuffed Kelly in the backseat, waited for Orga Syriac in front of the Fountain of Time monument in Washington Park west of the Midway Plaisance. Now Larry Cole, for the first time in his career, donned a disguise. He was wearing a fake thick mustache over his thinner one and a stick-on goatee that made his chin itch. The only other items he wore to complete the alteration of his appearance were a Chicago Bulls ball cap and a pair of rose-tinted glasses. To say the least, Blackie didn't like it.

"Boss, you should think twice about doing this," the lieutenant argued.

"Why?" Cole said, patting the fake hairpieces.

"Well, for one thing, you're the chief of detectives. You could get hurt."

Cole smiled. "I'm still a cop, Blackie." Then his smile vanished. "And I have a personal interest in this one."

Before Blackie could continue the argument, the WGN van pulled up behind the police cars. As Cole started to get out, Thomas Kelly spoke for the first time since he'd been arrested the previous night. "Once you go inside the Institute you're not coming out."

They turned to look at the deranged man for a moment before Cole went back to join Orga in the van.

After a moment Blackie's walkie-talkie crackled to life. Cole's voice came across loud and clear. "Testing one, two, three."

Blackie activated the instrument and said, "Are you picking up the boss, Manny?" Cole's device was only a transmitter.

In the Jeep behind them, Manny responded, "I read him five-by-five, Blackie, and the recorder's working perfectly."

"Good," the lieutenant said, emitting a sigh. "I hope it stays that way."

Again Thomas Kelly spoke. "Your friend is going to die in there."

Blackie placed a Parodi cigar in the corner of his mouth and sneered. Without turning around, he said, "Tom, you're probably new to this arrest thing, but I just want to remind you that you have the right to remain silent." Blackie fired up the cigar. "So why don't you do me and yourself a favor and exercise that right?"

The HDI electronic monitoring center picked up the WGN van while it was still a block from the Institute. One of the operators assigned to external surveillance of the facility noticed it. After verifying the markings he called Virginia Daley.

"They have arrived."

"Have them park in the south lot and monitor them every second they're in the building."

"Yes, ma'am."

*   *   *

Orga parked the van and they got out.

"You'll have to carry and operate the camera," she explained.

"That sounds simple enough." Cole opened the side door. The minicam was jammed inside the storage compartment, along with a great deal of other sophisticated-looking electronic equipment. Cole grabbed the camera. He proceeded to heft it onto his shoulder in the same manner as he had seen the operators of such devices do numerous times in the past.

"Carry it down at your side until you have to set it up," Orga instructed. "You also need to take the cases containing the tripod and sound equipment in with you."

Cole stopped. His confusion was evident as he squinted into the cramped area.

Orga knew that their every move was being watched. "The tripod is in the silver case, the sound equipment in the black one."

Cole struggled along behind Orga and whispered, "You could give me a hand with all this."

"Can't," she said flatly. "I'm the star."

They continued on to the rear entrance to the Human Development Institute.

Virginia Daley was waiting for them inside the entrance to the building, where a uniformed rent-a-cop was seated behind a desk. There was an open ledger in front of him.

"I need to see a photo ID and have you folks sign in."

Cole, carrying the TV equipment, became very still. He should have remembered that the last time he was here with Blackie, they'd both had to display their badges before they were permitted inside. He could have kicked himself for letting this slip his mind.

Orga smiled and said, "Dr. Gilbert Goldman is expecting us. We have an appointment to interview him at noon."

The rent-a-cop shook his head. "I can't help that, ma'am. Everybody that comes in has to show proper identification and sign in." He wasn't about to budge an inch.

The executive secretary stepped forward. "I'll take responsibility for these guests."

The rent-a-cop looked about to protest, thought better of it, and said to her, "What about the log?"

"That won't be necessary." Virginia Daley smiled coldly at her guests. "Ms. Syriac and her"—her eyes rested on Cole for a moment—"cameraman have been cleared by Dr. Goldman personally."

"Yes, ma'am," the rent-a-cop said with resignation. "Whatever you say."

She stepped forward and extended her hand to Orga. "I'm Virginia Daley, executive secretary to Dr. Goldman." She now ignored the man carrying the equipment. "I've admired your work on television, Ms. Syriac."

"Thank you," Orga said with ease.

"Please follow me and I'll take you to Dr. Goldman."

As the two women walked past the rent-a-cop's station, Larry Cole, lugging the equipment and keeping his head down, followed.

Cole's transmitter was contained in the tip of a Mont Blanc ballpoint pen he carried in his shirt pocket. It had a transmission radius of five miles and could be modified to send as well as receive. It was one of the most powerful pieces of equipment ever developed for American law enforcement communications.

So far, with Blackie and Manny listening, the reception had been crystal clear, as it was supposed to be. They heard the exchange between Orga and Cole in the HDI parking lot and then with Virginia Daley and the rent-a-cop. From their location a half mile from the Institute building, the cops had experienced the same tension as Cole and Orga when the rent-a-cop had demanded identification. However, they had no sooner breathed a sigh of relief when the transmission from Cole developed static.

Blackie snatched his walkie-talkie off the front seat. "Talk to me, Manny."

"I don't get it," the sergeant said. "The unit's working perfectly. I'm going to boost the power at this end."

The static dissipated momentarily before resuming. A few seconds later they lost Cole's signal completely.

"They're jamming us," Blackie said, crushing his cigar and tossing the remains out the window.

"What now?" Manny's forlorn voice came over the walkie-talkie.

"I don't know," Blackie said without picking up the radio.

"Maybe I can be of some assistance, Blackie," Thomas Kelly said from his handcuffed position in the backseat.

The lieutenant had forgotten that the HDI operative was there. With no other avenues open to him, Blackie said, "How?"

"I can get you inside the building without being seen."

Dr. Gilbert Goldman was waiting for them in his office. "Ms. Syriac," he said effusively as he got to his feet. Leaning on his cane, he came around the desk with his hand extended. "I've been looking forward to meeting you."

He ignored Cole, who was busy setting up the equipment in a corner of Goldman's office.

Orga flashed her most dazzling smile at Goldman. "It is an honor meeting you, Doctor. I'm really looking forward to this assignment."

Virginia Daley stood silently by watching the exchange between her boss and the reporter. The severe-mannered, somewhat plain executive secretary was definitely envious of the attractive black woman. This jealousy was heightened by the manner in which Goldman was fawning all over the TV newscaster. Neither Virginia Daley nor Gilbert Goldman was paying any attention at all to the cameraman.

Standing in front of the HDI director's desk, Goldman and Orga made idle chitchat for a few minutes. He seemed surprised when she told him that she had never met the president of the Tribune Company, who had recommended her for this assignment.

"Well, even if you haven't been formally introduced," the HDI head was saying, "he definitely knows of you and the excellent work you've been doing during the brief time you've been with Channel Nine."

"You are most kind, Dr. Goldman," she responded.

Cole and Virginia Daley had one thing in common at this

point. They both felt that Orga and Goldman were definitely overdoing it.

"My dear," Goldman said, taking the reporter's arm, "in order for you to better understand what we do here at the Institute, I want to take you on a brief tour of our facility."

"What about my cameraman?"

A crack appeared in Goldman's mask of perceived affability. "Some of the projects we are currently working on are confidential, Orga. I'm sure you can understand that. Why don't I take you on the tour now? Later, if there is anything that you would like to have on camera for your story and it doesn't compromise our research, I'm certain it can be arranged."

Orga didn't comment right away. Finally, she turned to Cole and said, "You can wait here until I get back." Turning to Goldman she added, "If that is acceptable with you, Doctor?"

"Of course," he gushed.

For the first time since he had entered the office, Cole became the object of their hosts' scrutiny. He kept his head down so that the bill of his cap cast his disguised face in shadow.

A frown crossed the executive secretary's face. "I don't think I caught this gentleman's name."

Orga crossed the office to stand beside Cole. "This is Dave Spurgeon. He's usually a very unobtrusive fellow. Of course, he's supposed to be. After all, I am the star."

"Naturally," Goldman said.

The sound of Virginia Daley's back teeth grinding together was almost audible in the office.

Dr. Goldman extended the arm opposite the one he used to support himself with his cane. "Shall we go?"

"Why not?" Orga said, taking the arm.

As they started for the door, Goldman said, "Virginia, are you going to join us?"

"No." She never took her eyes off Cole. "I think I'll stay here and keep Ms. Syriac's 'unobtrusive' video technician company."

When Orga and Goldman exited, Cole went back to fumbling with the equipment. Virginia Daley walked over and sat down in her usual chair in front of the director's desk. She never took her eyes off of him.

CHAPTER 71

The HDI guard came alone. He exited the elevator on the fifth sublevel below the Human Development Institute. He carried a paper sack containing cold cut sandwiches, cartons of fruit juice, and bags of potato chips. In appearance he was very similar to the other guards, with one exception. He looked younger than the rest, which, in fact, he was.

The Human Development Institute recruited its operatives in a manner that the cold war CIA had utilized. Certain types of individuals were identified for recruitment because they possessed traits that their potential employer desired.

Intelligence tests were designed and surreptitiously administered to high school and college students, as well as military recruits, job applicants, and civil servants. The Institute used its political weight and virtually unlimited funds to cajole and in some cases intimidate the parent institutions into not only administering the tests, but also turning over the results. A team of industrial psychologists went over these tests with an eye toward identifying certain traits. Primarily, they were looking for pliable personalities with a predisposition for following orders to an extreme. As a rule, the Institute wanted those who performed the security and nonspecialist field tasks to be of average intelligence. Even in the ranks of skilled operatives and educated researchers, high intelligence was considered suspect. Intelligent people were thinkers, and thinkers had a tendency to question actions which could at times be considered unethical and at other times out-and-out illegal.

The young man in the expensive, neatly pressed business suit who was delivering lunch to the three captives had been recruited from a junior college in Richmond, Virginia. He was targeted by the HDI because he was of average to slightly below average intelligence, had a tendency to become violent when met with adversity, and possessed an extremely pliable personality.

When he'd been given the assignment to go out and purchase lunch for the prisoners, he had done so without question or comment. He had driven an HDI sedan to a delicatessen on Fifty-fifth Street in Hyde Park, where he had purchased the sandwiches, making sure to obtain a receipt. The fact that he had been given this job to perform alone, whereas the two previous meals had been served by two guards operating as teams, did not register with him.

He was armed with a Sig Sauer 9-mm semiautomatic pistol, which he carried in a shoulder holster beneath his buttoned suit jacket. As he walked down the damp corridor toward the door of the sublevel cell, he carried a brown paper sack in one hand and an access control card to open the cell door in the other. The Institute was on a semialert status, which had never happened during his brief tenure here. As it had nothing to do with him, he didn't dwell on it.

Swiping the card through the access port, he waited for the audible click signaling that the electronic locking mechanism had disengaged before pushing open the door and entering.

He knew that there were supposed to be three people in the cell: a priest and two nuns. Why they were being held was irrelevant to him. He was an atheist. When he stepped inside he could see the priest and one of the nuns seated on the couch on the other side of the cell. He began a cursory search for the other nun when he felt a surprising, but instantly identifiable, object pressing against the side of his neck.

The young guard froze and dropped the paper bag and access card to the floor. Out of the corner of one eye he could see a portion of the nun's blue habit. He couldn't figure out where she had gotten the gun she was holding on him. Then he heard her say in a very nonreligious voice, "Now that's a good boy. I want you to raise your hands very, very slowly and I won't blow your head right off those broad shoulders."

With no other options available to him, the guard raised his hands.

The interior of the Human Development Institute was ultra-modern and extremely clean. Orga and Dr. Goldman started on the main floor, which was illuminated by a circular sky-light allowing the sun to shine down through the four-story atrium. All of the offices, chambers, and cubicles that were charged with performing the tasks of this organization led off from this atrium.

As they walked along slowly, Orga took it all in. Goldman was providing the public relations tour, which was undoubtedly rarely given, except to a select few.

"Here on the main floor we have our basic administrative and security functions."

Orga reached out and touched the wall. She could feel that there was much more going on than the alleged security and administrative tasks he'd mentioned. In fact, she knew that this was only the tip of the evil iceberg. She stopped at the center of the atrium and looked down at the floor.

"Dr. Goldman, are you aware that this building is built over some old subterranean train tunnels that were abandoned at the end of the nineteenth century?"

The director of the Human Development Institute appeared unaffected by this revelation. "My, my, you are quite a historian, Orga. I am impressed."

"The tunnels were supposed to be sealed off, yet almost a hundred years later they were still there and being used to carry out some very strange things."

Goldman smiled. "That is no more than an old wive's tale, my dear. And I assure you there are no old train tunnels beneath the Institute."

The reporter didn't move. "Then what is down there, Dr. Goldman?"

"Nothing, Orga. Nothing at all. Shall we continue the tour?" .

In Dr. Goldman's office Virginia Daley had grown increasingly suspicious of the TV technician who had accompanied Orga Syriac. Although for the most part he kept his back to her, she couldn't shake the impression that she had seen him before.

The HDI executive secretary was a cunning, devious woman who possessed a high IQ but very poor eyesight. Her glasses corrected her twenty-fifty vision to less than twenty-thirty. They generally gave her a view of the world which was more a soft blur than anything even remotely resembling crystal clarity. However, despite her being unable to see the cameraman as well as she would have liked, her indistinct sight of him was still disturbingly familiar.

Then a solution to the dilemma occurred to her.

She got up and went behind Dr. Goldman's desk. Activating his computer, she accessed the HDI mainframe, which Thomas Kelly had hacked into secretly. Using her access code, she called up the data the Institute had on WGN employees. She typed in the name "Spurgeon, Dave—Video Technician" and waited.

Blackie Silvestri and Manny Sherlock escorted the handcuffed Thomas Kelly through the main rotunda of the National Science and Space Museum at 5700 South Lake Shore Drive, approximately a mile east of the Human Development Institute. They proceeded to the museum basement, passing a number of visitors, who would have paid the plainclothes cops no attention at all had it not been for the bound, limping red-haired man walking between them. They also encountered a couple of National Science and Space Museum security guards, at whom Blackie flashed his badge, scowled, and snapped an abrupt, "Police business."

In the basement of the museum there was a plethora of exhibits on display. Most of them were of historical significance to the advancement of science and space exploration over the long history of mankind on the planet Earth. The centerpiece of the displays on the lower level was the "Transportation of Yesteryear" exhibit, which was a fully functional nineteenth-century train station. This exhibit was not a replica, but had originally been constructed by the National Science and Space Museum's founder, Ezra Rotheimer. The tunnels that Orga had mentioned to Gilbert Goldman had been built by Rotheimer. They were intended for trains that would connect his lakefront station with the Grand Railroad Crossing five miles away. However, the presence of an ancient cemetery between the origin and destination of the underground line halted this construction.

The tunnels and station had remained far below ground, virtually forgotten, while the building that was to become the National Science and Space Museum was constructed above. Blackie, Manny, and their prisoner knew this place well.

Entering the Transportation of Yesteryear exhibit, they descended to the main floor of the station. There were about fifty or sixty spectators, mostly children, viewing the exhibit. A few, noticing Kelly's handcuffs, turned to stare at the trio; no one approached them.

"Okay, where is it?" Blackie demanded.

"Over there."

They crossed the exhibit to an area where there was a roped-off display of a mannequin, dressed as a porter, loading baggage onto an iron-wheeled cart.

"We have to go inside," Kelly said, nodding at the exhibit.

Blackie reached down and removed one of the restraining ropes. Dropping it to the floor and grasping Kelly firmly by the arm, he led the way, with Manny following.

On the other side of the Transportation of Yesteryear train station, a museum guard saw the three men violate the rules by entering a restricted area.

"Hey!" she shouted. They ignored her.

She was a short woman with stumpy legs, but she managed to cross the area separating them with impressive speed. She reached the exhibit and was about to give the recalcitrants a firm but polite rebuke for the infraction. She was stunned speechless. The exhibit depicting the porter loading baggage on the cart with iron wheels was empty. The three men had vanished.

CHAPTER 72

JUNE 19, 2004
1:03 P.M.

"This is the heart of the Human Development Institute, Orga," Gilbert Goldman said expansively. He swung his arm up to take in the glass-enclosed, book-lined two-story room below them. The books were there only for show. It was apparent that the principal activity being performed in this area was accomplished by way of the computer operators manning the PCs arranged in banks of five around the room.

Orga noticed that there were thirty positions. Only three were not currently being manned. She stepped closer to the glass. She and Dr. Goldman were in an observation area on the second level behind the glass partition. All of the computer workstations were on the lower level.

She placed her hands on the wooden railing and leaned forward until her head was less than an inch from the glass.

"Exactly what are they doing down there?" Her voice came out a whisper, and Goldman had to strain to hear what she said.

"Research, my dear," he responded. "This is where we

collect the raw data which we utilize to formulate strategies to help some of the less fortunate of our brethren around the world."

Slowly, she turned toward him. When he looked into her face, particularly the eyes, he became frightened and took a step backward. She matched this maneuver by taking a step forward.

"Tell me about the plans you formulate here, Doctor."

He tried to speak, but found that his vocal cords were frozen with fear.

"Perhaps you'd like me to tell you," she said, as the face of the beautiful newscaster began to dissolve and the she-devil's formed. "This place has used the information that you have collected down there"—she pointed a taloned append-age at the glass—"to oppress innocent people all over the world for over one hundred and fifty years. Using your data collection system, you and your predecessors have identified and targeted individuals, organizations, racial groups, and whole segments of society for interference. And you have committed terrible crimes to achieve these ends. Crimes, Dr. Goldman, which have included murder."

Reaching for the terrified man, she concluded with, "To-day it all ends."

The computer screen in Dr. Goldman's office displayed a full-face photograph of WGN video technician Dave Spurgeon. Even with her poor vision, Virginia Daley could tell that the man setting up the equipment across the room was an impostor.

Turning away from the computer, she picked up the telephone to summon security.

"It'll never work," Father Phil said, donning the young security guard's suit jacket.

"We've got to chance it," Judy Daniels said as she tightened the strips of cloth binding the arms and feet of the guard. Judy had ripped up her slip to make the restraints. One of the strips was tied around the guard's mouth. The Mistress of Disguise/High Priestess of Mayhem had barely managed to conceal her exasperation when the priest had checked to make sure the guard's nose wasn't covered, so that he would have no problem breathing.

Now Father Phil was expressing second thoughts about Judy's plan to get them out of there.

"I'll never be able to pass for one of these people," he argued.

Sister Mary Louise stood by, not sure which side she should take.

Judy felt a headache coming on. Ignoring it, she said, "Father, these people have kidnapped us at gunpoint. Eventually they're going to have to decide what to do with us, and there are only two options. Let us go or kill us. Do you want to take that chance?"

She waited for it to sink in with not only him, but also Sister Mary Louise.

"I guess you're right," he said with resignation. "What do you want me to do?"

Blackie Silvestri and Manny Sherlock followed Thomas Kelly down a dark underground tunnel that seemed to go on for miles beneath the ground. There were no lights, so the cops utilized pocket flashlights casting beams that were quickly swallowed up by the darkness.

"How much farther?" Blackie asked in a slightly breathless voice. The lieutenant had an aversion to dark places.

"We're almost there," Kelly responded.

Then the tunnel came to an abrupt end.

"What now?" Manny said, shining his light on the damp walls and ceiling.

Kelly knelt down and felt around at the base of the wall. He found a hidden lever, which he pulled. The wall slid back to reveal a tunnel just like the one they had traversed. This one had plastic-encased lights illuminating it.

After they stepped through, the wall slid back into place. On the other side Kelly stopped.

"I've done what I promised," he said. "Now it's your turn to do something for me."

"Forget it," Blackie snapped.

"No, Blackie," Kelly said, standing his ground. "I won't go another step until you take these off." He held up his handcuffed wrists.

The heavyset lieutenant scowled. "You're a prisoner and you're going to remain that way until you stand trial for murder."

Kelly smiled. "I think you'd better think that over, Blackie." His Irish brogue had returned. "You see, when we came in here an alarm was triggered. In about thirty seconds you and Sergeant Sherlock are going to be surrounded by a small army of armed men, who shoot trespassers on sight."

"We've got guns too, Tom."

"But wouldn't that defeat the purpose of our little sojourn to rescue Larry Cole?"

Blackie's scowl did not waver, but his eyes flicked to Manny, who shrugged.

"Okay," Blackie said, "we'll do it your way." He removed a set of keys from his pocket. "But if you try to screw around or take off on us, I'm going to put a bullet right in your ear."

One of the computer operators in the HDI library happened to look up from her keyboard at the observation gallery above. Initially, she couldn't believe what she was seeing was real. But it looked like Dr. Goldman was being attacked by a monster, who dragged him away from the window of the gallery. As he vanished from view, she screamed. Every eye in the room became trained on her.

The HDI monitoring center also controlled security for the complex. Suddenly, a number of problems developed at once. The supervisor of the internal security function was about to send someone to look for the overdue guard who had been dispatched to provide lunch for the detainees on lower level five. But before he could do so a motion sensor went off in a deserted area of lower level three. The supervisor was about to dispatch a team to investigate when Virginia Daley called with a coded intruder alert signal. Then all hell broke loose in the HDI library.

CHAPTER 73

When the two guards came through the door to Dr. Gold-man's office, Larry Cole was ready for them. The two well-dressed, armed men were looking for trouble, but moving toward it with overconfidence. They charged in like the marines assaulting an entrenched enemy position. They saw Virginia Daley seated behind Goldman's desk and for just a brief instant thought that she was alone in the office. They didn't have the time for it to register in their well-disciplined minds that she was tied up and gagged before one of them caught the head of a minicam tripod in the gut. As he doubled over in pain, dropping his machine pistol to the floor, his companion spun to confront the threat. Still wielding the tripod, Cole lunged forward, first knocking the gun to one side before jabbing the guard in the stomach. The man bent at the waist and Cole uppercut him, knocking him back against the wall. He landed in an unconscious heap beside the other guard.

Cole disarmed them and discovered that they were both carrying sets of flex-cuffs attached to their belts. After binding their arms and using their designer ties as gags, he checked the HDI executive secretary. He had tied her up with an extension cord and used a roll of duct tape he'd found in the sound equipment case to cover her mouth. Finding her still secure, but glaring at him with wild-eyed fury, Cole hefted the two machine pistols and went in search of Orga Syriac.

*   *   *

The she-devil resumed her human form as she escorted a
terrified Gilbert Goldman through the corridors of the Institute. They were going to sublevel three, where the archives
of the Human Development Institute were kept. With this
information in her possession, she could cause the destruction of the Institute and expose its supporters.

They were crossing the first-floor corridor when four
guards came around a corner and began advancing.

"Tell them to stop, Doctor," Orga whispered, tightening
her grip on his arm.

He opened his mouth to speak, but no sound came out.

The guards stopped ten feet away from them and aimed
their guns.

"Are you okay, Dr. Goldman?" one of them demanded.

The HDI director stared with obvious terror from the
guards back at the woman. He still didn't respond.

The guards began moving to encircle them. Orga stepped
away from Goldman.

"Just stay where you are, ma'am," one of the guards ordered.

She kept moving.

The guard who had spoken began to tremble. "If you don't
stop we'll shoot."

Orga smiled at them and took another step.

The guards exchanged anxious glances, but didn't open
fire. By now she was in a position for the she-devil to take
them. By the time they did open fire, it was too late.

Kelly led them to a metal door next to a freight elevator. For
a man who walked with a pronounced limp, he was moving
much too fast for Blackie.

"Slow it down, Tom. Where's the fire?"

The prisoner didn't turn around as he went through the
door and disappeared into the darkness beyond.

"Hold it!" Blackie shouted, but the prisoner was gone.

The cops shined their lights into the dark. A stone staircase
led up as far as they could see.

"He couldn't have climbed up there that quick, Blackie," Manny said.

"I know." Blackie examined the damp walls of the stairwell. "There's got to be some type of secret passage in here, but I'll bet you dollars to doughnuts we won't be able to find it before Christmas."

"So what do we do now?"

Blackie checked the load on his revolver, slamming the cylinder shut with a loud click. "We go up there and find the boss."

CHAPTER 74

JUNE 19, 2004
1:10 P.M.

Larry Cole heard the gunshots echoing through the atrium of the Human Development Institute. Carrying the machine pistols he'd taken from the guards, he ran to the railing on the fourth floor and looked down. He could see the four guards lying below. He caught a glimpse of the she-devil dragging Goldman away. Cole went after them.

After escaping from Silvestri and Sherlock through one of the many secret passages that honeycombed the lower levels of the Institute, Kelly headed for the central heating and cooling plant. The complex was located three levels below the ground. Since he'd been taken into custody by Cole, Kelly had prayed for guidance. And through the haze of his mania the answer had come to him.

Actually, it had been Larry Cole who had given him the clue in the chapel last night. Now Kelly knew his true mission. He also realized that the acts of atonement he had previously engaged in, as Father James Lochran, were wrong. The reason for this error was the man who had sent him to plant explosives at the PAC dinner. That man was Dr. Gilbert Goldman of the Human Development Institute. So now Thomas Kelly had a new mission. Utilizing the massive independent cooling and heating system, he was going to blow up the Human Development Institute.

Judy and Sister Mary Louise walked in front of a very self-conscious Father Phil Cisco toward the freight elevator a short distance from the cell in which they had been held. When they reached the elevator gate, Judy examined the access control port mounted on the wall.

"Father, give me that computer card we took off the guard."

The priest fumbled in the pockets of the size-too-large jacket until he came up with the card.

Taking it, Judy was about to swipe it through the access port when they heard a noise coming from the stairwell door. As the nun and priest tensed, the Mistress of Disguise/High Priestess of Mayhem removed the detective special from the pocket of her habit and pointed it at the door. She motioned for the nun and priest to get behind her and held her breath as the door opened. She groaned with relief when Blackie and Manny entered the corridor.

The Human Development Institute had been reduced to a state of complete chaos. Without Dr. Goldman and Virginia Daley to rigidly guide it, the security function was rapidly breaking down. This situation was exacerbated by rumors that something "unnatural" had invaded this place on the University of Chicago campus. Something that was dangerous.

Suddenly there was too much happening at once, and the limited intellects were not reacting to it well. A few had even decided that discretion was the better part of valor and opted to vacate the building before they ended up like the four guards who had encountered Orga and Dr. Goldman earlier.

However, a number of security people remained. These men and women managed to overcome their fears and begin organizing themselves to combat and possibly kill the intruder or intruders who had invaded the Institute.

Ten guards, each carrying fully loaded machine pistols and equipped with extra ammunition clips, assembled on the main floor of the atrium. The guard who had been in charge when the Our Lady of Peace rectory had been invaded took command.

"Okay, we don't know what's going on, but we're going to find out. About an hour ago a TV reporter and a cameraman were admitted to the building and escorted to Dr. Goldman's office. We know that the doctor took the reporter on a tour of the facility and that the cameraman was not with them. A short time later Dr. Goldman and the woman were spotted on this floor. Now four of our comrades are dead, and they were apparently attacked by that woman." He paused a moment to study the faces of those around him. There was some fear there, but for the most part they appeared anxious, maybe even a bit eager, to encounter the intruder. They had been well chosen for their jobs.

The guard continued. "Now we're going to split into teams of two. One team will go up to Dr. Goldman's office and see if they can locate Ms. Daley. The rest of us are going to fan out, cover every square inch of this building, and find Dr. Goldman. Any unauthorized personnel are to be apprehended by any means necessary, to include the use of deadly force."

To emphasize the order, he raised the machine pistol over his head. As if returning a military salute, his armed companions duplicated this gesture. Then they separated.

Orga forced a terrified Gilbert Goldman to take her to the vault on lower level three below the atrium where the HDI's secret files were kept. The vault could only be entered through an enormous steel door set in the center of an iron wall. The wall appeared to be at least a foot thick.

"The files are in there," he said, pointing at the vault door. She turned to look at him. Frightened, he stumbled back-

ward and would have fallen to the floor if she hadn't reached
out and caught him.

"Open the door, Doctor."

He fumbled in his pockets for a computer access card and
a ring of keys. She watched him closely as he inserted the
card into a slot beside the door. He then inserted one of
the keys into a lock beneath the access port. When he turned
the key a humming noise sounded and the door began swinging open slowly.

There was a single metal box resting on a table at the
center of the vault.

"The archives are in that box," he said in a voice that came
out barely above a strangled croak.

"All of them?" she questioned.

He slumped against the wall. She noticed that he had gone
deathly pale and was sweating. "My secretary computerized
them five years ago. The entire history of the Institute, dating
back to the time it was known as the Consortium before the
Civil War, is contained on two disks."

She smiled. "That's just what I've been looking for, Doctor."

They stepped inside. Orga walked around the table, examining the metal box. It was secured by a simple metal
clasp. Reaching down, she unfastened the clasp and lifted the
lid. Inside there were a pair of computer disks inside transparent plastic cases. As she reached inside and removed them
a piercing alarm sounded.

CHAPTER 75

The freight elevator containing Blackie, Manny, Judy, Sister Mary Louise, and Father Phil rose from the depths of the Institute. When they reached the main floor, the elevator stopped. They were concealed from the main section of the Institute by a wall. Before they got off the car, Blackie cautioned, "Okay, we're going to find our way to the front door of this joint and walk out of here. In case there's any confusion, or anyone tries to stop us, I want Manny and Judy to pin their IDs in plain sight."

With a raised eyebrow, Judy said, "Do you think the people who kidnapped us care anything about cops?"

Blackie kept his gun down at his side, but he didn't need it to emphasize his words. "We're the law, Judy. If we get any kind of opposition, we're going to make them damned sorry." He turned to Sister Mary Louise. "Excuse me, Sister."

"I'm in complete agreement with you, Blackie," the nun said.

They got off the elevator and, with Blackie leading the way, entered the atrium. A couple of guards carrying machine pistols were running across the main floor away from them. Other than that, the atrium, all the way to the front of the glass-enclosed entrance to the building, was deserted.

For a moment they all considered the fact that this was just too easy. Before anyone appeared to challenge them, Blackie said, "Okay, we're going to walk out. Don't stop for anything. Judy, you're on point. Me and Manny will bring up the rear."

"Got you, Blackie," she said, feeling self-conscious wearing her Chicago police identification affixed to the nun's habit.

They skirted the edge of the four-story atrium and headed for the entrance. They proceeded along at a good pace, but did not run. At the inner door, Judy reached down and hit the release bar. The door opened onto the outer lobby, where a uniformed rent-a-cop was seated. He looked up at them and alarm registered on his features. But before he could react, Manny stepped forward and leveled a 9-mm Beretta at him.

"Get up," the sergeant barked. "And keep your hands where I can see them."

The rent-a-cop did as he was told.

"What are we going to do with him?" Judy asked.

Blackie looked back inside the Institute in time to see a couple of guards, carrying machine pistols, headed in their direction.

"Take him with us," the lieutenant responded, herding his charges toward the front door.

"What about Chief Cole?" Manny said, snatching the rent-a-cop's pistol from its holster and shoving him toward the exit onto the Midway Plaisance.

"We'll get some reinforcements and come back for him," Blackie said.

They stepped outside just as the armed guards reached the outer lobby. The guards took a moment to size up the situation and then retreated back inside the building. The nun, priest, and the cops had escaped.

Cole was not as fortunate as his colleagues had been in escaping from the Human Development Institute. He had followed Orga and Goldman into a damp staircase beside a freight elevator entrance adjacent to the atrium. The stairs descended from the main floor into a murky darkness below. Cole was carrying a pocket flashlight. Now he was forced to shove one of the machine pistols into his waistband so that he could activate the minitorch and illuminate his way.

He descended two flights of steps to a metal door marked with a Roman numeral "II." Carefully, he opened the door and peered into the corridor beyond. The area had fluorescent lights running across the ceiling and a tiled floor. Glass-enclosed cubicles lined this corridor, and people in white coats were visible inside them.

Although the actions of those present were indeed frenetic, Cole didn't believe that Orga had come this way. He decided to descend to the next level down.

As he moved through the darkness, he became aware of one of the walls beginning to vibrate slightly. He suspected that this was caused by the freight elevator being activated. He was unable to tell whether the car was rising or descending.

He arrived at the third level and found a door marked with the Roman numeral "III." Opening the door a crack, he found the exterior corridor to be much darker than the one he had encountered above. Also, this one was empty. Cole decided to investigate.

Turning off the flashlight and slipping it back into his pocket, he grabbed the other machine pistol from his belt. With both guns raised, he started down the corridor.

There were two doors set at thirty-foot intervals leading off the corridor. One of them was open, the other closed. The policeman was able to detect the hum of a powerful generator coming from someplace very close by. He walked a few more feet and could tell that the power source originated from behind the closed door. As he was closer to the open door, he decided to investigate what was beyond it first. He took a step in that direction when a loud, piercing alarm echoed through the corridor.

Cole quickly backed against the wall. He considered the possibility that he had triggered the alarm. Then he focused on the sound. It was coming from the other side of the open door. He was about to go through that door and investigate when the guards came.

They exited the stairwell and charged into the corridor with guns blazing. The bullets from their machine pistols ricocheted off the walls around him. The cop was splattered with splinters of stone and one of them opened a gash in his cheek. Ignoring the pain, Cole returned fire.

His aim was a great deal better than his adversaries'. He caught one of them across the chest with a pattern of three bullets that hurled him back into the dark stairwell. The other guard, whose rounds were missing Cole by at least a yard, was hit in the left arm and hip. Dropping his gun, the guard collapsed to the cement floor clutching his wounds.

Cole had no time to breathe a sigh of relief as four more guards showed up. Like their predecessors, they came through the stairwell door and opened fire the minute they spied the intruder. As the corridor became alive with steel-jacketed missiles of death, Cole sprinted through the open door from which the shrill alarm continued to scream.

There was a full-time engineer employed to maintain the Human Development Institute's internal and external facility. This man, now in his early sixties, had been recruited for this job with the same thoroughness as the security and research personnel.

The engineer's tasks included overseeing the maintenance of the external grounds, supervising the staff (provided by a private contractor) which cleaned the inside of the building five nights a week, and making sure that the heating and cooling units operated within normal parameters all year round.

Because of his position, the silver-haired black man had an office, of sorts, inside the power plant, located on lower levels three and four. He had outfitted the place quite nicely with leather furniture, a carpet, and even a minibar, which he kept well stocked and equally well concealed from the prying eyes of that "meddling bitch," as he referred to Virginia Daley.

Now, as the power that kept the Human Development Institute functioning hummed around him, the engineer was at his post. However, he was dead. He hadn't heard Thomas Kelly enter his domain and he was surprised when the red-headed intruder appeared standing over him with a crowbar in his hand. The last, incongruous thought that the engineer had in life was that if it had been Virginia Daley sneaking up on him he would have really been in trouble.

After killing the engineer and saying a prayer for the repose of his soul, Thomas Kelly went to work. From the hollow heels of his black oxfords he removed two small packages of Semtex. This was a plastic explosive which he would place sparingly at strategic locations in the sublevel HDI power plant. But first he would have to prepare the huge cooling and heating systems for the destructive tasks he wanted them to perform.

As he set about rewiring the apparatus and causing pressure flows to increase beyond the normal limits set by their manufacturers, he recalled the meeting he had attended over fifty years before. A meeting in which only two people had participated: the teenage orphan Thomas Kelly and a Catholic nun, whose name he could no longer remember.

They were in a small chapel in the basement of the orphanage where he had been raised from the day they'd found him as an infant on a church doorstep. The chapel was off-limits to the orphans except for special occasions when a member of the religious staff wished to speak with one of their charges in a totally secure and religiously uplifting environment.

Kelly recalled that he and the nun had prayed first, kneeling at the small altar adorned with the hand-carved wooden figure of the crucified Christ. Then she had sat with him in one of the pews. Even though her speech was impassioned, she never touched him. Touching for any reason was forbidden inside the orphanage and could result in a violator of this precept, whether an orphan or a member of the religious staff, being whipped so severely that blood was drawn.

Kelly could remember her words just as clearly at this moment as he had over fifty years ago.

"The Lord has taken both your father and your mother from you, which at this stage of your life must seem to be a great burden for someone as young as you are now."

The young Thomas Kelly had lowered his head and a thick comma of red hair fell across his face. He didn't brush the

hair away with his hand, because it effectively concealed the
tears welling in his eyes. He could hear the nun's voice, but
despite her sitting right next to him, the words seemed to be
coming from a great distance. It was as if she were speaking
to him from the sky, or more appropriately, heaven.

"Our Almighty Father has left you here on this earth alone,
shouldered with the heavy burden of being an orphan, because he wants to test your resolve. Do you understand what
I am saying to you, Thomas?"

"Yes, Sister," he replied without raising his head.

"There is some great task you must perform in his service.
What that task is I do not know, and it may be many years
before you learn of it yourself. But when you do become
aware of it, you will be given a sign."

In the present, while he worked to sabotage the environmental plant of the Human Development Institute to explode,
Thomas Kelly reflected on the sign the nun had mentioned.
A sign that only a few days ago he had erroneously believed
to have received in the trauma room of a hospital. A sign
that he had prayed for in the chapel of the Holy Name Mission on Clark Street last night, A sign which God had sent
him through the cop Larry Cole.

Thomas Kelly's work was almost finished when he heard
gunshots coming from the outer corridor. He had expected
the intruders to be discovered. Now they were near him, and
he wanted to see at least one of them once more before he
accomplished this final task of atonement.

Crossing the large two-story room, he entered the engineer's cubicle. The dead engineer's body was still lying in
the same position in which Kelly had left it. He pushed the
dead man to the side so that he had access to the power
control console. On this console there were five gauges
above circular knobs. Each gauge had a black needle which
scanned a dial reading "low," "medium," and "high" followed by an area marked in red. When the needles swung
to the far right and entered the red zone, the power plant,
aided by the Semtex explosive Kelly had applied at two very
critical locations, would explode with the force of a thousand
pounds of dynamite. Kelly knew that the plant would go

critical in two and a half to three minutes. Then, in a matter of seconds and with a blast that would be heard for miles, the building that housed the organization for which Thomas Kelly had labored for most of his life would be reduced to a very large hole in the ground.

Turning from his last completed act of destruction, Kelly went to the door, opened it, and stepped out into the corridor where the firefight was still in progress.

CHAPTER 76

JUNE 19, 2004
1:31 P.M.

After diving out of the corridor, Cole discovered that the HDI guards were not going to let him escape that easily. Landing on the floor and rolling over, he raised the machine pistols just as two guards attempted to come through the door after him. Opening fire, the cop hit one of them in the head and put three bullets close enough to the other to force him into a hasty retreat. A hasty retreat which was short-lived.

Two more guards appeared at opposite sides of the doorway and fired. Cole felt the whistle of bullets around his head and the whine of ricochets off the metal walls. Returning fire, he felt a sharp stinging sensation in the area of his upper right arm. He didn't have time to examine the inch-long graze wound that had been left there. He also realized that he couldn't stay where he was a second longer.

Cole emptied the remaining rounds from the pistol in his left hand while frantically searching for a way out of this trap. The metal corridor came to a dead end and the only remaining avenue open to him was inside the vault. Initially he rejected going that way because vaults were not known for having back doors. But it was impossible for him to go forward.

Scrambling quickly to his feet and firing short bursts from his remaining pistol, Cole backed into the vault.

The instant Cole left the corridor, three guards executed a coordinated assault, liberally spraying the area with steel jacketed rounds that nothing mortal could have survived. However, when they discovered that their prey had momentarily eluded them, they stopped. Cole was cornered. Now they could take him any time they wanted without getting hurt or killed for their trouble. They moved toward the vault cautiously. The alarm still sounded, but the rapid fire of their machine pistols had muted its clamor considerably.

Then the guards were attacked from behind.

Cole only caught a glimpse of the interior of the semidark vault, but it was enough. Orga and Dr. Goldman were there, two people whom he had set out to find an eternity ago. Now he had indeed found them, but they were not a priority at this moment. He was more absorbed with staying alive.

Cole ventured farther into the vault, keeping the gun raised. He estimated that he had eight to ten rounds left in the extended clip. When that ammunition was gone he would be at the mercy of his attackers.

Then suddenly the firing from outside the vault stopped. He was expecting a different tactic to the assault when a lone guard appeared at the vault entrance. Cole leveled his gun on the guard; however, the man's weapon hung limply at his side. He took a step into the vault before collapsing facedown on the floor. There was a large hole in his back and it was obvious that he was dead.

Cole continued to cover the guard, remaining aware of Orga and Goldman behind him. The shrill alarm stopped suddenly. For a long moment there was only silence. Then Kelly's voice carried to them from outside.

"Chief Cole, are you in there?"

Cole was shocked at hearing the killer's voice. "Where are Blackie and Manny?"

"I don't know the answer to that, but when I left them they were both well."

Cole didn't know whether to believe him or not. Orga stepped up beside him. He took a moment to examine the vault more closely. He saw the open box on the table and Goldman cringing in the far corner. Then the cop yelled, "What do you want, Kelly?"

"Is she in there with you?" the killer asked.

"Is who in here?"

Orga responded. "I'm here. I think you've been searching for me just as long as I've been hunting you and this evil place you work for."

Kelly paused. "I would like to see you one last time. May I come in?"

"One last time before what, Kelly?" Cole demanded.

"Let him in," Orga said.

Cole looked from her back at the open vault door. "Okay, come ahead, Kelly. But move slowly and I want your hands empty."

The murderer limped into view. He was dragging his bad leg behind him and his hands were raised. He stopped briefly at the entrance before stepping inside.

"Thomas," Goldman cried from where he remained crouched in the corner of the vault. "Why did you run away? You had me worried."

Kelly looked at the man who had meant more to him than any other human being in his life. There was definite sadness in the HDI operative's face. "I had a great deal of work to do, Gilbert. And I was confused."

Now Goldman struggled to his feet. He edged around the vault, keeping his distance from Orga and Cole. Leaning heavily on his cane, Goldman stopped in front of Kelly. "If you were having problems you should have come to me for help, as I have always come to you. After all, we have shared the same infirmities and passions for many, many years."

Kelly stared back at the director of the Human Development Institute. "My feet have been on the wrong path for most of my life. Part of that was your fault, Gilbert." He looked at Orga. "Part of it was her fault, whatever she is." Then his eyes swung to Cole. "And the rest of it was my fault. But God has been merciful to me and provided the means to atone."

Cole, sensing the danger, took a step forward. "Atone how, Kelly?"

At that instant the power plant blew up.

CHAPTER 77

JUNE 19, 2004
1:35 P.M.

Once clear of the Institute building, Judy's walkie-talkie worked perfectly. Switching to the citywide police frequency the detective division operated on, she put in an emergency call for assistance. This call was also broadcast to local police units in the area, and in a matter of seconds the scream of numerous sirens split the summer air. Marked and unmarked police cars began showing up in sufficient numbers to become a throng. Blackie and Manny Sherlock took charge and began organizing a raiding party on the Human Development Institute. Then the building blew up.

Most of the blast was directed inward and the building initially imploded with a force that shook the ground with the force of a major earthquake. All the cops and curious onlookers from the University of Chicago campus were knocked off their feet, and there were a few minor injuries sustained. Slowly, Blackie got to his feet and managed to peer through the thick smoke at the center of the huge crater in the ground where the Human Development Institute had once stood. With a sinking heart he realized that Larry Cole had been inside the building when it blew.

The explosion that destroyed the Institute possessed the destructive power of a ton of dynamite. The main force blew up and out, which demolished the two sublevels above the point where the blast originated and completely demolished the four-story building on the Midway Plaisance. The dynamics of the force, released by the elements Thomas Kelly had rigged, diminished as they dissipated sideways and down. The iron vault in which the HDI records had been kept received a far less substantial portion of the explosion. The walls of the vault were fireproof and sturdy. The blast failed to do much damage directly to it, but destroyed the stone floor and walls surrounding it and the levels below. The iron room was wrenched from its moorings and dropped into the cavern being formed by the force of the explosion.

The blast slammed the vault door shut, but the locking mechanism did not engage. The explosive debris became a swirling vortex and the vault's weight caused it to fall through the thick dust cloud until it struck bedrock some sixty feet below ground level. Debris covered the iron shell briefly and then rose into the air seeking the atmosphere above.

The four people trapped inside the vault were battered unmercifully, as they were thrown from the iron floor to the steel ceiling like toy dolls. Cole struck his head against the edge of the metal table and was knocked unconscious. Orga grabbed one of the table legs, which was anchored to the floor, wrapped one of her three-fingered appendages around it, and cradled the policeman in her free arm. This kept Cole from being smashed to death against the metal walls as the vault spun around and around. From her stationary vantage point she was able to witness the fate which befell Gilbert Goldman and Thomas Kelly.

The HDI director and his chief operative were smashed repeatedly against the hard surfaces. Blood formed a fine mist in the air and, when the vault finally came to rest, the corpses had been smashed to pulps.

Still holding the man whose life she had saved, the she-devil shoved the vault door open. The area outside was open to the sky far above, but no light could penetrate the dense cloud of dust and debris rising above the bomb crater. Then the Abo-Yorba saw the tunnel.

Carrying the unconscious Larry Cole, she entered the dark opening which had been constructed over a century ago that led to the Transportation of Yesteryear exhibit inside the National Science and Space Museum.

"I want as much fire department equipment and as many ambulances as you can spare," Blackie shouted into the walkie-talkie. "We've got a major explosion out here and it's possible that there could be some survivors."

Judy, Manny, Sister Mary Louise, and Father Philip Cisco were standing a short distance away from where the heavy-set, scowling lieutenant was pacing up and down on the park-way grass shouting into the radio. Judy had tears in her eyes and Sister Mary Louise had her arms around the Mistress of Disguise/High Priestess of Mayhem. Manny and Father Phil stood by exhibiting varying degrees of shock and horror over what had just occurred. There was still a great deal of dust in the air, which produced the effect of a pretwilight haze on this sunny afternoon. More curious onlookers were showing up and the media had put in an appearance attempting to get a statement from anyone who had witnessed the explosion.

Manny watched Blackie continue to shout orders into the walkie-talkie. The young sergeant knew that no amount of rescue personnel could help anyone who had been in that building at the time of the explosion. Blackie would eventually realize that, but Manny knew the lieutenant would have to do so in his own time. Manny himself was having a difficult time coming to grips with the fact that Larry Cole was dead.

Blackie had finally run out of steam. He lowered the radio to his side and looked across the street at the huge crater. For a moment his shoulders sagged and he lowered his head. Then, quickly he straightened up and spun around, scanning the phalanx of cops and firefighters standing around looking confused. If a rescue could be carried out they would certainly attempt it, but from the looks of this disaster scene there was no one to rescue.

Blackie spied a uniformed sergeant standing a short distance away talking to a fire department battalion chief. The lieutenant was starting toward them when Father Phil spoke for the first time since they had escaped from inside the Human Development Institute. Although the priest's words were meant for all, he was primarily addressing Blackie. "Before we go any further in our efforts to rescue those we care for, perhaps we should pray?"

Without hesitation Sister Mary Louise reached out and took her pastor's hand. Judy and Manny followed suit, and even the HDI rent-a-cop joined in. Blackie paused for a moment, his scowl deepening. It appeared that he was going to shout a rebuke at the people who had joined hands and lowered their heads just a short distance from where he stood. But again his shoulders sagged and slowly he came over to join them. No one looked at him. If they had they would have seen tears of pain, anguish, and loss in his eyes.

Father Phil began the Our Father. The priest was about halfway through the prayer when Blackie squared his shoulders again and snapped, "Be quiet, Father."

Puzzled and alarmed by his rudeness, the other members of the circle looked up to stare at him.

Ignoring them, he said to Manny, "Can't you hear that?"

Manny looked dumbfounded before he realized what Blackie was talking about. The walkie-talkie attached to Manny's belt was still broadcasting on the frequency Cole's ballpoint pen transmitter was set to. While he had been inside the Institute, the signal was jammed. Now it was working, and Cole's voice was coming through loud and clear.

Snatching the radio from its holster, Manny held it up for them all to hear.

". . . entering the lower level of the National Science and Space Museum. I don't remember how I got here, but I've got a pretty good idea. The tunnel I came to in is full of smoke and debris. Apparently, Kelly rigged the Institute to explode. Kelly and Goldman are dead."

Another voice could be heard coming across the frequency. "You are in a restricted area, sir," a stern-sounding female said. "What you are doing is a serious violation of museum regulations. If you don't leave right now I'm going to call the police."

"I am the police," Cole responded, "and I am leaving." Then he again addressed the cops listening a mile away. "If you guys are reading me, I'll be out in front of the museum in about two minutes. Oh, Blackie, I'll need a bit of first aid. I picked up a scratch or two before the Institute blew up."

"Okay, let's go," Blackie said to Manny and Judy. "We'll get somebody to take you folks back to Our Lady of Peace," he said to Sister Mary Louise and Father Phil. "And, Father, that was one heckuva prayer."

The cops were running for the nearest squad car they could find to take them to meet Cole when the former HDI rent-a-copy said a dismayed, "What about me?"

Tossing his gun to him, Manny responded, "I guess this means you're out of a job."

CHAPTER 78

JUNE 19, 2004
2:15 P.M.

Despite the explosion of the Human Development Institute being a hot story, the Dubcek murder case, as it was being called, commanded the center stage of media coverage not only in Chicago, but nationally. On television sets from coast to coast the human drama was played out before millions of viewers. The twenty-four-hour-a-day news stations carried continuous coverage of the triple murder in which Pete Dubcek was considered the prime suspect. In Chicago regular programming was preempted and the story was covered continuously. In-studio commentators, supplemented by sports figures, engaged in inane and at times stupid dialogue about Dubcek, his late wife, and the two people who were brutally murdered with her. Most of the commentary was carried on a voice-over of the basketball player's videotaped exploits on the court. The last game he played the previous night in Atlanta attracted particular interest.

Jack Carlisle and Sonny Balfour were watching the coverage in the fixer's Dragon's Lair office. The crew the Vegas book had sent had collected on their bet an hour ago. Carlisle had come up with the two million in cold hard cash. He hadn't gone through a bank to cover the amount of the debt, because doing so would have drawn too much scrutiny. But he had come up with it in two suitcases, which the Mob banker had opened and proceeded to count right in front of him. Two muscular armed men stood by until the collection process was completed. Then the trio had left the nightclub, leaving Jack Carlisle the poorer for his foray into Olympic competition wagering.

"Don't take it so hard, boss," Sonny Balfour said when he returned to the office after escorting the collector out the front door. The club wouldn't be open until after six o'clock. "After all, Pete Dubcek is going to be paying for what happened last night for a long time."

Carlisle was staring blankly at the TV set. He was obviously not uplifted by the ex-boxer's words of comfort. It took him a while to come out of his mood of brooding contemplation. "Maybe I've been too hard on Pete," Carlisle said.

Balfour's eyebrows knitted in confusion, but he made no comment.

The fixer spun his chair around in a complete circle and one of his patented smiles appeared on his face. "Sonny, I might have just come up with a way to get my money back. Where's that tape you made of our favorite newscaster?"

*   *   *

After rescuing Cole and leaving him unconscious in the tunnel, Orga had barely made her way into the National Science and Space Museum's Transportation of Yesteryear exhibit. She had concealed herself in one of the displays until a group of spectators walked by before slipping out without the guard seeing her. She made it to the rear entrance to the building and out into the park. She was forced to brace herself against the railing of the bridge leading onto the island behind the museum or she would have fallen into the lagoon. Finally, she made it onto the small island and stumbled a short distance to where the trees and dense shrubbery concealed her from prying eyes. At that point the image of the she-devil descended on her and she fell to the ground.

Orga could feel the faint, irregular thumping of her heart. She was very close to the end, which had a beginning over 150 years ago in the rain forests of the Congo. She was the last of her kind, and when she was gone there would be no more. Now she could die with the knowledge that she had accomplished what she had set out to do. The Human Development Institute had been destroyed, which was fitting retribution for what had happened in Diggstown, Mississippi, so many years ago. Had it not been for the interference of the three strangers who had shown up unexpectedly on that night, she would have lived out her days in that small southern town. Instead she had spent decades on a mission of vengeance.

But the curtain of death would not come down on the Abo-Yorba's life. She still had Blessing's death to avenge. Slowly, she managed to get to her feet. She was weak, but would find the strength to do what she had to. The she-devil made her way off the island behind the National Science and Space Museum.

Kate Ford was working at her computer while keeping half an eye on the Dubcek murder case coverage on the TV when her telephone rang.

"Hello."

"Ms. Ford?" a male voice said.

"Yes."

"I have some information that you will find interesting."

"What kind of information?"

"It is my understanding that you're investigating an African legend called an Abo-Yorba."

Kate made no comment.

"I have positive proof that not only does such a creature exist, but it is also responsible for killing Vanessa Dubcek and the two people who were murdered with her."

Kate forced herself to remain calm. "What kind of proof?"

"I have her in action on videotape."

"I want to see it."

The caller laughed. "And so you shall, but it's going to cost. I'm sure you and your publisher can come up with the appropriate sum."

"And what is an appropriate sum?"

"I'd put it in the seven-figure range."

"You've got to be kidding."

The voice turned harsh and in that abrupt attitude change Kate recognized her caller. "Do I sound like I'm kidding, lady? Now I can take what I've got to a number of other media outlets, but I figure, since you're already working on this thing, I'll give you the inside track."

"Before I can convince my publisher to come up with that kind of money I'll need to take a look at what you've got."

"This is how we're going to work this. You get me a down payment of two hundred thousand dollars and I'll give you a preview that you'll never forget."

"Where do you think I can get my hands on two hundred thousand dollars?"

"From that very successful New York publishing firm that has published your last three books and made a bundle of money for themselves and you."

"Suppose they're not interested."

Again the laugh. "You'll convince them, Ms. Ford, because you're interested. If you weren't, this conversation would have been over a long time ago."

"Okay, so I'm interested," Kate said. "How can I get in touch with you?"

"You don't. I'll call you back in about an hour."

The line went dead.

Kate sat back and stared at the phone. She wasn't one hundred percent certain, but she strongly believed the man on the other end of the strange call she'd just received was Jack Carlisle. And he was claiming to have a videotape of Orga in her she-devil form. Somehow she couldn't see him running a bluff on this, so he probably could make good on his claim. In addition to that, he had connected Orga with the Dubcek case. This reminded Kate of something Larry Cole had said this morning about the man killed in the Dubcek house. There was a connection between Ronnie Skyles and Paige Albritton. And Paige Albritton had worked for none other than Jack Carlisle.

Kate's mind was racing with possibilities as she reached for the telephone and dialed Larry Cole's apartment.

CHAPTER 79

JUNE 19, 2004
2:30 P.M.

Butch Cole returned to the apartment after playing tennis with friends. He let himself in and went into the bathroom to wash up. He was running water in the tub when he heard Paige talking on the telephone in his bedroom. He could easily hear what she was saying.

"I know Jack wanted to blackmail Pete Dubcek. He even tried to get me to seduce him. I don't know what Jack and that thug Balfour have been up to since I walked out, but Dubcek wasn't playing very well for most of the game last night. Jack could have gotten to him to make him play so badly. Then Dubcek caught fire, which could have been a double cross from Carlisle's perspective." Paige paused and emitted a deep sigh. "Jack Carlisle owned Fuzzy Dubcek and I know he had some dealings with Ronnie Skyles. Killing them and that black woman, then setting up Pete Dubcek to take the fall is something that Jack would do and even enjoy."

Butch was so stunned he didn't realize that he was eavesdropping, which his father would find totally unacceptable. He was about to shut the bathroom door when Paige said, "I'd be willing to bet my life that Jack and Sonny are involved in this thing and that tape he's trying to sell you is a fake. I think I know a way we can find out. There's a Dunkin' Donuts a block from the Dragon's Lair. Meet me there in half an hour."

Butch turned the water off and stepped out into the hall just as Paige came out of the bedroom with her purse in one hand and her car keys in the other. She was surprised to see him.

"I didn't hear you come in, Butch."

"I've only been here a minute or so," he said awkwardly. "You going out?"

"Yes. I've got some errands to run."

"Can I come along?"

She smiled. "No. You need to get out of those sweaty clothes and take a shower. I'll be back before you know it."

With that she walked past him and out the front door.

He dashed to the telephone and dialed his father's office on the private line. The phone rang without being answered. He hung up and started to dial his father's beeper number, but that would take too long. He decided that there was no time to wait. Paige was placing herself in danger and needed his help, whether she wanted it or not. He rushed to change clothes.

"This could use a stitch, Chief," the ambulance attendant said as she placed a bandage over the wound on Cole's left cheek. "The antiseptic will reduce the chances of infection, but you should see your own doctor for further treatment."

"Thanks," Cole said, climbing out of the ambulance,

which was parked in front of the National Science and Space Museum. A short distance away, the *Constellation* space shuttle was on display overlooking Lake Shore Drive. As Cole stepped to the ground he recalled being given first aid in this exact same spot some years ago after he'd almost drowned inside the museum in the area where the Transportation of Yesteryear exhibit was now located. Before he could dwell too long on past events, Blackie came rushing over to him.

"The WGN van that was parked in the lot behind the Institute is gone," the lieutenant said. "It probably sustained some damage from the blast that destroyed the building, but it's got to be still drivable. Where do you suppose Orga went?"

Cole thought for a moment. "I think we'll have to guess on that one for the time being, but there are a couple of things I want done, Blackie. Check with Sven-Erik Voman and have him call us immediately if she shows up at the studio."

"Do you think he'll cooperate?"

"Probably, but you never can tell. Newspeople have loyalties just like cops. But she did steal his van, so he won't be too happy with her right now. Then there's the strong possibility that she won't go back to the studio at all. When the Institute was destroyed, her self-appointed mission was completed. She might be moving on, but somehow I've got a funny feeling that there's something else she has to do."

A lopsided grin spread across Blackie's face. "A hunch, boss? You know what I always say about them."

"Yeah," Cole said. "Cop hunches aren't hard evidence. But humor me on this one. After you talk to Voman put out a lookout on city-wide for the van. I want it emphasized in the message that she is not to be apprehended. Tell any unit sighting her to take no action, keep her under surveillance, and notify us immediately."

After Blackie left, Cole called his apartment. There was no answer. He knew that Butch had plans for the afternoon, but he had expected Paige to be there. She had wanted to talk to him about something that morning, but he hadn't had time to discuss it. Now he intended to find out what was on her mind, but she wasn't at the apartment. Next he called Kate Ford and received a voice message that she was not at home; however, the call was being forwarded to a portable unit. After a series of beeps another recording told him that she was unavailable and instructed the caller to leave a message. Smiling at the intricacies of this age of modern communications, Cole decided to head back to police headquarters.

Paige was sitting in a booth sipping coffee when Kate Ford entered the Dunkin' Donuts. Taking a seat across from her, the investigative journalist said a slightly breathless, "Hi."

"Hi, Kate." But Paige's attention was focused on a group of punk rockers who were walking past the doughnut shop. "You got fifty bucks on you?"

Surprised, Kate said, "I think so." Fumbling in her purse, she came up with a twenty and three tens.

Taking the money, Paige said, "Jack's got one of those speed video copying recording machines in his office. If we can find the tape he's trying to sell you, we can make a copy right there and give it to Larry. He'll be able to tie Jack and Sonny into Fuzzy's death somehow and get Pete Dubcek off the hook for murder."

"Okay," Kate said, "I'll go along with that, but how are we going to get inside the nightclub?"

"The back way. I've still got a key."

"But won't Carlisle and Balfour be there?"

Paige smiled and raised the money Kate had given her. "That's what this is for. When you get an advance for the book you're going to write about all of this, you can claim the fifty as a business expense."

With that Paige got up, went outside, and called to the punk rockers. Recognizing Paige from the Dragon's Lair, they came over to her.

"I've got a real plan on this one, Sonny," Jack Carlisle said with an enthusiasm that the ex-boxer had not seen the fixer display since he first got the idea to fix the Olympic basketball game. "This she-devil thing is going to end up making me more money than sports gambling ever did."

Balfour was less than enthused with his boss's plan. "How are we going to explain me making that video, Jack? The cops find out that I was at the scene of a triple murder they'll start asking me some very embarrassing questions."

Carlisle's grin lit up the room. "Nobody's going to put you at the scene. We're going to tie up all the loose ends to include your friend the doorman at Orga Syriac's apartment building and the guy who went with you last night to the Dubcek house."

Balfour raised his hand and made a fake gun out of his index finger and cocked thumb. He dropped the thumb and said, "Bang, bang?"

"You got it."

Balfour was still far from convinced. "The cops are still going to want to know who made the tape."

"By the time that becomes an issue I'll have everything taken care of and we'll own the rights to a video that will be worth more in the long run than the Zapruder film of the Kennedy assassination or the video of the LAPD cops beating up on Rodney King."

Carlisle had always been straight with Balfour in the past, so the ex-pug decided to go along with him for the time being. But at that instant he decided that if the fixer ever tried to double-cross him, Balfour would make a deal with the cops so fast Carlisle wouldn't have the time to say "witness protection program" before the prison doors slammed shut on him.

The buzzer sounded at the front entrance to the club. The eyes of both the fixer and the ex-boxer went to the monitor covering the front exterior of the Dragon's Lair. There four punk rockers were visible standing out on the sidewalk. One of them, a woman with aqua blue spiked hair and a large silver earring piercing her lower lip, was leaning on the bell.

"What in the hell do they want?" Carlisle said with a frown. "We're not scheduled to open for hours."

"They're some of the regulars," Balfour said. "They know

what time we open. A couple of them usually hang around until we close."

"Go down there and get rid of them. I've got to call Kate Ford back in a little while."

Without a word Balfour left the office and headed for the Dragon's Lair's main entrance.

Alone in the office Jack Carlisle continued to study the monitor screens. He wasn't the type of man who relaxed his vigilance at crucial moments. Maybe the "freaks" ringing the bell were just acting goofy, which was not unusual for Dragon's Lair clientele. However, he wasn't about to take any chances. This time he wasn't going to lose control of this deal like the one which had gotten away from him in Atlanta last night.

Suddenly, all of his monitors went blank. Stunned, Carlisle stared at them before frantically looking around the office. He vividly remembered Orga Syriac's unannounced visit to his office last night. Now he was alone. Very much alone, with an odd sense of eerie isolation, which he had never experienced before. He quickly realized that this odd feeling was because the usually undetectable hum the air-conditioning unit made was no longer audible. It too had gone out.

Was the punk rockers' showing up at the same time that the security monitors and air-conditioning unit went out merely a coincidence? The lights in the office were still on and the television and video recorders worked. So this was a selective power failure, which could have been caused by an unusual equipment malfunction or . . . something or someone else.

Quickly, the fixer got up from behind his desk and went to a locked closet across the room. From it he removed an M16 military rifle with a collapsible stock. If the mechanical problems being experienced inside his nightclub were caused by anything other than a malfunction he planned to deal with the source in a most severe manner.

CHAPTER 80

Boss," Blackie said over the intercom, "we've found the WGN van."

"Where?"

"On the North Side about two blocks from that Dragon's Lair nightspot Jack Carlisle owns."

Butch Cole was a block away when he saw Paige talking to the punk rockers. He stepped into the doorway of an antique store and watched her give them money. Then they walked away and Paige went back inside the doughnut shop. She emerged a few minutes later with Kate Ford. The two women went quickly down the block toward the Dragon's Lair. They disappeared into the alley running behind the nightclub, and by the time he got to the mouth of the alley they were gone. He figured that they had managed to get inside the building, and he was about to start looking for a rear entrance when he heard a commotion coming from the front of the club. Crossing the street he watched the four punk rockers arguing with a muscular black man. Butch remembered that this same man had been sitting with Paige the night that he and Judy had gone to the club.

A woman in tight leather pants with spiked aqua blue hair was shouting. "I'm not going anywhere until I can go inside and look for my sister's purse. She left it under her chair last night and when she came back to get it the club was closed."

"So come back after six o'clock when the club is open."

"Why can't I come in now and look?"

"Because I said so."

The others began joining in the argument and it was obvious that the big guy was starting to get angry. Finally, he reached the limit of his patience and stepped from the club doorway out onto the street. His shoulder muscles bulged beneath his suit jacket and his massive hands were clenched into fists. "If you people don't get the hell out of here right now you're going to be missing some teeth along with that purse."

"You can't threaten us like that," the aqua-haired woman said, but she slipped behind one of her male companions, who didn't look too eager to take on the bigger man.

Butch crossed the street and entered the alley. Less than thirty seconds later he found an unlocked back door leading off a loading dock. He entered the Dragon's Lair.

The controls for the electrical equipment operating inside the Dragon's Lair were in a utility room at the rear of the main section of the nightclub. After Paige and Kate snuck inside, they proceeded directly to this room.

"Here it is," Paige said, going to a metal cabinet mounted on the far wall. Opening it revealed two rows of switches with a diagram printed on a sheet of cardboard on the inside of the cabinet door.

With her index finger, Paige traced the circuit breaker switches until she found the ones that controlled the air-conditioning and the video monitors in Carlisle's office.

"Won't he come down to investigate why he lost power?" Kate asked.

"I'm counting on it," Paige said, closing the cabinet. "But he won't be too quick about rushing in here. He's afraid of the dark."

A naked lightbulb in the ceiling provided illumination to the small stone-walled room. "Cover your face," Paige said, before swinging her purse like a club and smashing the bulb. Slivers of glass cascaded down on them and the floor.

Paige was brushing glass out of her hair as she led Kate

out of the utility room. "C'mon, he'll be down here any minute."

They crossed a corridor and entered the rear of the darkened nightclub kitchen. There they crouched until they heard footsteps. Paige pulled Kate farther into the empty kitchen. A shadow passed the doors, but they were unable to see who it was.

"This way," Paige whispered, pulling Kate through the dark. They exited through a door leading into the main section of the nightclub.

They went quickly to the fixer's office.

Sonny Balfour was forced to chase the four punk rockers a quarter of a block before he could finally get rid of them. Unlike the fixer, he did not see any ulterior motive behind their badgering him to let them inside the Dragon's Lair. But, he wasn't paid to think.

He had left the door open when he pursued the intruders, and when he returned it was closed. He figured that the wind had blown it shut. Going back inside, he crossed the lobby and was about to enter the main section of the club when Orga Syriac stepped from the shadows. Balfour froze.

"You killed . . . Blessing," she said, haltingly. "For that . . ." She took a step toward him, but was having trouble keeping her balance. He began backing away. She continued to advance.

Remembering what she had done to Ronnie Skyles last night, Balfour didn't hesitate a second longer. Turning, he bolted through the door out onto the street. With every step he expected her to grab him from behind and kill him. When he looked back she was not pursuing.

Balfour kept running and veered out into the street in front of an oncoming black Chevy. The car was forced to skid to a stop to keep from hitting him. He kept running until he heard the shouted, "Police officer! Stop right there, Balfour!"

The ex-boxer halted and raised his hands. Turning around he saw Larry Cole and Blackie Silvestri emerge from the car with their guns drawn. Balfour was actually glad to see the cops. And he had a lot to tell them.

*   *   *

Jack Carlisle reached the utility room and attempted to turn on the overhead light from a switch inside the door. When nothing happened he stood at the entrance peering into the darkness. Since childhood he'd had a phobia about dark places. He could always return to his office for a flashlight, but he realized that there was something going on here. He turned to go back down the corridor when he stepped on something that crunched beneath his shoe. Looking down he saw slivers of broken glass from the smashed lightbulb.

A cruel smile crossed the fixer's face. Hefting the M16, he headed back for his office.

"I bet this is the tape," Paige said, removing an unmarked videocassette from the recorder in Carlisle's office.

"Shouldn't we check to be sure?" Kate asked.

"It's the right one all right. Jack has everything else labeled." Paige slipped the cassette into her purse.

"I thought we were going to copy it."

"No time," Paige said. "We've got to get out of here."

They started for the door and were about to exit into the corridor when Butch walked in.

Gasping, Paige said, "What are you doing here?"

"I wanted to help you and Kate clear Pete Dubcek."

Before Paige or Kate could respond, Jack Carlisle appeared behind Butch.

"How nice," the fixer said, leveling his gun on the intruders. "Uninvited guests. Now isn't this cozy."

CHAPTER 81

Look, I'll tell you guys anything you want to know, but you've got to protect me," Balfour raged from the backseat of Cole's car, where he sat with his arms handcuffed behind him.

"Protect you from what, Sonny?" Cole asked from the passenger side of the front seat. "You and the fixer have a falling-out?"

Balfour was sweating as if he'd just run a marathon. "I'm not worried about Jack. It's the broad. The one that can change into a monster."

"What about her?" Blackie demanded.

"She's in the club. She came after me, but I managed to get away."

"Why is she after you?" Cole said.

Balfour lowered his head.

"Talk to us, Sonny," Blackie prompted.

"Okay," the ex-boxer said in a voice that was very close to tears. "I'll tell it. I killed Fuzzy and the broad who lived with Orga Syriac. It was in retaliation for Dubcek not throwing the basketball game in Atlanta last night. Jack had the fix in by threatening to kill Fuzzy if Dubcek didn't shave points. Dubcek went along with it for part of the game, but then something happened to him and he started playing like a madman. When Jack lost the two million he'd bet, he decided to follow through on the threat."

"So you killed the two women and Ronnie Skyles?" Blackie said.

"I didn't kill Skyles. Your female monster did after I splashed the black chick's blood on him. Jack's got a videotape of the whole thing. Now she's in there, but she was after me."

"We'll protect you, Sonny," Cole said, opening the door.

"Where are you going, boss?" Blackie asked with evident concern.

"I'm going to take a look inside. Don't worry, I won't get into trouble. I've had enough of that for one day."

They were forced to sit on the couch in Carlisle's office. Paige, Butch, and Kate didn't like the broad smile etched on the fixer's face. The smile and the M16 rifle he kept pointed at them were frightening.

"Now tell me, what brings you three here on such a nice day?" he asked.

"I came back to get my stuff, Jack," Paige lied.

"And you needed these two to help you carry it away?" He swung the gun carelessly over their heads.

Paige had no response.

"What have you got to say, Ms. Ford?" Carlisle said to the journalist.

Kate glared at him. "I couldn't wait to see the evidence you were going to show me."

"So you came down here to steal it. Now is that ethical conduct for a prominent journalist like yourself?"

"Look who's talking about ethics," she said defiantly.

Carlisle's grin faded momentarily before brightening again. "I like spunk in a woman. Even if it does prove fatal." He pointed the rifle at Kate's chest.

"Leave her alone," Butch said.

Jack swung the gun to point at him. "And the man of the group. Now who might you be?"

Before Butch could answer there was a noise originating outside in the club.

"Sonny," Carlisle yelled, "is that you?"

There was no answer.

"Sonny?!"

Still nothing.

"Could there be another member of this surprise party?" he said to the captives. Then he snarled, "Get up."

The fixer made them form a single-file line in front of him with Paige in front and Butch bringing up the rear. "Let's see what's happening out in the club. Walk real slow and remember that I'm holding the rifle. One bullet can go through all three of you."

Orga summoned all the strength she had left and the visage of the Abo-Yorba descended on her. She had lost the man who had killed Blessing, but she knew that Jack Carlisle was responsible for her death. She began moving across the nightclub toward the fixer's office. She lost her balance and would have fallen if she hadn't braced herself against a nearby table. She knocked over a chair, which clattered to the floor. Righting herself, she kept going.

Larry Cole entered the front door of the Dragon's Lair just as Carlisle exited the office with Paige, Kate, and Butch in front of him. Cole pulled his gun when he saw the rifle the fixer was holding. Then he saw the she-devil.

As if frozen in time, everyone inside the Dragon's Lair stopped. Paige and Butch were shocked speechless at the sight of the she-devil. Carlisle was terrified. Cole and Kate Ford could tell that Orga was critically ill. Then the suspended moment passed and Jack Carlisle opened fire.

"Stop!" Cole yelled, but it was too late.

The bullets from the assault rifle slammed into the Abo-Yorba and knocked her down. Paige, Kate, and Butch quickly ducked out of the line of fire and Cole raised his gun and shot the fixer through the left forearm. Carlisle dropped the gun and grabbed his injured arm. He backed into the wall as Cole approached and spun him around. The fixer cried out when the cop began cuffing his hands behind his back.

Kate rushed over to assist Orga, but it was too late. The she-devil was dead.

EPILOGUE

The arraignment of Pete Dubcek on charges of murdering three people drew so much public scrutiny and worldwide media coverage that the affair looked more like a sporting event than a criminal trial. Reporters, both from the print and electronic media, were chosen by drawing lots for selected seating in the courtroom. Spectators were allowed in on a first-come, first-served basis. Although this was merely to be a preliminary hearing for the purposes of setting bail, if any was allowed, the attention the proceeding was getting was unprecedented. The world waited with no little degree of impatience for their first look at the accused celebrity murderer.

Dubcek was transported from the jail ward of Cook County Hospital to the Markham branch of the circuit court at 151st and Kedzie in a sheriff's police van. He was dressed in the same clothes he had been wearing on the night of the murders and bloodstains were visible on his pants and shirt. As he shuffled in the back door of the courthouse with his head down, a number of cameras focused on the dark spots.

The judge selected to preside at the hearing was the Honorable Anjelica Pate, a no-nonsense female jurist who was determined not to permit the Dubcek hearing to turn into a media fiasco. She entered and took her seat on the bench. Instead of banging the gavel to get the attention of the throng assembled before her, she sat stock-still and fixed her aging but still pretty features into the most severe judicial scowl she could muster. Quickly, the room quieted to the point a partially deaf person could hear a pin drop.

The judge cleared her throat and began. "Before we begin these proceedings, I would like to set the ground rules for the prosecution, the defense, the media, and spectators." Then she began to recite a litany of taboos that made those in attendance certain that they were as much on trial as Pete Dubcek. She was concluding when the door to the courtroom opened and Larry Cole, accompanied by Judy Daniels, pushed his way inside.

They proceeded up the main aisle to the prosecution table. Judge Pate knew Larry Cole, but couldn't fathom why he was here. The Dubcek case was a suburban affair.

Cole leaned down and whispered to the state's attorney assigned to try the case. The judge watched the prosecutor first appear surprised, then incredulous, and finally awestruck.

"Mr. State's Attorney," Judge Pate said, "is there something you would like to share with the court?"

Shakily, he got to his feet. "I know this is highly irregular, Your Honor, but I must request a short recess to confer with the Chicago Police Department regarding this case."

"You have ten minutes. No more." With that she left the bench.

Exactly ten minutes later Judge Pate returned to the courtroom. "Is the state ready to proceed in this matter?"

"Yes, Your Honor," the state's attorney replied. "Due to evidence that has come to our attention in the last few minutes, the state is dropping all charges against Piotr Dubcek."

The courtroom erupted in bedlam and not even Judge Pate's gavel could bring it back under control.

The Midway Plaisance had been cordoned off for four square blocks around the huge crater in the ground where the Human Development Institute had once stood. A construction company had been employed to excavate the crater and sift through the debris. Tight security had been put into place under the auspices of an unnamed government security agency. If any of the Human Development Institute's secrets had survived the blast, they intended to find them. However, as the day wore on into early afternoon it appeared doubtful that anything at all would be discovered in the rubble.

Two men were standing a short distance from the site of the excavation. One was black and muscular, the other blond and slender. The blond walked with a stiff gait. To some extent they were vastly different in appearance; however, there was one thing about them that was identical. That was the color of their eyes, which was a startling blue-gray. The black man and the white man were brothers. They shared the same father and had different names, but they were very similar in their approach to problems. That was one of the reasons why the United States government found them to be of such great value for covert operations.

"This place was pulverized," Ernest Steiger said, squinting to keep the dust from a bulldozer from blowing into his eyes. "What kind of explosive could do that kind of damage?"

"It was rigged to blow," Reggie Stanton said. "And by someone who knew exactly what they were doing."

A third voice entered the conversation. "A workman is only as good as the material he uses, and it's my understanding that the man who did this sabotaged the environmental plant. Maybe he had a bit of plastique at his disposal, but nothing capable of this much destruction."

The two government agents turned around to find Dr. Silvernail Smith, the historian from the Museum of Natural History, standing a short distance away. How he'd gotten inside the tight security perimeter imposed around the area was a mystery. But Stanton and Steiger had had dealings with this gentleman in the past, so they knew that they could expect the unexpected and unusual from him.

Stanton decided to let the historian have his say. "So, what do you think happened here, Doctor?"

Silvernail turned around and looked back at the Institute crater. "As Mr. Steiger said, the structure was pulverized. Debris is almost nonexistent except for that steel vault that was found in a tunnel sixty feet below the ground."

"Would you like to tell us how you know about that?" Steiger said in a voice containing measured menace.

"Oh," Silvernail said innocently, "is that information classified?"

The matching blue-gray eyes of the brothers locked on him. "No, it's not classified," Stanton said, "but we'd still like to know how you came by that information."

Silvernail smiled. "I have my sources. Sources which also told me that there was something missing from that vault. Something that has all this high-priced security and you two very formidable gentlemen prowling around the ruins."

"You still didn't answer my question," Stanton said. "What caused all this damage?"

"The Human Development Institute didn't develop anything for mankind at all. In fact, they did more to retard the advancement of humanity than anything else. So I would speculate that they were doing some unusual experiments in there. Experiments which could have very destructive consequences." Silvernail squinted at the crater. "I suggest that you have those workmen put on protective suits because I'd be willing to wager there is a great deal of radiation in this area."

Steiger laughed. "If a nuclear device had gone off in there, half this town would be gone."

Silvernail smiled. "Perhaps if the files that are missing from the Institute are ever found, they might disclose that Dr. Gilbert Goldman was working on some very unusual uses for nuclear power, and although he would never allow explosives inside the Institute, there was probably enough nuclear material present to cause the pulverization effect for everything but that specially designed steel vault."

Stanton and Steiger exchanged looks. A short time later they had the area checked for radiation. Although the yield was not life-threatening there were indications that some type of nuclear event had occurred. This was another mystery left by the destruction of the Human Development Institute.

JULY 3, 2004

J. Ellis Montgomery was one of the most prominent and successful criminal attorneys in America. A silver-haired black man of sixty, Montgomery was a graduate of Harvard Law School and had tried cases from coast to coast, before the United States Supreme Court, and before the Court of International Law at The Hague in the Netherlands. He was adept at getting hopelessly guilty defendants acquitted. It was to Montgomery that Jack Carlisle turned after his arrest.

The prominent attorney was a resident of Atlanta, Georgia, but maintained a license to practice law in the state of Illinois. He had flown to Chicago immediately upon being contacted by the jailed gambler. After conferring with his client in the Cook County Jail and agreeing on his fifty-thousand-dollar retainer, Montgomery had set out to obtain Carlisle's acquittal.

Two weeks later he returned to meet with the fixer. The bandage on Carlisle's arm had recently been changed, but he would take the scar made by Larry Cole's bullet to the grave. After Carlisle was ushered into an attorney-client interview room by a jail guard, the fixer took a seat across from Montgomery. Carlisle's confident smile was in place.

"We need to discuss a couple of things, Mr. Carlisle," the perpetually formal defense attorney said, pulling a sheaf of documents from his worn leather briefcase.

"Sure thing. I've reserved the whole afternoon for you," the fixer quipped.

Montgomery glanced up at Carlisle, but did not smile. He did not find anything amusing about this case or his client.

"I've been having difficulty verifying the details of the story you told me. Perhaps you'd like to start at the beginning and tell me again."

Carlisle was smart enough to know better than to lie to his lawyer, so he told it all, from his attempt to fix the Olympic basketball game between the Americans and Italians, to his sending Sonny to kidnap and kill Orga Syriac's companion, to the murder of Fuzzy Dubcek. He then went on to the frame he'd put on Pete Dubcek to take the fall for the triple murder. And then there was Orga Syriac.

The fixer concluded with, "Paige, Kate Ford, and Cole's son broke into my club, probably to steal the tape and protect this she-devil thing. I got the drop on them and then the monster showed up. I shot that thing in self-defense and then Cole shot me. I want you to file a multimillion-dollar damage suit against the CPD. That cop has got to be in this thing with them."

J. Ellis Montgomery never took his eyes off his client. When Carlisle finished, the attorney said, "I checked out your story about this she-devil and I've been unable to substantiate any of it. You say that when she's in human form she's Orga Syriac, a local TV newscaster?"

Carlisle's smile faded. "That's right, and I've got her in her monster form killing a guy on videotape back at my office."

"I went to your office and looked for that tape. It's not there."

"What about Orga Syriac?"

"Sven-Erik Voman received a formal letter of resignation from her dated the same day that you say you killed her. Voman also said that he was going to terminate her employment prior to receiving the letter of resignation. He said that they had what he termed 'professional differences.' "

"What about her body?" Carlisle was becoming increasingly irritated with each passing second. "I emptied a clip from an M16 rifle into that monster. That's why Cole gave me this." The fixer held up his bandaged arm for emphasis.

Montgomery flipped through the documents in front of him. Selecting one, he scanned it while saying, "There is no body. According to Chief of Detectives Larry Cole, he fired at you because you had discharged a fully automatic"—he looked over the top of the page at his client—"and, by the way, illegal firearm in the vicinity of three unarmed civilians, to wit, Paige Albritton, Katherine Anne Ford, and Larry Cole Jr. There is nothing about Orga Syriac in the police report."

"Hell, they broke into my club. They were trespassing, for

Christ's sake. I had a right to defend my property."

The attorney put the paper down and said, "Wasn't Paige Albritton an employee of the Dragon's Lair?"

"She quit."

"When?"

"A couple days before this whole thing went down."

"Did either of you enter into a formal agreement of employment termination?"

A shadow of Carlisle's former smile returned. "Paige was a hooker, Mr. Montgomery. For most of her life she made her living on her back."

Nonplussed, the attorney said, "Are you aware that she still had keys to your nightclub in her possession?"

"Look," the fixer said, banging his palm on the table and drawing a disapproving frown from his counselor, "we can cut right to the chase on this one. Sonny Balfour will back up everything I've said."

"Mr. Balfour is currently being held in protective custody, Mr. Carlisle. There are strong indications that he's made a deal with the state's attorney and is going to testify against you."

That one stopped Carlisle dead in his tracks. "I don't believe it."

J. Ellis Montgomery began shoving the papers back into his briefcase. "Believe it, Mr. Carlisle; but what Mr. Balfour can do, we also can do."

"I don't get you."

Montgomery stood up. "We can also make a deal."

"What have I got to deal with?"

"I don't know," the attorney said, motioning to the guard on the other side of the iron-barred gate that he was ready to leave, "but I'll never be able to effectively defend you based on what you've told me so far. Our only option is a deal followed by a negotiated plea. Sleep on it and I'll see you tomorrow."

Once back in his cell, Jack Carlisle considered his options. There were things that he knew that the cops and state's attorney's office would like to know. He hadn't spent his entire adult life on the fringes of illegality without finding

out a thing or two. The only other avenue open to him was
a long prison sentence, or worse, a lethal injection. The irony
of it made him laugh. For once the famous Fixer Jack Carlisle had been fixed.

LOUISE, MISSISSIPPI
AUGUST 4, 2004
Dusk

The small Baptist church was located on the outskirts of the
town of Louise, Mississippi. Behind the church there was a
graveyard, which had headstones dating back to the Civil
War. All of those interred in this area were African Americans, and some of the markers bore the label "Colored." Isaac
Diggs, the long-dead founder of Diggstown, which had been
located a short distance from Louise, was buried in this cemetery.

The church was poor, which was evidenced by the peeling
paint and porous roof, so the young pastor was happy to
accommodate the party from "up north" for a substantial burial fee.

They arrived just as the sun was going down, which was
an unusual but not unheard-of time for a funeral. There were
five in the party, three men and two women. The tallest male
in the quintet was the only African American. He also appeared to be the one in charge. He identified himself as Larry
Cole, which was the name the small-town pastor had been
given by the woman who had called him. Her name was Kate
Ford and she had made the arrangements for the funeral. She
introduced the others, whom the pastor recalled as being
Judy, Manny, and Blackie. This Blackie looked like a gangster in the pastor's opinion.

Cole met with the pastor in the church office. There the
agreed-upon sum in cash for the service was handed over.

"We'd like to have the funeral performed as soon as possible," Cole said.

"Do you have a properly notarized certificate of death,
sir?"

Cole removed a white envelope from his inside pocket and handed it over. It contained a death certificate issued in Cook County, Illinois, and signed by a Dr. Silvernail Smith, for a black female named Orga Syriac. To the pastor it appeared quite proper, with one exception. No age was listed for the deceased. He brought this discrepancy to Cole's attention.

The tall black man said a subdued, "We don't know how old she was when she died. I was told that it wouldn't prevent her from being buried."

Something about his visitor's manner made the pastor apprehensive. "The age isn't necessary, but it is usually estimated in such cases."

When Cole didn't comment, the pastor said, "Was she a relative?"

"No."

His curiosity raged. "You must have been very close for you and your friends to bring her all this way for burial."

Cole looked at the pastor and responded. "We were close, Reverend. May we now proceed?"

The casket had been heremetically sealed, and they all joined in to act as pallbearers. The grave had been dug by a couple of local laborers. Using ropes, the casket was lowered into the ground. Then, as darkness fell on the Mississippi countryside, the young pastor opened his Bible and began with, "Ashes to ashes, dust to dust . . ."

They were driving back to the Jackson, Mississippi, airport on the same road that the Buick Roadmaster bearing the HDI operatives had driven to Diggstown on a half century ago. The highway was now a four-lane blacktop with a double yellow line bisecting the center. Cole drove the GMC van they had rented to transport the coffin from the airport to the Louise, Mississippi cemetery.

Kate Ford was seated in the bucket seat beside Cole. Blackie, Manny, and Judy were dozing in the rear of the large vehicle.

Kate sighed. "It all seems like such a waste, Larry."

He glanced at her briefly before turning his attention back to the road. "What seems like a waste?"

"Orga's death. She was an authentic historical legend. To die in the manner she did was a tragedy."

"I wouldn't say that," he said. "You've got your book to write about her and then"—he unzipped the breast pocket of his nylon jacket and removed two disks—"you have these."

She took them and said, "What's on them?"

"The files of the Human Development Institute. Orga must have slipped them into my pocket when she left me in the tunnel after the explosion. They were encoded, but I got a friend of mine in the FBI lab in Washington to decode them for me. I think you'll find the information they contain is very interesting. In fact, you're holding the story of the century in your hands."

And she was.